Point of Departure

Based on the life
Of Charlotte Mailliard
1827-1921

This book is a work of fiction. Any resemblance to actual events or persons, living or dead, is entirely coincidental.

"Point of Departure," by Dianne Kirtley. ISBN 978-1-62137-188-5 (Softcover) 978-1-62137-189-2 (Ebook).

Published 2013 by Virtualbookworm.com Publishing Inc., P.O. Box 9949, College Station, TX 77842, US.

Manufactured in the United States of America.

. . .they are founding in the valleys of the Mississippi a new society which has no analogy with the past and is connected to Europe only in language. It's here one must come to judge the most singular state of affairs that has doubtless existed under the sun.

. . . one can't restrain one's astonishment at the influence exercised by the point of departure on the good or evil destinies of peoples.

I have no hesitation in saying that although the American woman never leaves her domestic sphere and is in some respects very dependent within it, nowhere does she enjoy a higher station. And if anyone asks me what I think the chief cause of the extraordinary prosperity and growing power of this nation [is], I should answer that it is due to the superiority of their women.

Alexis de Tocqueville, 1832

Chapter Titles

Foreword

Perhaps it was the letter to her granddaughter in Charlotte's own beautifully scripted handwriting that firmly cemented my interest in this woman whose life had changed so dramatically at such a critical age. I had heard the stories of one strain of my husband's lineage which connected him with the family of Napoleon Bonaparte, specifically his brother Joseph, but it wasn't until I found the papers of my own father-in law which charted Charlotte's experiences that the pieces of the story began to fall into place.

Charlotte Mailliard was raised and educated with Bonaparte princes, had lived in their residence in Florence and the royal chateau outside Paris, but at age fourteen in 1841, she, her parents and two brothers left behind the elegance of their surroundings, where the family had served as personal secretaries. Charlotte's father had already transported three other daughters to Illinois to his in-laws three years earlier. But now he made the decision to forever make their lives in Illinois, the western frontier of America.

Here was a land of opportunity, a land where property was cheap. Fortunately for the Mailliards, their transition to the new land was made comfortable by gifts and money from the family of Joseph Bonaparte and his daughter Charlotte, after whom Charlotte Mailliard had been named.

The western frontier, Illinois, had had other French come before the settlers, the trappers who made peace with the natives and often lived among them. These Europeans were not the settlers, did not seek to farm lands, build towns and exact permanence for their families. When the settlers came, they drove out the natives, and after the Blackhawk War in 1832, forced them to cross the Mississippi.

That challenge faced, the wave of immigrants flourished, but the underlying scourge that festered at the core of the new nation, the issue of slavery, which had been sidestepped by the founding fathers, came to an unavoidable upheaval in the Civil War. Illinois watched as its native son grew from his backwoods roots to achieve prominence as the great Union leader of that war.

Charlotte Mailliard and her family, like so many others, were an intrinsic part of that history. Yet played against that larger stage, their lives were fraught with the same problems we currently face as each of us struggles to find love, deal with family issues, confront prejudice, and ultimately cope with the challenge of each new day.

October 17, 2012

Part 1

Leaving Survilliers, Mortefontaine, France, 1841

Charlotte sat in the huge window seat with her head buried in her knees. Mama would of course reprimand her for such an unlady-like posture, but at this point she was beyond caring about what Mama—or Papa, for that matter—would think.

She wanted to be angry at someone for this terrible upheaval in her life, and they were the two most likely candidates. She could also be equally angry at her incredibly annoying brother Amedee, at twelve, two years younger than she, and yes, even Napoleon, who at one made her life miserable with his incessant squalling.

Even the baby's name was an irritant.

"I'm supposed to be speaking nothing but English for practice, they tell me, and yet they name the infant Napoleon," Charlotte said outloud. "What possible sense does that make?"

When one is fourteen, well, actually thirteen and a half, parents can indeed be most troublesome and unreasonable.

In a few minutes the carriage would come to begin the Mailliard family's journey to Calais, then to Liverpool, England, where they would board the steam ship *Commerce*, which would take them to America, their new home. Papa said first they would stop at New Jersey to visit Uncle Louis at King Joseph's estate at Point Breeze, then westward from there. They would be traveling for three months before they reached their final destination.

In a few minutes gone would be the life she had known: Florence, Paris, the residence of Mortefontaine, the splendor and ceremony of royal society, the coddling by Princess Charlotte, the tutors she had shared with the princes.

She also knew she would miss the teasing of those princes. Annoying and condescending as they could be, Charlotte had begun to appreciate their attention, and though she was still "the servants' child," all the Mailliards had been treated more like family than servants. Indeed Papa and Mama, Eloi and Amanda Mailliard, had served the Bonaparte family as confidential attendants for many years, including the difficult ones after Emperor Napoleon's demise. She had also heard of Papa's brother, Uncle Louis, and the dangerous journey he had undertaken to transport many of the riches of the Bonaparate family to a safe Swiss hideaway. Papa had told Charlotte that the royal family had promised that the bond between them and the Mailliards would never be forgotten.

As Charlotte looked out the beautiful large window of the chateau, she could remember so easily the many times she had anxiously anticipated the sounds of carriages that brought so many elegant ladies to the very room where she now dreaded hearing those sounds.

She remembered seeing the beautiful Princess Charlotte, for whom she was named, walking through the doors.

Mama would say in her most elegant French, "This is your godmother, Charlotte. What an honor has been given to you to be named for one of the Emperor's nieces. And our dear Prince Napoleon Louis is your godfather."

But Charlotte's name was not the only benefit for the Mailliard family. She had heard Papa mention the yearly stipend that they would receive from the Bonapartes. Charlotte had also seen Mama sewing opals and rubies, more gifts from the illustrious family, into the hem of her dress. She also realized that the greatest treasure they would be carrying was perhaps the most remarkable gift, Raphael's painting *Ecce Homo*, with which Papa had taken great care as he wrapped the priceless work. He had told Charlotte that he hoped these treasures would help to establish them in their new home, Illinois.

The name of that American state was so strange to her tongue, a tongue used to forming the beautiful, melodious sounds of her two native languages, French and Italian. How incredible that within a short time she must abandon those words and be speaking only the ugly sounds of English. She might as well be made to speak German!

Two large trunks were dragged into the foyer of the chateau as Papa began to say his farewells to the other staff members. Now as he walked towards Charlotte, he inquired about the new traveling shoes he had purchased.

"Are they comfortable, Charlotte? These will be the only shoes you will wear until we reach our destination."

"Yes, Papa, they are fine. But for new shoes they look rather shabby, I think, as if someone else has already worn them. But thank you for making the heel a bit higher. You have begun to believe me, I think, when I say I am becoming a woman."

"My dear, Charlotte, I have no doubt that you are a woman already. As far as the shabbiness of the shoes goes, I thought it would be better for them to appear a bit worn. With five of us traveling together, we are already creating a commotion and drawing attention to ourselves. We do not want to appear too rich, too opulent, or we may be easy marks for thieves. You must be polite and inconspicuous. I am counting on you because Amedee, well, Amedee is twelve and a boy. And the baby, of course, will take all of Mama's attention. Mama is still not well. The changes, the deaths, have taken their toll, you understand. You are my rock, Charlotte. You are a young woman, not a child. Above all, you must always have those shoes either on your feet or within your sight. Do you understand, *mon cherie*?"

Before Charlotte was able to answer, Amedee came running into the foyer.

"Papa, I hear the carriage coming. Are you ready? Is Mama ready? Isn't it time for us to go?"

Clearly Amedee was ready for his "adventure" and not feeling Charlotte's anxiety.

The horses' hooves echoed on the stone road in front of the Chateau Surveilliers, the sentinel. Charlotte's stomach felt as if it had traveled to the back of her throat, and despite Papa's speech of confidence, she did not feel like a brave young woman. She longed simply to have life the way it was last year, last month, last week.

"Amanda, are you ready, my dear? Our carriage is here," called Papa.

Holding little Napoleon by his hand as he faltered in his steps, Mama, pale and drawn, but still controlled, answered with an affirming sigh.

Charlotte looked at her Mama lovingly and tried to understand the losses her mother had experienced. In the last few months, Charlotte's brother Jules had died of a fever. Then Mama's dear friend and childhood companion, Princess Charlotte, and Charlotte's husband had died suddenly. Perhaps America would take Mama away from this sadness. She looked at Mama's blue eyes filling with tears as they had so frequently in the last months.

Charlotte had told Papa she was now a young woman, and if that were true, she must now try to be his rock, as he had said. Besides, when they did arrive in Illinois, she wanted to be sure that she was as mature as two older sisters, Heloise and Pauline, and Charlotte's younger sister, Amanda, Mama's namesake, who had already been living with their grandparents in Illinois for three years.

Charlotte saw Papa tenderly take Mama's hand. "Are you ready, my dearest Amanda?"

Mama nodded, but did not speak. Papa lifted the baby into his arms and gently guided his wife towards the door.

Trunks lashed to the back of the coach, and all five Mailliards in their places, the carriage set off speedily as the four grays snorted and panted, their breaths taking shape in the early morning air.

Charlotte, sitting next to Papa, looked for the last time at the Chateau Survilliers. The sun shone full as it cast a startling light on the eight peaks of the edifice. The brilliant blue April sky was a stark contrast to the heaviness of her heart.

Traveling to Paris and Calais

Although neither Mama nor Papa expressed Charlotte's worry, the extended stay in Paris was surely due to the fact that the Mailliard family, she thought, may never come to that beautiful and fascinating city again.

Charlotte absorbed once more the rooms of Versailles, the Petit Trianon, the very path that Marie Antoinette had taken to the guillotine. Charlotte thought of the tragic life of "the Austrian," as she came to be called, who was just her own age when she had come to Paris for the first time.

As Charlotte put her own feet on the pavement of that street, she shuddered and nearly stumbled.

"What is it, Charlotte? Are you alright?" questioned Papa solicitously.

"I am fine, Papa. I cannot help but think of the poor queen and the children she left behind."

"Yes, that is so much like you, Charlotte. We, Mama and I, have always sensed that about you. Sometimes we worry that your decisions will be made, well, with others more in mind, than for yourself."

"But, Papa, is that not how you have made decisions also?" Charlotte asked

"I would like to think that is so. But," Papa paused choosing his words carefully, "sometimes the practical side of life causes one to act, well, cautiously."

Charlotte noticed a strange look on his face as he spoke. Surely, her Papa had always done the "right" thing. It was impossible to think any other way. Perhaps he was thinking about something else.

"Papa, don't be worried about my decisions. You and Mama worry about all your children, but I know Mama is already thinking about where her girls will find husbands. Well, at least we don't have to worry about political marriages. I have already observed that life can be much simpler when titles are not involved. In any case, I doubt if I shall ever marry," she sighed. "I doubt any man my age could share my interests."

"Perhaps, you are correct, Charlotte. Although Mama, I am sure, would think otherwise in a few years, of course," said Papa smiling.

As Mama and little Napoleon stopped at a small café for a rest, Charlotte, Papa and a still annoyingly ebullient Amedee proceeded to the Arc deTriomphe, one of the many accomplishments of the famous Bonaparte. Papa warned Amedee to speak quietly, for one never knew who was listening, and even in 1841 the Bonaparte name could cause unpleasant discussion with those whose sympathies were not with the former royal family.

Charlotte closed her eyes tightly and tried to impress on her mind the many sites she had seen in these recent days. She would force herself to recall them; she would never forget this country, where the last six years had been so very secure and comfortable.

For four long days on the road from Paris, the Mailliard coach bucked, jumped and fought its way on the road to Calais. Oblivious to the tension felt by the three older members of his family, Amedee wanted to share everything he had heard about the country that was to be his new home.

"Charlotte, do you know that the American Indians scalp people when they capture them? I am sure they would love to have a trophy made of your long, brown curls."

"Really, Amedee, I would think that your blonde, tight little curls would look so much better attached to some savage's belt." Charlotte had also had her head filled with gory stories.

"Children, children," said Papa wanting to change quickly the tone of the conversation for Amanda's sake, "in Illinois, where we will make our home, the Indians have been quiet for several years. Do not immerse yourself in such drivel. Charlotte, I sincerely hope you brought the papers I suggested you read."

"Of course, Papa." Yes, reading the Americans' *Declaration of Independence* and some Thomas piece called *Common Sense* would definitely keep a young woman company on a stormy Atlantic night.

"And what will Amedee be reading, father?" asked Charlotte deliberately emphasizing her brother's name and the English word "father."

"I hope that he will, of course, read the same things you will in time, but he is just a boy," said Papa, taking off Amedee's cap and tousling his hair.

Amedee responded with that wonderfully engaging smile, only too ready to accept his father's indulgence.

"One story that I know is true about America, Papa, is that the southern part still keeps African people as slaves. How can this be true since I have heard that the Declaration document speaks of equality for all?"

"Surely you know, Charlotte, that governments often profess one thing, but practice another. But again, the slavery issue will not concern us. Illinois, does not allow slaves."

"But if only one part of the country allows this practice, does not every part share in the shame?"

"We have so many other things to worry about, Charlotte. We will deal with that issue when we must. Hopefully never."

Papa was right of course, as he was about so many things. Though he had not a large stature, in his daughter's eyes he was strong, fair to others and a good man. To Charlotte, as to many daughters of her age, her father was a hero. He did seem to indulge Amedee a bit, but then he was more spirited and unpredictable than she was. And now with Jules's death, he was the only son except for the baby, who was too young to have captured Papa's fancy. She was the eldest of this group, but what would occur when they reached Illinois?

Then she would be one of four girls, for her three sisters were already with *Grandmere* and *Grandpere* Gallet, who had been in Woodsville for the past three years. Heloise at seventeen and Pauline, sixteen, would most likely be haughty toward their younger sister. Amanda, nine, could be . . . pesty. The three sisters had traveled with Papa during an earlier American visit and stayed with their grandparents. Now, persuaded by them and Mama's brother John, Papa was convinced that America was indeed "the land of opportunity."

How could "opportunity" improve the experiences of the life Charlotte had known? Indeed she had been the Mailliard child who had reveled in the attention of the Bonaparte family. Her time with them in Florence seemed etched in her mind: their treating her with chocolate candies, the prince calling Charlotte "his little wife," the exposure to wonderful teachers in Italian history and language, and the joy of participating in the sketching class.

Thinking of those lessons, she unconsciously touched her small bag and felt the reassuring shape of her graphite sticks. Though she was forced to leave her beloved France, she vowed to recreate the trees and flowers of her native countryside once she was settled.

Florence had been so much more than lessons, though. Thinking of the carnival atmosphere of that city seemed much more real than looking ahead. She remembered fondly the colorful, vivid gowns of reds, yellows and deep blue worn by European nobles. Once she too had dressed as a little Turkish girl and the sultan from the Turkish embassy had brought her a box of candy. She could still recall the strange, sweet juice that had invaded her mouth with that delicacy.

What royalty would parade through Woodsville, Illinois? The answer to that question was all too clear.

She closed her eyes tightly and tried to think of what lay ahead: sisters she barely remembered, the house they would live in, the town (*Grandmere* said it was simple, but beautiful), that she could not project. She doubted that there would be anything as grand as the chateau of Survillier. Her eyes were wet with tears, but she would not let Mama, Papa, and especially Amedee, see her anxiety. Today, at least, she was the eldest child; she must also be the strongest.

Her eyes turned to Mama. Mama and Papa had made many trips with the Bonaparte family. How happy she seemed then, but now she looked so sad and pale. Mama had already traveled to America several times to visit her brother-in-law, Louis Mailliard, the steward and friend to King Joseph, Napoleon's brother. Charlotte remembered how her parents had told her that at Joseph's home in New Jersey, Point Breeze, the royal family had entertained America's own celebrities, including future presidents, and Uncle Louis was the one in charge of all receptions.

But Mama's last few years had not been healthy. She had spent months at the Bonapartes' resort at Montmelian, France, trying to regain her strength. Charlotte had heard her parents agree that the three girls must stay with their grandparents in America. Certainly the older two could guide and take care of little Amanda, they had said. Besides, they had been born in America, whereas she had been born in that beautiful city of Florence. Always traveling with Princess Charlotte, the Mailliards had been with the noble family wherever they lived or visited.

However, when her beloved Princess Charlotte, Joseph Bonaparte's daughter, had died suddenly, Mama had become completely disconsolate, no longer seeing a reason to stay in France. She agreed to reunite with her mother, father, and brother John

Charlotte had also heard Mama whisper that she was worried that Charlotte was becoming too "bookish, too much like a man with her independent thinking. It will be good for her to be with older girls, to do girl things together."

Charlotte remembered thinking, "girl things" sounded very boring and silly. She hoped Mama would soon forget that idea when they arrived in Illinois.

Now, as she looked at her Mama sitting on the opposite side of the carriage, she noticed how lovingly she hugged Napoleon, who had thankfully fallen asleep, close to her breast. His round, little faced, framed by small blonde curls, was totally at peace. Indeed, he looked a true angel in repose with no concerns. Charlotte returned the smile that she shared with Mama, a smile that seemed to say, "Yes, how wonderful to be so young and never need to worry."

Stopping after hours of travel on this fourth day, the family once again rested at an inn. Due to the expanse of their accommodations, each night Charlotte had been able to find a corner for herself. This solitude, Charlotte knew, would be absent once they boarded their ship to cross the Atlantic.

To Liverpool, England

The paddle-ferry carrying the Mailliard family crossed the short distance from Calais to Dover without incident and only a small wind had accompanied them on their sixty league trip.

Disembarking with the other passengers, Amedee rushed past several people, brushing against them and causing several to cast disparaging glances in his direction.

Surely Papa would say something, but he was too busy trying to arrange for the transfer of the Mailliard trunks while Mama sat quietly, holding Napoleon close.

"Charlotte, Amedee, I need your help here," called Papa.

His exuberance still at a high pitch, Amedee raced back to assist his father. "Isn't this a wonderful day?" he exclaimed. "We are so lucky to be making this journey."

Perhaps, thought Charlotte, I should take a lesson from Amedee's positive spirit. Maybe she would save that thought for another day.

It was true, however, that, compared to what the day could be, the late April weather was at least amenable, neither too hot nor cold. Thank goodness for that, for their traveling clothes were heavy and cumbersome—Mama and she were wearing their sturdy wool dresses with petticoats, their hats and gloves, and those shoes. Despite what Papa said, they really did look as if they had been worn.

The luggage transferred from one conveyance to another, the Mailliard family would travel by coach from Dover to London then by train from London to Birmingham and onto Liverpool, a distance of two hundred leagues, a trip that could take several days. The dried foods that Mama had brought would have to sustain them until they reached the inn at Liverpool. Amedee already had begun to complain about the lack of food early in the voyage. On the Bonaparte farms in Mortefontaine, meat, breads and fruits were easily accessible to the Mailliard children.

At last, thought Charlotte, we will finally get to see Amedee's sickening enthusiasm fade.

Though a bit hungry herself, Charlotte sat back in her seat and looked at the faces of her parents and thought of the journeys that their lives had taken. As a boy of ten, her father had followed his older brother into the service of the Bonapartes. There he had learned to be a barber and attendant to the royal family. Later, his role expanded as he learned to read and write and serve as a secretary and "personal confidante" to the Bonapartes.

Charlotte knew that her father's honesty and loyalty had rewarded not only him, but also his family. He was now forty-four years old, and no matter how busy his life was, she admired his always striving for self-improvement, reading and learning whatever he could. Charlotte reveled in the attention he had given her and his attempt with Amedee to plant the idea of intellectual curiosity firmly in his children's minds. She often heard him speak of what might be happening with the daughters who were already in America.

"Don't worry, Eloi," Mama would say. "There are more things to learn about in life than books."

Yes, thought Charlotte, art, drawing, singing, all the refinements of life. Perhaps with life in France and Florence, but Illinois, hardly.

Yet as she evaluated her parents, Charlotte sensed that they were a good match for each other. Surely part of Papa's success and spirit was due to Mama. Eight years younger than he, she seemed a refined and delicate woman, and except for the last few months, a smiling companion to Papa. It often amazed Charlotte that despite Mama's apparent fragileness, she had given birth to seven children. Mama would often tell Charlotte that she understood her place as a woman, to support and bring joy to the man in her life.

They had met when Mama was still a teenager. As she and her parents, the Gallets, were also servants to the Bonaparte family, the match seemed not only likely, but also one of love and respect. In Charlotte's eyes, though Mama could be a bit too preoccupied with her dear princess or her own children, she felt that her parents' union was one in which both seemed happy.

Train travel in 1841 was quite a marvel to even seasoned travelers like Mama and Papa. The London and Birmingham Railway, opened in 1838, linked the rapidly growing city to the country's capital. Gone was the tenuous trip up the east coast of England into the temperamental North Sea or the seemingly endless coach ride through the mid country of England.

Travelers could now experience the safe and more reliable train travel, where the exposure to weather and lingering highway robbers did not exist. Even more dangerous on coach travel was the fear of overturning due to careless drivers or unexpected changes in the roads. Coaches could also become easily mired in the mud-sodden trenches caused by rain. More than once Papa himself had told his children how he had been forced to disembark with other passengers as a coach toiled up a muddy hill, horses straining to bring their loads forward.

In comparison, train travel was luxurious. Seats were firm, rocking was almost forgotten with the smooth tracks, and if an occasional spark coming from an open window burned a hole in one's garments, the trade-off was well worth the price.

The family boarded at Euston Station in London, then traveled north-northwest until Rugby, where it turned west to Coventry and then to Birmingham, a mere one hundred eighty kilometers. Yes, Charlotte had learned she must now address distances in kilometers, not leagues as she had done in France.

Having traced the path of their travel before the start of their voyage, Charlotte looked forward to the next leg of their journey, the Birmingham Curzon Street Station, where they switched to the Liverpool and Manchester Railway.

Liverpool, on the Irish Sea, looking almost directly west to Dublin, was teeming with immigrants of many nationalities waiting to set sail for America. Many carried little more than the very clothes on their bodies. Charlotte could not help but notice the signs of days on the road, the dirt that had collected in the lines of their tanned faces.

"Papa, where have these other people come from?" she asked, her voice easily betraying the sympathy she felt.

"What, what is that you say, Charlotte?" he inquired. "Oh, yes, the other travelers. Well, I am not quite sure. Perhaps, like us, they are going to America to visit relatives."

Charlotte was startled by Papa's dismissiveness. To her it was obvious that these "travelers" were not off on some excursions for pleasure.

"Now, now, there's that look again, Charlotte," Papa said. "You must not concern yourself with others. We have enough to do today just to take care of ourselves."

But it wasn't that easy, thought Charlotte. For some reason situations that seemed unfair had always bothered her. She remembered an instance a few years ago when she had stood up to a much older boy, one of the farm hand's sons, who was teasing a dog by pulling its tail and making it fall. Without thinking, she had run up to him and yelled at him to stop. At first, Gerard (yes, that was his name) had just laughed. She had not moved, and even as he came close to her, she stubbornly planted her feet, though she could remember how her heart raced, and she feared she would be shoved to the ground. Instead, Gerard made an angry face at her and then spit at the dog. Charlotte knew Mama would have definitely called her actions "unladylike."

Now Charlotte looked at these weathered faces, and though she tried not to stare, she somehow felt guilty for all that she was fortunate enough to have.

"Come along now, Charlotte," Papa said gently. "We will be going to one of the local inns to rest before our journey across the ocean. We want to be refreshed before we begin."

Yes, thought Charlotte. We will be "refreshed," but the only shelter these other travelers could expect was the street.

Liverpool, England, "The Steed and Stirrup"

Henry Wallingham, the proprietor of "The Steed and Stirrup," had learned early in life to convey an air of congeniality and yet be extremely wary of all who came into his establishment. More than once he had been taken advantage of by a guest who not only could not pay for lodging, but also managed to take several room items with him or her as they "checked out" through a back window.

Eloi Mailliard, however, did not look the part of a desperate man. His attire, though not rich, was decent and clean. Henry judged a man first by his clothing, especially his shoes, and in Mailliard, Henry saw a man whose life seemed, if not luxurious, at least of some substance.

And what could charm any man more than a wife with a beautiful, if somewhat wan, appearance? The three children also seemed well-fed and well-dressed, unlike some poor street urchins who begged for the food at his door each day. Turning his attention back to the Mailliard family, Henry had to wonder why a family of apparent sufficient means would be traveling, especially with a child so young. As a curious and cautious innkeeper, he intended to learn.

After resting from their journey, the Mailliards were served their dinner in the anteroom of the inn. Here they ate cheese and drank hot tea, for to drink water of questionable purity could prove unwise before their long journey.

Jane Wallingham, a congenial peer of her husband, served them their food. She too wondered about this family: French, obviously from their speech, and the three attractive children, the boy somewhat excitable, the girl quiet and cautious and the beautiful baby.

"Madam," asked Jane, "what is your baby's name?"

Amanda opened her mouth to speak, but suddenly breathed in as her eyes grew large and questioning towards Eloi.

"His name is . . . ," butted in Amedee, who was stopped abruptly by a stern glance from his father. It may have been the first time that Amedee, had received so harsh and silencing a look.

"Excuse me, Mrs. Wallingham, for not introducing myself and my family earlier. As your husband may have told you, I am Eloi, this is my wife Amanda, my children Charlotte and Amedee, and our baby Leon."

Amedee's head turned swiftly when his father said the baby's name. Charlotte raised her eyes but restrained any other show of emotion.

Amanda merely smiled and added, "Yes, Leon has been such a good traveler so far as, of course, have our other two children here.

Children, a common ground for mothers' conversation, had broken the barrier of strangeness, and now Jane gushed with information of her own family.

"Oh, yes, Henry and I also have our brood. Young Henry has gone to work the mines in Birmingham, I'm afraid. Elizabeth is soon to be married and George and William are still being schooled. The Lord only knows what for. And then, of course, we had young Jane. She only lived to her fifth year before the fever got her."

"I am so very sorry," said Amanda. "We, too, have lost a child, our Jules, when he was seven. But we have three other daughters, who are living with my parents in America. We look forward to being reunited with them in a short time."

Henry, whose ears had picked up when the women began to speak, now understood part of the Mailliard mystery, yet there still were questions he longed to ask—perhaps not now, but later when the men might share a bit of ale.

With dinner ended, Amanda, the baby, and Charlotte retired to their large room on the second floor.

From Mama's look, Charlotte realized that her mother was exhausted from the journey already. Although she was a bit upset that she had been told to come upstairs before her brother, Charlotte admitted, to herself only, of course, that she was also tired. She felt a tightness in her stomach. Was the cheese at dinner not fresh or was the bread too coarse? Perhaps she did need some rest.

She had fallen asleep quickly, but suddenly Charlotte awoke to a darkened room and then quickly remembered where she was. This was the inn in Liverpool, England. Across the room, Mama and baby Napo- no, baby Leon- now slept close to Mama. Amedee too was on his bed, still in his traveling clothes, sound asleep. But there was no Papa. Charlotte surveyed the room again, thinking she had missed him. But she was right, no Papa.

Quietly making her way out of bed, Charlotte moved to the door and as noiselessly as possible, peered into the hall. Looking back into the Mailliard family room, she saw Mama stir slightly and Amedee mumble something in his sleep. Fortunately, the baby was a good sleeper once he was tucked in for the night.

Charlotte saw her shoes and remembered Papa's odd admonition to never let the shoes out of her sight. Mama could be watching them now, Charlotte rationalized.

Moving furtively out the door, she heard voices, Papa and Mr. Wallingham's, coming from the downstairs dining area.

Charlotte crept towards the stairway and settled down beside the wall, feet tucked under her.

"So I must now ask you, my friend, why are you making this trip? I do not understand. You obviously are a refined man, a good family man with a dutiful wife. To travel across that unfriendly ocean, that is quite a feat."

Shaking his head, Papa responded, "What do you see in me, Henry? Do you see a learned man? Hardly. All of my life, since the age of ten, I have worked for others, as a barber, personal attendant, then a secretary. Never in my life have I worked for myself."

Charlotte wondered why the room became so silent. Then she heard her father speaking in a voice that was barely audible. "I have seen . . . I have seen too much. It is often difficult for a man with no means, and then with a wife and family to, to speak up. I have had to agree to pretend I do not see many things. Now, I hope to make a new life for me, for my family."

"Let me ask you," Papa continued. "Do you own this inn?"

"Yes," Henry replied. "It has been in my family for three generations. I hope when I am gone that George and William will keep it alive."

"You see. You are working for yourself, for something that is part of you. I have never been in that position. My brother-in-law in America has written that I can purchase land cheaply and build my own home. Do you know that that will be the first time I will live in my own home? Always I live in others' places, not my own," said Papa.

Charlotte reflected on her father's words: things he had seen, others' places, not his own. She suddenly began to understand, perhaps for the first time, why her father had decided to make this huge change in their lives. Someone's servant, doing others' bidding all his life. No, that could not be very satisfying. But building his own home or doing that kind of physical work, what could he possibly know? Maybe Uncle John, Mama's brother, would be able to help him. Her grandparents would surely be too old.

More disturbing were her father's other words: "I have had to agree to pretend I do not see many things." She thought of the many gifts her family had received from the Bonapartes and wondered if they were given at the cost of silence. The thought was stunning and now Charlotte looked at her father and her family's situation with a new awareness.

"Charlotte, Charlotte, what are you doing out here?" asked Papa. "This is not where you should be sleeping. Come inside, quickly. You must be more careful."

"Papa, I knew you were not far away. Don't worry so much," Charlotte whispered.

As she rose from her crouched position, Charlotte once again felt that strange pain in her stomach. Was her discomfort physical, or uneasiness caused by a revised perception of her family's relationship with the Bonapartes? She must not be ill now, and she prayed to God to please let her be strong in the weeks ahead.

Crossing the Atlantic, the *Commerce*

With trunks loaded and their goodbyes to the Wallinghams complete, the five Mailliards set upon their journey once more. A short coach ride to the dock brought them to the vessel that would be their home for, God willing, the next two weeks.

They would be accommodated alongside the other hundred or so first-class passengers crossing this huge sea. The Mailliards were shown to their suite by a young boy, perhaps no older than Charlotte herself. Their cabin on the *Commerce* was extremely compact, perhaps no more than twelve by twelve, Charlotte surmised, with a screen around another small room that would serve for their toilette.

As he did each morning since the start of their journey, Papa asked everyone if they had said their morning prayers. Charlotte replied, "Of course, Papa," while Amedee shrugged his shoulders in a bit of an assent. Since this particular day was Sunday, the family knelt together (actually, Mama sat and Napoleon crawled aimlessly around the kneeling trio) and professed their thanks to the Lord and made some special requests.

Papa spoke deliberately in his most precise English, "Thank you, Lord, for our many gifts. We pray for a peaceful journey."

Mama, in halting English, spoke for herself and Napoleon. "Dear Lord, thank you for my dear husband (she shot a loving look to Papa) and these three children. Napoleon says thank you for the tasty fingers to chew."

Both Charlotte and Amedee smiled at Mama's comment.

When Charlotte's turn to speak came, she silently hoped that she would not be sick from the constant rocking of the ship (she reasoned that was why she felt ill), but aloud she said, "I thank you, Lord, for my Mama and Papa, who love me. I hope our journey is safe."

Ready to capitalize on any weakness in his sister's comments, Amedee said, "Thank you, Lord, for the best parents in the world, and I hope our journey is filled with surprises."

Surprises! Yes, Charlotte thought, it was surprising how clever her brother's English could be when he tried.

Once again, Charlotte experienced the strange feeling in her stomach and longed for prayer to be finished so she could be more comfortable. Oh, what a time to become ill! Please, God, don't let me die now, she thought.

As they waited on deck for the launch to begin, Charlotte noticed the intense focus of the crew. There were nearly as many hands as passengers who would guide the vessel to its destination, Boston, by way of Halifax. Papa, who had made many trips across the ocean, had told both Amedee and her about the history of this ship. The steamship, run by John Cunard, had been making crossings since 1838, and although crossings could be dangerous, this vessel with steam power was more or less in charge of its own destiny. Papa quickly added that though the sea was always to be respected for its strength, traveling at this time of the year was considered the safest.

The two-decked ship would travel at a top speed of nine knots, and hopefully arrive at its first port in fourteen days. On the main deck, were the passengers' rooms and two dining rooms. The hold carried over two hundred tons of cargo, including mail.

And, although the vessel was officially a steamship, steering was controlled at the helm by the crew—steam power simply propelled the boat. If a storm arose, several seamen would be required at the helm to keep the ship in check. Captain John Hokin, in Papa's estimation, was a forthright and capable leader as he oversaw his officers and crew readying for the launch.

Papa commented on the size and power of the ship, which, he professed, was much more reliable than the ships he had previously ridden. Even Mama seemed impressed by the apparent safety of the ship as her manner had relaxed.

Charlotte wanted to enjoy the splendor of the adventure on this cloudless day in May, but she could not overcome the queasiness in her stomach. When the family dined for their evening meal with their most cordial captain, she was barely able to sit erect. After dinner she excused herself to her cabin and hoped that this illness would subside.

Alone in her cabin, Charlotte readied herself for her first night on the ocean. Though the shifting of the boat as it made its way through the north Atlantic was very light, each motion seemed to exacerbate the sick feeling in her stomach. Soon, however, the source of the discomfort became evident as Charlotte noticed the dark brown stain in her linen. She should have known what the cause was. Mama had noted earlier this year that Charlotte had not begun her courses, and now, today, they had started. In a way she was relieved to know the cause was not serious, but why today of all days?

Now she could only hope that Mama returned to the cabin before Papa and Amedee. Fortunately, her wish was granted.

"Mama, I am so glad you are here. I have begun my courses. What should I do?" inquired Charlotte.

"Oh, my dear daughter. Finally, you are a true woman. Do not worry. We use the rags especially cut for this purpose. Also it is best that for the first few days, you remain in the cabin and rest," said Mama, drawing Charlotte to her breast. "God indeed has given us a gift, to be able to bear his children."

"Children? I don't want any children! I shall never want children of my own," shouted Charlotte. She had seen enough of the farm animals "creating children" to know that she would never, could never, let anyone treat her in that manner.

"Yes," nodded Mama. "I know how you are feeling now, but someday you will love someone enough to want to share your entire being with him. But, until you are married, you must let no man touch you. Do you understand? You must not disgrace yourself and your family with sinful behavior." Mama's voice suddenly had lost its concerned tone and become adamant and strong.

"Of course, I understand," Charlotte replied somewhat insulted. "Please, don't tell Papa, and make sure Amedee never knows."

"They couldn't possibly be interested," replied Amanda.

When the Mailliard family awoke after a relatively calm first night on the Atlantic, Charlotte remained in the cabin with Leon while Papa, Mama and Amedee enjoyed their breakfast. Feeling depressed about her current situation, Charlotte asked the question that many girls have asked: "Why couldn't I have been a boy and escaped all this trouble? Why do I have to go through this when I never want any children of my own?"

She looked at little Napoleon. As he sat there amusing himself with some small wooden figures, he looked up and, with a slight giggle and drool running down his chin, gave her his best four-toothed grin, a smile that would have melted even the coldest of hearts.

Despite his baby charm and smile, Charlotte would not let her mood be changed. She looked at Napoleon, the documents placed close to her by Papa for *her* (Amedee was not quite ready, Papa had said) reading while she was "ill," and those ugly, ugly shoes that Papa had insisted she wear.

Since the day was already lost, Charlotte reasoned she might as well begin the laborious reading Papa was insistent upon.

"Reading will improve your English, Charlotte. Besides, these are such important papers to Americans. You should begin to learn about the people who will be your neighbors in a short time," Papa had said.

Yes, she would read these American papers, but become one of them. . . . she didn't think so.

"*When in the course of human events, it becomes necessary . . . .*"

Despite the reticence with which she approached her task, she found the tract compelling and specific. She also knew that the primary writer, Thomas Jefferson, had later become the president of his country. This in itself added interest. Charlotte also faintly remembered hearing of the positive impression Jefferson had made with the French.

The document stated that all men were born free and that Life, Liberty, and the Pursuit of Happiness were given to men not by any government but by the Creator himself.

However, Charlotte already had noted to Papa that not all people in America were free; those with dark skins were subjugated by others, so the document was laden with hypocrisy from the start. Papa had said the slavery issue was sidestepped to expedite concurrence on other matters, to rally the original revolutionaries in their goal of expulsion of the hated taxes of the King. But she already knew that now, over a half-century later, slavery still existed in the American South.

The English King, of course, was the real focus of the document, his unjust laws, taxes, quartering of soldiers, etc. etc., and the inciting of the Indian savages.

There it was again--the talk of the savages, the topic that Amedee loved to mention. Despite Papa's opinion on this topic (there were no savages in Illinois) Charlotte was again bothered. Something about the word itself conjured a fearsome image in her mind.

Once Charlotte finished this reading, she was attracted to the names of the signers. She loved the name Josiah. It was so melodious and soothing. "Josiah Bartlett of New Hampshire (wherever *that* is,)" spoke Charlotte aloud. "Mr. Josiah, I would like you to meet my brother Leon, formerly Napoleon, of France and Italy."

From across the room, Leon, hearing his name, crawled towards Charlotte. He tried to pull himself up to her knees, but simply slid down and leaned against her leg.

She gave him a dismissive pat on the head, much as she might have petted a dog, and returned to her reading.

The names again intrigued her—so many of those Williams and Georges. There was even a William Williams, such redundancy! But it was the Georges that were most annoying. What a harsh, harsh, sounding name, and the Brits and now Americans seemed so entranced with it. She would certainly never name any son of hers George, but then she was never going to have children anyway.

Well, Jefferson was at least quite readable, and short, but this other Thomas, Paine, was much more longwinded. Papa had also said that Paine had spent much time in France—to the extent that he had become immersed in French politics and almost lost his head at the guillotine. Papa was intent, Charlotte surmised, on showing the strong connection between France and America with the writers he had chosen for her to read.

To most fourteen-year-olds, these readings may have presented an insurmountable task, and Charlotte admitted to herself that her reading choice would have been her favorite book, *The History of Maria Antoinette*, but she would not disappoint

Papa and was determined to complete these "assignments" today, vowing not to become too side-tracked.

Paine's *Common Sense* proved to be much more challenging, not only due to its length but also to its emotional ranting. While the Jefferson treatise was directed to the English king, Paine was truly incensed by the mere *idea* of monarchy. It was, in his mind, illogical and insulting to think that by mere birth alone, someone could rule others.

Yes, Charlotte thought, she could understand that grievance, but she also knew that some rulers, whether by birth or not, achieved their status through popularity or force and then abused their power. She recalled Robespierre and ironically learned in Paine's biographical profile that he, Paine, had been imprisoned during that horrible time, the Reign of Terror. Paine's support for any government that overthrew a monarch was so avid that he had become a part of the French government in the years immediately following the disposition of the King, thus becoming entrenched in French politics.

Ironically, although Paine had rejoiced in the downfall of King Louis XVI, he thoroughly denounced regicide, thus turning suspicion towards himself. How tenuous were French, and apparently other, lives during that turbulent time. She recalled again the killing of Louis and his queen, Marie Antoinette. And then the time of Napoleon Bonaparte, who brought order to his country. Unlike the admiration for his older brother Joseph, the Mailliard family patron, Charlotte always sensed the ambivalence with which her family had addressed Napoleon. Papa's curious remarks in Liverpool about "seeing too much" now weighed on her mind also. She remembered the caution with her little brother's name. There seemed so much to be sorted out that she had not thought of before.

Charlotte's mind returned to the young woman, Marie Antoinette, once again. She had often felt drawn to the story of the queen. How odd, she thought, at fourteen, just my age, Marie had been forced to leave her home, Austria, and become French.

Now she, Charlotte, was forced to leave her country. Ugh! She would never again see her beautiful France and Florence. She hated America, a country of savages. Because of those savages, she knew one could lose a head, or least part of one, by ways other than the guillotine.

Power and corruption, kings and rulers, how unimportant, how trivial it all seemed. How horrible to be imprisoned in any place against one's will, including this incredibly small room, first-class or not.

With an unexplained fury, but careful to miss the baby lying asleep on the floor, she flung one of her shoes across the cabin releasing all the frustration that had been building for weeks.

The result was quite startling.

The baby, scared by the sudden noise, burst into yells, not to be comforted the least by the ministrations of Charlotte as she grabbed him up and rocked him in her arms.

Despite the concerted efforts to quiet the baby, Charlotte's attention focused on the more remarkable scene at the wall where the shoe had met its impact. The heel of one shoe lay open, ajar as it were, and there on the floor were several opals and rubies, just the right size to fit inside a high-heeled shoe.

Charlotte gasped at the contents and gathering them with one hand, she placed them safely in the bottom of her dress pocket. She hurriedly placed the baby on his bed.

He quieted and fell back asleep.

Charlotte returned to the shoe, rubbing her hand lightly on the floor searching for any other fallen gems. She counted eight stones of various sizes. This was the reason Papa had made these shoes dull and with a higher heel! While she was flattered that she was entrusted with these jewels, she felt annoyed that he had not told her the truth.

The other shoe then became Charlotte's focus. She grabbed it roughly, trying to effect the same result. It did not open. She wanted to throw it at the wall, but waking the baby was too much of a risk.

Turning the shoe in her hand, she felt the heel carefully for the place where it would also open.

She then tried pressing various parts of the heel with her hand, pushing first at the inside of the heel and then the back. Perhaps only one shoe held jewels.

Just when she was about to abandon the possibility of another secret chamber, Charlotte felt a slight rise on the bottom arch of the shoe. She pressed the rise and the heel of the shoe slid open. There she saw more stones, eight of them in their undisturbed bed. Cautiously, she slid the heel closed.

The other shoe had to be tried to make sure it worked. She closed the chamber, pressed the rise in the arch, and it opened again. Hearing voices in the hall, she transferred the gems in her pocket back to the heel, counting each as it got replaced.

Not a minute too soon, she placed the shoes neatly beside her bed and picked up one of the pamphlets. Quickly she turned the tract. Reading English right side up would draw fewer questions than reading upside down.

And if Papa felt he had a secret, now she had one also.

As the days passed on the ocean, Charlotte's spirit suffered many transitions, from times of melancholy to positivity about the adventure ahead. She tried to hide her feelings from her family, for she knew there truly would be no one with whom she could commiserate.

Night on the ocean was terrifying for Charlotte. She had never seen blackness so thick and comprehensive. As the vessel moved stalwartly through the night, she felt a loneliness and isolation that was overwhelming. Not one single light, other than on the vessel, could be seen. How easily a life could be lost with just a slight shift in the waves. One could fall into that blackness and disappear forever.

As the breeze of the evening passed over her body, Charlotte shivered involuntarily with the thought of forever being alone in some great deep dark. Unconsciously, she stepped farther back from the railing and resolved never to look at this vast darkness again.

"Charlotte, Charlotte, come back inside, please," Mama requested.

For once, Charlotte was glad to acquiesce.

Halifax and Boston, 1841

On the fourteenth morning, the cry of "Land Ho" was heard throughout the ship. The first sighting of Halifax in the distance brought smiles to all those on board.

The Maillards would not stay in Halifax, Nova Scotia, but would travel on another day's journey into Boston, America. However, the opportunity to walk on solid earth for a short while would be a welcome relief for all travelers continuing their journeys.

Once the cargo and disembarking passengers had left the ship, the Mailliard family made their way down the gangplank of the ship to the pier.

Captain Hokin assumed his station at the end of the runway. The captain served as both an emissary for the Cunard line and an immigration officer.

"Have you enjoyed your journey so far, my dear Mailliards?" inquired the captain.

"Oh, yes, most agreeable," responded Eloi. "How long do we have to walk about here in Halifax?"

"I would suggest no more than an hour. We want to use the daylight hours as much as possible as we will be traveling closer to the shore now. What about you younger Mailliards, Charlotte and Amedee, I believe, have you enjoyed your adventure so far?"

Before Charlotte could respond, Amedee shoved forward and offered his thoughts.

"*Merci*, Captain Hokin. I mean, thank you, sir. I loved this experience. I especially loved the night and looking at the stars. They are so incredibly bright and large, much larger than at home," said Amedee.

Charlotte remembered her fear of the interminable blackness and truly wished she had been imbued with her brother's positive outlook.

"Mademoiselle Mailliard, what are your thoughts on these past two weeks?"

"It has truly been a time of many changes for me, captain. I shall never forget this experience. And thank you very much for keeping us from any storms," said Charlotte with a smile.

"Yes, well, I am afraid I cannot take credit for the positive weather any more than I can be responsible for the storms, which inevitably do come. The Atlantic can be a challenge, and June is the hurricane season, but crossing at this time of year certainly decreases our chances of a challenging trip," replied Captain Hokin. "Please, now enjoy the respite and I will see you in a short time."

As they walked away from the ship, Charlotte heard the captain entertaining the next group with the same questions. Despite feeling less special than she had a moment ago, she continued to entertain her good opinion of the captain. After all, he was answerable to many passengers and crew.

Back on board the *Commerce*, Mama admitted she was glad to be back in the Mailliard cabin, for it is very difficult to subdue a squirmy one-year old, who insists on crawling or trying to walk on his own in an uncontained area. Napoleon was generally a good baby, but two weeks of confinement had registered on his little psyche. It was easy to see, he longed to just *go* without holding anyone's hand or being carried.

Charlotte had a keen sense of her own confinement. Though her world certainly had larger limits than Napoleon's, she was very aware of her boundaries, the limitations of her life and being completely subject to her parents', at least Papa's, decisions. How wonderful it must be to be an adult and in charge of one's own life.

The sense of smallness and insignificance weighed on her mind. Why couldn't she feel the ebullience that was so intrinsic to Amedee? Perhaps she would feel less encumbered around her sisters when she would no longer being the oldest, as she had been for three years. But she really was not looking forward to being the younger sister again, either.

Charlotte felt she would definitely be better once her family reached Point Breeze and were able to rest at the Bonaparte estate before setting out on the next leg of their journey.

Yes, she thought, Point Breeze will provide just the freedom one needs. However, she still needed to survive two days in Boston.

When the ship docked in the Boston harbor, the Mailliards waited for others to disembark. Though Papa was an experienced traveler, he told Charlotte and Amedee that the family should not draw attention to itself. This country would be their home certainly, but for now, well, one never knew what to expect in a strange city. He arranged for the trunks to be once more lashed to a carriage that would take the family to an inn where they would be staying for the next few days.

"Ah, the dear Mailliard family. Please let me officially welcome you to Boston, Massachusetts and America. I hope your stay here will be pleasant," said the captain.

"Actually, Captain Hokin, we may not make another crossing for a long time. We intend to make this country our home," replied Papa.

At the sound of that word "home," Charlotte felt that sense of resentment well. Her eyes began to fill slightly, but she swallowed back any sign of tears. She must overcome this melancholy, she decided.

Pleasantly surprised by the hilly terrain, Charlotte also felt comfortable with the many French influences in this city of 60,000. She heard her beautiful tongue intermixed with the English sounds and witnessed the grand ceremony of the consecration of two flags being sent to people of Poland. Somehow the elegance of the ceremony lessened the apprehension that she felt about the savageness of this country.

As the flags were unfurled, Charlotte was close enough to see the last words of a Polish hero inscribed on one: "It is better to die with glory than to surrender." The meaning of that phrase struck her keenly, and she wondered if she could ever be brave enough to do anything courageous. In this new country perhaps the chances for glory occurred more frequently.

When the name of Lafayette, to whom the flags were entrusted, was mentioned, Charlotte felt a swell of pride for her native country. Here in the American city of Boston, she experienced her first connection to this land.

They continued to observe the proceedings as six companies of infantry and a corps of cavalry joined in the parade. Once a Rev. Dr. Beecher had invoked a Divine Blessing on the cause of the Poles, the dedication was completed as two bands played celebratory songs.

How fortunate that we were here to see this ceremony, Charlotte thought. Perhaps this was indeed a good omen.

Amedee was definitely excited by the events of the day, and Charlotte had to admit, but only to herself, that she enjoyed watching others and learning about America. Mama was tiring already, however, and they all accompanied her back to their inn, where she would rest with Napoleon.

Charlotte and Amedee had convinced their father to continue a walk through the streets of Boston. They sat quietly in the front room of the inn and waited for Papa as he settled Mama and the baby in their room.

"Are you children new travelers to our city? Excuse me, I say, have you just come to our city?"

Charlotte and Amedee looked in the direction of the voice, which appeared to be coming from a rather elderly man sitting in a chair across the room.

"Yes, sir, we have come from Paris, across the ocean. We are going to our new home in Illinois," gushed an enthusiastic Amedee.

"Who are you traveling with?" continued the man.

Charlotte now turned her full attention to the inquisitor and wasn't quite sure how much information she should reveal. His face was friendly enough, but she had never been in a position to answer directly to a stranger, for when they traveled, Papa was always there to provide answers to others' questions.

"This is my sister Charlotte. Papa and Mama are upstairs with our brother, our little brother. We are just waiting to go for a walk."

"You remind me very much of my own grandchildren, Susan and Thomas. My name is John Redding and I have lived in this inn for almost two years. I see many travelers and like to learn about them and then write about them in my journal. It gives me something to do, you know."

"Now, Mr. Redding, you're not getting too nosy with our new visitors, are you?" asked the proprietor of the inn, George Knox, who had just come into the waiting room.

"Just keeping myself occupied with a few questions, George," replied Mr. Redding. "And you, miss, do you always let your brother do the talking for you?" he asked teasingly.

"Not at all, sir. We were told by our Papa to wait quietly to go for a walk," said Charlotte quite deliberately while looking directly at her brother.

"Well, well, I do see a bit of spark there," said Mr. Redding laughingly. "Don't mind my questions, Miss Charlotte. I'm just an old man who tends to be a bit lonely."

The laughter in the man's voice and his kind eyes now touched Charlotte's heart.

"I'm sorry you are alone. Have you no family here in Boston?" asked Charlotte kindly.

"I did once, but my wife and son are both," he paused as if the word still pained his heart, "gone."

"I'm so sorry," said Charlotte sincerely.

"Well, you are a one, aren't you," added Mr. Redding. "I can see by that look on your face that you feel some of the pain that I still feel when I think of my losses."

"Where are your grandchildren now?" asked Charlotte.

"They are in New York with my daughter-in-law and her new husband. I don't get to see them very often. I don't blame her, of course, for marrying again. She found a good man. It is not good for a young woman to be without a man to protect her and her children."

Charlotte and Amedee were so taken by Mr. Redding's story that they did not see Papa enter the room.

"Children, children, please do not disturb the other visitors," Papa's distressed voice and disapproving look quickly interrupted the conversation. "I am so sorry, sir. Charlotte, I am so surprised by your behavior, and Amedee. Forgive me, sir. My name is Eloi Mailliard. We will be staying here a short time. Please forgive my chidren's behavior."

"Mr. Mailliard, it is I who should apologize. I struck up the conversation with your children. I live in the inn here, and one sees youngsters so rarely. Please forgive me my impertinence. I did not mean to cause trouble or to pry," said Mr. Redding.

"Yes, well, we have been traveling quite a while now, and I was just making sure my wife and young child were settled in our room before these children and I go walking," replied Papa.

During the conversation the front door had opened quietly, and a young woman with tinted lips and cheeks entered and sat quietly in one of chairs near the door.

John Redding noticed the young woman first and shook his head.

At almost the same moment the proprietor shouted in the direction of the young woman. "You don't belong here, not in my place. Take your wares somewhere else, I say."

Startled by the shouting, the Mailliards now turned their eyes to the young woman who seemed impervious to the shouts of George Knox.

Wanting to avoid any scene, Papa moved Charlotte and Amedee towards the door.

John Redding also rose from his chair as if he were about to embark on a walk with the family.

The young woman sat unmoving, seemingly unaware of the commotion beginning to brew around her.

As they passed, Charlotte noticed how young she was, not much older, if any, than Charlotte herself. She was not a woman, but a girl. Her youth and flawless skin, however, were in stark contrast to the cheap, bold color painted on her face. As Charlotte, Papa and Amedee came close to the door, the girl rose and looked boldly at Papa and Mr. Redding.

Charlotte now understood what her business was. She had seen women like these while in Paris, even though Papa had tried to guide the family away from their corners and pretend that they did not exist.

Now, as the entire group converged at the door, the girl placed her hand on Papa's, came close to his ear and spoke in a throaty voice, "Perhaps you would like someone to show you the city later, sir, after you send your children to bed."

"Get out, you trollop, or I'll take this stick to you." George Knox shouted into the woman's face, his voice echoing throughout the small room as he raised a broom.

For a moment, fear registered on her face, but then she regained her composure and with a practiced bravado, spoke loudly enough for all to hear, "It wouldn't be the first time I've been slapped by a gentleman."

Though her words were brave, she moved towards the door, smiled and stared boldly into the innkeeper eyes. With a toss of her hair and her brown curls shielding her face, she exited the building and began walking straight into the street and into the path of a carriage.

She screamed and the driver pulled tightly on the reins. The horses reared and snorted as they strained against their constraints.

"You stupid girl," the driver shouted. "I might have injured my horses."

Papa, Charlotte, Amedee and Mr. Redding (who seemed intent on joining the Mailliard family's excursion) emerged from the inn just as the driver yelled at the woman.

Charlotte loosened her grip from Papa's hand and moved towards the girl. She noticed the mud on the girl's face and the look of obvious terror in her eyes. But as their eyes met, the girl quickly changed her expression to one of defiance, looking at Charlotte as if she were a mere child to be ignored.

The girl rose quickly, straightened her clothes and walked purposefully down the street.

Charlotte stepped back and leaned against the wall of the inn.

Amedee, whose eyes had widened, spoke first. "Will we go for our walk now, Papa?"

Charlotte turned her head sharply towards her brother and gasped at his insensibility, or was it incomprehension, of the entire scene.

"It's a pity, that's what it is, a real pity." The voice of John Redding filled the silence that engulfed Papa and Charlotte, and the impatient Amedee, who was waiting for an answer.

"These young girls come to the city from the northeast, many of them from families too large to support their brood. They come here looking for work, but there just aren't enough jobs, legitimate jobs, for them all, and, more often than not, they fall to the streets."

Though Papa seemed to want to move away from Redding's unsolicited explanation, the man was intent on having his views heard.

"I have no idea where their families came from . . . . I, and I speak for many of us here in Boston, we are very proud to trace our roots back to England (remember, it's just the king, we hated), but these girls, well, I just don't understand their lack of morals, no matter how bad the situation."

"Now, I must say, Mr. Mailliard, we don't mind an occasional Frenchie, such as yourself, and your beautiful children settling in these parts, although I must say the French seem to move further west. But, mark my words, if that mess in Ireland doesn't resolve itself, we'll find ourselves beset by those Irish Papists too. I just don't see how that would be good for any of us," added Redding.

Papa stiffened a bit, but did not respond. Charlotte noticed how he turned his hands over and over. She waited anxiously to hear Papa's comment, his response, anything.

"Mr. Redding, yes, thank you so much again for your compliment to my children, but I am afraid I must return to my wife now. Perhaps we will see you again before our departure," said Papa.

With that comment, he spoke quickly to Charlotte and Amedee in French. "*Eh bien, enfants. Ce n'est pas notre affaire.*"

It was the first time Charlotte had heard her father speak French since they had left Mortefontaine.

Papa tipped his hat to Mr. Redding, and then, grabbing each of his children by one hand, he returned to the inn.

Charlotte felt that surely there would be some discussion about the scene when they returned to their room. But Papa forbade both Charlotte and Amedee from any mention of the scene and any comment on Mr. Redding's remarks.

Instead, Papa allowed Mama to effusively describe every "adorable" behavior that Napoleon had exhibited during the time they had been gone. His new word, "*oui*," ("imagine that, French, too," she gushed), how long he had slept, how sweet was his smile, etc. Given any opening, Mama always filled silence with the talk of her darling babies.

During dinner Amedee was somewhat subdued, but soon his appetite returned and it seemed he had forgotten the earlier incident.

Charlotte searched Papa's face to see if he would meet her eyes, thus providing an opening to discuss the scene. However, he deliberately stirred all conversation to anything other than the afternoon's experience. He talked of how lucky they had been in their recent crossing, and then related in every detail, or so it seemed to Charlotte, the occurrences on his previous three crossings. How lucky the family had been to be on a steam-powered vessel this time. She believed she had never heard her father speak so much.

Charlotte poked at the food set before her. She did not feel the least bit hungry. She wondered where the young girl had gone, and what Mr. Redding had thought of Papa's odd behavior. She thought, too, about the man's loneliness, but the hurtful comments he had made about Catholics resurfaced, leaving her confused.

Suddenly, between mouthfuls, Amedee questioned, "Papa, what is a Papist?"

Charlotte immediately looked at her father, who had taken a slow deliberate sip of his wine.

"A Papist is someone who believes that the pope in Rome is the leader of his religion."

"But, Papa, isn't that what we believe? Isn't that just being a Catholic?" Charlotte dared not ask anymore, although she hoped that this opening would lead the way for more of an explanation of the day's events.

"Well, yes, my dear Charlotte, I suppose we are Catholic in that way. But we don't want to worry ourselves or Mama, especially by any trivial discussion." Papa emphasized the word *Mama*, telling Charlotte that any conversation that might disturb her mother was not to be tolerated. The subject was undeniably closed.

Charlotte looked in Amedee's direction. He was already engaged in deciding which of the sweets to eat. As quickly as he had thrown the word Papist into the discussion, he seemed to have forgotten.

The day had started so positively, but the afternoon would forever be etched in her mind, and it was clear nothing further about this day would ever be mentioned, at least not by Papa nor Amedee.

Looking from face to face at the table, Charlotte wondered if there would ever be anyone in whom she could confide.

Point Breeze, New Jersey, Uncle Louis and Cousin Antoine

At times it seemed to Charlotte as if this place called New Jersey would never actually materialize. Traveling on a much smaller ship, the Mailliards boarded once again for a port called Perth Amboy. Unlike many passengers who traveled from Boston to New York via the Atlantic and then right up the Hudson River, the French family had left their ship at this Jersey port.

Here Charlotte read the historical marker that related the history of the town, settled in 1651, when one August Herman had bought land from the Algonquin Indians. Evidently there were some natives who were willing to do business with the early settlers, she reasoned.

In Perth Amboy, Papa made arrangements for a private coach to take them sixty miles southwest to Trenton, from which they would travel the few short miles south following the Delaware River to Bordentown and, finally, Point Breeze. With luck, the final leg of this journey would take no more than three days.

The late May weather blessed the Mailliards. The pungent smells of thriving farms and blossoming trees filled the air as they traveled. Once in Trenton, they lodged at Bow Hill, the red-brick structure where Joseph Bonaparte had resided for a time. With the mention of the Mailliard name, the family was treated almost as royalty themselves. Uncle Louis's name, it seemed, opened doors to expansive civility. Louis Mailliard was well known as the kindly and efficient steward for Joseph Bonaparte, or, as he was called in this world, Count de Survilliers.

Though Papa had told the story before, he now recounted again the story of the Mailliard's patron, Joseph Bonaparte. Established first as the king of Naples and then of Spain and ousted from both *and* his native France, the "gentle"[1] Bonaparte, as Papa called him, older brother of Napoleon, had come to New Jersey in 1816 and built a three-story mansion near Bordentown. The property encompassed 1700 acres with farms, orchards, and wetlands and twelve miles of carriage roads.

Charlotte loved the story and listened graciously. She noticed that Amedee looked anxiously from one side of their carriage to the other, waiting to see the residence that Papa had promised.

As they neared the end of their journey, Papa drew their attention to the dam on Crosswick Creek, a tributary of the Delaware that created a half-mile lake adjacent to the property. Islands dotted the lake and here the Count had planted rare trees and shrubs. European swans glided on the lake while small swan-shaped pleasure boats floated through its waters. So gracious and generous was the Count that he opened his estate to all. Admiring his generosity and the surroundings, families came to picnic on Sundays.

As Papa continued his story, he told of the fire in 1820, when the mansion had burned to the ground. Neighbors helped save the many pieces of art that had adorned the walls inside. The Count's kindness was rewarded as not one artifact was stolen. A rumor circulated that a certain Russian countess had perhaps started the fire out of jealousy. For, in addition to his admiration of the world of art, the Count was also an admirer of women.

"Yes, though loyal to his Queen Julie," Papa said, "the Queen disliked America and seldom stayed more than a few weeks at a time. And the Count," Papa selected his words carefully, "was always popular with ladies."

Charlotte noticed Mama gave Papa a very annoying look. "Now, now, Eloi, be careful of your words. We have children here, you know." Mama's English may have been tenuous, but there was no mistaking the tone of her words.

"Yes, of course," Papa continued."

Charlotte waited for the story to continue, not only to hear how the home had been rebuilt, but also possibly to catch another more interesting detail from Papa's story. Unfortunately, he merely recounted the history lesson.

"When the Count rebuilt after the fire, he employed the French master Theodore Mauroy to build a second house, more secluded from the site of the first and designed after the Bonaparte estate in Prangins, Switzerland. I know that neither of you, Charlotte and Amedee, have been to that home, but for Mama and me, when we visit Point Breeze, it is as if we can smell the very air of the Alps in this corner of America."

Charlotte smiled at the apparent enjoyment that lit Papa's face. Yes, so much beauty here and in Europe, she thought, but where did those riches come from?

As if reading her thoughts, Papa continued. "Remember children, it was to that Switzerland chateau that the faithful steward of the Bonaparte family, your Uncle Louis, risked his own life on a mission transferring much of the Bonaparte treasure safely when the royal family's fortunes had been threatened," continued Papa.

Yes, Uncle Louis had risked his life, but how many lives had been sacrificed for the Bonapartes to acquire those treasures? It was a thought that Charlotte could not escape.

The trip from Trenton to Point Breeze seemed to have lightened the hearts of the Mailliard travelers, and, on arrival, Charlotte felt that she was in a place that truly looked like her home in France. They stopped at the site of the first mansion, where now the only remains were a belvedere, a vantage point from which to view the Delaware River and the surrounding lands. Across the river and to the south was the city of Philadelphia. Papa had promised that the family would make a visit to that city, which housed another residence of the Count.

At long last the carriage arrived at the American home of Joseph Bonaparte, Count de Survilliers. Charlotte, despite the long journey, sat still in the carriage and appraised the three-story structure that clearly dominated the lands and sat between the home built for one of his daughters, Zenaide, and her husband Prince Charles Lucien, and the lesser one, set back and to the right of the chateau, built for Uncle Louis. This was to be the place where her family would rest for the next month or so.

Yes, she thought, it was quite remarkable for this place called New Jersey, but in Florence or Paris, it would have been merely one of many.

Two servants from the chateau rushed from the door to welcome Papa and Mama. It was obvious to Charlotte that her parents were greeted as old friends. Then two others emerged from the home, one so much like her father, the other a much younger version.

"Eloi, Amanda, and children, welcome, welcome. We have waited so long for you to come. How was your journey? I know you must be tired now, but you must tell us everything at dinner. How wonderful it is to see you," said the older man, obviously her Papa's brother. "Surely you remember my son, Antoine? He has grown so tall since your last visit. He has become my right hand man."

Uncle Louis kissed Mama and Papa on both cheeks as a now squirming Napoleon managed to pry himself from Mama's grip.

Normally, Charlotte might have been more reserved, but it was very difficult not to be warmed by her uncle's warmth.

Kissing her hand, the younger man, her cousin Antoine, looked at Charlotte with a curious expression on his face.

"Father, I thought you said my nine-year old cousin was coming? I think this cousin is definitely not nine."

"I am almost fourteen," replied Charlotte.

"She's not even thirteen and a half," interjected Amedee. "We're really only a year apart."

"Well, yes, there it is, eh, Eloi. The children—always wanting to be a different age, just as you and I argued," laughed Uncle Louis. "I really thought you were bringing the baby, Amedee and the younger Amanda."

"That was our original plan, but then we decided that three older daughters would be too much of a challenge for my dear wife's parents. And besides, Charlotte was so adapted to Florence, her Italian is quite remarkable, or so everyone says, that it is she that has remained with us," replied Papa.

"How wonderful. Perhaps, Charlotte, you will be able to help me through my struggles with that language," said Antoine.

Charlotte could hardly imagine anything she wanted to do more. With his charming manners, pleasing smile, merry eyes and curly, brown locks, spending hours speaking Italian would be most pleasurable indeed.

Smiling, she replied in as even a tone as possible, "*Cerchero di fare del mio meglio.*"[2]

Amedee sighed audibly and tried very hard to look bored.

But their uncle seemed not to notice.

"Hearing your name, Charlotte," said a wistful Uncle Louis, "I cannot but be reminded of our dear Princess Charlotte. How incredible that she died so suddenly. I have heard that it was a brain hemorrhage, and she was only thirty-seven. It is because of her death that the Count has returned to Florence to be with his wife, Queen Julie. I'm not sure he will ever return to this world again."

"But how insensitive of me. Your little Jules too is gone, and he was how old?"

"He had just turned seven. Yes, our little one, named for the Queen, of course. It was the fever, you know. We thought he would survive, but then he went so fast. Leaving him in the cemetery at Survillier was . . . was most difficult," said Mama, her eyes moistening.

It was the first time Charlotte had heard her mother speak of Jules' death in such detail.

"It is so very sad. Life is so tenuous, and, for the very young and very old, never to be taken for granted," commented Uncle Louis.

"But now, please come inside. For some reason, life has been incredibly good to me in so many ways, not the least of which is this wonderful home that the Count built for us," he continued.

Uncle Louis's words were indeed true. Compared to where they had been staying for the past few weeks, this home was tremendously expansive, a rectangular, yellow-bricked structure with square windows, three rooms downstairs and four rooms up. Papa and Mama would have their own room, Antoine and Amedee would share a room, and Charlotte would be with Napoleon. She also knew that if Napoleon fussed in the least, Mama would come and take him into her own room. For a short time, it was possible that Charlotte might have a room to herself, a rare delight.

For their first evening in Point Breeze, supper, a most welcome meal of mutton and potatoes, was served by Mary, one of the servants borrowed from the main house during the Mailliard visit. Of course, during the ensuing time, Mama and Charlotte would prepare the family meals.

This evening, however, as Mama descended the stairs, almost like a princess herself, Charlotte noticed how lovely she looked. Mama had taken particular care with her hair, piled stylishly on top of her head with small, curling tendrils down her back. She wore her Sunday gown of medium blue, her favorite color, and had added color to her face and lips, giving her a young, refreshed appearance. Charlotte felt her mother looked quite lovely, for an older person of thirty-six years.

In this comfortable setting, Charlotte felt that she and everyone else at their table, seemed to shed the tension that had filled so much of their time since leaving Survilliers.

Uncle Louis told of the many visitors he had seen to Point Breeze, some of whom who had become quite famous in this country: Admiral Charles Stewart, commander of the *U.S.S. Constitution* during the war with the British in 1812; John Quincy Adams (before becoming president); Henry Clay and Daniel Webster. Many ornithologists had also been guests at the estate, for King Joseph, or "the Count," was a true lover of nature and, especially, birds.

Her uncle Louis also told of one humorous *faux pas*, however, that had occurred when a company of ladies from the American Temperance Society were mistakenly offered wine.

"These immoral French," mimicked Uncle Louis in a falsetto voice, "they shall be the ruination of our country."

Was it the story or her uncle's strange voice that had everyone laughing, including little Napoleon who seemed to mimic the smiles and giggles around the table. It had been quite some time since Charlotte had heard his and her parents' laughter. And Amedee, of course, laughed more heartily than anyone.

"Yes, that was quite an experience," added Antoine. "Perhaps we were too quick to assume that all our guests are as, well, comfortable with our French style as we are, including our custom of serving wine with meals. There are so many things to learn when running a household such as this. I only hope I can be as adept as my father. He has taught me so well. I have learned to be a careful shopper and am trying to learn to be a judge of character as I listen to my father speaking to people about possible employment. There are so many employed here, you know—house staff, gardeners, carpenters, brick workers. We need to rely so much on the honesty of others as we are often away. My father is teaching me to not only listen to what others say, but how they speak and what their manners reveal. It is very interesting."

Unconsciously, Charlotte stopped toying with the spoon left at her plate, straightened her posture and turned her eyes in Antoine's direction. He smiled at her, in a reassuring manner, and she returned his smile. He seemed so much wiser and much, much older than she. She couldn't possibly imagine how Antoine and Amedee would have any conversation in the room they would be sharing.

"Amanda and Charlotte, you have let us monopolize the conversation. I cannot tell you how wonderful it is to have two lovely ladies with whom to share our dinner. My dear Hortensia has been gone for many years. It has been so long since we two bachelors had a lady guest in this home. It may have been the last time you were here, some six years ago, I believe," said Uncle Louis.

Charlotte waited for Mama to respond.

"Louis and Antoine, I find my feelings so difficult to put into words, and English words, at that. But I will try my best." Mama smiled a bit at she looked deliberately at Papa. "I know I must put the things of Europe behind me, and yet my heart is still there, at least partially. I must look ahead to seeing my three other children, children that will almost be like strangers. Will *they* still know their Mama? I feel so, so uneasy. And yet, tonight, at this table, my dear husband, my three wonderful children, you Louis and Antoine, I thank God for the family that is here with me, this day," she said.

She flashed a beautiful smile towards her little Napoleon, who automatically laughed at his mother's loving face. The sweet sound of his laughter broke the heavy spell of Mama's words.

Charlotte was amazed at her mother's speech, so profound and so true to the melancholy on Mama's face. Charlotte had focused on changes in her life so intensely and had not stopped to think about the conflicts that existed in her mother's heart.

Charlotte would have loved for time to stop right here, right now at Point Breeze. Short trips into Bordentown, boating and fishing (for the men), enjoying the art of the main house, and the company of an interesting, older cousin made life incredibly pleasant.

But change of various kinds was always there. For Charlotte, it was also a time of change of another sort. Mama had noticed that the seams of all of Charlotte's dresses needed to be let out and then the hem let down. Amedee's voice often cracked when he started to speak, and he gladly accepted the shoes that had grown too small for Antoine.

Shoes—Charlotte's shoes still were her secret, hers and Papa's, of course. She doubted even Mama knew about the sliding chamber hidden so deftly.

On many days Charlotte and Amedee would accompany Antoine to the markets of nearby Bordentown, shopping for staples not grown on the estate grounds. Antoine had told his two cousins to stay close and learn how to deal with merchants. He told them that he had worked very hard to speak unaccented English when bargaining or paying.

"Accent, what accent?" asked Charlotte. "I do not hear any accent in your voice."

"My dear Charlotte," laughed Antoine, "that's because your accent is much stronger than mine, and Amedee's, of course."

"What do you mean?" Charlotte inquired.

"Listen. I will try to say 'Good morning, Madam Smith,' in the American way. First of all, I would not say 'Madam.' What would I say instead, Amedee?" questioned Antoine.

Amedee's mind had obviously been lost about three sentences earlier, so he merely replied with a shrug.

"Oh, Amedee, aren't you paying attention? Antoine is trying to get us to be more like Americans, although I'm not convinced that is necessarily a good thing," said Charlotte.

"Well, my feeling is," replied Amedee sprightly, "that people will like me just the way I am."

After a look of disgust from Charlotte and a laugh from Antoine, he continued the lesson.

Giving up on Amedee, however, at least for today, Antoine turned to Charlotte. "Do you know the answer, my lady cousin?"

"I believe that you would address the lady as missus, instead of madam. Is that not correct?" she questioned.

"Yes," replied Antoine. "But also listen to how I say the phrase. 'Good morning, Missus Smith.'"

Charlotte noticed immediately that the expression was, well, . . . flat would be the best word, without that lilt or song in his voice.

Following Antoine's example, she mimicked the phrase perfectly, much to her delight.

"Wonderful, Charlotte," replied Antoine. "We just may make an American out of you yet."

Not if she could help it, thought Charlotte.

The three cousins spent other days picnicking and fishing in the small lake. Often, Charlotte and Antoine would try to have their conversations in Italian, but soon he would become too impatient with his own inadequacy, and the language slipped into French or English.

Not that Charlotte cared in the least, but conversing in Italian did just about eliminate Amedee from the conversation. However, she had seen a change in her brother, probably a positive effect from staying with Antoine, she surmised. Charlotte noticed that Amedee, in attempting to emulate his cousin, had become definitely less annoying. He had stopped his sudden blurting out, apparently becoming aware that one should actually wait to be addressed. Mama and Papa had indulged his childlike habits far too long to suit Charlotte, at least.

For her part, in Antoine Charlotte had found someone with whom she could relate some of the experiences of the family's trip so far. She especially wanted to listen to Antoine's thoughts on the episode in Boston.

One day, as the three sat on the lake's shore, Charlotte felt the opportunity to tell the story had arrived. While Amedee was intently engaged in fishing, she and Antoine sat nearby on the grass. Putting her sketching materials aside, she asked if she could share a troubling story with him.

"Of course, Charlotte. From the look on your face, this must be something very important," replied Antoine.

Charlotte then recounted the story of Mr. Redding and the young woman, replete with every detail she could remember: the old man's comments on Irish Papists, the young woman's obvious situation in life, her near death encounter with the carriage horses.

"It all happened so fast, and Papa did nothing but tell us to move away because it was not our affair. I was so disappointed in him. I was so disappointed that I didn't do anything myself," confessed Charlotte.

"And what should your Papa have done? He had two of his own children with him, in a strange city. He had to think of your safety first, don't you think?"

"Maybe, but then we couldn't even talk about it later because he implied that the incident would have upset Mama," said Charlotte.

"Yes, well, you see, adults, too make choices at all times. Sometimes we may not think they are the best choices, but we may not understand all the responsibilities that each person carries," replied Antoine. "Your father is a gentle man and very caring about your mother. Also, Charlotte, what could you have done?"

Thinking for a while before answering, she replied, "I could have told the girl I was sorry. I could have offered her my hankie to wipe the mud from her face. The strange thing was, however, that as soon as she saw I wanted to help, she, she made me feel that she didn't want my help, that I was just a child. "

Grabbing her hand, Antoine replied, "Charlotte, you are a young woman of great heart. That would have been a sweet act of kindness. Sometimes it is just such a small act of kindness done by one individual that can change lives. Yet, often if people accept acts of kindness, they show their own vulnerability. Whatever her situation was, I suppose she felt she couldn't let that happen."

"But I didn't do anything. That's the disappointment. Maybe the next time I will be braver," Charlotte said.

Although he seemed unaware of the conversation, Amedee now added, "I thought the girl was going to get her brains smashed by the horses."

In almost the same breath, he yelled, "Antoine, could you come here and get this line untangled? I've got a mess here."

Perhaps there was no hope for Amedee after all, Charlotte thought.

———

Time passed so swiftly. Was it really almost two months since their leaving France? As the day approached for their leaving, Uncle Louis reminded Papa that the family had not taken the opportunity to view the splendid works of art which still adorned the halls of the Count's home.

With little Napoleon safely ensconced with Mary back in his home, Uncle Louis and Antoine led the Mailliards throughout the house that, with its central block edifice and two perpendicular wings, was a recreation of the Count's chateau in Prangins, Switzerland. In her uncle's estimation, the focal point of the entryway was the eight and half by seven foot painting of Napoleon crossing the Alps by Jacques Louis-David. Recreating the 1800 victory of the emperor, the artist had captured that look on Napoleon's face, at once compelling and commanding, turned toward the observer, pointing forward towards the mountains, his tan cape spread wide in the wind, his white horse reared on its back feet as if ready to charge.

"One can see why that face enticed others to do his bidding," said Uncle Louis quite soberly.

"Yes," continued Antoine, "much good, and yet much that was . . . not good."

Charlotte noticed her uncle look sternly at her cousin.

"Not now, Antoine," replied Uncle Louis.

It was an awkward moment, Charlotte felt, for she had not heard such a tone from her uncle in the entire time they had spent at Pointe Breeze.

Antoine merely nodded at his father and led the family forward. "You also can see the beautiful paintings by Frans Snyder and Charles Joseph Natorie. The Count also brought this huge desk in Empire style and a table with an Italian marble top from Florence, of course. The white curtains bordered in green on the windows are made with fabric imported from Belgium.

The red and white rug comes from Spain, and four gilt-copper chandeliers hanging from the ceiling are from Paris."

Her cousin's voice now sounded strange, decisive and cryptic, quite emotionless. Her uncle continued to stare disapprovingly at Antoine.

As the Mailliard family moved from one room to another (seven on the first floor) Uncle Louis detailed each of the many acquisitions that had been brought to the home. Curiously, thought Charlotte, he did not mention from where they had come as had Antoine.

"When first built," continued Uncle Louis, "nearly two hundred paintings had decorated these walls, including five by Rubens, and one each by da Vinci and Velasquez. These busts and statues of our royal family are truly magnificent, also. To me, they stand here in the halls as marble sentinels almost ready to burst into life."

As they moved into the grand salon, Uncle Louis drew their attention toward many paintings of the royal family by Francois Gerard including Napoleon, in his court robes and his brother Joseph as King of Spain.

"Yes, our dear benefactor, Joseph Bonaparte, a good man, a generous man," added her uncle.

Charlotte noticed the look that he directed toward his son.

"And, dear Amanda, I know this must be difficult for you," Uncle Louis stopped in front of a painting with a young woman and two small girls. "Yes, this is your friend, of course, Queen Julie with the two young daughters, Charlotte and Zenaide. If you remember, the scene is said to recreate the tender moment in the life of the Queen and her two daughters when they received a letter from Philadelphia from their father."

Charlotte's eyes were drawn immediately to the young Queen, seated in a flowing red dress with a front panel of white, her feet propped up on a green cushion, staring stately in the direction of the painter. Zenaide, seven years of age, smiled serenely at the painter, David, while the younger, Charlotte's namesake, looked lovingly at her mother.

She stared at that younger daughter for whom she had been named. The little face seemed to have such a sense of expectation of and adoration for her mother.

Charlotte recalled her own sketching teacher's comments when she expressed the desire to draw faces. "Young ladies do not draw the bodies of people. It would be inappropriate. Besides women do not have the talent or the passion for such challenges."

At the time, Charlotte had accepted that idea, but now, looking at these paintings, she wondered why she should be limited in her choice of subjects just because she happened to be female. Someday, she thought, there will be a face that I will draw.

Breaking her reverie, Charlotte glanced in the direction of her mother to see how she would react to this moment of seeing her dear friend and patroness depicted in the portrait.

Mama, holding onto Papa's arm, began to weep softly, muttering, "So young, so young. She was so good, so kind to me. It was as if she were my older sister."

As Charlotte looked at the picture of her godmother, who had been so very loving to her, she strained to remember that face in real life, in Florence.

The artifacts were not the only remarkable acquisitions. Charlotte was amazed to see the expansive library that housed some 8,000 volumes.

"Yes," remarked Uncle Louis, "the Count has been most gracious in extending the use of those works to both me and Antoine. They have not only helped us pass the time in the evenings, but also to make us appreciate King Joseph's love of the arts. The books include many writings by American authors also: Thomas Paine, Benjamin Franklin, just to name a few."

"Of course, Louis, I have recently recommended Paine to Charlotte on our crossing. I felt his passion and dual citizenship of sorts would be particularly interesting to her," replied Papa.

"Really, that is most impressive. Paine could be a bit of a challenge for a younger reader. But I keep forgetting Charlotte's excellent education," responded a smiling Uncle Louis. "I must remember that she is no longer a child, but indeed a young woman.

"Uncle, would it be possible for Antoine and me to perhaps look at some of these while you continue on the tour? I would, if nothing else, enjoy seeing whom the King felt important enough to place in his library," asked Charlotte, seizing on the opportunity to see how versed cousin Antoine was in this area.

After the others had left the library, Antoine selected the book by the young Frenchman, Alexis de Tocqueville, who, with his friend Beaumont, had come to America in 1832.

"I think you will find this good reading, Charlotte, for Tocqueville seems to have an especially perceptive eye for addressing the plight of emigrants who leave their own histories and travel to this country. He contends that these emigrants, as your family will do, travel to the valleys of this river called the Mississippi and are founding a new society. Yes, they keep some of their traditions, but they strike a new path without limits or obstacles."

"Tocqueville also commented on that path that you will soon take down the Ohio River, the river that separates the two states, Ohio and Kentucky, the former a slave-free state, the latter one with slavery. Listen to what he says, Charlotte. I have read it often because it seems an issue that is a cancer in this country. Yes, here it is: 'The state of Ohio is separated from that of Kentucky by one single river. On the two sides the soil is equally fertile, the position as favourable, yet everything is different. . . .'"

"And," continued Antoine, "those differences of energy against sloth, of enterprise and rapid growth against stagnation and brutality, he attributed to slavery. 'It brutalizes the black population and debilitates the white. . . . Man is not made for servitude. That verity is perhaps even better established by the master than the slave.'"

"I can see you are very passionate on this topic, Antoine. Have you seen slavery?"

"No, in fact, in Philadelphia, across the river, there are anti-slavery groups. But I have heard stories, stories, that, that I should not repeat for you. But I feel someday before too long that this slavery issue must come to a head. I'm sorry, though, to have become so serious on this subject. I do not mean to scare you, and as Uncle Eloi has said, there is no slavery in Illinois. It is a free state."

"The truth is, Charlotte," continued Antoine, "I envy your family this experience, what Tocqueville has named 'the point of departure,' for here in New Jersey it seems as if we have simply transported a small piece of France to this estate," continued Antoine.

"Then come with us, Antoine," suggested Charlotte.

It was a bold comment and one that she hoped would not betray the attachment she felt for this engaging cousin of hers.

"Perhaps someday I will come to visit you in this town of Woodsville, where you are going, but for now I must stay with my father. He needs me here and in Philadelphia. For so many years, it has been just the two of us. We have truly worked together as partners in these last few years. I could not think of going anywhere without him. But it is a most kind invitation," said Antoine, grasping Charlotte's hand and bringing it to his lips.

The tenderness of the moment was abruptly broken by the sound of a door slammed and a strong woman's voice in the foyer. Charlotte looked startled and carefully closed her book as Antoine ran from the library.

"Well, isn't there anyone here to greet me in this palace?" questioned the voice as rapid steps paced in the hall.

Charlotte moved closer to the foyer where she now saw Antoine bowing to a woman, perhaps a bit older than her mother, dressed in a beautiful crimson gown. She untied her black cape and tossed it at Antoine, apparently not caring whether he caught it or not. Her black hair was styled carefully in a cascade of curls that hung gracefully about the olive-skin of her bare neck and throat.

"Antoine," she said as she extended her hand to be kissed, "what a handsome young man you have become."

Her huge, dark eyes became openly flirtatious, an action, Charlotte surmised, that played easily on the woman's part.

"Madam Delafolie," stammered Antoine, "I did not know you were expected."

"Yes, well, that's how things go, life's little unexpected adventures. I have come to see your father, of course, on an urgent and pressing matter: finances. Would you like to find him for me, or should I start looking from one room to the next? I am quite familiar with *all* the rooms in this place, of course," she continued.

"I will find him immediately," replied Antoine.

As Antoine hurriedly left, the woman called to Charlotte. "And you, over there, trying to be inconspicuous, come out where I can see you."

Cautiously Charlotte emerged from the library. Keeping a distance, Charlotte curtsied as delicately as she could, for she felt she was about to be evaluated.

"Who are you? One of Antoine's *young* lady loves come for an afternoon tryst?" asked the woman emphasizing the word "young" as if it were particularly distasteful.

"Madam, I am Charlotte Mailliard, Antoine's cousin, Louis's niece. My family and I are visiting Uncle Louis," replied Charlotte in a voice she hoped was steadier than she felt.

"Charlotte, named for one of his daughters, I suppose, his and his dear Queen."

"Yes, that is correct. Princess Charlotte was my godmother."

"Unfortunate, yes, I heard of her death. But come closer where I can get a better look at you," demanded the woman.

"Well, you are pretty, in a pale sort of way. However, you don't have the color and fire of my daughter. Yes, mine, and King Joseph's. Don't look so shocked, my dear. That's what they do to you, these royals. Use you and then toss you aside, marry you off to some conveniently handy aide."

Without the least bit of hesitation and slipping easily into French, the woman told Charlotte her story. Her name was Annette Savage. (Savage! Charlotte wanted to yell.) She was a descendant of Pocahontas, the Indian princess. (Entirely believable, Charlotte thought.) She had been raised in Philadelphia by well-regarded parents, but met and fell in love with King Joseph in 1821 and her daughter (and Joseph's) was born in 1822. Her beautiful daughter Caroline, Caroline Bonaparte Delafolie, was married in 1839 to Colonel Zebulon Howell Benton.

"Yes, it was perhaps the most elaborate wedding Watertown has ever seen. I must say that Joseph did provide a dowry. And why not? Caroline is just as much his daughter as are Charlotte and Zenaide," continued Annette.

"Does this surprise you? At, what are you fourteen, fifteen? You surely have seen women tossed aside after being used?"

Charlotte simply replied, "Yes, madam," although, in truth, she had not heard of Joseph's affair before. She also could not quite imagine anyone "tossing aside" Annette Savage.

"Well, I do intend to collect my due—financially, at least. I will not be dismissed," said Annette. "They take what they want, when they want it, to suit their needs. Then they toss us a few crumbs to keep us quiet, to satisfy us for a while. And it's not just people, of course. Look at this place with its art works, its furniture, and all the riches. Surely you don't think the previous owners gave them to the Bonapartes of their own free wills? If you do believe all the stories about the Bonaparte family's largesse, then you are younger than I thought."

Charlotte's head turned quickly as Uncle Louis rushed into the foyer.

"My dear Madam Delafolie, how can I possibly assist you?" Louis inquired.

"You know me well enough, Louis. I have written, pleaded, for Joseph's help. I will not be put off any longer. I told Joseph the price is $20,000, or I will expose this whole sordid business. The difference in age when our tryst began would surely be of interest to someone," replied Annette coming directly in front of Uncle Louis's face.

"Please, please, let us retire to the study. Surely we do not want to discuss such private matters in front of the children," replied Uncle Louis as he tried to usher Annette out of the foyer.

"Oh, the children, yes, yes, I was a child once too," hissed Annette, as reluctantly she followed him into the study.

Once both had safely left the room, Charlotte looked immediately to Antoine, who had returned from searching for his father.

"I'm so sorry, Charlotte, that this occurred while you were here. This is sad business. I'm not quite sure what will happen," replied Antoine.

"Actually, she is quite a fascinating woman. What a story to tell! Is it true? And don't answer as if I am a child, Antoine. I think you know better than that."

"The truth is I don't know if King Joseph can truly pay such an outrageous amount—or if he wants to pay anything at all. He most likely believes he has done everything he can, and especially for his and Annette's, Madam Delafolie's, daughter. I'm sure my father will soothe her in some way."

With a smile Charlotte added, "Her last name is so appropriate too—Savage. I believe I have met my first American 'savage'. It has certainly been quite interesting."

"Yes, well, speaking of savages and our upcoming trip to Philadelphia, I have something by Benjamin Franklin for you to read. Don't twist that lovely face. If you are going to be an American, you must surely read something by Franklin, perhaps the most enigmatic man of his age—writer, philosopher, diplomat, inventor. I think if there were one of these Americans I would want to have a conversation with, it would be Franklin. But, that is impossible, of course. Here is the piece, Charlotte. It is entitled, *Remarks Concerning the Savages.* We'll discuss the ideas when you finish."

"Savages? Is this a joke?" Charlotte replied laughingly as she took the book of Franklin's essays.

"Charlotte, Charlotte," yelled Amedee running into the foyer. We have just had the most wonderful adventure. We found a secret tunnel leading to another house. It was to pass from King Joseph's house to the house built for his daughter. It was damp and dark, but we used torches to light it. It was so exciting. You have really missed all the excitement."

"Oh, have I really missed all the excitement again, Amedee? I just never seem to be in the right place," replied Charlotte, patronizing her brother as much as she possibly could without arousing too much suspicion from her parents.

The dinner in the Mailliard home was somewhat unsettled, for Uncle Louis was visibly disturbed by the episode with Mrs. Delafolie. Though reluctant to share the details of the meeting, Charlotte heard him mutter to her father, "That is one devil of a woman."[3]

The tension seemed to infect all as Leon fussed through much of the meal, Amedee was completely unbridled in his recreating of the adventure in the tunnel, and Mama was visibly tired by the walk through the mansion and grounds and seeing the pictures of the Bonaparte family.

Only Charlotte seemed to be invigorated by the day's occurrences, and she eagerly awaited discussing Franklin's essay with her cousin, whom she had drawn from the dining room after the meal was finished.

"It is a curious writing, Antoine. It seems as if Franklin is telling us that the manners of those who are deemed 'society' are actually less desirable than the customs of those who are called 'savages'. Am I reading this correctly?" asked Charlotte.

"Yes, that is right. The savages are more democratic, more welcoming, than those of our world. At least that is Franklin's supposition."

"He does present some logical arguments. But how do you explain the savage practice of scalping? That is surely an evil custom," commented Charlotte.

"Well, that is another 'custom' that can be attributed to French trappers, so I have heard."

"I cannot believe that we will actually be going soon to a place, this Illinois, where savages, Indians, have been so recently. At any rate, Papa says the Indians have left Illinois. I hope I really never meet one," added Charlotte. "I think I have had enough savages to last a life time."

A farewell to Point Breeze and a short trip on Count Survellier's personal ferry across the Delaware River brought the Mailliards to the city of Philadelphia. All were to stay in the Count's home in Philadelphia for the good part of a month. In the three-story structure at 260 South 9th Street, the Mailliards were treated as honored guests by the house staff. It was clear that Uncle Louis and Antoine were well respected by their peers.

The days spent in this city were filled with visits to the famous places of American history including stops at Independence Hall and the Liberty Bell, and the home of Benjamin Franklin. As they talked of the momentous occurrences in those days of 1776, Charlotte was glad to have read the Declaration of Independence as Papa had suggested.

She mentioned her fascination with the names of the signers of the document, and Antoine smiled and said, "Yes, and do we realize that, had the outcome of that war been different, each of those men had signed their own death warrants, for they surely would have been hunted down by the British and ended their lives hanging as traitors."

How true, Charlotte thought. Traitors or patriots, the label depended on which side had the stronger army.

In Philadelphia, the Mailliards also learned that the city had a large, free African-American population of 20,000 and heard of the famous Pennsylvania Abolition Society—the PAS—which worked to protect black people from being kidnapped and sent back into slavery in the South. Antoine informed the Mailliards that Benjamin Franklin had been president of the society in the 1780s.

"Yes, another of his accomplishments was his work for the abolition of slavery. It is said that when he died in 1790, over 20,000 people came to his funeral," added Antoine.

In his own way Amedee, too, seemed impressed by sights which he had seen. Though his perspective was vastly different from Charlotte's, he reveled in hearing of the events in the actual war: Lexington, Concord, the Boston Tea Party, Washington's crossing the Delaware River.

The day following the end of the city tour and bags once more securely packed, the coach arrived to take the five journeyers on the next leg of their trek, to Pittsburgh and the Ohio River.

For Charlotte, the good-bye was indeed a sad one because she realized that perhaps she would never see Antoine again. For almost two months, she had had a true friend, a confidante, who shared her ideas. She felt as comfortable talking to Antoine about her parents, her fears, her frustrations as it was possible to talk to anyone. Did he feel the same? She wasn't quite sure, for his manners and apparent concern for all in the Mailliard family were equally warm. If she had made a mistake in sharing confidences with him, then so be it. At least for eight weeks there had been a friend with whom to talk. Perhaps one of those distant sisters would take his place in the future, but for now, her heart was feeling very empty.

With a wry smile on his face, Papa embraced his brother and nephew and then turned to his own family saying, "Alright, my stalwarts, it is just another thousand miles, miles remember, down and up the Ohio. Well, of course after we travel the road from Philadelphia to Pittsburgh, a mere three hundred miles."

"Papa, surely that is not true," gasped Charlotte.

"My dear, it is just that. This America is nothing if it is not large," he replied.

Antoine assisted all the family into the coach—Mama with Leon, Amedee, Papa, and lastly, Charlotte.

Charlotte could not bear to think of embracing her cousin for the last time.

"We will meet again, dear cousin. And we must always write," said Antoine.

"Yes, yes, of course. I will always write, and perhaps I shall also send you drawings of the flowers in Illinois," whispered Charlotte. "Papa, there will be flowers in Illinois, won't there?" she asked.

Amedee, delighting in Charlotte's apparent discomfort, blurted a menacing response before Papa could reply. "Yes, of course, flowers, and Indians with human scalps on their belts." He put his hands in his waist, pretending to be checking the ornaments on his belt.

Charlotte tried her most sophisticated look, but with her heart truly aching, she stepped into the coach and took her place next to Papa. She waved to Antoine, and then the sound of horses' hooves on the stones signaled the end of another chapter of the journey.

A 19th Century Turnpike

There is nothing like a velvet-lined seat and iron springs in a coach designed for nine passengers and filled only with five to distract the sad heart of a young woman. Charlotte leaned her head cautiously at first, but then comfortably, in this large conveyance and thanked the Bonaparte family silently.

For the sum of twenty American dollars, Papa had managed to hire the stagecoach and driver for this journey across the state of Pennsylvania. The trip would take over a week with stops at inns along the way.

At the entrance to the turnpike, a long pole blocked the roadway, and only after paying their respective tolls could travelers, both two-legged and four-legged, be admitted to the road. Foot travelers and sheepherders walked side by side as faster conveyances passed as they could. Carriages and those on horseback somehow made their ways together in this mélange of activity. For those traveling by carriage, horses were changed after every ten miles. Food and lodging could be obtained from various stops.

Charlotte had often seen animals and carriages on the same road, but perhaps her senses were now keener than they had been before. The strong smells of both animals and humans permeated the air, and more than once she wanted to complain of the smell and heat that was beginning to become oppressive on this warm, early July day. She thought of how wonderful it would be to shed these ugly, hot shoes and wiggle her toes in some cool water, quite unthinkable, of course.

As their carriage passed the animals, Charlotte peered her head further out the window of the carriage and looked closely into the faces of the sheepherders. Her eyes became arrested by the sight of a slim-figured young woman. As the Mailliard vehicle passed closer to the figure, Charlotte looked directly into the eyes of a girl, much the age of Charlotte herself. Suddenly the carriage jolted to a stop as the driver called to the horses. One of the sheep from the flock had strayed into the path of the coach and narrowly missed being stomped.

All traffic on the road stopped, and Charlotte now looked closely at the girl who had attracted her attention. Yes, she was certainly no older, perhaps even younger, than Charlotte herself, but she seemed older. The pale blue eyes of the girl were vacant and her lank, dark blond hair poked out from beneath the dirty cap on her head. In that moment Charlotte felt such a rush of empathy she wanted to leave the coach immediately and run to her aid. And do what, she thought futilely?

In an instant, however, the girl's eyes met Charlotte's and were filled with a sense of defiance. The girl rebuffed Charlotte's stare, much as the girl in Boston had done, when her vulnerability was exposed.

The scene was broken as a rough-looking, tall man came up behind the girl and smacked her soundly on her rear.

"What's the stall here, girlie? Do ya think we got all day to walk this stupid road? The sheep are due to be delivered by noon. Stop your dawdlin' and move along now," he yelled, wiping the spittle from his lips as he spoke.

With the sound of his strident words, the sheep began to bleat noisily as they were pushed on.

Amedee, his head out of the carriage, began to imitate the sheep to his and Leon's amusement. Mama joined in the laughter, delighted to see both her boys in such good dispositions.

"Baaa, baaa, baaa," shouted Amedee. "Baaaaaa, baaaa, baaaaa," he reiterated more loudly and longer than before.

"Please, Papa, make Amedee stop. He, he is making people stare at us," for certainly Amedee's noise had drawn attention to the Mailliard coach.

"Oh, Charlotte, do not be so serious. Amedee is just having a bit of fun," said Papa.

It was not the animals that Charlotte was anxious for. She had seen the girl's eyes, the harsh words of the man, his familiar smack on her body, her feet in the worn clumsy shoes. What is her life, Charlotte wondered, when she is not with the sheep?

Looking at her own shoes, which she had so recently wished to be without, Charlotte slunk down within her seat, hoping the strangers could no longer see her head. She snuggled down tightly into her velvet seat and grew silent.

Lulled by the rhythmic turn of the carriage wheels, Charlotte fell into a fitful sleep. In her dream, she became the shepherdess of the road, while her family laughed heartily at her as the carriage rolled by. She called, but they were unable to hear her voice because it was drowned out by the baaing of the sheep.

Jarred by a bump in the road, Charlotte sat up quickly, only to be faced with the sound of baaing by Amedee, whose face was a mere hand-span from hers. Involuntarily she screamed, delighting her brother immensely.

The next stop could not come soon enough for Charlotte, who longed to escape the confines of the coach and the teasing of her brother. Yet when the stop was reached, she sat unmoving in her seat. Amedee rushed from the coach followed by Papa, who assisted Mama and Leon as they alighted from the vehicle. Charlotte waited for her family to leave the carriage. Hoping she could distance herself from the other four, she waited as long as she could. Perhaps others would think she was a lone traveler and not connected to the entourage.

As Papa purchased some fresh fruit and water for the family, Charlotte continued to distance herself from each of them. How could her parents be so unaware of her loneliness, the rudeness of Amedee, and yes, even the annoyance of Leon? Despite the baby's charming grins and smiles, and his attempts at speech, English now mixed with French, he was a ball of squirminess, refusing to be contained as he now could proudly walk a cautious few steps. Walking as quickly as his chubby little legs could manage, Leon ran from Mama and Papa. They, of course, pursued him, much to his delight.

Traveling the Ohio

"This is it, my weary ones, La Belle Riviere,"[4] said Papa trying to bolster the spirits of his little group as he gestured towards the huge Ohio River. "Soon, just ten or so more days, we will come to our new home, Illinois. And we will have a most luxurious room on this steamship as we move down this waterway."

Yes, true, the room could be "luxurious" by some standards, but what Eloi did not tell his family was that travel by steamship could also be extremely dangerous as the pressure from the steam often became uncontrollable, causing boilers to burst apart or catch fire. Ships sank and crew and passengers died from scalding burns or went to watery deaths. On his previous journeys west, he had heard the stories of the steamships *Motto*, *Monmouth*, *Belle of Missouri*, *Dubuque*, and *Wilmington*, that had been destroyed by carelessness and poor planning.

In addition to steamships, the river was host to a large number of the flatboats that carried trade and immigrants making their way westward. Upon landing at their destinations, these settlers would then dismantle their boats and use the wood for their new homes.

On this particular, already uncomfortably warm and humid, day in July, 1841, where the Allegheny and the Monogahela joined together to form the Ohio, Pittsburgh teemed with ship activity. Passengers boarded for Cairo, Illinois; Natchez, Mississippi; New Orleans, Louisiana; and St. Paul, Minnesota. Only the waterways of those great lakes north of the Ohio—Huron, Ontario, Michigan, Erie and Superior—rivaled the paths taken by European immigrants and Americans from Eastern seaboard states traveling westward. The city, one of the largest west of the Allegheny Mountains, was indeed, as Tocqueville had said, a "point of departure."

Papa had bought passage for his family on the *Prairie*, a steamer that could run from eighteen to twenty-four miles per hour. He requested the room as far away from the paddle wheel as possible, for he viewed it as a possible danger for both of his sons, one out of curiosity, the other from ignorance. The five Mailliards would be situated in a stateroom on the salon, deck, ten feet above the main deck. From this level rose the promenade with more staterooms and the pilot house situated at the front. Chandeliers hung in the salon while the women's salon was equipped with velvet chairs.

Since the vessel was still in port, the family was invited by Captain Horace Bixby to view the pilot house, a roomy, glassed-in structure, decorated with an oil painting of the vessel itself. The two huge smoke stacks rose another thirty feet billowing black smoke.

"Thank you, Mr. Mailliard, for joining us on this lovely day," welcomed the captain. "My crew has secured your trunks safely into our hold, and in a short while we will be ready to leave. I hope we can provide enough entertainment to keep your family happy for the next few days. We are very proud of our ship and the care we take to make all our passengers comfortable."

"Yes, thank you, Captain Bixby. My older children, Charlotte and Amedee, will be very interested, I am sure, in all the stops we make. As new Americans, I want them to learn and absorb as much as possible on this voyage," said Papa with a concerted look at both of them. "And my wife and I will keep our younger child out of harm's way."

As the Mailliards settled into their stateroom, Charlotte chose a corner as her own and then quickly asked for permission to observe the activity from the outside promenade.

She saw Captain Bixby greeting the passengers as they made their way on the gangplank to their assigned rooms. Did his manner seem to become less cordial as the dress or lack of belongings of passengers became apparent? The line of humanity ascending the ship was indeed interesting. She speculated on the country of origin, straining to hear how they spoke, how many were traveling together and what their relationships might be.

Unconsciously, her eyes moved to a young man standing in the back of the line. He was looking directly at Charlotte, yet when she looked at him, he quickly moved his eyes downward and shuffled forward. She saw that he was dressed neatly, but in well-worn clothes, and carried just two small cloth bags, one obviously heavier than the other as it weighed down his right side.

As the young man approached the captain, he began to speak quickly and seemed to earnestly be making his case. The captain shook his head, but the youth would not be dissuaded and followed the captain as he moved away. The young man opened one of the bags and reached inside, displaying some sort of tool to the captain.

Charlotte was enrapt with the scene. She wanted the youth to convince the captain despite not knowing what his plea was. As the captain moved away again, he glanced at Charlotte, who now felt somehow she must also convince him to move in favor of the young man's request. She waved to both the captain and the young man, hoping that this ridiculous and futile intervention would somehow make a difference.

The captain nodded to Charlotte and then, turning back to the youth, furthered his questioning. As the youth seemed to be nodding an affirmation, the captain brought his book out, wrote quickly, and directed the young man to the forecastle, where other crew members were assigned.

Charlotte wondered what had occurred and if she indeed had played a part, but when the youth disappeared she began to once again notice other passengers.

"Miss Mallard, excuse me please, may I speak with you quickly?" a young male voice spoke behind her.

Somewhat startled, Charlotte turned rapidly and came face to face with the youth to whom she had waved. She saw more closely the same interesting, if not even a bit handsome, face of a young man, several inches taller than she. Removing his tan cap, his brown hair fell forward around his face. His blue eyes were intensely focused on her.

"Oh," she gasped, "it's you."

"Yes, yes, but I am confused. Do you know me?" asked the young man.

"No, I don't," said Charlotte. "But I just felt that I had to do something to, to help you. I certainly did not want to cause you any trouble. My name is Charlotte Mailliard, (Charlotte deliberately pronounced the *three* syllables of her surname) and I am traveling with my family. Did I do something wrong?"

"Oh, my absolutely no, Miss Mailliard," said the youth trying to emulate Charlotte's pronunciation. "You have, in fact, helped me to obtain work on this vessel. The captain was not going to hire me because, because I have no experience, but when you waved, he assumed I knew you."

Pausing, he continued, "I hope you will not betray my secret. I didn't dissuade him from his assumption. But I am a hard worker. I won't do anything to embarrass myself nor involve you."

Charlotte, delighted by the outcome, simply smiled and said, "I'm sure you will be an excellent crew man. Perhaps it might be good for me to know your name, however."

"Of course, I have forgotten my manners," he said with a slight bow. "Please, forgive me. My name is George, George Simmons."

Charlotte offered a slight curtsey, and with that the youth quickly moved down the stairs to the lower deck.

Smiling to herself, Charlotte felt that the pleasantness of the encounter was offset, just slightly, by his name, her least favorite, of course, because it was just so English. And, if possible, she resolved to keep the meeting with this new "friend" entirely to herself.

"Charlotte, have you been enjoying yourself out here?" asked Papa accompanied by a surprisingly quiet Amedee.

"Yes, Papa. I have been very interested in watching the passengers come aboard. How many do you think will be on this boat?"

"The captain has told us there will be around three hundred passengers and a crew of forty. Yes, and I also want you to be aware of something else. There is a black crewman on this ship, Charlotte. His name is Jonas Williams. The captain did not want us to be startled or shocked by seeing him here."

"Papa," interjected Charlotte, "I have seen people with dark skin before once or twice in Paris and then in New Jersey at the markets. Is this man one of these poor American slaves?"

"No, not at all," replied Papa. "In fact, that is what makes his position so difficult. He is a free man, but traveling this river, which is banked by free states on one side and slave states on the other, he is constantly in danger of being kidnapped and sold again because he is such a remarkably strong worker. There already has been one attempt to take him, but he managed to spoil the effort by wounding his would-be kidnappers. Even sadder, his wife and two daughters were kidnapped. And his wife was an octoroon."

"Yes, I didn't know what that was either," replied Papa to Charlotte's quizzical look. "It means she was only one-eighth black, but it was enough to bring her to slavery. I just had no idea that this slavery issue, what the captain called this 'peculiar institution' would touch us so personally. There may be some of these kidnappers riding on this very ship, so we must be very wary of strangers. Jonas has tried to learn of his family's whereabouts but to no avail. And he must do so without drawing too much attention to himself."

"I cannot begin to imagine the pain and turmoil that he feels. I try to imagine myself in that position, thinking of you and Amedee living a life where you would be abused and 'owned' by someone. The mere thought is too painful," continued Papa.

Turning to Amedee, Papa said, "Are you alright? The captain's story contained so, so many vivid details of Jonas's life that I am afraid you are not well. I should have sheltered you from hearing them."

"Papa, could I be made a slave too?" asked a pale Amedee.

"No, no," said Papa. "You are boy with white skin. You do not need to worry."

Charlotte thought again of her father's behavior in Boston. *Ce n'est pas notre affaire*, it is not our affair. But then whose affair was that?

"Above all, children, you must, absolutely must not, disturb Mama with these stories. She has endured so much lately. She must not be told of evil things that we are powerless to control. We will make our way to Woodsville as calmly and peacefully as possible, not looking for trouble. I will tell her that a black man works as a crew member on the ship and end the story there. Do you both understand?"

"Yes, of course, Papa," answered Charlotte.

Amedee nodded, but his face, Charlotte noted, was still visibly distraught by what he had heard, and he said nothing. She wondered why this particular sad episode had disturbed him more than the girl on the street in Boston. Was he indeed developing some empathy for others? She turned to him and tried to read the still ashen and impassive face, so unlike Amedee. She saw no answers.

As the *Prairie* launched north up the Ohio and then finally made its turn to the south and its final destination Cairo, Charlotte settled into the routine of the journey. In the morning the family would breakfast together; then she would help Mama with Leon. In the afternoon, she tried to sketch some of the flora she remembered from the time at Point Breeze as Mama and Leon napped as the ever-increasing heat seemed to cause days to move very slowly.

Charlotte knew that members of the crew would be working to fire the boilers and could not even begin to imagine their discomfort. She wondered what exactly George Simmons' job was. She had heard the crew worked in four-hour shifts. How long those four hours must seem when the external heat was nearing one hundred, and boilers were waiting to be fed.

The vessel rolled past several towns—Steubenville (once called La Belle), Moundsville, where an eighty foot mound containing Indian remains rose from the earth. Everything was so expansive in the country: this river, a mound. By comparison she remembered one of the family's last trips down the Seine in Paris, where Amedee had called "*Bon Jour*" to people on the shore, and they had smiled and returned his greeting. Here a whole chorus could scream and not be heard on shore.

She tried to sit on the lower deck where she might possibly meet or see others, but though other families were traveling, Charlotte had not seen other passengers her own age. And, yes, she also hoped to see George Simmons and ask him so many questions. She was not sure of his work hours, but she felt that he must truly be exhausted after his shift.

On the third day the ship stopped at the town of Marietta, established in 1790, and, in gratitude for the French help during the Revolutionary War, named for Marie Antoinette. Alighting from their ship, Captain Bixby reminded them to make the ship's call in four hours.

"Thank you, Captain," replied Papa. "We have no desire to make our trip any longer than necessary."

The shops and walks in Marietta were a pleasant respite from the confinement of the ship. Amedee, restored to his positive self, entertained little Leon as they romped in the town park while Papa watched.

Mama and Charlotte visited the small stores that displayed the crafts of local merchants while a general store displayed staples such as salt, sugar and spices. Having learned how to purchase and use the American coins while shopping with Antoine, Charlotte helped her mother buy some chocolate.

As they were leaving the store, Charlotte noticed George Simmons crossing the street coming towards her and Mama. Had he seen them before or was this merely a chance encounter? She could not move Mama quickly enough to avoid introduction and decided to speak although George addressed them first. How American, Charlotte thought.

"Miss Mailliard," said George, "how very nice to see you again."

"Mr. Simmons, I imagine you have been very busy the past few days. Permit me to introduce my mother, Mrs. Eloi Mailliard."

"Mr. Simmons, you are a friend of my daughter's?" questioned a rather surprised Amanda.

"I do hope I may be her friend, madam. I did meet her when I came on the *Prairie*," answered George.

"Well, how very nice to see a person of my daughter's age traveling with us. Would it be possible for you to dine with us this evening?" asked Mama.

Charlotte gasped, a bit surprised at Mama's forwardness.

"Thank you sincerely for your kind offer, but I am afraid that would be impossible. I am merely a member of the ship's crew," replied George.

"Oh, a crew member," answered Mama with a hint of disdain. "What is someone as young as you doing working on this ship? Where is your family?"

Charlotte wanted to roll her eyes. Truth be told, however, she longed to hear his answers.

"Madam Mailliard," said George with a slight bow, "I am not *that* young actually. I am eighteen years old and have come from New York. As so many others, I am traveling west. I hope to perfect my trade as a carpenter and also become a teacher in St. Louis."

"A carpenter and teacher, those are fine goals, Mr. Simmons. And how did you come to know my daughter?"

"We met, Mama," Charlotte injected, "when Mr. Simmons was coming onto the ship. He seemed to be so earnest in his need for a job that I, I implied to the captain that I knew Mr. Simmons."

"And just how did you do that, Charlotte?"

"Well, I waved to them."

"You waved?"

"Yes, Mama," continued Charlotte looking directly at her mother and hoping that her eyes would tell Mama to end this somewhat embarrassing interrogation. "I waved."

"Madam Mailliard," implored George, "there was nothing inappropriate on your daughter's part. I hope you would not be offended by my allowing the captain to think I, I was acquainted with your family."

"Oh, this country is just so very forward. I will never get used to this. I suppose it was all very innocent. I must say you are a very well-spoken and polite young man. You say you want to be a teacher?"

"Yes, yes, madam. In fact, would you allow me to discuss with your daughter the book that I have just purchased? It is a new edition of essays by Ralph Waldo Emerson. I also have my other favorite book, *Poor Richard's Almanack* by, of course, Benjamin Franklin."

"You wish to discuss books with my daughter? Now, I think, you have met her, us, before, for she is just the person to engage in such a talk. She has been groomed by her father and her cousin, most recently, to be a reader of books."

Nothing Mama said could have delighted Charlotte more.

"Have you, by chance, read any of Franklin's works, Miss Mailliard?" inquired George. "I do know that the Almanack has been translated into French."

"No, I have not read the Almanack, but I have read, in English, (Charlotte stressed that fact) Franklin's writing, *Remarks Concerning the Savages of North America.* I look forward to your comments soon, Mr. Simmons."

Charlotte wanted to shout, Thank you, thank you, Antoine, for having me read that piece by Franklin, but she knew she could not. She would, however, be sure to write her cousin a very thankful letter.

"You may come by after your shift tomorrow, then, Mr. Simmons. My daughter will be ready to discuss . . . books."

Although the summer heat of the Ohio was becoming more oppressive each day, and the evenings were filled with the incessant attacks of ravenous mosquitoes, Charlotte now looked forward to five in the afternoon, the time when George Simmons would come to "discuss books."

It seemed to Charlotte, however, that she actually did most of the talking—and although she would tactfully, she thought, try to learn of his family, Mr. Simmons, George, was not one to divulge much of his personal life.

She did enjoy Franklin's witticisms, though, from the Almanack, but whereas Charlotte might see the humor in the sayings, George would be much more serious about their content. Sometimes she could see the frustration building in his manner as she made a flippant comment on something George regarded as serious.

"Miss Mailliard, this is one of my favorites from Franklin: 'A Plowman on his Legs is higher than a Gentleman on his Knees.' Do you see how this idea gives each occupation a nobility that is greater than the work itself?"

"Yes, Mr. Simmons, I believe I do understand the impact of that statement, and how, in this country particularly, it has impact, but I am afraid that in my mind I see a rather rotund farmer stepping on the back of a foppish gentleman whose greatest concern is now the dirtying of his socks from the, the . . . soiled bottom on the farmer's shoe. And, of course, we know what is most likely to be on the bottom of a farmer's shoe."

Charlotte often surprised herself with her behavior toward George. He was so very intent and serious that she frequently felt the need to lighten their conversation.

"Well, yes, I suppose. One could see the image as somewhat comical," said George. But his face did not smile, and he said no more.

George clearly took to heart, Charlotte felt, Franklin's aphorism, "Well done is better than well said."

When he spoke, he already seemed a teacher, so convinced was he of his ideas. He spoke with an assurance that she felt she would never have. Moreover, when she had spoken with Antoine, she felt comfortable voicing an opinion. With Mr. Simmons, George, she felt ill-equipped to argue with his ideas.

Emerson, George professed, had taught that a man must be self-reliant, must not conform to traditions or society for the mere sake of pomp or notoriety. Man should not be concerned by what others think. Institutions, yes, even friends, seek to influence and destroy our state, but men cannot allow confusion into their lives.

"We must belong to no one but truth. When those around us, even those to whom we are closest to in our family, seek to separate us from the truth, then we must still be ourselves," uttered George.

"Oh, my, Mr. Simmons. But what is 'truth'? How do I know when I see it? Do I not learn from my parents, from their example? Do I not learn from Jesus's example?" replied a very distraught Charlotte.

"I certainly do not claim the answers for you, Miss Mailliard," answered George. "I only know, and perhaps this is because I am older than you, that what I seek is not in the form of material wants or society's institutions. Each man must be self-reliant, in every sense. That is what I have learned. Thank you for your company, this evening."

With that George bowed slightly to Charlotte and made his way down to the crew's quarters.

Charlotte felt a pang of guilt as she went forward to join her family, her "society" at its reserved table in the dining room. What would Mr. Simmons think if he knew that her family was tied to the Bonapartes? Even more, what would he think if he knew that they were "Papists?" The very word seemed to imply a non-self-reliance that she had never thought of before.

Without Charlotte's knowledge, Papa had already inquired about Mr. Simmons after Mama's urging.

Privy to Charlotte's "waving," incident, Papa asked the captain one evening, "How is our young friend, George Simmons, working on the ship?"

The captain was only too glad to report that Simmons was a hard worker who kept to himself and did not join in the card games of other crew members. He seemed solicitous of his money and apparently had little with him. His carpentry skills had been used to repair and replace boards on the vessel. He did this with ease and capability, reported the captain.

"I see that the two young people have been spending time with each other in the evening. Were they good friends before?" inquired the captain.

"Yes, well, somewhat, one could say." Not wanting to continue the charade too deeply, Papa turned the discussion to an island mansion that suddenly came into view as the boat turned.

"My word, Captain Bixby, are my eyes deceiving me or do I truly see a most spectacular building appearing on the horizon?" inquired Papa.

"Yes, we must be nearing the Blennerhassett house. You are quite right in what you are seeing. At one time the edifice was called Paradise, and, indeed, its owner, Harman Blennerhassett, built it, no expense spared, so they say, for his wife *and* cousin Margaret. I never saw them myself, but supposedly they were a most attractive and romantic couple who came from Ireland at the end of the century. But poor decisions and an alliance involving Aaron Burr and a General James Wilkinson in some fool scheme to separate the state of Kentucky from the United States led to Mr. Blennerhassett's getting himself thrown in prison. As the story goes, Harmann was acquitted, but his fortunes were depleted, and then bad growing seasons led to further depletion of resources. The couple abandoned the house in 1831, and the house has not been occupied since. Each time I come to this part of the river, I look at its fading beauty, a monument to love, and extreme bad judgment and foolishness."

"Not that I have anywhere near the man's resources," continued Captain Bixby, "but my tastes run to not displaying any fortune in such ostentatious ways. My wife and I live a simple life. Perhaps our good rapport with each other has much to do with the fact that, for many months of the year, I am home infrequently," said the captain laughingly.

"If you don't mind my asking, Mr. Mailliard, what is your trade?"

"My trade, ah, yes, well, I hope to become a farmer," replied Papa.

"Glory be!" exclaimed the captain. "That would have been my last guess. You look and behave as if you are from some of that dang royalty in Europe, probably French from your speech."

"But you see, captain, that is the beauty of this country, I am told. It does not matter who a man's father was, but only that he is willing to work and be a good member of society," replied Papa.

"Sure, that's a great founding principle of ours, I guess. But from what I have observed in this country, the real royalty is money. It's a somewhat jaded view, is it not? Perhaps I have guided too many ships down too many rivers. I hope I have not bored you with my stories and views. You have a lovely family, and that, too, is its own richness. Good evening, then, Mr. and Mrs. Mailliard. Perhaps we can share more time before your journey is ended," said the captain.

As the captain moved to the tables of other passengers, Papa looked from one family member's face to the next.

"We are not rich in the sense of money; that is very true. But we have the greatest richness of all, this family. We have had our family in France, our family that will help us once we arrive in Woodsville. And each of us gives to the family in our own way. Mama, you are the heart. Charlotte, your generosity and concern for others causes us to consider those who may be less fortunate. Amedee, you bring a liveliness to our lives that I hope you never lose, although at times it could be a bit more subtle," he said, looking at Amedee and tousling his hair.

"I hope that as little Leon grows, he will add his own special quality to our family and that my two sons will become good friends, just as my brother and I have been. When our journey is finally ended, we will have three more daughters to add their joy to our group. Yes, we are truly blessed," added Papa. "Amedee, would you please help Mama take that little brother for a walk now? He really is becoming quite curious in his exploring."

"Of course, Papa." Amedee seemed very delighted to be given this responsibility as he smiled broadly towards his father and rushed away from the table, following Mama and Leon.

"Charlotte, I feel there is something which I have hidden from you, something that perhaps you are ready to hear. With Heloise and Pauline gone for these past three years and Mama ill so often, I feel perhaps that I have relied on you, given you too much responsibility. When we finally reach Woodsville, I will share a secret with you and I hope we will laugh together then."

"A secret, Papa? Really, now you are just teasing me, I am afraid," smiled Charlotte in return. "Well, then I suppose I will just have to wait until that time, won't I?"

Charlotte thought, I believe I already know your secret, Papa, and consequently she did not press further for the information, but unconsciously shuffled her feet under the table.

"Thank you, Charlotte, for being so understanding. I cannot help but think of your sisters in Woodsville and how they will have changed during the three years since we have seen them. Heloise, seventeen, and Pauline at sixteen, so close in age, good companions for each other. My word, they might even be thinking of marriage, although your Gramere Gallet did not say so. Did you know your dear Mama was only eighteen when we married? And her namesake, our little Amanda, was only six when we left her with her grandparents. The last time I saw her she was so very much like Amedee, in spirit and looks."

A slight touch on his arm, and Papa jumped.

"So deep in thought, I see that I surprised you, *mon chere*," said Mama. "What is it you see out there?"

"I was just thinking about our children. Please don't cry, Amanda, about Jules. He was a precious gift for those seven years. And we are so blessed with the six children we have. I have just been talking about our family with our dear Charlotte."

"Children are our blessing, but one never stops thinking about those that are taken away nor worrying about what their futures bring. Do you realize how old Heloise and Pauline are already? We should be searching for husbands for them."

"You know, my dear, there already is a small French community in our new home. Perhaps our task will be easier than we think," said Papa. "But we must remember. This is America. Our families will be remade in this new land."

"Yes, I know it is true. What do you think of this George Simmons who has taken to 'discussing books' with our Charlotte? Surely this is some guise, or young men have changed greatly. But then he is English, of course," said Mama, looking directly at her daughter.

Laughing and taking her hand in his, Papa replied, "Yes, he is English. But he is like us, a traveler, looking to change his life. I must admit I would like to know more about his family, however. Perhaps we should have Amedee engage him in conversation. What do you think, Charlotte?"

"You want Amedee to join our conversation, Papa?" questioned a rather incredulous and disapproving Charlotte.

"Do not be so hard on your brother, my dear. His manner may be not as sophisticated as yours, but he has a good heart. And perhaps he may actually bring a different perspective into your conversation. With your permission may I introduce him to your friend?"

"Papa, I have no claim on Mr. Simmons. But are you not worried about how much Amedee could reveal about us? Is there anything that you could say to him to control his tongue? Are you not worried about our safety?" said Charlotte. Secretly, however, she had to admit, her blunt brother might just be able to draw out the somewhat tight-lipped Simmons.

"I will give Amedee specific instructions about what not to speak of. I am afraid, however, that if he does not speak with someone who is close to his own age and interesting, he will simply find more mischief."

And as the *Prairie* moved tentatively down the stretches of the Ohio, Charlotte made two observations: the French had definitely contributed to the history of the river and its towns, and one, twelve-year old former Frenchman had definitely changed the dynamics of her time with George Simmons.

George seemed to be more at ease and smiling when Amedee would appear. A certain tenseness that had existed between her and George had subsided. She also had to admit that Amedee's direct questions drew responses from people. In the two days time since he had joined their late afternoon meetings, Charlotte had learned much. As they passed Gallipolis, George related the story he had heard from other crew members about the settling of the community in 1790 by Frenchmen, known as the French Five Hundred.

"The men have told me that they arrived in the dead of winter. They were not farmers by trade, most were shopkeepers and businessmen. But their spirit was undaunted. When they came, supposedly after unpacking their clothes, they threw a dance," said George.

"That would be great, don't you think, George," said Amedee. (Amedee and George had achieved first-name basis after a very short time.) "You definitely would want to do something that was fun after a long journey. You certainly couldn't plant any seeds in the winter also."

"Yes, Amedee, that is a very perceptive statement. And if one thought dancing were fun, then it would be the thing to do," replied George.

"Do you not dance, George? I have only been allowed to dance with Charlotte, but when we get to Woodsville, I will dance with my three other sisters also. Their names are Heloise, Pauline and Amanda. Heloise and Pauline are even older than Charlotte, but Amanda is younger. I'm sure they will dance much better than Charlotte. Do you not have sisters to teach you to dance?" gushed an animated Amedee.

"I do have sisters."

"How many? Are they older or younger? I certainly hope they are younger. That is much better, I think," continued Amedee.

There was a long pause as both Charlotte and Amedee turned in George's direction. Was he waiting to speak because he felt there could be more questions coming from Amedee, or was he waiting because he simply did not want to reveal anything about himself? Charlotte could not be sure.

"I have two sisters, who are older," replied George.

"What are their names?" pursued an undaunted Amedee.

"Their names are Sarah and Mary." George responded so deliberately as if to speak the names was to almost feel some physical pain.

With just a slight pause in his thought pattern, Amedee announced, "Me and Charlotte have other names also. My name is Amedee Joseph, Joseph for the king, of course. And Charlotte is named for the king's daughter, but her other names are Louise and Josephine. Josephine is for the empress, I think. Our little brother's name is . . . (finally realizing that he might have crossed into forbidden territory after a startled look from Charlotte) well, you have heard it, Leon," said Amedee, completely pleased with himself that he had been very careful in not revealing too much.

"King Joseph? The empress Josephine? You are named for people in Napoleon's family?" questioned the rather surprised George.

"Yes, well, we are French, of course. I'm sure you have detected that by our speech, if not Amedee's and mine, then surely by our mother's. Many people took the names of the royal family," interjected Charlotte, trying to intercede in Amedee's revelations. "You yourself have the names of several of your English kings, George."

"I believe that is the first time, Miss Mailliard that you have spoken my name, and somehow it sounds . . . different," replied George with a smile.

Charlotte could not quite interpret the smile and wishing to extricate herself and Amedee from other uncomfortable circumstances, she said, "I'm afraid we have taken up so much of your free time already, Mr. Simmons. Thank you. Amedee and I must return to our parents now. Good evening."

"Good evening, then, Miss Mailliard and Master Mailliard," said George, careful to pronounce their name correctly. "I look forward to meeting with you again tomorrow."

"I do too," replied a sprightly Amedee. Tomorrow you can tell us all about your job on the ship here. Perhaps when I get as old as you, I should be part of a ship's crew, instead of a farmer."

Back in their room, Charlotte related to Papa how Amedee had almost revealed too much about their family.

"Yes, Charlotte, you have done well in recovering for your brother, and for that I am most grateful. But you must also think of Amedee as well, a steam boiler. If the pressure is not released regularly, it can explode. Be patient with him. Our journey will come to a close before too long. When we finally reach our new home, we will all be so busy that his energy will be focused on so many chores. For the two or three weeks that are left, please try your best with him. As I have said, he has a good heart," concluded Papa, taking her hand and pleading with her with his eyes.

"Oh, alright, then, I'll try my best. But for you Papa, not Amedee," said a disgruntled Charlotte.

The *Prairie* slowly traveled its way westward: Huntington, Virginia, on the south; the new town of Ashland, Kentucky, where the boat made a north turn and then set on a northwest pattern; then past Portsmouth in the state of Ohio; Maysville, Kentucky, to the south; Ripley, Ohio, on the north side.

On most days Captain Bixby seemed to find some time to spend with the Mailliard family.

"Perhaps it the fact that we are newcomers to his land and he feels comfortable sharing the history he knows so well," said Papa. "I hope you children enjoy his stories. I think there is a bit of loneliness about the man. He has told me that he has no family at home. We must be generous and share the joy of our own family with him when we can."

On one particular evening as the boat made its way past Ripley, the captain warned the family of a possible brush with slavery as they traveled through Kentucky.

"It is such a turmoil, this slavery thing. In Kentucky, on the south as we travel in Kentucky, we have the legal status of slavery, but on the north is the free state of Ohio. I've heard tell that some of these negroes have tried to swim this actual river to reach the shores of freedom. Can anyone imagine doing that? Look at the size of this water, the eddies, the current, the snags. I will tell you this about the current also. You can feel its strength against a vessel this size. And the eddies working against the current can pull a man down in no time. What would that pressure be against the human body? But imagine yourself enslaved, and able to *see* freedom within your reach. What a temptation it would be to try," said the impassioned captain.

"I am sorry, Mr. Mailliard. I do not mean to frighten your wife or your children, but it is an issue that cannot be ignored, especially as we travel this great river. And then, of course, Jonas Williams, a negro works on this ship. He is a free man, of course," continued the captain.

Charlotte and Amedee were silent, but then Papa asked the very question that Charlotte would have loved to ask.

"And what of your crew man Jonas, how did he make his way to freedom?"

"Jonas," replied the captain, "was one of the lucky ones, though you couldn't tell that if you ever saw his back, which bears the scars of a whipping. Despite the cruel punishment he received when he was a slave, when the master died, having no sons to inherit his property, he freed his slaves. Maybe the old man was trying to gain redemption for his eternal soul. For I know this: That despite what the 'good book' says about slaves and masters, there is something wrong in the whole setup. The problem is that it has become so entrenched in our South."

Charlotte knew it was a bit inappropriate for her to comment, but nonetheless, she said, "My cousin has read to me from Tocqueville's book, Captain Bixby, that slavery not only is evil of itself, but it also ruins those who keep the slaves, causing them to lack industry and initiative of their own."

"My goodness, Mr. Mailliard, you must be very proud of this little lady. Not only is she pretty as a picture, but she quotes from Tocqueville," replied a surprised captain.

"Yes, well, that is our Charlotte. She has always been a reader," said Papa.

"I can see, then, why you were acquainted with our Mr. Simmons. He spends much of his time on his own reading," continued the captain. "Bettering one's self, that is what has made our country so strong. I see that each time we reach our next city, Cincinnati, in Ohio, of course, which has become such a thriving port and contributed to our cargo tonnage that American vessels now rival all the ships of Britain. Now that's what you call American ingenuity, my dear Mailliards. It is also one of the loveliest cities on our route."

"Just across the river the town of Covington is not doing as well. The problem there, however, for us ships is that her water is just too shallow. I'm not sure that she will ever make it as big as Cincinnati," continued the captain. "Speaking of our approach to that great city, it is definitely time for me to check on our progress. I take your leave for now, then."

"Dear Captain Bixby, you have made us feel so comfortable and welcomed on this part of our journey. Please know that we are happy to see you whenever you can afford the time to be with us," answered Mama.

As the captain moved away from the Mailliards, Mama turned to Charlotte. "Reading Toqueville? Really, Charlotte, what else did your cousin expose you to? I keep telling you and your Papa," Mama glanced disapprovingly at her spouse, "that you must spend more time in ladylike pursuits. Reading and thinking should be left to the men. Eloi, I fear you may have done too much damage already."

Charlotte was very still. She noticed the smug look on her brother's face.

"There, there, Amanda. Don't worry about our Charlotte. She does all that is expected of a girl, no, young woman her age. The reading is simply a plus," said Papa.

Not wishing to be a part of this old discussion, Charlotte asked permission to walk the decks of the boat. She had learned that smiling and furtively listening to others' conversations was an interesting way to hear more stories about this country. She moved away from her family, and leaning on the rail of her deck, she peered into the distance as if looking for some landmark. Two older gentlemen were sitting within earshot.

"We'll be coming into Cincinnati before too long, Thomas," said one of the men. "I have confidence in our captain, unlike that hapless soul who piloted the *Moselle* into the port three years ago. Do you remember that story?"

"How could one forget?" replied his companion. "One hundred and fifty people lost, and just after they had boarded. The explosion was so forceful, they say, that the pilot's body was found clear on the Kentucky side."

Her eyes suddenly wide and her hands visibly shaking, Charlotte moved away from the two men and hoped that a check on the steam boiler pressure was one of the captain's chores this evening. She decided that eavesdropping definitely could reap unwarranted information.

North, south, but always westward, the *Prairie* continued onward without incident. There definitely was the heat, yes, but then it was July, what else could be expected? No snags had yet to be encountered, and Captain Bixby felt incredibly lucky to have contracted with Horace Wilson as his pilot. The man knew the river like the back of his hand, as the saying goes, guiding his vessel by the sight of familiar trees, hills, rocks, structures. Passing Vevay and Ghent, he moved the ship gracefully onward, now gliding by Madison, the capital of Indiana, where the Kentucky River contributed its water to the ever-building Ohio. The next stop, Louisville, was only a few miles ahead.

Louisville, Kentucky

Perhaps, Charlotte thought, life in America might not be that horrible after all. There were so many obvious French influences and connections: Point Breeze, soon St. Louis, and now this town, Louisville, also named for the French king. Tonight, after the sun had mercifully begun to set and the heat had somewhat abated, she hoped to find some wares at one of the open-air markets, a souvenir from this city in this strangely named state.

"Charlotte, please do not stray too far from Papa. I know we have felt very safe on the boat, but the shore, well, we don't know what to expect here," said Mama. "I don't suppose I could ask you to please watch out for Amedee?"

"Oh, Mama, please. How could you possibly ask me that? And he never listens to anything I say, anyway."

"Yes, yes, I suppose I can agree. Papa must keep him close at hand. He is liable to go anywhere and do anything. But do keep your Papa within sight."

With Mama's approval, or so Charlotte reasoned, she moved quickly to rid herself of Amedee and worked her way more deeply into the crowd. The heat of the day had taken its toll on the strolling people, and she brought her handkerchief to her nose as she moved from one display of meat, sweets, and crafts to another.

At one stand she noticed a woman selling hand mirrors. "Please, please, young lady, don't you want to see how beautiful you are?" said the vendor, shoving one of the mirrors into Charlotte's hand.

Unthinkingly, Charlotte brought the mirror to her face. She looked at that face. Though somewhat distorted by the poor quality of the object, she noticed that her hair looked full and far curlier than usual as it absorbed some of the humidity of the Kentucky evening. Mama would, perhaps, scold her for removing her bonnet, but the mild breeze felt wonderful as it moved her dark locks. Her skin also had taken on a healthy hue from the days aboard the *Prairie.*

Assessing the face before her, objectively, she thought, it would not be called beautiful or remarkable, but merely the face of any young woman. Wistfully, she thought, she would never be as lovely as Mama, whose features were more delicate and refined than her own.

As she continued to look in the mirror, she saw the face of someone smile and quickly she returned the mirror to the woman and looked behind her. Feeling very foolish, she quickly walked away from the stand.

Charlotte had been perusing the wares for about a half-hour when she suddenly realized that the crowd was becoming more male-dominated although there were still a few women to be seen. The sweep of humanity moved toward one area where a platform had been erected. Charlotte's curiosity was piqued; she wondered what possible items could be displayed here.

She turned and saw Captain Bixby standing not too far from her with the black man from the boat, Jonas Williams.

"And what have we here, sir? Another slave to be auctioned?" inquired a most disagreeable looking, short, bald man.

"Decidedly not, sir. This is Jonas Williams, a free man. We are here looking for his wife and daughter, now about eight, who were stolen by kidnappers in Virginia," replied the captain.

"Now see here," replied the small man. "We run a strictly legal business. You know, sir, we have, unfortunately, not been able to import slaves for sale from any other state since 1833, harmful to an honest man's business as that dang rule may be."

Charlotte tried to fade away from the crowd that had gathered in the area, for she now realized what "items" were to be sold. The man who had accosted the captain, she realized, was an auctioneer. She wondered how a man dressed as elegantly as he was dressed could be engaged in such a heinous business. He brought out two, black-skinned men in shackles, and as if someone were selling a piece of furniture or livestock, the men were disposed of and dragged off by their new owners.

Charlotte scanned the crowd and wanted to move towards the captain, but the crowd was too dense. She noticed some people were shaking their heads. Why didn't they do something to stop it? It was unthinkable, inhuman.

She could not believe she had just seen the "sale" of human beings, all this in a manner of minutes. She had to leave quickly, for the horror of this scene was beginning to overwhelm her and she felt light-headed. I must leave and get back to Papa, she thought.

But she could not retreat as the push of the crowd pressed forward to the platform. Suddenly the wave of people was split by a tall, strikingly handsome young man who walked with an air of arrogance toward the auctioneer.

"Good evening, Mr. Parker. I believe we have something here that will greatly interest you," said the auctioneer.

Moving towards the platform, Parker passed by Charlotte, nodded and handed her a handkerchief. "I believe you dropped this, mademoiselle, at the booth that was selling the mirrors," he said smoothly with more than a hint of condescension. His hand grasped Charlotte's as he pushed the handkerchief in her fist.

Charlotte gasped a thank you and, in that moment, she stared deeply into the most spectacular and arresting blue eyes she had ever seen. Coupled with the dark blond hair that hung to his shoulders, Charlotte felt those eyes had learned to hold the attention of anyone, particularly women.

"Delightful as this moment is, I believe I have a little business to attend to this evening," said Parker mockingly.

"Mr. Parker, this is the young slave I mentioned earlier today," said the auctioneer. "She just came to us from Lexington a few days ago—all very legal, of course, no importing," as he glanced in the captain's direction.

Parker quickly moved away from Charlotte, and then she saw that the attention had turned toward the young woman and child who had ascended the platform.

"A young female, fourteen years of age, and with a child of approximately one, her own, which is not yet weaned. An investment, surely, one can see, with many years of child-bearing ahead. At any price, certainly a bargain, but we will start at $1500."

At the mention of fourteen years of age, Charlotte also pressed toward the platform. There she saw a very tall, beautiful dark young woman, *just her own age.* The girl's skin was a deep golden bronze. Her garments consisted of a course, worn, brown apron over a soiled white loose dress, with a red turban tied around her hair, curly dark wisps of hair escaping around her face. The child, clinging to his mother's legs, was naked except for a small pair of pants. Both were barefooted.

The dark woman scanned the crowd and in that moment, her eyes met Charlotte's. She would not turn her gaze, and Charlotte could not turn away.

"What is your name, girl?" shouted Parker.

No answer.

"I said, what is your name?" he repeated.

"You must answer the man for your own good, and if you want that boy of yours to go with you."

The thought of the possible separation forced the girl to respond. "My name is Savannah."

As the young black woman turned to answer, Charlotte saw a fresh scar, three lines like lightening streaks, running down her right cheek.

"Well, well, you do have a tongue. And from the way you answered, I would guess you might even read and write a bit. Is that true?"

Reluctantly the young woman again answered, "Yes, sir"

"Judging from those streaks down the side of your face and the color of that baby, I would say that you got a bit too close to the master and your mistress threw you out," commented Parker.

The child at Savannah's feet began to whine and twist around his mother's legs, then held his arms to be lifted up. Automatically, the young mother responded, and Charlotte sensed that the young mother's manner had changed from one of defiance to supplication for the sake of the child. Holding the child deftly with one arm, she scanned the crowd as if desperately searching for one kind face. Again, her eyes met Charlotte's.

"Alright, Mr. Carstens, I'll open the bidding with a generous offer of $1600," bellowed Parker.

Silence struck the crowd with the sound of the opening bid, and Parker scanned faces, a look of confidence on his own, clearly not expecting anyone to oppose him.

"I bid $1601." Charlotte could not believe how small her voice sounded when, in her own mind, she had wanted her bid to resound throughout the crowd.

"Now see here, young lady, females are not allowed to participate in this auction," replied Carstens.

"Well, perhaps our mademoiselle, even a very young and pretty one, just doesn't understand what is proper in our great state. After all, she probably thought she was coming to watch the guillotine this evening," joked Parker, although his voice expressed annoyance.

Some in the crowd responded with a muted laugh, apparently approving his cleverness.

Suddenly Charlotte was grabbed tightly around the waist, and, as she tried to loosen herself from the grip, she met Papa's eyes staring straight into hers.

"What are you doing here, Charlotte?" he demanded as quietly but as firmly as he possibly could utter.

Trying to implore his sense of justice, Charlotte whispered, "But Papa, they are selling, *selling* this young woman, Savannah, and her son. She is just fourteen, like me Papa. We must do something. We must help her. I know we can help her."

"I have told you before, Charlotte. This is not our argument," said Papa.

"If it is not ours, then whose is it?" retorted Charlotte. "Perhaps I could trade her for my shoes," said Charlotte as she glared back at her father.

Charlotte and Papa were beginning to draw attention as their conversation grew in volume, each of them staring in the other's eyes.

"Now look here, Frenchie. As amusing as this may be, we are doing business. I suggest you take your young lady away from this auction before she finds herself in a very uncomfortable position," said Parker, his guise of friendliness now completely gone.

Parker's comment once again drew some laughs from the crowd.

"Alright, let's conclude the deal, Carstens. I believe there will be no more interruptions. Here is my case. Count out your $1600. Savannah will carry the rest for me. Won't you, Savannah? I'm sure she'll get use to carrying my weight in many ways," smirked Parker.

Charlotte, pulled by her father, continued to look at Savannah and her child. "I will never forget this. Or you," she spoke softly.

When they had left the auction area, Papa began to reprimand Charlotte again.

"I have told you we must not draw attention to ourselves. We are foreigners still to these people. How could you endanger us all?" he questioned.

"How did you find me?" was Charlotte's only reply.

"George Simmons was kind enough to find me and tell me you were in danger. He is standing right over there," replied Papa. "You should be grateful he found himself in the same place as you. Please express your thanks to him."

As they approached George, Charlotte petulantly said, "Thank you, Mr. Simmons, for guiding my father to save me. Perhaps someone should have also thought to save the slave girl and her baby."

That evening as the family was gathered for dinner, Charlotte could not eat any food. The spectacle she had seen that day had completely drained her of any energy. Mama asked where she had been, if she had made any purchases on shore, but neither Charlotte nor Papa spoke of the incident.

As she replayed the day's events over and over in her mind, she realized how foolish she must have seemed, especially to that despicable Clayton Parker. She had heard the people speak of the many horses he bred for some famous Louisville races. It was clear in her mind, that he would treat his new "acquisition" as simply a two-legged animal.

Charlotte could not put out of her mind, also, how he had known she was French. Had he been in the crowd watching her as she passed through the market and heard her mistakenly speak French when she asked the price of items? Then she remembered. He had spoken of "dropping her handkerchief at the stand with the mirror." Yes, that was it. His was the face she had seen for a moment in the background of the mirror. The thought was quite upsetting.

With a great sense of shame, she then remembered how trivial her embarrassment was compared to the horror of Savannah's life. Charlotte had understood the meaning of Parker's "carrying my weight" and the thought of *that* she could not forget.

At bedtime Charlotte could not read nor sleep for many hours. When she finally did fall asleep, the scene in the market was relived through her nightmare as she and Napoleon stood on a platform to be auctioned by Carstens as a laughing Parker bid for her. She awoke with a cry and reached for the slop pot where she vomited what little food had been in her stomach.

Of George Simmons, she had not dreamt at all.

To Cairo

For days afterward Charlotte could not bear to talk to anyone. She felt foolish, small, and insignificant. She wanted to talk about the incident with someone, but there was absolutely no one in whom she could confide. The afternoon conversations with George Simmons had subsided, for she had not seen or heard about him since Papa had told her that it was George who had seen her at the slave auction. She wondered what George thought about the slavery issue and how it fit into his grand scheme of being true to one's own thinking. Did he approve of slavery? Surely not, she thought, he seemed too kind for that. But there were people who appeared to be kind who were also slave owners. She had heard that even some of the first American presidents were slave owners. How could this be?

Her confused thoughts swirled endlessly in her head. When she brought her paper and pencil to try to draw some of the flowers she remembered from Point Breeze, she could not. When she closed her eyes, the only scene in her mind was of the slave woman and her child. Though she knew her fingers were not skilled, she moved them deliberately to recreate the incident: the child with hands upraised, the girl's eyes looking at the crowd, the three streaks down her right cheek.

"What are you drawing, Charlotte?"

Her father's voice startled her so that she nearly fell from her chair. Quickly gathering her papers in her folder and turning her face from him, she replied, "Nothing, nothing that I can draw well, nor make any better."

"Life is often so overwhelming, Charlotte. I am so sorry you had to see that, that misery," he said, taking her hand.

"But you see, Papa, we could have done something to make things better. We could have bought the girl and her baby and set them free. I know we could do that," said Charlotte, glancing at her shoes.

"But let me ask you this, then, Charlotte, would you have the money to buy all the slaves in the world? Surely you can see that would be impossible. Yes, and then the shoes. Well, now you know my little secret. I didn't want to burden you with the responsibility. I thought we would laugh together once we reached Woodsville," said Papa.

"I'm not sure I will ever laugh again," she replied softly. She wanted to also say that she would never quite think of her father in the same way also, but she did not.

Perhaps Papa was right. She could not buy all the slaves in the world, but, remembering what Antoine had said, she knew that one kind act was the way to begin.

During the next few days Charlotte kept to herself as much as she could. Papa stayed away from her, she managed to escape Mama's attention, and, thankfully, Amedee had interested himself in exploring more of the boat. Perhaps, she thought, he had even found George Simmons to occupy his time, for she had also been careful to avoid him. She now felt that what she had done in the ridiculous 'bid' was incredibly childish. The confidence and passion she had experienced in Louisville had evaporated as the ship moved steadily away from the scene. That was how people avoided evil, she felt. They simply refused to acknowledge its existence.

Remembering the small book she had brought with her, Charlotte found a remote seat at the back of the second deck and buried herself into Abbott's *History of Maria Antoinette.* The book was a gift from Papa and was to be reserved for reading only when she "could find nothing else to do," according to his instructions. "For surely," he had said, "there will always be something to keep you busy."

Now, she hoped that the book would help to distract her thoughts, for the young queen's story was also one filled with misery and suffering. And wasn't she also, in a much different way, of course, a marriage pawn for her mother, a kind of a slave? However, Charlotte knew that some of Maria's troubles were due to her own unwise decisions.

As Charlotte read, she also tried to remember the expansiveness of Versailles, the lush saloons with incredible furnishings that Abbott described, the extravagance of the Petit Trianon, where the queen sought to escape the pomp of court only to further enflame the peasants of France. In her own naiveté Maria Antoinette thought to regain a simpler life. "One can then be one's own companion, and find society in one's own thoughts."

How very true was that idea from the book, thought Charlotte. "When all possible confidants fail, I must rely on myself."

"Miss Mailliard, I am sorry to disturb you. You seem so deep in thought." George almost whispered the words. "May I please join you?"

"Oh, Mr. Simmons, yes, you may join me if you wish although I do not think I will be very good company," replied Charlotte. Her unease with this young man was especially keen as she felt he would assess and judge her actions at the slave market.

For what seemed like an endless time, no one spoke. Charlotte resolved, despite the silent tension, she would not speak first.

Finally, George said, "I wanted to say so many things about what you did and what I did back in Louisville. First, I hope you will believe me when I say that I was not following you. I happened onto that horrible scene just as you did. I did not realize you were there until I heard your voice. Your gesture was, I believe, and I have thought very long as to how to say this . . . it was a noble act, but dangerous."

"The oddest thing, Mr. Simmons, is that I had no idea that I would speak. My passion was so strong; my words came from my heart, not my mind. The uselessness of my actions, however, haunts me. But my own discomfort is so small compared to the evil that occurred that evening and must occur every day throughout this land. You are older. Perhaps, you have learned not to be concerned with the established acceptance of slavery."

"You are incorrect, Miss Mailliard. That was my first encounter with a slave dealing. I have heard stories, of course. But slavery in my state of New York has not existed in my lifetime. My own feeling in Louisville was one of frustration, for I saw the evil but was not capable of making a difference. I have no money to bid, so any action was impossible. Furthermore, saving one slave does not change the system. I am but one person. How can I change a whole philosophy of life? You see, I also feel very, very insignificant, as you put it."

The words seemed so sincere and thoughtful. They showed a vulnerability that she had not seen before in this young man, who appeared at times so righteous in his beliefs.

"George, Charlotte, there you are!" shouted Amedee. "The captain has told the best story about this place we are just passing. Do you see it there? On that hill? Up there? It is called Cave-in-Rock." (He lowered his voice and spoke the name in a deliberately deep and onerous tone.) "And Charlotte, it is in Illinois, this Illinois where we shall live. There used to be a big band of outlaws here." (Again Amedee said the words slowly, making sure to repeat them exactly as the captain had spoken them.)

"These outlaws had so many men in their gang" (another new word he had learned) "that the boats could not even travel here without being attacked. The worst outlaws were the two Harpe brothers. They captured one man and made him jump into flames off the hill. Once they took a baby, like the Indians use to do" (deliberately looking in Charlotte's face) "and dashed its brains out against a rock. But one brother was shot and the other brother had his head cut off and told the man doing it that he wasn't doing a very good job. Isn't that a great story?" concluded Amedee as he smiled, wide-eyed apparently proud of having remembered so many graphic details.

Charlotte covered the Marie Antoinette biography with her hands. She would save reading about that unfortunate woman for another day.

As quickly as he had interrupted their conversation, Amedee ran down the deck, perhaps rehearsing his story for its next rendition.

Smiling, George said, "Your brother has a way of, well, certainly changing the tone of one's thoughts. You are so very different from each other. Amedee smiles his way through all encounters and treats them as adventures. You, Miss Mailliard, seem far more serious, as I fear I am, also."

"Perhaps that comes from being the older sibling. That will change for me, of course, when we come to Woodsville, where my two older sisters are already living," replied Charlotte.

"Yes, you to Woodsville, and I will be traveling onto St. Louis, where I hope to secure work on another ship. The opportunity of working on this vessel will surely help me find another job. I hope you will not think me too forward, but, for helping me when this journey began with your wave, I would like to thank you with this gift."

George withdrew a small box from his sack and handed it to Charlotte. For a moment their hands touched, and then, just as quickly, George pulled his back.

Holding the gift in her hand, Charlotte could not have been more surprised. "Oh, my, Mr. Simmons, it is truly lovely." She held a small box of dark wood with her initials burned into the top. The workmanship was not that of a master craftsman, perhaps, but nonetheless showed attention to detail. The initials were set into a pattern: The "C" and "M" encased the smaller "L" and "J."

"I cannot believe you remembered all my names. You are indeed very attentive, Mr. Simmons."

For what seemed an endless moment, Charlotte held the box in her hand and then decided to speak. "Mr. Simmons, perhaps you may not want me to have this gift when I explain some things about my name. My family is French. We have also lived in Italy."

"Yes, I realized you were from France from your name, and the, the," George smiled, "the special quality of your speaking."

Charlotte returned his smile, but then said, very seriously, "But what you do not know is that I am named for Charlotte, the daughter of the Count de Survilliers, as he is called in this country. In Europe he was known as the King of Spain for a while, Joseph Bonaparte, the older brother of Napoleon."

"Many people are named for despots, my name for instance."

"True, but it is much more than that. My mother was Charlotte Bonaparte's personal secretary. Princess Charlotte, as she was called, was also my godparent at my Catholic baptism. Of course, you can guess why the Josephine is part of my name. And my little brother's name is shortened from the emperor's. In truth, Mr. Simmons, two generations of my family have been attached to the Bonapartes in some form of service. They have been our benefactors in many ways. Even now my uncle is the steward for Joseph at his estate in New Jersey," said Charlotte, now handing the box back to George.

She could not read the look on his face, and the silence seemed interminable.

Finally, George shook his head and pressed the box more forcefully in her hand. "My small gift was made not for one in service to the Bonapartes, but for a young woman who waved kindly to me, who had the courage to speak against an injustice when everyone else was silent. That is the wonderful thing about this country. It does not matter who you were before, or to whom you were in debt. This is the place where a new start is always possible. "

Smiling, Charlotte looked directly into his eyes. "Then, thank you. I will certainly think of you whenever I see your gift."

He returned her smile. "That is my hope. I do wish to pay my respects to your parents and say farewell to Amedee, but, if I do not have the opportunity, please tell them your family has made my time most pleasant," said George with a slight bow.

"I will do so. You also have made my, our time very interesting. Good-bye, Mr. Simmons. Good-bye, George." If it was forward to call him by his first name so be it. For better or worse, this was America, after all.

Awkwardly, he took her hand and brought it to his lips. "Good-bye, Miss Charlotte."

To St. Louis

Charlotte had been so absorbed with her own thoughts that she barely noticed the change in rivers as they moved from the *Prairie* to another steamship headed north to St. Louis. The accommodations were just as luxurious, but only on the third and final day of their journey did she take notice of this dirty, sluggish river called the Mississippi. It was the largest of the American rivers, she was told, but its beauty in no way compared to the Ohio's. She barely noticed, at the confluence of the two waters, that the Ohio was also much larger and yet the Mississippi, another Indian word she surmised, was the more prominent.

As she looked south, back toward Cairo, she wondered about George Simmons. She unconsciously reached for the wood box in her sack. She had examined it many times since they had parted. The wood was so very smooth; he must have worked very diligently. More interestingly, was the perfect way the lid fit on the box, snug and tight, so that even if shaken, it would not dislodge. Inside was a carefully laid bright red, velvet lining. The color was curiously similar to the large divans in the salon. She wondered how long it had taken him to complete the project. When did he begin? What had he really thought of her family's connection with the Bonapartes?

One man's benefactor could certainly be another man's despot.

"Is this something new I have not seen before, Charlotte?" said Mama. "I am afraid I have been so occupied with Leon that I have neglected my other two children."

Sooner or later, Charlotte knew that Mama would notice the box, so Charlotte was ready. "Yes, Mama, I received this wood box from George Simmons, as a thank you, for helping him secure his job on the *Prairie*. It is nothing special, really," replied

Charlotte. She didn't want Mama to see the initials, so she turned the box on its side.

"What a nice gesture. Yes, he did seem like a polite, young man. May I see it?"

Shrugging, Charlotte said, "Of course."

"Oh, yes, I can see it is nothing special, especially since it has four letters that just happen to be your initials burned into the lid."

What woman can resist opening a box? Mama held the gift in her hand, carefully opened the lid, looked inside, sighing a very pleased, "Oh," and then closed the lid.

"It is actually quite lovely, in a simple way. 'Just a gesture, of course,'" said Mama mockingly. "My dear Charlotte, no young man gives a young lady any gift that is totally innocent."

"It is a box, Mama."

"Tell me this, my daughter. How many times have you opened and closed it since you said good-bye?"

"Well, perhaps, five or so." Fifteen would have been more accurate. It would take at least fifteen examinations to know precisely which corners fit best together, to feel the smoothness of every surface, to feel the softness of the velvet inside.

"Yes, five, of course," said Mama. "And who did you think of each time? Something tells me I know the answer. This December, you will be fourteen, the precise age I was when I met your Papa. Of course, this George is English, but then . . . . "

"Oh, Mama, tell me, are all mothers matchmakers?"

"Perhaps. We do worry about our daughters, especially. There is no world, particularly this one, I believe, where a woman can survive alone. At least we have family. But our family has four daughters. When we arrive in Woodsville, we may be pleasantly surprised to learn that Heloise and Pauline already have beaus. What a joy that would be! Or *Grandmere* may have already been building a list of suitors for them," said Mama laughingly.

Despite the topic, Charlotte joined in her mother's lightheartedness.

The August heat of St. Louis was something the Mailliards had never before experienced. Other trips by Papa and Mama had been taken earlier or later in the year. Now there was no escaping the wet heat that caused even their cotton clothes to stick to their bodies.

Charlotte could tell that Papa tried his best to ease his family's discomfort. They dined at a port restaurant, hoping to be refreshed by the open air rather than the ship's closed salon. She could tell her father tried to maintain his positive tone, but his energy, too, had begun to wane.

"Do you know, children, that this very city was started by our French many years ago? It was named for one of our saints, and the University was founded by the Jesuits. Perhaps, Amedee, it is a place where you will go to learn in a few years."

Amedee simply stared over his father's face and supported his head with his hand. He looked too tired, too hot, to deny or agree with anything Papa said.

"I know you are trying, Eloi, but the trip has seemed endless. Perhaps we will talk about education another time," said Mama, trying to smile reassuringly.

"Yes, perhaps, education is not the appropriate topic. Amedee, would you like to go to the stores and see the beautiful furs that the trappers have brought in? I remember that it was quite exciting to look at the bear, wildcat, and beaver hanging on the wall. There may come a day when we would all love to have a warm coat made of some animal, as distant as that seems today. If only we could save this warmth."

"If you want to, Papa," replied a very compliant Amedee.

Dinner completed, Mama, Charlotte and Leon walked back to the boat. Charlotte held Leon's little hand as he moved quickly to keep pace with his sister. She noticed how delicate and small the little hand was, how well it fit into hers, despite the fact that it was now most sweaty.

As if realizing her thoughts, the little one smiled up at his big sister, "Char, Char," he uttered.

"Le, Le," she replied, laughingly. Picking up the tyke, Charlotte ran ahead of Mama. Her legs ached as she ran, but it felt wonderful to move quickly, to be unconfined before they had to return to their cabin.

And in the morning, Papa had told them, they would switch to the packet boat with even less space. Tonight, however, despite the heat, they would try for one more good night's rest.

To Peoria

Mercifully, the day dawned somewhat cooler than the last few days, and, once aboard the *Exchange*, Papa tried his best to bolster the family with his enthusiasm. This was the very last boat on their journey. Although their cabin was much smaller than the steamers on the Ohio and Mississippi, here on the Illinois River, the fare was much more reasonable, a mere $6, he told the family.

"We are very fortunate," he said "to be able to afford the cabin. I have chosen this route, unlike the time I came up the Wabash River, because often the roads west from that river are no more than Indian trails or paths used by some French trappers. Since my last trip here, when I traveled with your three sisters, the packet now runs daily from St. Louis and goes to the towns of Peru, LaSalle and Ottawa. We will leave the boat at the town of Peoria and lessen our trip overland considerably."

Charlotte tried to muster a little support for Papa's attempt, but even she was a bit overwhelmed by this day's lesson.

North, west, then north again, passing Alton, Grafton, the settlements of Illinois appeared as little enclaves of activity. Childs' Landing, Beercreek, Meredosia—the miles on the journey clicked away. The French influence was so easy to see, especially at Meredosia, named for the French priest, Antoine D'Osia, who lived in his cabin near the Indian village. When the settlers began coming after 1832, they named their community for the priest and added the French word *mere* for "lake."

Charlotte questioned why Mama's family had not settled here along the river instead of traveling further northwest to their settlement.

"Perhaps the soil was better. Or, despite our previous lives, we are farmers at heart," answered Papa. "I hope that, once we are settled, we will soon see the fruits of our labor in the fields as our crops will be harvested. The river traffic is the focus of much life here with crops being brought to markets in the east and pelts traded by the trappers. But land that is already clear and level, such as it is in Woodsville, will make our efforts easier," said Papa, "and that is what we will find as we travel further away from the river."

Charlotte tried to imagine her Papa behind a plow, her delicate Mama following, spreading seeds and sowing young plants. These images were simply too incongruous to the life she had known before.

She also noticed the difference in life aboard the packet, for trips tended to be short for most passengers, and business was completed quickly, unlike the luxury and ease of life on the Ohio. The mail was part of the cargo, and the boat would pick up and deposit passengers along the waterway. Flags were hung along the shore, signaling the captain to make arrangements for docking at the ports.

"I have also learned that a new railroad line has come into existence in Meredosia since my last trip. The Northern Cross Railroad now runs the twelve miles between Meredosia and Morgan City. Just this year another line from to Jacksonville to Springfield, east of Meredosia has begun its run. Each year this country makes such strides," added Papa.

After two days on the packet, the Mailliards were able to stop at the town of Beardstown, named for its founder, Thomas Beard, who settled in 1819. The first name had been French, *Beau Tertre Village*, Beautiful Mound Village, so called for the large Indian burial mounds that had been there. The town was large compared to many settlements along the river. Here, twenty-one blocks stretched along the water front, three blocks deep with the city square in the center.

Charlotte sat on the bench at the city square with her parents as Amedee and Leon ran in the adjacent yard. She thought, is this what Woodsville will be like? She looked at the people that walked by. There were no Indians, no Negroes, no slave markets. The large, two-story, red brick building looked somewhat like buildings she had seen in Boston and Philadelphia. If her town were like this one, she reasoned, she may not be completely satisfied, but perhaps somewhat content.

When they once again settled into their cabin, eating the food that they had purchased at Beardstown, Papa announced positively, "My dear ones, we have been so very fortunate. Our journey has been without incident. We are now two-thirds on our way to Peoria. Once we reach Peoria, we have simply another fifty miles—yes miles we must remember—to our new home, our family. Let us pray and thank God for our good fortune."

Joining hands, the family prayed their simple prayers, the Roman Catholic "Our Father" and "Hail Mary."

"Before too long," Papa said, "we shall be saying these prayers on solid ground in our own home."

Peoria, on to Woodsville

Despite her initial disinterest, when Papa began to tell the history of the town of Peoria, Charlotte's attention was definitely drawn to the story. The saga of its people told an interesting tale.

The French had come first to this beautiful area along the Illinois River in the late 17th century. They lived peaceably among the Peoria Indians, traded their furs and brought their Catholic faith. In 1680, Robert LaSalle and Henri Toni built Fort Creveceour, on the east bank of the pristine waterway. In addition to the trading post, soon a blacksmith shop, a church, winepress and a windmill became part of the settlement. Although the French & Indian War had relinquished many of the French lands to the British, the new village still retained the French settlers. Post-war British General George Clark appointed Jean Baptiste Maillet, a French-Canadian military man commander of the settlement, and it became known as LaVille de Maillet. Log houses, gardens, orchards, and roaming farm animals added to the peaceful setting.

A French-Haitian, Jean Baptiste DuSable expanded the town and owned over eight hundred acres of nearby land, but he then left for the Great Lakes area and founded the settlement named Chicago, much smaller than the village he had left.

The peaceful scene did not survive as the War of 1812 left its mark upon the village. The Americans suspected the French villagers of supporting the Indians, who were suspected of attacks upon western-bound American pioneers.

"It is a terrible part, unfortunately, of this city's history, for it was then believed that the American army killed the inhabitants of Chief Black Partridge's village and then burned the homes of the French settlers, taking any survivors to a prison in Alton. It seems no matter where we live on this earth, war is an inescapable part of man's history," said Papa.

Charlotte noticed a concerned look pass Mama's face.

"But, of course, we do not have to worry about that problem because that war is long over and the Indians are no longer allowed to live in Illinois," continued Papa.

"What happened after the war?" Charlotte asked.

"Yes, finishing the story . . . ," said Papa, "Fort Clark replaced LaVille de Maillet and in 1825 the village name was officially changed to Peoria. In 1832, a defeated Chief Blackhawk and all Indian tribes were forced to move west of the Mississippi. That is why Woodsville is now very safe. And this town of Peoria has certainly thrived. Since my last visit here there are many new buildings."

A short walk from the pier, Papa settled the family into the Clark Livery Stable, where he would make arrangements for the last part of the journey.

"Good morning, sir, I am Eloi Mailliard. I have been informed by my wife's brother, John Gallet, that you are the man to see about hiring a covered wagon and horses to travel to Woodsville."

"Well, howdy. It's good ta' meet you, sir," said a friendly face. "I'm Elias Black, owner of this here place. I have met John, a good man. And, if memory serves me right, I've taken a few of your country folk to that settlement. And just when would you want to make this trip?"

Charlotte could not help but notice the man's way of speaking. It was English, of course, but he used words she hadn't heard before, and his voice had something of a twang to it.

"As soon as possible, Mr. Black. I would need a wagon large enough for my wife, two older children, and a baby. Oh, yes, I also have two rather large trunks."

"Well, that sounds like a pretty heavy load. Plus we'll have to have two drivers. One to drive the wagon—no offense, sir, but I'm thinkin' you haven't done that before—and then one on horseback for the return trip. I never send a man out alone, ya' know. The bears are mostly gone, I hear tell, but them wolves can be downright nasty, alone or in a group. Do you have your own rifle?"

"A rifle, no, I do not," replied Papa.

"Well, that might be one of the first things you think about gettin' and learnin' how to use. I'm a peaceful man myself, but I mean to protect what is mine, and all with me, especially my horses. So, I expect I could see about them drivers today and let you know tomorra'. Where did you say you was stayin'?"

"Thank you so much, Mr. Black. My family is staying at the boarding house on River Street. What will the fee be for your service?" asked Papa.

"Well, now that depends. Are you just vistin' or do you plan to stay for a spell?"

Stay for a spell? Charlotte thought. She wondered just how many weeks constituted a spell.

"My family and I intend to live in Woodsville, sir. Three of my daughters are already there with their grandparents Gallet," replied Papa.

"Well, then, welcome to Illinois, Eloi, is it? Eloi? Well, I never did hear that name before, but since you're related to John, I spect I can trust ya'," said a smiling Mr. Black. "The round trip will cost you $15 and that includes the feed for the horses. And please call me Elias."

Two days later the group headed to Woodsville, fifty miles mostly west followed by a turn to the south. Crossing the creeks, which they would have to do twice before reaching their destination, would not pose a problem since by this third week of August most of the small water beds were completely dry. The wagon carried two barrels of water for the trip, for people and horses.

Charlotte looked at the new mode of conveyance with concern, but it would not be the first time she had ridden in a country wagon, of course. Fifty miles seemed liked a long way, however, and she wasn't sure what would happen if the journey could not be completed in a day.

Fortunately, the day dawned with a brilliant blue sky and a warm summer breeze, not too uncomfortable at the start of the trip, with a mild wind, just enough to dry the sweat that Charlotte could feel running down the sides of her bonnet. She heard the two men from the livery stable introduce themselves to Papa.

Caleb Martin would drive the wagon, and Abner Douglas would ride alongside on his horse called Whiteside. They assured Papa that each man was a good shot.

"Yes, sir, Mr. Mallard, I keep ma' rifle on my right side lyin' in the wagon, and Abner's is slung over his shoulder with the trigger near his right hand. He bein' right-handed, a course," said Mr. Martin. "Gosh a'mighty, you got yerself quite a load here," he added as the two men struggled to lash the trunks to the wagon.

Charlotte noticed the spittle running down Caleb's chin. As they settled, one into the wagon and the other astride his horse, each man packed his mouth with a wad of tobacco, obviously the source of the brown stream emitting from the man's mouth.

As the wagon moved away from the town, Charlotte seemed to feel every bump on the road. Now she understood what Papa meant when he talked about the advantage of shortening the overland part of their journey. She noticed the strained look on Mama's face, and Leon was not satisfied sitting on Mama's lap. He tried walking on the floor of the cart only to fall down as quickly as he would stand.

Charlotte unconsciously sat to the back of the wagon, blocking the opening as much as she could. She also wanted to stay as far as possible from the men and their spitting. She had seen the spittoons, certainly, on the boats, but these two seemed to be constantly engaged in this disagreeable habit. Every time she heard the disgusting expulsion of the juice, her stomach jumped.

When the wagon crossed a creek for the first time, she grabbed as tightly as she could to the rough seat for she feared she would soon find herself lying down in the shallow, rock-filled crossing.

Once again, Charlotte also noted how easily Amedee responded to this new adventure. In no time he was sitting next to Caleb, asking about the road, the animals, the Indians he might have seen.

Turning his face to the back of the wagon, her brother asked, "Who do you think can spit farther?" He seemed to be fascinated with the way both men were able to project the tobacco juice.

She also noticed how the man seemed to be enjoying her brother's company. How typical of Amedee to have found a friend in the most unlikely of places.

The wagon was unable to travel for longer than an hour, which, Charlotte thought, was actually a remarkable pace, considering the condition of the trail. Legs were stretched and horses watered at each respite.

After the second stop, a change in the sky became apparent as the sun was hidden behind clouds, any breeze had completely disappeared, and haze seemed to hang in the air. Suddenly, the wind began to stir and the dry prairie grass waved, first slowly, but then more strongly, bending the stalks to nearly touch the earth as the storm clouds grew.

Caleb called to Abner, "It looks like we're in fer it here in a bit. Do ya know any settlers nearby?"

"Not by name, I don't. But it seems to me some new family has settled in that place a bit farther west, if my memory serves me right," answered his companion.

"Well, I just have to hope we make it there before this thing really lets loose. I'll keep ma' eyes open."

The darkened sky now flashed its warnings at close intervals, and in every direction the blue that had dawned earlier disappeared completely. The sounds of thunder rolled through the open prairie as if some great god were bellowing his displeasure at the violators of his pristine land.

The wind's speed increased, and then the rain began to assault the wagon and the single rider. The team of horses tried to forge ahead, but they shook their heads and snorted, racing as fast as they could to escape the driving rain.

Amedee scurried to the back of the wagon, his eyes wide. Charlotte rocked from side to side, and the rain drenched the travelers as the water penetrated the canvas. Mama held Leon close to her breast, trying, futilely, to shield his little body from the storm. He whimpered and mouthed the word, "Mama," but his small voice could not be heard. Papa yelled to Charlotte and Amedee to hold tightly.

"Caleb, Caleb, do ya see that house on the left? I see a shed now, too. Maybe we could stop there a piece," yelled Abner, keeping his head as low as he could but still patting his horse and trying to keep him from rearing.

Charlotte looked toward the front of the wagon and saw Caleb move the reins of the team, driving the horses as fast as he could, following Abner. The single rider moved ahead and drove Whiteside into the barn. She could see him tie his horse quickly and begin wiping him down with his hat.

When the wagon got to the shed, Caleb told Papa to get his family out of the cart and into the shelter. He unhitched the wagon and brought the team into the shack. The five horses filled the small area quickly.

Abner, trying to soothe his mount, spoke into the horse's ear, "There, there, boy, you'll just have to get calm now and learn to share."

The Mailliards huddled closely. Once his family seemed to be safe, Charlotte saw Papa peer into the wagon, obviously checking that both trunks were still inside. He nodded his head as if in thanks.

The door of the cabin suddenly opened and a man's voice rang out, "Matthew, is that you?" A gun in the man's hand was pointed toward the shed and the horses.

Caleb yelled, "Now hold on there, man. I'm Caleb and this here is Abner. We're bringin' a family to Woodsville and were just lookin' for a place durin' the bad weather."

"You say you have a family there?" he yelled over the din of the storm.

"Yes, sir, we have Eloi and Amanda Mailliard and their three children. They're related to that John Gallet."

"Well, come on over here to the house. We've got a problem."

Abner said, "You all go on in. I'm stayin' with the boys here. They're a bit riled up."

"Is there a missus in yer group?" questioned the man at the door, putting down his rifle. "I'm sorry about that, but ya can't be too careful."

"I'm Mrs. Mailliard, Amanda," said Mama as she stood on the porch and shook the water from her clothes.

"It's my wife, ma'am. Her baby isn't due for a few weeks, or so we thought. But her pains have been bad since yesterday. I sent my son fer help, but the storm must 'ave held him up. My name is Luke, Luke Cooper. That's my wife Jessie on the bed. Do you think you could help her?"

Mama moved cautiously into the small cabin, stepping ahead of the rest the family. "Charlotte, come with me, please."

Charlotte was startled by her Mama's request, but responded obediently. The closeness of the small cabin hit Charlotte's face immediately. She peered around the house and could not believe any house for four would be this small. It was the bed in the corner, however, that quickly arrested her eyes. There a woman lay moaning, her hair wet with sweat, her eyes closed, her belly swollen.

Mama moved towards the bed, felt the woman's pulse and shook her head. Then she spoke the woman's name. "Jessie, Jessie, can you hear me?"

The woman breathed shallowly and made no response.

Mama moved closer to the bed while Charlotte hung back. She saw her Mama raise the woman's dress, spreading the woman's legs slowly, and then gasping and saying, "*Mon Dieu.*"

Charlotte would not look at the bed. She did not want to be a part of this, but her mother motioned her to come closer.

She heard Mama say, "Your wife is almost exhausted, and I am afraid the baby is in trouble. I can try to save your wife, if you wish, but know that I am not a midwife.

"Is she close to death?"

"I think that may be. If she has been with pain since yesterday, then it is possible."

"Please, then, missus. Do what ya can. I'm afraid now fer my boy too since I sent him fer help. I can't afford to lose my wife."

Going back to the porch, Mama quickly spoke to Papa in French.

Charlotte stood uncomfortably between the bed and the open door. She wanted to run back outside, but she knew that was not going an option. As she looked outside, she noticed that the rain had mercifully begun to slow.

"This woman is trying to have her baby, Charlotte. We are going to help her," said Mama.

Suddenly Mama's speech changed to rapid French. She told Charlotte how she had assisted a midwife in just such a birth, a birth where the baby does not turn and the feet come before the head. She was going to put her hand inside the woman's birth canal and turn the baby around. She was afraid, however, from what she saw that the baby was already dead. Mama admitted she was very frightened, but she knew that Charlotte could help her just as she had helped the midwife.

In clear English, Mama said, "This is what women do for each other. You are a bit young to learn this so soon, but we have no choice. You must be very brave. This is your chance to help someone. I want you to look into her birth canal now and tell me what you see."

Charlotte was aghast. She wanted to shake her head violently, "No," but something in her mother's words told her she had no choice but to obey. She came to the side of the woman's bed, saw her mother lift the clothes, and spread the legs.

"Closer, Charlotte. Do you see?"

Charlotte tried to breathe evenly and then, bending down, she saw the tiny blue foot, not as large as her little finger.

Charlotte nodded. Her eyes filled with tears. She would try her best.

"I will need clean water, heated, a knife to cut the cord, and the soap in my bag," said Mama. "Bring the slop pot over for the afterbirth."

Nodding to Mama's commands, Charlotte told Luke to bring what she had ordered. He had known enough to keep the pot boiling despite the heat of the day.

Mama then took two deep breaths, washed her hands thoroughly, made the sign of the cross, and told Charlotte to do the same.

"Keep her still now, Charlotte. When I tell you, you will get behind her on the bed and help her sit up a bit. Then you will tell her to push."

"*Mon Dieu*," Mama whispered, "please make me strong enough to do this and turn the baby."

Charlotte saw her mother, eyes closed, reach into the birth canal. Beads of sweat rolled down Mama's cheeks and she wiped at them with the sleeve of her dress. The woman moaned occasionally but was still unconscious. Mama continued the movement for several minutes, one hand inside, another on top of the woman's belly.

She spoke to Charlotte, "You must take over. I no longer have the strength. We cannot ask the men. Their hands are too large. Wash your hands, first. The dust is not good."

Charlotte breathed deeply, "I will try, Mama."

For several minutes Charlotte worked her hands the way she had seen her mother's, one inside, one moving over the woman's belly. She felt something hard, and Mama nodded.

"It is the head, Charlotte. You must slowly turn it toward the birth canal."

Charlotte could see the hard portion of the woman's belly moving.

"Now, Charlotte, I will take over. Get on the bed behind her, and when I tell you, raise her body (thank God she is not a large woman) and tell her to push. You are definitely stronger than I. You may need to slap her face a little to waken her."

Charlotte climbed on the bed behind the woman and tried to retain her balance as the mattress tipped and moved. She nodded to her mother, letting her know she was ready.

"Alright, lift her," said Mama.

Charlotte lifted the body, hoping to keep the woman and herself steady. She hoped she could hold that position. "Push, Jessie," she said.

The woman made no sound.

"Slap her cheek a bit. She must help now, or I am afraid all will be lost," said Mama.

Charlotte struck the cheek more forcefully and called the woman's name again, this time almost shouting in her ear, "Push, Jessie, push."

The woman eyes opened and looked into Charlotte's face. "You must push now, Jessie, please."

The woman gritted her teeth and pushed with all her might.

"I see the head now," said Mama. "Push, push again, Jessie."

Charlotte could feel the sweat dripping from her face as she exerted all her strength to support the woman.

"It's coming, it's coming. Yes, more and more. I see the head fully now. Just one more push," said Mama. "Hopefully, we will hear some cries soon."

But there was no sound as the child finally fell completely into Mama's arms. She grabbed the little girl by her feet and slapped her on the back as quickly as she could.

Charlotte had seen animals born in the barn, but never was she as close to any birth as she was now. She saw the birth cord trailing grotesquely after the baby. Charlotte could not believe how thick, how sinewy it was. Now she understood why some infants became entangled in them. It looked like a strong, menacing snake.

The infant's blue body swayed slightly as Mama continued her efforts, but the only sound heard was the breathing of the three women in the small cabin.

"She did not make it. Bring me that chair quickly, Charlotte. I must clean the baby up and let her rest in her mother's arms even if she is not breathing."

Mama, using the seat of the wood chair next to the bed, cut the cord deftly and threw it and the afterbirth in the slop pot.

Charlotte could not believe how adept Mama had seemed during the birth. She had not thought of Mama as being particular equipped to do anything, let alone anything so human, so bloody. Mama had given birth to seven children, of course, but Charlotte had not even thought of the process, nor had she ever been allowed, or near, the same room when the children were born.

Charlotte looked at her right hand, the blood that was smeared there, the blood that had gathered under her nails. Unconsciously she opened and closed the hand as if trying to erase the work it had just accomplished.

Jessie had fallen back on the bed, but managed to mutter, "My baby, please, my baby."

Mama gave the wrapped child to the mother, and, with tears in her eyes, "I am so sorry. Your little girl did not survive the birth."

No, she did not survive the birth, Charlotte thought. How can one survive life in this place if she is not strong enough to survive birth?

Jessie looked at the infant and began to moan, "My little girl, my little girl."

Charlotte wiped the woman's face, and then seeing her startled look, said, "I am Charlotte. Mama and I helped deliver your baby. I am very, very sorry."

The woman nodded her head a bit. Mama looked at Charlotte and signaled to call in the husband.

Running to his wife's bed, Luke grabbed her hand and said, "I'm so sorry, Jess. She jes didn't make it. But she is a beauty, ain't she? Jes like her ma."

The tears continued to roll down Jessie's cheeks. "Well, we still got us our boy."

"Yes, yes, that's fer sure."

But Charlotte knew the boy had not returned.

"Say yer good-byes now, Jess. We'll need to say some prayers over her grave."

As the mother gave up her child to her husband, the sound of shovels could already be heard as the two men from the livery began digging a grave.

They took the tiny body, now wrapped in a sack, and placed it reverently into the hole. Shovelful by shovelful, the men replaced the dirt and covered the mound with huge rocks they had brought from the creek. Then they placed a cross made of two tied twigs into the grave.

"Mr. Mailliard," called Caleb, "we think ya might be the best one to say some here prayers for the babe."

The little assembly, all except Jessie, stood at the site with their heads bowed. Papa spoke the words of the "Our Father" more reverently than Charlotte had heard them spoken before.

"Take her, dear God, and make her one of your little angels," he said.

The scene was abruptly broken by the sounds of a wagon rushing up to the cabin. "Pa, pa, is ma, okay?"

Luke ran to his boy and hugged him, crying, "Oh, Matty, my boy, you're safe. Yes, your maw's okay, but the Good Lord decided your baby sister jes wasn't ready for this here world. These kind folks helped your maw to make it through."

Charlotte stared at the boy, younger than Amedee, who had been sent in the storm to find the neighbor woman.

The boy excitedly told his father how, when he got to the Wilsons, Mrs. Wilson had not been at home. She had gone to visit her mother in Peoria three days ago. Then the storm came, and Mr. Wilson said he could not leave until it was over.

"That was the right thing to do, Matt. I am jes glad that you're safe," said Luke.

From the cabin doorway, Jess called weakly to the group, "Ya all come in now, and Luke will fix up some eats."

Mama ran to her side. "Now, now, Jessie, you must not worry about us. You need to take care of yourself and make sure you don't get the fever or the milk leg. Be sensible, now. Charlotte and I will take care of things."

After their supper was finished, the sun set brilliantly in the western sky. Evening came quickly and the hum of crickets could be heard as the little cabin became the resting place for the Coopers and the travelers. The Coopers slept on one side of the cabin while the Mailliards slept on the other on blankets they had carried in their trunk, blankets that had kept safe a small painting. Caleb and Abner slept in the stable with the horses.

Charlotte had never slept in anything less than a bed in all her life, but as she put her head down on the blanket, she felt her mother's hand stroke her back. Sleep came quickly.

In the morning the travelers gathered their belongings and once more climbed into the wagon. Thank-yous were exchanged and then the vehicle began moving west once again.

Amedee relinquished his place beside Caleb and sat quietly next to his father. Papa and Mama sat strangely silent also, their bodies swaying with the motion of the wagon. Charlotte noticed that even little Leon seemed to be somewhat subdued by the experiences of the previous day.

She huddled her bag between her feet and noticed the corner of the wood box. How long ago it seemed since she had been given that gift. Was it three days, three weeks? She wasn't sure. She closed her eyes and tried to see George's face in her mind, but the image was not clear. Were his eyes blue or brown? She could not remember, and she hated herself for her ingratitude.

As Charlotte sat in the back of the wagon and looked towards the Coopers' cabin, she saw Luke, his arm around Matt, waving. As she returned their wave, her eyes were drawn to the little grave. It was then that she noticed a second grave, not far from the baby's, where a large, black crow had perched on its cross. As the bird shifted its weight, the old cross broke, and it moved swiftly to the newer marker. Here, cawing defiantly, it seemed to stare back at Charlotte.

Traveling west, then moving south for the final few miles, the wagon labored over the hard ground. Caleb stopped at the second crossing for the horses to water. The shallow creek was greedily invaded as the horses drank and snorted their approval.

The only other sound was that of Amedee, who had removed his shoes, moving his left leg back and forth in the stream. The water ripples cascaded over his foot in a peaceful cadence. Then he picked some small stones from the edge of the water and tossed them into the creek, each time trying to reach the other side.

Normally, Charlotte thought, Amedee would have played to his audience, describing and embellishing his actions with vivid commentary, often slipping casually into French. But today he was silent. It was as if the events of yesterday had captured his voice.

Charlotte's eyes welled. As much as she often hated the sound of Amedee's voice, today it would have been a welcome respite from her thoughts.

"Well, folks, it's time to get underway. Not too fer, now. Woodsville is just up the road apiece," said Caleb.

The trail wound its way south widening as the wagon progressed. Soon dwellings appeared in the west and Papa stood tentatively to peer over Caleb's shoulder.

"Amanda, children, I think I am seeing places I remember. Yes, yes, some of these homes belong to the Woods families. If I remember right, yes, there is the hill that has the stable for the animals. There it is in the distance, your grandparents' house, the one built by your uncle. Amanda, Amanda, do you see?" cried Papa excitedly.

Mama began to laugh and rock Leon back and forth in her arms.

Amedee grabbed Charlotte's hand and said excitedly, "We are here, Charlotte. This is our new home. Do you see it?"

And then Mama screamed.

In the distance a young girl was guiding cows toward a stable. She had turned to look at the wagon, and now was breaking into a run towards the vehicle.

Charlotte strained to see the girl's face, but it was not a face she knew.

The wagon stopped and Mama quickly moved to be lifted out. She scooped Leon into her arms and running as fast as she could, she yelled, "*Oh, mon enfant, mon enfant.*"[5]

Mama was running, thought Charlotte, *Mama running.* And now they were all running, Papa, Amedee, even little Leon, running on his own.

Charlotte stood at the wagon, where Caleb and Abner had begun to unload the trunks. She looked at the five figures, silhouetted in the sun, converging on the hill. This was it, Woodsville. No more journey, no more adventure.

She had never felt so alone in her life.

Part 2

Paris, 1804

Henri grasped the bags more closely to his body and ran as fast as his legs could carry him away from the gendarme's whistle. He felt for his sling shot, hoping it was attached securely to his waist. Yes, still there, no need to worry.

He quickly slipped into one of the alleys, the alleys he had known so well since he was a child. He had started these daily runs long ago. Was he only four when Mama had instructed him how to steal and scrounge for every piece of food or dropped coin? In the early years he had been able to don the disguise of a girl, looking forlorn and vulnerable, and then running quickly after he had pilfered food or some small item. But now he was much too tall to pose as a girl and the dark fuzz beginning to appear on his upper lip would soon have to be trimmed or shaved.

Yes, for ten years he had been able to ply his trade, finding food and bringing valuables back to their room. He kept two bags for their distinct purposes: one for their treasures, the other for the rats that he would catch.

It wasn't that he necessarily hated the rats, but they were always in the way, competing for food that should be his. He had learned to use his sling shot well, to aim for their eyes and then let go. Once inside the bag, he would make sure they were dead by slamming the bag against a wall or the ground. He would empty the bag in the Seine, then methodically replace any stones he had lost when stunning the beasts.

Once the bag was emptied, he wrapped his gloves in the outside of the sack. He loved these gloves which had been given to him by the *capitiane* when that soldier had come to see Mama. They were too big for Henri then, but now they fit as if they had been made especially for him. He remembered when the *capitiane* had asked Henri if he would like to wear his gloves, Henri had simply replied that he would like to wear them all the time.

Laughing and looking back at Marie, still in bed, the *capitiane* complimented her on her smart boy and said in his coarse French, "So they are yours then. And what will you do with them, Henri? Wear them to the ball?"

"I shall use them when I catch the rats," replied Henri honestly.

Yes, the gloves had saved him from many nips by the ugly creatures.

The *capitiane* was gone now, but other boyfriends had come to take his place. For a long time now, Mama had insisted that he call her Marie, her given name. Having a fourteen-year old son as tall as Henri would not have helped Mama with the sewing that she did for many of the soldiers.

His mother was not that old. She was only 17 when Henri was born. She said he was her greatest joy and used to call him her Bastille present when he was little. When he became older and could understand what that meant, it had made him uncomfortable. Now, however, he understood and didn't care. There were many children his age, children that had been born nine months after the rioting at the hated prison.

He didn't blame his mother. Like himself, she too had been a creature of the streets. Her own mother had died when she was born; her father came and went as it fit his moods. When he was little, Henri had met his grandfather, a meeting he would just as soon forget. The man had sat on the side of the street, drinking his bottle then hugging it to his body. His red eyes stared in Henri's direction, and when Marie told him this was his grandson, he simply laughed and swatted her rear.

Henri had never met his father. Marie had only said that he was a handsome and tall soldier who had said that he would take care of her and her son when he returned from his campaign. He had died, she said. Perhaps, Henri thought. It didn't matter.

The boy knew he could take care of himself.

Tonight, as he walked the last few streets towards their room, he wondered what he would find. He did not like Marie's new boyfriend. The man never spoke to him directly, but Henri could hear him whispering to his mother and saying his name at times. She would shake her head, and then the man would take her in his arms and draw her behind the bed curtain.

Henri came into his building and walked the last few steps slowly. He listened to the door, but heard no sound, and then went inside.

The smell of closeness and sweat mingled with half-eaten food left on the small table was always a shock at first. The food was gone tonight, but he could still see a few crumbs.

He called for his mother, but there was no answer. Crossing the few steps to her bed, he pulled back the curtain and held his breath. But still there was no sound. He called her name a few more times, but he knew it was futile. There was simply no place to hide in the small room.

Henri was reluctant to move down the hall to Josette's room, but now there was no other choice. Despite the woman's repugnance, she seemed to be his mother's confidant.

Cautiously he knocked on Josette's door, half-hoping she would not answer.

When she opened the door, she was only too pleased to see the handsome young boy.

"Oh my dear Henri, at last you have come home. Yes, yes, come in. I have something for you from Marie."

"Do you know where my mother is?" asked Henri, stopping at the threshold.

Please, please, Henri, come in. Don't tell me you are afraid of your dear Josette?" asked the woman teasingly.

"Of course I am not afraid. I am not afraid of anything," said Henri, moving into the room. Yet even as he said the words he could feel the tenseness coming into his body, a tenseness he always felt in Josette's presence.

Josette closed the door behind him as Henri stepped into the room. The woman had once been attractive, but now her bulk seemed to hang in folds as the too-tight dress clung to her body. Her face was heavily rouged and the lip coloring was smeared.

"Sit down, dear boy. I have a note for you from Marie, a note and some coins. You can read, Henri, can't you?"

"Yes, Marie always made me read."

He could read a minimum of words, but he would not admit his inability to this woman.

"Well, then, here. This is from your precious Marie," the woman's tone had suddenly become defensive. She wrestled with herself over the number of coins she would actually give to the boy. Marie had given Josette twenty sou, expressingly asking Josette to promise that she would give the boy half.

Why should he have half, Josette reasoned? He is young and strong; his legs can carry him fast. Besides, he is too unfriendly. He thinks he is something he is not.

Shoving the note into his hand, Josette decided she would give the boy five of the precious coins.

Henri steadied his hand as he read. Though he could not understand every word, he knew that his mother had left with Gerard, and Henri could not come with them. She was sorry and hoped he would forgive her, but she knew Henri would be alright.

Henri held the note, trying to decipher its contents.

Josette grabbed the paper from his hand and confidently read it for him.

"Your mother says she knows you are a clever boy and handsome, so much like your father. Gerard has been so generous in giving us the coins, which would surely help with food. You can always turn to Josette if you have a problem." The woman smiled and ran her finger down the side of his arm.

Henri would not allow the sick feeling in his stomach to rise to his throat. He looked at Josette and simply said, "Give me my coins."

The woman decided she would try one more time. "Perhaps if you would like to stay with me, we could discuss the coins later."

"I will take my coins, now," said Henri evenly.

"Fine. Then here are your five coins," she said sarcastically, slamming the sou into his hand.

Back in his room, Henri breathed deeply against the door and bit his lip. He positioned the plank they used to block the door and threw himself down on the bed face first. Only then would he allow himself to cry quietly.

In the early morning before Paris was completely awake, Henri already was carrying out the plan that he had devised the previous night.

Feeling like a king, he *bought* bread and cheese from an early morning vendor. The man who ran the stand was wary when he saw Henri approach. Surely this boy had stolen from him before. Well, if he could pay now, so be it. Perhaps his coins were pilfered, but that was not his problem.

Henri carefully ate half of the food and then securely placed the rest in the clean bag. He made his way through the streets and alleys of the city and then stood half-hidden close to the gates where the carriages passed. He did not know where the carriages went, but he knew he was sick of Paris, sick of its smell, sick of Josette. He never wanted to see again the close room that he had shared with his mother.

As the first carriage slowed to pass through the gates, the boy moved into position to jump on the rear, and then he quickly and deftly became part of vehicle.

The driver noticed a slight jerk as the weight shifted, but then righted the carriage and assured the travelers their trip to Calais would be a comfortable one.

Calais and the Caroline

Traveling on the carriage west and north had proved more challenging than Henri had imagined, and yet he was undaunted by the numerous times he was sworn at and forced to leave his perch. No matter, he felt, for a new coach always seemed to be not too far behind.

Some drivers realized the extra weight and, upon investigation, allowed him to ride beside them. This was a luxury Henri had not anticipated. In Paris, drivers were always wary of street boys catching rides for a lark. On this route some drivers were actually friendly. Perhaps the longer trips gave rise to the need for conversation.

When a scheduled stop was reached, however, Henri would have to leave that particular carriage, for a bad report could result in a driver losing his job. The boy seemed not to care. Perhaps the warm June days, the open air, the smell of the countryside made any challenge seem like an adventure.

In all, Henri rode five different carriages to Calais. The trip, which might have taken a paying passenger only a half day, took Henri a day and a half. At one point, he took a nap in a nearby field only to be awakened by a friendly dog licking his face. Henri smiled and welcomed the wet on his cheeks. Perhaps it was the openness of the French countryside that made him forget for a while the loneliness he kept pushing from his mind.

When he jumped on another carriage, he waved to his new four-legged friend and held up his arm, shaking his head no, for he did not want the dog to follow. As much as he longed for companionship, for now it could not be.

The smell of the fields and manure gradually changed as a new aura spread throughout the air. For the first time in his life, Henri inhaled the smell of the sea air, and as he peered around the side of this carriage, he saw the port of Calais and the channel ahead. Carefully steadying himself, he alighted from the coach and decided to walk the last distance to the port.

The old familiar feeling of hunger gripped Henri, and he searched again in the bag hoping to gain a few missed crumbs. He had not been prudent in reserving his food and now both coins and scraps were gone.

Henri assessed the activity at the port of Calais. Braced up against a support on the side of the pier, he noticed the vessels and passengers bustling about, preoccupied with thoughts of their own business. He surmised he easily could pick some pockets or grab food from some nearby stand, but he did not want to begin that again unless absolutely necessary. He was sick of running from the vendors, the whistles of the gendarmes.

For nearly an hour, Henri stood and watched the passengers boarding and alighting from the boats. First the passengers would disembark from the boats; then the crew would follow. He examined the crews of the ship, scruffy looking men, but certainly no worse than the street people of Paris. Sometimes the crew included a boy, no older than Henri.

What would life be like on a boat? he questioned himself. Would skills be needed? What skills could I offer?

Gathering his courage and hoping the man spoke French, Henri walked to the end of the pier and spoke to one of the crew. "Monsieur, I am Henri Moreau. I want to work on the boat."

"What? What's that you say?" questioned the surprised first mate, Jonathan Wakeman, as he looked at this too-thin, young face. The boy's height did not match the youth and innocence of his face.

"And if you're speaking that foolish French, I never bother with that jibberish," he continued. "Well, you might be lookin' for someone and from that lean look I hope you find who you're lookin' for," said the mate, raising his hand and motioning the boy forward as he finished supervising tying down his ropes. "Just a minute here and I'll find the captain for you."

Not quite sure what to expect, Henri stood and waited. Paying little heed to the tall boy, other crew members now left the vessel and made their way into the streets of the port city.

As he surveyed the boat, Henri examined the many ropes attached to the packet's sails. How fascinating would it be to learn to control those sails and fly across the water to one's destination.

Following one particular sail down to the base, Henri saw a familiar site, a scurrying beady-eyed beast that walked across the railing of the boat and then facilely jumped from the vessel to the pier.

Yes, that will be my skill, mused Henri.

"You there, boy, you wish to speak with me," said a large man in a dark blue uniform, his gray beard and shaggy hair escaping from his captain's hat. "My first mate seems to think you might be looking for someone," said the man as he motioned Henri towards him.

Again Henri repeated his introduction with a slight bow of his head. "Monsieur, I am Henri Moreau. I want to work on this ship."

Fortunately for Henri, Captain Christopher Tyler had bothered to learn some of that "French jibberish," as the first mate had called it.

Switching to his rather rudimentary French, the captain was able to ascertain that this young lad wanted a job on his boat. Somewhat jokingly, he asked Henri what he knew about ships, even a ship as small as this packet.

Henri spoke directly to the man's face, a kindly face, he discerned, for if there were a skill that Henri had already acquired, it was the ability to read a man's eyes. "I do not know anything of ships, *capitiane*, but I wish to learn. I do know how to catch rats, sir. I believe you have some on your boat," replied Henri.

"Rats, you say. Yes, they are the bane of any boat. So you think, Monsieur Henri Moreau, that you can catch rats. Let's see what you do in one hour," said the captain. "One hour, do you hear?"

"*Merci, capitiane*," said Henri with a slight bow.

Carefully he jumped onto the vessel, a smile on his young face as the captain led him forward.

Captain Tyler led him down to the lower deck of the vessel and then to the hold, watching the boy's face, a face that he, too, had read. He surmised the boy could be fourteen or sixteen, but there still was an eagerness that he had not seen in a long time. He thought of his own boy, his only son now gone four years, who would be close to this boy's age.

Once they reached the lowest deck, the captain nodded and showed him where the creatures might be found. In his mind Christopher Tyler already knew he had found a new cabin boy.

Henri detached his sling shot from around his waist and began searching for the stones in his bag. Then he put on his gloves. He crawled in the lowest recesses of the hold and listened patiently. In a short time his eyes adjusted to the dark, and he could hear the scurrying of the beasts as they began to come close and sniff this new creature to their haunt.

From above, Captain Tyler would hear an occasional thump, but no other sound from the area where he had left the boy. He looked at his watch; a half hour had passed. He smiled to himself. "Well, we will see."

In a little under the allotted time, Henri emerged onto the main deck of the packet, his bag proudly held at the top, but not too close. He then dumped the contents of the bag at the captain's feet. Eight rats lay in a heap on the wooden boards of the vessel. One of them began to twitch a bit, and quickly Henri stomped at the base of its skull.

"There is no need for them to suffer," he said decisively in French.

In English, the captain replied, "A wise and kind remark, Mr. Moreau. You are now the official cabin boy of this vessel, the *Caroline.* And if I have anything to say about it, you will begin to learn English, and most likely very quickly."

Aboard the packet, Henri learned every aspect of sailing and managing a small vessel. He learned all facets of the ship itself—to scale the ropes, to unfurl the sails, to cope with the motion of the boat, to carry his weight as a man. When the air was particularly positive, he was even allowed—under close supervision—to have a short turn at the helm. To feel the power of the wheel and to experience the control of the boat were the most exciting times for Henri.

He also learned how to cope within a given society. He knew which men to take at face value, which men to be wary of.

Most importantly, in Captain Tyler, Henri found a surrogate father, the first positive man in his life. The captain also brought Henri to his home in London, where Henri realized that, while a man could rule his own world on the sea, on land he became, at best, the second mate.

Mrs. Caroline Tyler, for whom the packet had been named, was a warm, friendly woman who had had to manage her home and daughters during the times when her husband was away. She was not about to relinquish that position just because her man walked through the front door occasionally.

Caroline Tyler at once realized why John had taken to Henri. It was not that he looked like their son, although his age was close, but his intelligence and curiosity were so like their own boy. She would have loved to know about Henri's roots, but she resisted the obvious questions. If the boy did not willingly divulge this information, then it most likely was a subject too painful to discuss.

The Tyler home was a busy one, with three grown daughters, all married, who lived close to their parents. There were some small grandchildren—Henri was never quite sure which children belonged to which daughter—but they took to Henri immediately, sensing someone who had not quite crossed the chasm into adulthood.

For Henri, the shock of family life was alien. He had guarded his emotions so keenly in early life that now the warmth of this comfortable surrounding could not invade his spirit deeply.

It is truly impossible to give one's heart completely when it has not been nourished in childhood.

Westward

When Henri told Captain Tyler that he would be leaving the *Caroline* soon, the announcement did not surprise the older man. The captain had taught the boy everything he knew about sailing the small vessel and had shared the many books that he had with his protégé. Indeed, Christopher himself looked westward also and would have relished a new adventure across the Atlantic, but success and duty necessitated a more conservative path for the captain. At twenty, Henri had no such obligations or commitments.

However, the parting with the Tyler family was more difficult than Henri had imagined. Yet he realized that, if he did not leave the comfort of this life, he would regret it forever. He longed to be part of the larger ships, the challenge of the sea that sailors spoke of with awe, a challenge for which he felt prepared.

At the helm of the *Carleton*, Henri yelled for help as the wind washed wave after wave upon the deck. In the many crossings that he had made from Liverpool to Halifax, he had never experienced such fierce winds and sheets of rain. Every muscle in his body struggled to keep the wheel under control, but he felt his arms being ripped from his torso. Williams finally assisted him with the wheel, but the storm was just too fierce.

In one huge wash over the vessel, he saw two of his crew mates pushed off the deck as if they were sticks. He heard their screams, and then they disappeared forever into the waves. Captain Thomas had come to help with the helm and the three of them managed to keep hold of the wheel.

As the cold sea washed over Henri again and again, he realized that fighting the fury of the Atlantic was not what he wanted to do for the rest of his life. Now twenty-five years old, he resolved that once on the western shore, he would leave this life and follow the paths of fellow countrymen who traveled the quieter waters of the inland lakes. He had heard of the vastness and richness of the young United States and no longer felt the need to prove himself among the crew of the sailing vessels.

Although he never had any formal schooling, Henri had heard of the tale of his fellow countryman, Jacques Cartier, who three hundred years earlier had traveled the path that he, Henri, had now chosen. Cartier had been searching for the Northwest Passage. Henri's ultimate goal was to reach the western frontier, Illinois.

He made his way from Halifax northward and then turned west at the St. Lawrence River. When he tired of his solo journey, he would abandon his loneliness and seek the company of other adventurers traveling in larger bateux, flat-bottomed boats that could range from eighteen to fifty feet. Here, other men marveled at Henri's prowess in dealing with the oars and sails of the vessel. He could have shared his tales of harrowing Atlantic crossings, but he had learned early that fellow sailors admired one's skills, more than words.

As Henri traveled westward on the St. Lawrence River, the towns of Quebec and Montreal offered respite from the constant challenge of the trek. This area, once entirely ruled by the French, had been ceded to the English in the French and Indian War. The natives of the region, primarily the Iroquois nation, had been decimated by European diseases and forced to move west. One particularly heinous story related the tale of British General Lord Jeffrey Amherst, whose troops used blankets infected with smallpox as a weapon of genocide against the Indians.

The French, on the other hand, entrenched themselves in the St. Lawrence towns. In 1815, the town of Quebec, once called Stadacona by the natives but now heavy with a French population, carried the resentment of its English rule.

Henri, walking a cautious line between his French roots and his English sea experiences, kept ever close to his own thoughts. His English was not native, but practiced enough to handle any encounters. From the French, he learned to hunt and trap, often exceeding his teachers' ability. His strength, coordination and guile, an adjunct of his early life, all served him well.

Blessed with these qualities, Henri also bore the curse of good looks, penetrating blue eyes that averted their stare for no one, hair bleached by days in the sea, muscles that had been earned by strenuous work. Women stared at his handsomeness with unabashed admiration. But he had seen the rigors of life with women, such as Josette and his own mother, the devastation of syphilis that snared the lives of many of the older sailors, the constant sores, the swelling, and, in some, eventual madness.

Henri learned to hide his face with a beard and avoided the whores that employed their wares near the harbors, but if an occasional country maiden came his way, he was not above an amorous encounter. None of the liaisons touched him, however, and he kept at his forefront the goal to the west.

Peoria, 1823

Henri could hear the shouts of the young braves of the Peoria tribe playing baggataway as he rode his horse into the natives' camp. The two teams, cheering and shouting, passed the small ball from hand-held nets as they moved down towards their opponents' goal. Henri smiled to himself, thinking how it would be good to be that young again, to play games, to not feel the aches that crept into his bones when he slept on the bare ground.

He had reached his goal, this new frontier called Illinois, and yet he felt he had accomplished nothing. His trek through the lakes and, now, down this Illinois River had not brought the contentment he had hoped. The longing, the emptiness remained.

As he dismounted and greeted the tribe's chief, a ritual that had become part of his itinerant life style, he knew his life could extend many more years, yet a great wash of futility suffocated his body. He was only one man, one life, but felt his existence should count for something. One more hunt, one more village—whether native or settler—fit into a pattern of dull sameness.

Fair Moon had watched as the tall, bearded man rode into the camp. She was careful to make sure her furtive glances in the man's direction would not be noticed by the other girls. She had learned to be wary of all others, both male and female, since her father's death. As a single young woman with no brothers on whom to rely, she was pursued by several of the braves in her tribe, but she would have none of them. She tried to keep her independence, tend her own crops, and be left alone, but she had known for some time that her position in the tribe was becoming much more tenuous.

The women hated her, too. She was too aloof and much too winsome to not be a threat. Lately, she had noticed some of the crops that she tended—maize, beans and squash—were stomped by human footprints. When she asked the other women if they had seen what happened, they glared and turned away. Even in this communal existence, that which is "other" is not accepted.

Henri could not help but feel the stares of the dark eyes upon him, as he took his saddle, gun, pelts and bedroll from his horse's back. "There, there, old boy, we'll get you rested for a few days and then be on our way again."

Though his tone was light for effect, he still felt the heaviness weighing upon him. A tugging on Henri's pant leg turned him around to face a bevy of youngsters that had crowded around the newcomer to the camp. Though many of the children had seen the faces of other white men, the event always brought stares. As Henri bent down to shake some of their hands or touch the tops of their heads, they tugged at his beard.

"So, you don't like this old thing, do you?" he laughed. "Well, I think I might just get rid of it and see who actually lives under here. What do you think?"

Though they could not understand his speech, their curiosity overcame their shyness. One small girl held her arms out to be lifted up, and Henri obliged.

"Senka, Senka," called the mother, racing towards the tall stranger and her daughter.

"I meant no harm, ma'am," assured Henri as he handed the child to her mother.

As he looked across the group of women who were now calling to their children, he noticed one tall, young woman that stood apart from the others. She moved towards him cautiously in graceful movements, brushing back the long black strands of hair that blew in her slender face.

Henri could not take his eyes away from her. As she came closer, she nodded slightly and then, just when he felt she might say something, she turned abruptly away.

"Wait, please. Don't go. Won't you tell me your name? Please, I am Henri Moreau," Henri said, placing his right hand on his chest.

She stopped, and then turned her head towards Henri. Speaking in halting English, she replied, "Fair Moon."

Perhaps it was because his soul had felt such great emptiness, but when Henri heard her voice, he almost shivered.

As the weeks passed and Henri stayed with the tribe, he and Fair Moon spent more and more time together. When he had shaved his beard, his face took on the appearance of some young novice, quite belying the experiences that had etched years in Henri's persona. Fair Moon touched the whiteness of his face, that part protected by the beard for so long, the cheeks and chin, and then looked searchingly into his eyes. She sensed a sorrow hidden behind the façade of bravado.

Her very finger tips on his face brought a sensation to his soul that was completely new. He took those fingers, the rough hand calloused by farming, and brought them tenderly to his lips.

Henri knew he was expected to bring gifts to a woman's brother as a symbol of a desire to marry, but without a father or brother, Henri offered several choice animal pelts and a hunting knife to the tribe's chief, Running Bear.

The chief had known for some time of the white man's attraction to Fair Moon. He looked at the pelts and nodded. Then he carefully examined the proffered knife. He touched knowingly and appreciated the scars and wearing. He sensed the richness of its history and the value that it must have to the owner. Shaking his head, he returned the knife, clutched the pelts and nodded yes in the direction of Fair Moon. A man, Running Bear reasoned, can always find a wife, but a good hunting knife could be used to save one's life. He smiled at the white man's ardor, but not his wisdom.

In truth, Running Bear was glad to see Fair Moon attached to a man. Without parents and siblings and now too old to be accepted into another unit, she had become a distraction to the tribe, causing jealousy among the women and rivalry among the men. Henri Moreau's proposal was a viable solution to a problematic situation.

For three days Fair Moon was escorted by Soweto, the wife of Running Bear, to the tepee where Henri had lived for the past two months. Taking pride in her new guardianship of Fair Moon, Soweto adorned the bride-to-be with glass beads and bells and ceremoniously walked her each day to her intended. Members of the tribe witnessed the ceremony and, as in all rites of passage among communities, they nodded their approval or forecasted the grief destined to be part of the new couple's life.

On the fourth day, Soweto left Fair Moon with Henri. The two were now officially man and wife.

Fair Moon and Henri

In both mind and spirit Fair Moon and Henri were completely suited to each other. Raised to be independent by the very nature of their disparate circumstances, their joining made one complete person. Neither had ever imagined that life could be so happy and content. When separated, they continued the motions of their lives, but thoughts of the days when they would be together were always foremost.

Henri continued his hunting and trapping, sometimes traveling with the men of the tribe for several days at a time. As he had learned in dealing with other groups of men, he trusted others warily, and did not draw attention to his skills or prowess in tracking animals and capitalized on the knowledge of this new society. In hunting with the braves, he learned to recognize more keenly the tracks of Illinois's animals and to be aware of changes in smells as they tracked their prey, the small red wolf, the grey wolf and the occasional bear.

Once, when Close Eyes's rifle had jammed as a cornered grey wolf was about to pounce, Henri had calmly and efficiently shot the beast cleanly between its eyes, earning the respect of the other hunters. As aptly as he had handled his slingshot, Henri had learned to dispatch other, larger prey with a rifle.

For her part, now joined formally in tribal custom, the women no longer felt Fair Moon to be a threat, and, though they might still be envious of her because of her independence, they accepted her into their world of attached women. When Fair Moon learned she would soon bear a child, they welcomed her more completely into their circle. The women smiled and nodded knowingly when Fair Moon became listless and melancholy during Henri's absences. She will learn, they reasoned, that life can be less hectic and challenging when the men are gone, though they secretly envied the unusual relationship of this white man and their Fair Moon.

The women would not allow Henri inside the tepee where Fair Moon now lay almost unconscious as she labored to give birth to the baby that struggled to be free of her womb. The black head of the child was thankfully visible as Watsika's deft hands massaged the young woman's belly. Yes, she thought, it is fine to be tall and graceful as Fair Moon was, but she much preferred the short, stout women to bear children. Watsika looked at the blood that pooled beneath Fair Moon and knew that much damage had been done inside the young woman.

There was no choice, however; she had to use her hands to grab the back of the head just beginning to peer into the cold world. She slapped the face of the semi-conscious woman and, shouting, told her to push. Fair Moon instinctively obeyed the command, and the hands of the woman reached and ripped out the slick body, which fell into the blood.

Watsika smiled and nodded and slapped the bottom of the strong son that was now in her arms. After cutting the cord, she called to Henri and proudly handed him the boy. Looking in Fair Moon's direction, she shook her head and mumbled words that, to Henri, were unintelligible.

Henri looked at this bundle that had caused so much trouble to his Fair Moon and could not bring himself to feel the excitement of others. Yes, he had checked to make sure the little body was whole, but he had returned the bundle to one of the women and then held the hand of Fair Moon and kissed it tenderly.

Her eyes opened slightly and she tried to whisper to him.

"No, no, be quiet. Save your energy. Our son is beautiful, so much like you," Henri lied. He had no idea what the face of the little creature looked like.

With her hair matted with the sweat of her labor, her copper-colored skin looking so very pale, and the limpness of her body so apparent, Henri was shocked to face the idea that she could have died. It should be a happy time, but the sight of his wife clinging to life so tenuously struck him as surely as any blow he had ever received before from man or nature. He could not lose her. If she lived, he would never make her go through this again.

Though the child was named for his father, Henri Moreau, the native village had soon given him the name of Swift Eagle, for he seemed to be running from the time of his first step. His long legs, even as a child, carried him more quickly than other children of the same age. Though his skin was lighter than his mother's, his hair was dark, like hers, but with enough wave to let one know that he was not just a native. His face was clearly defined by his mother's face, however, the dark, deep soulful eyes, the chiseled nose and high cheek bones. The faces were so similar that all who came into the village could not fail to recognize the child as belonging to none other than Fair Moon.

As the child grew, he learned the skills of his father and his tribe. There were some in the tribe who would have rejected the child due to the white skin of his father, but both father and now six-year old son were recognized for their prowess in hunting and tracking, and thus accepted by the other braves and young boys. Occasionally when an older native boy would be put to shame by Swift Eagle's catches and begin to beat the younger boy, other braves would come to the child's defense.

For the three members of the Moreau family, it was an idyllic existence. They seemed complete in themselves, but could depend on the tribe for extended protection.

Life, however, was about to change as the ever-growing white population challenged the nomadic existence of the natives. As tribes pushed back and atrocities occurred on both sides, as happens in all wars, the peaceful existence of the plains' tribes came to an abrupt end. Convinced that his people were going to starve due to the less fertile lands where they had been forced to move, the Sauk tribe chief Blackhawk, as he was called by the white population, decided to test the resolve of the U.S. army. The natives were defeated in major battles, resulting in the edict that all Indian populations had to travel west and join those who had already crossed the Mississippi. The year was 1832.

Woodsville

As the native village where the Moreau family had lived was forced to dissolve, Henri faced a choice for not only himself, but also for his family. Fair Moon and Swift Eagle would, of course, accept any decision Henri made, but this was a new experience for him. Before he had only himself to consider; now he was accountable for three lives. In his heart, he knew he could not be comfortable forever in the Indian lifestyle. Yes, the three had sufficed nicely, almost for eight years in the tribe, but he could not envision that life forever. He had also visited the white settlements that were quickly sprouting up along the rivers and creeks of Illinois and sensed that his family would not be accepted in the white man's world completely.

The French that had settled were more accepting of the Moreau family. Young Henri had only to speak a few words of his father's native land and he would be smiled at or patted on the head by the French men and women. But the new Illinois settlers, the English and German, were not as welcoming to this peculiar, in their minds, mixed family.

It would be a new venture for Henri as he decided to settle, a word still alien to his nature, on the fertile land west of Peoria that could easily be claimed as one's own. He, Fair Moon and young Henri built a small cabin in the fashion of other settlers along a small creek. The land was rich and welcoming. Crops grew easily. Yes, dangers were always present, the threat of prairie fires, the wolves that could be heard howling their ominous songs at night, but the three were complete in themselves.

In Henri's mind, life passed amiably. He had his dear Fair Moon and the boy, now nine, grew every day into a role of accepting all responsibility that his father gave to him. He could fish, hunt, shoot, and, unlike the native boys that he had grown up with, was not insulted by having to plant crops. In the evenings, his father also made sure that he could read the pamphlets from the trading posts where they bartered for supplies.

When the family began making trips to the new settlement of Woodsville, not far from their cabin, Fair Moon told Henri she could feel the eyes of the white women staring at her. Though some tried to be kind, the memories of the recent war were still keen in the minds of many. When the family left, the women of the town would conjecture as to why such a handsome man would marry an Indian.

"Did you see her touching all those combs and ribbons, Mary?" asked Mavis Tripp. "I don't think any one of us will want to buy those things now."

"Others have touched those ribbons before," replied Mary, the wife of the general store's owner, Owen Willis. "Besides, she has raised a good and obedient son. Anyone can see that."

Yes, most in the town felt that the Moreau boy was one any family could be proud of, despite his obvious looks, so like his mother. He seemed respectful and strong. He easily lifted the sacks that his father purchased from Owen Willis.

"Mr. Moreau," commented Willis, "you have no idea how blessed you are to have a youngin' so strong. My wife Mary and I have not had your good fortune to have a son, or any children, for that matter. You just never know how much you could use another hand. Many children would be the greatest of blessings, but you at least have the one."

"Yes, Mr. Willis. I suppose you are correct. He has always been a good child. I never really thought about it, but, yes, I am blessed with such a son," agreed Henri.

Illinois summers could bring the stifling, humid heat, but it was the winters that tested the mettle of the stalwart settler. In the second year of their life on the prairie, the cold penetrated the very core of the Moreau cabin. The fire inside was no protection against the temperatures, which fell below zero, or the cruel prairie winds that easily penetrated the logs of the little home.

Her cough began just as the temperatures reached new lows. Then the fever and chills assaulted Fair Moon's frail body. In the four years since her tribe had been forced to leave, Fair Moon's health had faded. Henri could not understand why she had not adjusted to their new life, but, in truth, she was never a true settler. While Henri, who had learned to adjust to new challenges throughout his life, thrived in that role, Fair Moon could not. On some evenings, even when the ground became cold and hard after frost, she would take her blanket and sleep outside. Henri would wake suddenly during the night, reach for her, and, when he didn't find her, would run outside looking for his wife. She would be asleep, a few feet away from the home.

Was it her sleeping on the cold ground that had started her illness, or had she faded because life was so changed? Henri did not ask himself this question, but instead ordered his son to tend to his mother while he traveled to Woodsville to secure the doctor. Bringing the only leeches he could find, the doctor bled the woman, believing this treatment would rid her body of the sickness.

When Fair Moon died in early winter, Henri and young Henri pounded the almost frozen ground under the large walnut tree as they dug the hole for her body. It was as if life jeered at their attempts to control their destinies. They wrapped her body in the blanket she had been given by the midwife Soweto, the last token of her life in the tribal village. Then the two covered the grave with large rocks from the ice-covered creek.

Henri sat in the cabin, staring at the bed where his wife had died, while young Henri cooked some of the meat from the rabbits they had trapped. Neither spoke. The only sound in the desolate cabin was the chewing of young Henri, who refused to wipe away the tears rolling down his face.

The dreams began not many days after Fair Moon's death. Henri found himself in a dark hole while the eyes of rats stared menacingly at him. He would reach for his sling shot or his gun and be unable to find either. He would begin yelling at them and fighting back.

For months he was plagued by the wild dreams, but he thought that, when spring finally came, when life returned in March, he could shake the torment.

Each day he would plow his fields, working from sunrise to sun down, hoping to exhaust himself physically so that he could sleep at night. Working close to his side, young Henri would keep step with his father, proving to him that he was becoming a man.

However, Henri seemed not to be able to fight the overwhelming loneliness and anxiety that surrounded every corner of his life. When he returned from a day of plowing, he would pass her grave and tears would well in his eyes. Each time he opened the door, he expected to see her dark face, and the realization that she was not there was like a fresh wound. He heard her voice as she used to sing when mixing the cornmeal for their dinner. He was quite sure he had seen the rocker, where she had spent so many evenings, moving when he looked up from his reading.

Perhaps he should have been comforted by his son's company. But even as the young boy took every stride with his father in the field or helped inside their house, how could the father tell his son that the mere look of his face, a replica of his mother's, was like a sword to his heart?

On one evening when Henri was particularly tired, he fell to sleep quickly. But once again it was a fretful sleep, plagued by the threat of rats, which scurried under his bed. Then a wolf howling in the night slipped into his dream and began charging and scratching the door. Henri reached for the rifle, which was always close to the bed.

The click of the rifle as it was cocked by his father's hand startled the boy. He awoke to see his father with the gun pointed straight into his young face.

"Pa, Pa, don't shoot. It's me, Henri. Pa, please, don't shoot."

The screams of his son mercifully woke the anguished man. "*Mon, Dieu*," he said, sinking to his knees.

Henri Moreau sobbed as he had never cried in his entire life, not when his mother had left him, not when he had been bitten by rats—and not even when Fair Moon had died.

Young Henri knelt at his father's side and tried to comfort this man that he admired so completely. But, in that instance, the father knew what he must do.

"Mr. Willis, Owen, I wonder if I might speak to you about a situation, a problem, that I find myself faced with."

"Yes, yes, of course, Henri. I know how difficult life has been for you since your wife died. Thank God you have the boy, though. Do you need less seed for planting or to repair the yoke for the oxen? I'm afraid I can't promise any more payment for your crops this year. It seems everyone had a bumper crop," replied Owen.

"No, it is not anything with the farming." Henri paused, searching for the words to explain the terrible decision that he had made. "You mentioned my son, young Henri. I have been so troubled about him lately. He is eleven now, you know, and I feel he needs more than I can give him."

"Really?" said Owen. "He always looks healthy when I see him. He is getting so tall these days."

"No, I can give him the food, Owen. That is not the problem. What he is missing is, is his mother." Henri hoped the lie would not be as transparent as he felt it must be, for indeed the boy had not cried for, nor talked of his mother. He seemed to accept the fact of her loss as he did everything else, without question.

"Yes, boys can miss their mothers, but he seems to be very attached to you. In time, I'm sure he will deal with his loss," replied Owen.

There was no way for Henri to admit that he was the one who had nearly murdered his own son due to the grief.

"What I was thinking, Owen, was that, perhaps, while I do some hunting across the Mississippi, that maybe you and Mrs. Willis would be so kind and have my boy come and stay with you. I could give what I have saved in the last few years, $30, to help pay for his food. I notice you have a store room out back where, maybe, Henri could stay."

It was only then that Owen realized the incredible proposition that the man was suggesting. Yes, he and Mary had always longed for a child, especially a boy, a strong young boy, to help with the chores, but this proposal was something he could not imagine. What would Mary think?

"Well, Henri, I, I just don't know what to say. I will, of course, have to talk with Mary, but what does young Henri say to this idea?"

"I have not mentioned it to him yet. I wanted to see what your reaction would be," replied Henri.

"Yes, yes, well, I can see how that would be the thing to do first. I will talk to Mary tonight." He looked in her direction as she waited on a customer in the store. What a wonderful companion she had been for these past fifteen years. Her manner always friendly, but forthright, her body a bit rounded by age, the hair showing strands of gray, but always someone he could confide in. Their lives were truly blessed, except for the absence of children. Now this opportunity had suddenly appeared. In truth, he did not know how his wife would react to this most strange idea.

"The man wants to do what?" Mary questioned as she let the bread drop from her hand onto her plate.

"Yes, you heard me right. He has suggested that we take in young Henri while, while he is off hunting, hunting west of the Mississippi."

"Hunting west of the Mississippi, he says. My word, this poor child. First he loses his mother, now his father wants to abandon him. Oh, don't shake your head. I know what abandonment is when I see it," said Mary.

How true were Mary's words, for she too had lost both parents when she was eight years old only to be raised by a cold, distant pair of cousins who expected the child to do all the housework of an adult. When Owen saw her working in their store, he saw a person of industry and comeliness, someone who could make a perfect companion for his desire to run a struggling business. Moreover, despite the absence of love which the cousins had shown toward the orphan, Mary's loving environment with her parents had prevailed in her personality.

She was especially kind to children and had always wanted some of her own, but a cruel irony had determined that was not to be.

"He has offered us $30 to take care of the boy," Owen replied.

"Thirty pieces . . . ," Mary's voice trailed off. "How has the boy reacted to this . . . exchange?"

"Well, he said he hasn't told him yet. He wanted to run the idea by us first."

"You know I always wanted a child, but this is just so, so troubling for the lad. Let's be sure to do some extra prayers for the youngin'. I'm afraid he'll be needing all the help he can get," said Mary.

She also knew she would be saying some extra prayers for Owen and herself, for although her heart was already beginning to feel the excitement of having a child in her household, she knew there would be challenges ahead for all of them.

As if reading her mind, Owen said, "You know, Mary, there are some in this town that hate the Injuns, and I've heard them refer to the boy as the half-breed many a time. We could be bringing trouble into our lives on that score. I just want you to look ahead and be sure about our decision."

"I figure there are always gonna' be those who find something to gripe over. I know I can get by their comments. And if the boy hears them, which he probably already has, we'll just explain to him about the stupidity of others."

Owen smiled and shook his head. "Well, it looks as if some mother-like instincts have already kicked in. We've got to remember though, Mary, that we'll be easing into this situation with the boy. We can't expect him to take to us too quickly."

"Yes, of course I know that," replied a smiling Mary in return.

"But I am a good hunter, Pa. Not as good as you perhaps, but I am gettin' better every day. And I promise to do everything you tell me. I know I can be better," pleaded young Henri.

"You are the best son anyone could ever hope for. Do you understand that, Henri? I am not leaving because you have done anything wrong. It is me. I am the one who, who must leave. It just wouldn't be fair to you to face the kind of life that I have ahead."

"Yes, yes, it would, Pa. I would love it. We wouldn't be plantin' crops, we wouldn't have to lug all the stuff to the store. Please, please, take me with you," the boy pleaded.

"Don't you like the Wilsons? They are good people. They have a place for you in their home behind the store. They know how to read. You would learn so much."

"The only things I want to learn, Pa, are from you," said the boy softly. He had come to learn that, once his father had decided an issue, he could not change his mind. And the boy was too proud to plead further.

For two days the father and son worked side by side, mostly in silence, as they closed the cabin that had been their home for the past four years. They boarded the windows, packed the seed that was left, and loaded the meager dried foods that they had along with the bag of cornmeal into the small wagon. If the two did speak, it was only to ask practical questions about the packing and emptying of the cabin.

On the third day, the boy and his father climbed into the wagon as they had so many times before and road west and south towards Woodsville. Young Henri looked back at his mother's grave and a sudden feeling of anger, an anger he had never felt before, welled up within him.

It is her fault, he thought. If only she hadn't gotten sick and died, my Pa wouldn't be leaving.

The feeling of anger surprised the boy, and, as quickly as it had come, he realized that she had not chosen to die and leave them both. Closing his eyes tightly, he promised he would never forget her and her beautiful face. He turned toward his father and, in that instant, he realized without a doubt that this day would be the last time he would see him.

With a steady motion, the wheels of the wagon creaked toward Woodsville and young Henri's new life.

Part 3

Woodsville, 1841

"You must come and meet our Henri, well, everyone calls him Henry now, dear Charlotte," smiled Heloise coyly. "He is sooo beautiful, right, Pauline?"

"Oh, definitely," replied a giggling Pauline. "He is absolutely the most handsome looking boy I have ever seen."

"And you have seen so very many," laughed Heloise.

Charlotte looked up from her mending, something she had been doing diligently for the five days since her arrival in Woodsville. She needed something to do with her hands, an excuse to keep to herself , for she was so uncomfortable with these new sisters. She had tried reading, but Heloise and Pauline were so talkative and busy, Charlotte could not find the quiet she needed.

Now, as the two giggling ones looked anxiously in her direction and seemed to be asking for some sort of response, she thought hard about what names went with the two similar faces. She finally devised her crutch: Heloise, seventeen, the older by one year and slightly taller, had the name that was higher in the alphabet, while Pauline, "P," was sixteen. Other than that, Charlotte saw them as one entity. They seemed to speak together, walk everywhere together, often laughing about someone or something, read little or nothing at all, and always be not more than two feet apart. Even now, sitting here in their grandparents Gallets' home, they moved their chairs together so they could nudge and jab at each other as they half-heartedly attempted to tat a small doily.

Their faces echoed each other, also: pointed chins, playful blue eyes, brown hair gathered carefully at the nape of their narrow necks with ribbons, small mouths that constantly seemed to be "oohing" or "aahing" at the merest suggestion of an idea. They seemed to be so happy and content with everything that Charlotte found their demeanor quite annoying.

Across the room the younger sister Amanda, a sullen nine, was nothing like the two older sisters. Though her face bore some similarities to the older two, there was "a squareness" that made her look quite like a boy, despite the dress that she was forced to wear. She had confided in Charlotte, quite unexpectedly and unsolicited on Charlotte's part, that Uncle John Gallet had allowed her to wear boys' breeches when riding a horse, much more to her liking, thank you, than silly dresses. As they prepared to share the loft's bed on their first night, the younger sister was quite pleased by the shock her secret had caused Charlotte. She was careful to speak quietly so that Heloise and Pauline, in the adjoining bed, could not hear her startling revelation.

Now, Amanda, struggling to finish what could only be described as very clumsy stitches, tsked disgustingly at the two gigglers across the way and added, "Henry is very tall and strong." As soon as she had opened her mouth, she knew it was a mistake.

"Oh, yes, Charlotte. We forgot to tell you that our *little* sister has quite a little crush on our Henry, or should I say Swift Eagle," said Pauline teasingly as she made sure to emphasize the word "little."

"He is my friend," shouted a disgusted Amanda, who now threw her stitching into a pile on the floor as she turned her face from those two annoying sisters. She looked at the face of this new sister, Charlotte, and wasn't sure just where she would fit into her life. When she first saw Charlotte and noticed that she didn't giggle and talk incessantly as her other two sisters did, she hoped that she might have a friend, a friend who was a sister also. She looked in Charlotte's direction to see how she would respond to this teasing. Would she be a friend, or just another annoyance?

"But why do you also call him Swift Eagle?" questioned Charlotte in as even a tone as she could muster.

"Well, that is the really interesting and soooo sad story about him," gushed a ready Heloise. "He is half-Indian and half-French, thank goodness. His father was Henri Moreau, some mysterious French trapper or something like that, and he married, we think he married, this Indian woman called Fair Moon. So they had our Henry, but his Indian name was Swift Eagle while they lived with her tribe."

"Yes, can you imagine that?" butted in an excited Pauline. "A Frenchman actually living with an Indian tribe."

"And," continued Heloise, who was slightly miffed at being interrupted, "they built some cabin not too far from here where she died and her grave is under a tree close to the cabin. And then the father just left one day, and, since then, our Henry has stayed with the Willises, who run the general store. The father was supposed to come back some day, but he has been gone for a long time, five or six years is what I heard, and no one has ever heard from him. Henry is now sixteen, just like Pauline."

Charlotte tried very hard not to show how shocked she was to hear that a half-savage boy was living in Woodsville. She remembered, however, Franklin's ironic essay on "savages" and realized that one does not always know the complete story, but then she also recalled the Annette Savage she had encountered so recently. Well, she reasoned, one could never be quite sure about anything in this strange land.

Then she grasped that this person had been left with strangers for the last few years. "It sounds so very, very sad," responded a visibly moved Charlotte. She couldn't imagine being without one or the other of her parents. Even when Mama was gone for the year or so when she was ill, she had been with Papa. But then, with a sudden awareness, she realized that these three sisters had been left with their grandparents for three years. How difficult for them also, although Charlotte felt their spirits hadn't been dampened. Of course, they were with their grandparents. There was also Uncle John, their mother's brother, who had been the first of their family to pioneer this area.

Still wanting to best herself in front of these older sisters, Amanda could not resist the last coup, in her mind. "Henry and I, with Uncle John, of course, have ridden to the cabin where they lived. I think a family called the Coopers live there now, and Henry has put some wildflowers on his mother's grave."

"You went *riding* with him," said Pauline, feigning a shock she certainly didn't feel. In her mind, the little sister barely existed at all. Still, she herself would have loved to go *riding* with Henry.

"You, you are always making fun of me. I am so tired of being your little sister," shouted an indignant Amanda, looking at Charlotte, who she hoped would come to her rescue.

Charlotte felt this was a pivotal moment and needed to say something in the younger girl's defense, but she just wasn't sure what the wise course would be. However, she felt a strong sense of sympathy for this younger sister.

"Girls, girls, what is all this shouting about? Is this how you have behaved in my absence? Have you simply not learned to be kind and gentle with each other? What have your grandparents allowed you to become?" asked their curious mother.

"Oh, dear Mama, we are just teasing Amanda a bit about her . . . friendship with the Indian boy in town. Well, half-Indian, anyway," responded Heloise.

"Indian boy! Here in Woodsville? Papa told us that all the Indians had been forced to leave. What will become of us living here in this uncivilized place? I cannot believe that these wild people are here and my girls are shouting and teasing each other. Have you not learned to be ladies?" replied the distraught mother. She wasn't quite sure what was more of a problem, the wild people or her shouting daughters.

"Oh, Mama, don't be so worried. It is just one boy, and we promise we will be kinder to each other," soothed Heloise, who in just five days had learned how to handle her mother just as she had managed her grandparents for the last three years.

"We have learned to do all the things that young ladies must do. We can draw, play, sew and even cook once in a while," continued Heloise, smiling and charming her way straight into her mother's heart.

Taking her cue from her older sister, who nodded in her direction, Pauline added, "We are so happy you are finally here, Mama. We will definitely be able to refine our ladylike pursuits with your guidance."

Mama was dully appeased. How could one not like these two lovely faces? So charming, so feminine, so . . . unbookish. Not at all like Charlotte. And then her own namesake, Amanda. She wasn't quite sure what to make of this poor child. When she had left these girls three years ago, she was just a baby, only six. Perhaps she should have stayed with Eloi, but a girl needs a woman's guidance at that early an age, and he had not insisted on keeping the youngest daughter with him as he had insisted on Charlotte, and their son, of course. Even now, though, as she looked in that youngest daughter's direction, she recognized a face that was not as comely as the other girls' and hands and feet that seemed too large for the body. She resolved to spend more time with that child. Perhaps, with the right supervision, she could change her.

Deciding to begin her crusade at that moment, Mama smiled her most dazzling smile in her younger daughter's direction, hoping to foster a change in the child's behavior.

But the girl only looked at her mother's face, a face that she hardly knew, and thought it was just an older version of Heloise and Pauline.

"Mama," Charlotte remarked, "the story that my sisters have been telling me is so interesting and sad. The Cooper house, where we helped deliver the baby who died, seems to be the very house where this boy and his parents, a Frenchman and an Indian woman lived. It is the woman's grave that we must have seen next to the baby's."

"You delivered a baby, Mama?" inquired Heloise.

"Yes, we did. Charlotte and I helped the woman, but the baby . . . ," she paused, choosing her words carefully while all four girls stared. She had to be very cautious with the story. It would be so much easier in French, but she had promised Eloi to speak English. And then there was the issue of the nine-year old listening. "Yes, the mother was just fine, but the baby was not strong enough to live."

Charlotte sat very still, the mending resting in her hands, as she stared forward, not wishing to make eye contact with anyone. The scene of the birth and death which had faded somewhat in the last few days suddenly rushed forward in her mind, and she swallowed hard to keep the tears from coming into her eyes.

Her reverie was broken as Heloise spoke, "You must give Pauline and me all the details at another time, Charlotte." She nodded knowingly in her nine-year old sister's direction already assuming a confederacy with this new sister.

Charlotte's voice was soft but firm, her large blue eyes wide and direct. "I don't think I can do that."

Heloise and Pauline looked at each other with unabashed surprise.

Amanda looked at this new sister with a sudden admiration. No one, not *Grandmere*, *Grandpere*, not even Uncle John, had spoken in that tone to either Heloise or Pauline before.

The Gallets, as many other residents of Woodsville, raised much of their own food. Their meals were filled with fruits from the seeds and trees they had planted: strawberries; grapes, for eating and homemade wines; cherries; peaches and the fall apples.

Other fruits grew wild on the prairie: blackberries, plums and crab apples. All were used for preserves for immediate and future use. During the summer the wonderful vegetables grew on the fertile soil: beans, corn, peas, potatoes, turnips. They also tended their own chickens and milked their cows. Wild game, especially the favored quail, often augmented their food. Johnnycake, made of corn meal, sugar and water, was present at most meals.

The general store, however, sold the staples settlers relied on and also the delicacies that could not be made at home. Salt, sugar and spices could be purchased from the large sacks in the store while beer, whiskey, molasses and vinegar were stored in barrels and flowed from the spigots. Tea, coffee and chocolate, the latter a favorite of the Mailliard girls, could also be found. Pies and homemade cakes, made by the store owner or other ladies, often were sold. Quinine, the remedy for many ills, was also a basic item on the shelf.

Though almost all clothing was made in the home, the general store was also the place to purchase the fabric for a family's apparel, and a woman's fancy could be arrested by the display of ribbons for decorating their homemade bonnets, dresses and petticoats.

On a typical, sunny September morning, the five Mailliard women, Amanda and her four daughters, walked to the general store run by Owen and Mary Willis. It was a short walk, yet the girls did not go without their bonnets, for, indeed, the strong sun could color one's skin decidedly, and Amanda had noted to her brother that her youngest daughter's skin was already spoiled by the strong sun.

It was a strange little parade: the mother, flanked by Heloise and Pauline, followed by a reluctant Charlotte, pulled away from listening to a conversation between Papa and Uncle John, who were speaking of immediate plans for the new Mailliard cabin. Papa was insisting there be a cookhouse behind the cabin while

Uncle John argued against it. Amedee had assumed a new prominence in this world and was constantly at his father's and uncle's sides. The boy seemed to fit so easily into this new setting and the world of men that it appeared he had been here from the start of his life. Charlotte truly envied her brother's position.

"That is men's talk, and you will come with us, Charlotte," said Mama in her no-use-in-arguing-with-me voice.

Behind Charlotte trailed the youngest sister, a conflicted Amanda, who would much rather have picked the ripe grapes, but who always looked forward to seeing Henry, the one person besides Uncle John, who did not speak to her as if she were a child.

As they entered the store, the various, welcoming smells wafted towards them. The store was small but orderly, surmised Charlotte, and she wound her way through the opened spaces, becoming familiar with the pleasant array of food and dry goods. She had brought the family sugar jar to be refilled. The bags rested on the floor while the barrels were set on benches to facilitate the drawing of various liquids.

Close by, she heard the high voices of Heloise and Pauline speaking rapidly, and then Heloise calling to her quite demandingly, "Charlotte, come here. We want you to meet someone."

Charlotte deliberately delayed responding to the request as she read intently the markings on the bag of sugar to see how far it had traveled, checking to see if it had come the same route as her own journey. She finally walked toward her sisters, making sure to tighten the lid on her now-filled jar.

As she turned the corner around one barrel, she walked straight into the chest of a very tall person. "Oh, excuse me, sir," she replied automatically. Stepping back and very embarrassed, she looked up into a pair of deep-set, young, dark eyes, high cheek bones, long, dark, wavy hair, and a most kind smile. Without question, it was the most astoundingly handsome face she had ever seen. It took all of her restraint to keep from gasping at this most pleasant countenance.

"Oh, there you are, Charlotte," gushed Heloise. "I see you have already met Henry, not in a formal sense of course. Well, that will never do. Henry Moreau, this is another younger sister, Charlotte. She has just arrived from Europe with our parents and two brothers. She wasn't even born here in America as we were. I guess it was France where she was born."

"Actually, I was born in Florence . . . Italy," replied a rattled Charlotte. She wasn't quite sure why she was feeling so insecure and tentative, but the pair of eyes that continued to focus on her had elicited a particularly unnerving feeling in the pit of her stomach. She also hoped her response did not imply that the young man did not know where Florence was. She was just being informative.

"I am very glad to meet you, Miss Charlotte," replied Henry. "Perhaps someday you will be able to tell me about Florence, Italy, and the journey you have taken. I have never been far from this very town."

The words were spoken in such a strong voice, a voice that, to Charlotte, tried to be cordial and light-hearted but was filled with sadness.

She grasped the sugar jar tightly, for she felt she must hold something to keep her hands from shaking. In as even a voice as she could rally, she replied, "It is very nice to meet you also, Henry. Perhaps we will speak sometime in the future."

Charlotte continued to look at his incredibly handsome face as her mother, who had been making her introductions to Mary Willis, came upon the scene that was playing out between Henry and her daughters. She looked at the face of the young man and immediately recognized him as the boy of mixed parentage.

"Oh, Mama, this is the Henry Moreau we told you about," said Pauline, anxious to be included in the affair.

With a slight nod, Amanda responded politely, although not entirely friendly, "Henry, yes, we have heard of you."

"How do you do, Missus Mailliard. It is a pleasure to meet you," said Henry formally.

In her mind Amanda was grateful that the young man had at least been given some manners by the Willises, but she could not overcome the obvious savage influence that his appearance decried.

Turning away from his face and towards her girls, she said, "Come along now, ladies. We have much yet to do this afternoon."

"Good-bye, Henry, we shall see you very soon," said a beaming Heloise.

"Yes, yes, very soon," echoed Pauline.

But as the two older sisters gathered their wares and followed closely behind their mother, Charlotte noticed that her younger sister was now talking in an animated fashion to a very attentive Henry. The nine-year old girl shook her head and tugged on Henry's sleeve while he, in a most solicitous manner, listened attentively to her words. He then laughed slightly and patted Amanda on her head, a gesture that the young girl clearly enjoyed.

Charlotte looked at the two and smiled also, for she could appreciate how they seemed to have some innocent confederacy at work. She felt like an eavesdropper, but could not turn her eyes. As Amanda started to walk towards Charlotte, Henry looked full in Charlotte's direction, nodded and smiled.

He was hardly a savage in any sense of the word, and in that moment, Charlotte knew she had found the face she would someday draw.

Autumn in Woodsville was a beehive of activity as the settlers prepared for the winter months ahead. If lucky, only two months, January, with its long nights, and February, would test the mettle of central Illinois residents. Yes, there could definitely be some below zero days in December, but they usually didn't last a long period.

September and October, however, required a concerted effort from all residents, both young and old. There was little time for leisure activities as each person contributed what he or she could to the oncoming onslaught of winter. From Gabriel and Therese Gallet, Amanda and John's parents, now in their 60s, to little Leon (no one seemed to ever say his full name), tasks were assigned to prepare for the challenge of survival. Food must be harvested and stored. Root cellars held dried fruits and vegetables and salted meats. Wood had to be cut and then hauled by oxen to a place near cabins. Blue stemmed grass, cut and hauled from nearby Lewiston and stacked on a brush sled, was brought to Woodsville for feed for the few cattle and horses, the most valuable of all new world possessions. Corn, harvested mostly in October and November, also was used to feed those animals plus ever more prominent sheep.

Due to the winter preparations, John had convinced his brother-in-law Eloi to abandon plans to begin building the Mailliard home although Eloi had purchased a large tract of land, slightly east and south of the main part of town, from the county seat in Quincy for the price of $1.25 an acre. The home would sit on a small hill, close to the Gallet home and not far from the creek named for John Gallet.

To Eloi, John was somewhat of an enigma. The brother-in-law had been educated to be the secretary to King Joseph's daughter, Princess Zenaide. But after Napoleon's demise, he had been the first of the family to travel alone to America. Settling first in Ohio, he then traveled on the Wabash River through Indiana. Like so many of his fellow adventurers, he was called by the lure of the western frontier, Illinois, and was part of the swell that increased Illinois' population from 157,000 in 1830 to 476,000 by 1840. He had been married for a short time, but his wife Louisa, who was expecting their first child, had died during an outbreak of diphtheria in 1837. Urging his parents and his sister's family to follow in his footsteps, he seemed to want to fill his life with his remaining family.

"But where will we all sleep during this long winter you have warned us of?" questioned Eloi. "There are so many of us Mailliards. You have graciously shared your home with us for the past two months."

"In this world, my dear Eloi, the Gallet cabin is a mansion. Though, of course, you are used to the palaces of kings, here we have, if not spaces, the blessing of family. Mama and Papa will keep their room, you and Amanda with Leon will take the storage room where I have slept, the girls will sleep in the attic as they have done before Charlotte came, and Amedee and I will sleep in the main room. Believe me when I say that in winter we will all be thankful for our many bodies together. You have no idea how I envy you your family, and now you will let me share in it, won't you?" asked John.

Yes, this is the blessing, six healthy children, that I have, thought Eloi. How could he possibly refuse anything to this man who had none of his own. "Of course, John, you are most kind and generous."

It was decided, then. The eleven members of the Gallet and Mailliard families would winter together. The remaining valuables of the Mailliard family were finally unpacked. The Raphael painting now adorned an inside wall in Eloi and Amanda's room as distant as possible from the smoke of the cabin interior. How strange a home for this rare work that had once hung on the walls of the palaces of kings. But here, the poignancy of the face of Jesus, eyes raised toward heaven, still penetrated the observer. Though not large in size, perhaps only fourteen by eleven inches, "Ecce Homo," "Behold the Man," based on the words of Pontius Pilate, conveyed the suffering already borne by Christ, now adorned with the crown of thorns, while compelling the viewer to think of the ignominious death ahead. The work of art was a stark contrast to the general tone of happiness that permeated the home.

In addition to the painting, the opals and rubies that Amanda had sewn into her hems were secreted in cabinets. There were, however, some other stones that Eloi had not spoken of that now he felt he must address.

One early October evening, as Charlotte sat quietly reading from her *History of Maria Antionette* on the front porch, Eloi sat next to this daughter, whom he believed he understood so much more than any of his other children.

"And so, Charlotte, we are here for almost three months now, and we have not even talked once to each other," began Eloi.

"Yes, Papa, I have missed our time together. We have been so very busy preparing for this winter everyone speaks of. Then, in the evenings, we seem to be so tired and so, so filled with everyone. There is little opportunity for quiet."

"How is to have three sisters so suddenly?" questioned Eloi.

"I'm not really sure. Heloise and Pauline are so very close, and I really do not understand Amanda. I think I have forgotten what it is like to be nine," Charlotte replied.

"Oh, yes. And, of course, you will be the ripe old age of fourteen this December. Is this not so?" chided a smiling Eloi. But then, as he teased this daughter, he had a difficult time thinking of her at nine. Even as a small child, she seemed to have an "old soul," wise and tender beyond her years.

As he reflected on this child, he remembered the purpose of his talk with her and recalled their confrontation in Louisville. She saw the complete and evil picture at that time; he saw only the safety of his family. Her words then, "I could have traded her for my shoes," still cut through him each time he remembered the terrible experience.

"It is your shoes, Charlotte, that I feel we must talk about. I know you have not been wearing them since our arrival, and that the stones are safely stored. But I would like to explain why I kept them secret from you. The only reason I give, but I believe it to be very valid, is that for you to know their secret was to put you in great danger. I thought it would change your behavior and make you more likely to act, well, unnatural and protective. You have such a sensitive and often transparent heart, Charlotte, that I only sought to keep you from harm."

"Of course, Papa, you are right," agreed Charlotte. But in that moment, it was not the secret that troubled her, but rather that her father had not expressed any concern for the poor girl and her child who had been *bought*. The word still made her cringe.

Eloi sensed the tension in her reply. "I am one man, Charlotte, and most likely not a very brave one at that. I am not a hero. I am simply a father with a lovely, good wife, and the good fortune to be blest with six children."

Charlotte nodded in agreement, but the sadness she felt could not be kept inside. She raised her moist eyes to her father, and he enfolded her in his arms. "It is a gift and a curse, Charlotte, to feel as deeply as you do."

With that, Charlotte began to cry in earnest. She moved away from her father and toward the vineyard away from the house.

Eloi watched as her slim body moved along the vines and she began to pick aimlessly over the already stripped vines.

He reached for the book she had been reading, which she had forgotten, and opened it to marked page. There in the margin he saw the words she had written lightly: "To be one's own companion, thus have I been."

Were those the words of his own Charlotte, or the empathy she had felt for another fourteen-year-old girl?

1842

Had it truly been five months since the activity of life had been restricted to the confines of the Gallet house? Charlotte could not believe that such a long period of time could pass so quickly. Yes, she always felt she was bumping into one family member or another in the Gallet home, but it did not seem as horribly uncomfortable as she thought it would be.

She enjoyed listening to the French conversation of her grandparents. Though Uncle John and Mama, still struggling with her own English at times, reminded their parents that they should try at least to speak with the girls in English, they merely shrugged their shoulders and continued their chattering comfortably in their native tongue.

During this time Mama and *Grandmere* showed the girls how to spin, twist and dye the wool for stockings, and then each female would contribute what knitting she could to the final product. Each finished piece seemed to depict the personality of the creator. Mama's were, of course, done with great care and quite perfect. *Grandmere* could not only produce hers with great speed, despite what she said were the growing pains in her hands, but she could do so while critiquing the work of her granddaughters. Heloise and Pauline's finished products diminished in direct relation to the intensity of their talk, which was quite prolific. Charlotte worked diligently at her task, but with mixed results. Though she wished heartily to be as proficient as her mother and grandmother, her fingers lacked their talents. She much preferred to be drawing some of the landscape she had encountered during this past year. And always when she thought of drawing, she envisioned that one face that had so impressed her.

Thinking of that face, Charlotte turned to her sister Amanda, who openly struggled with her task, at times throwing her efforts in exasperation onto the floor. Charlotte wondered if she also thought of that face which they had not seen during this winter's passage. Somehow, she always felt too hesitant to ask Amanda about the young man, who came into her own mind so often.

While the women were busy sewing and repairing the family's clothes, *Grandpere*, Eloi and John smoked their pipes and planned for the spring: the building of the home, the planting of the crops, the tools and supplies that they would need for all their activities. They repaired the smaller implements as best they could—sharpening and oiling the knives and saws that would be used in the coming growing season. They cleaned and oiled the barrels of their rifles, stored above the front door. John spent much time teaching his brother-in-law how to use the weapon for it was not something either had needed in their previous lives. But, on the frontier, there was no question. A man must have and be prepared to use a rifle at all times. The sound of her father practicing never ceased to jar Charlotte while Amedee repeatedly asked when he could also learn how to shoot.

"Next summer. When you will be thirteen, when I will be able to teach you, that will be time enough," replied his father.

Amedee had been changing in many ways, Charlotte noticed, becoming a good companion in many ways for the young Leon, now a very busy two-year-old, who spoke in a mixture of English and French, delighting the close-knit group with his childish gibberish. He was entertained easily by the very energy of Amedee, who seemed to please the baby. Amedee, in turn, realized his newfound job and gladly accepted the role, particularly because he was then not besieged by Papa to spend time reading.

Yes, it was difficult to find space and light for reading, especially during the short days of winter, but Charlotte eagerly read the few new pamphlets and even copies of the *Prairie Farmer* that her father had been able to secure from the general store.

Often with the arrival of infrequent mail, a letter from Uncle Louis would be greeted with delight by the entire family. The older Mailliard brother would relay the latest news of King Joseph and his unfortunate failing health following his stroke and Louis's own challenges facing the stewardship of Point Breeze. How fortunate, their uncle added, that he had Antoine's continued support. The letters would also tell of the latest news of Philadelphia and the ever-growing anti-slavery sentiment that was gripping the east.

Louis would also include other reading material for the Gallet and Mailliard families: *Poor Richard's Almanack*, portions of which were often read aloud by Charlotte, (to herself she recalled her discussions with George Simmons) and Franklin's virtues, as they were called. She also remembered the essay that Antoine had given her, *Remarks Concerning the Savages.* How different were her thoughts now compared to when she had first heard the title of the piece.

One delivery was especially appreciated by many of the family, a copy of William Shakespeare's *Romeo and Juliet.* This provided entertainment for many evenings, and the parts were vigorously read by almost all. Of course, Heloise and Pauline insisted on reading Juliet, although Charlotte did remind them, in her wide-eyed most charitable way, that they were both too old for the part, and that she was, without question, the closest to Juliet's age, just fourteen. Why did fourteen always seem to be such a pivotal age for so many?

Amedee actually loved reading, with much adlibbing, of course, the part of Mercutio, not Romeo, whom he considered a whiner, and played with vigor his favorite character's death scene as surely as any Shakespearean actor ever had, with moaning, groaning and rolling on the floor, much to the delight of Leon, who joined him in the rolling. Amedee especially enjoyed Mercutio's lament, "Ask for me tomorrow and you shall find me a grave man," a line which he had learned to perfection, and therefore inserted whenever *he,* Amedee, felt appropriate.

They also did not forget their religious roots. With the absence of a priest in their community, the family recited the prayers of the Catholic Mass not only on Sundays, but on many days. They read their Bible, a French Bible, the one significant tie to their native language the family did not relinquish. The treasured book had traveled to all their residences—Paris, Bordentown, Florence—and showed the wear of time. In the front section the births of the Gallets and Mailliards were duly recorded. It was not only a recording of the stories of the Old and New Testament, but a veritable history of one strain of America's settlers.

Despite the cold surrounding the home, the security of the family provided the warmth of life. Unknowingly, Charlotte's loneliness diminished as the days began to lengthen and winter's hold on life waned.

With the arrival of March, the threshold of survival had been crossed, and life began anew. Charlotte noticed the change in the fields as the greening of the earth began in earnest, birds chirped more freely, and the small animals suddenly began appearing in greater abundance. Even the howling of wolves and coyotes at night did not sound quite as forlorn and ominous as they did in the long winter nights.

For the Mailliard family, there was one task that was at the forefront, the building of their own cabin. As soon as possible, Eloi, with John's help, arranged to have logs brought from nearby Ellisville for the start of the cabin. A daunting task for just the two, Eloi secured the help of other strong helpers, among these, to Heloise, Pauline and Amanda's open delight, was young Henry Moreau.

If anything during the passage of winter, the seventeen-year-old had become more handsome. Charlotte exerted every ounce of control to keep from visibly showing how much his mere arrival on the building site would cause her to tremble. When he would arrive each morning to begin work and nod in the sisters' direction, Charlotte deliberately breathed slowly and steadily.

Henry, along with Orlando Woods and Alexander McFarland, two young men of Woodsville, moved logs from the wagons into place while Eloi and John struggled to keep pace with them. The level site chosen for the structure would measure over twenty feet on any side. Logs were put on the ground first to see how to best fit the pieces together. The first logs laid were cut in half, and then subsequent ones were notched to bring ends more closely together. Gaps between logs would be filled with small slabs while mud was daubed inside and out to form as solid a wall as possible.

The two-story cabin, really one story with an attic, would be similar in style to the Gallet cabin: a large fireplace; floors of puncheons, (boards smoothed on one side) and doors hung with wooden hinges. The men worked from sunup until sundown, stopping to drink water from the well that would be shared by the families and for the meals that the women provided. Charlotte noticed that, often when the crew stopped for dinner, Heloise would make sure that the lunch she brought was given to Orlando while Pauline could be found sitting next to Alexander.

Charlotte tried to seem casual in bringing food to her Papa and Uncle, but somehow she always managed to bring food last to Henry, and they would spend their time together. There also was always a third person who ate with them, sister Amanda. She, of course, had been Henry's friend long before Charlotte had come to Woodsville. Charlotte actually welcomed her younger sister into this little circle, for it eased the tension that she, at least, seemed to feel. Amanda spoke so naturally and comfortably with Henry that Charlotte quite envied her little sister. Despite her discomfort, however, the lunch breaks always seemed quite short.

As the building began to reach completion, Charlotte was disappointed on several accounts: that she would no longer see Henry every day, and that she had not begun to try drawing his face. She resolved that this was a task she would definitely start each day, but, as if reading her mind, Mama seemed to fill Charlotte's days more than she did her older sisters. In fact, to Charlotte, it appeared that Mama would find reasons for Heloise and Pauline to remain in Orlando and Alexander's company without interruption, while she, Charlotte, was constantly being sidetracked from staying with Henry. Surely Mama would not be that devious, she reasoned.

When the days of spring lengthened and the fields dried, Eloi and John arranged to borrow a team of oxen to help seed the families' crops. The teams consisted of three to four of the sturdy animals slowly but steadily dragging the plows. How strange for these two men, who had been raised in the courts of French royalty, to be driving the yoked animals behind the plow, creating the furrows in the rich loam of the Illinois soil. One man would drive the team while the other guided the plow and supervised, keeping the depth of each furrow, about two and a half feet, even. Amedee, now a strapping thirteen, looked much more natural behind the reins of the plow when he proudly took his turn driving the team.

The women, with their bonnets fastened securely to protect them from the rigors of the sun and their hands protected by the gloves sewn during the winter, nurtured the grape vines and the strawberry beds. They fed the farm animals that brought the family fresh eggs and milk.

The kindness of spring gradually changed into the heat and humidity so intrinsic to the central Illinois climate. Often, the clear mornings would change into the strong storms of afternoon as the humidity of the rivers collected and then unleashed itself into the torrents of rain. Overall, however, it was a fruitful growing season as crops were not lost in overflowing streams or excessively long dry periods.

Charlotte's life fell into a comfortable pattern. Her relationship with her sisters had warmed considerably, and what she had at first thought of as silly and immature in their behavior now she regarded as warm and comforting. Had she changed that much, she wondered, or had they grown to accept her into their world? Even Amanda seemed to soften into more of a girl and had not worn her breeches, as she called them, since last year.

Whenever Charlotte thought of Amanda, however, she always thought of Henry. She now admitted to herself that she would like to be in Henry's presence without the ever-present Amanda. If Charlotte invented a reason to walk to the general store, Amanda would be sure to follow. If Charlotte met Henry in the store and engaged him in conversation, Amanda was surely there. If Charlotte informed Henry that she would be walking in the area of Gallet Creek, Amanda would take the very same walk.

On one day the group of three was walking along that very creek. Amanda led the way, as usual, and Charlotte followed with Henry behind the two sisters. As Charlotte paused atop a rock, she suddenly started to lose her balance. With swiftness and agility, Henry caught Charlotte easily and swept her away from her slippery perch to the shore. For just a few seconds, Charlotte's face was close to his. She saw the dark, long lashes that adorned the tanned skin of his face, the short dark hair that was gathering above his lips, the beads of sweat that had collected on his wide forehead, the strands of hair that fell into his eyes. She felt the warmth of his breath close to her own.

When he gently set her down on dry land, she felt both relieved and very disappointed.

"Are you alright, Miss Charlotte?" he inquired solicitously.

"Yes, yes. I am sorry to be so clumsy and cause you such trouble," replied Charlotte, desperately trying to keep her voice low and steady.

Henry grabbed her hands in his. She felt small and insignificant, powerless to move away.

Rocks scraping off to the right, quick footsteps running to where the two stand, Amanda sees her sister and Henry. The younger sister begins to question, "Where have you . . . ?" but then stops moving and speaking. As the older sister and Henry look in Amanda's direction, they see the younger sister's face, at once startled and betrayed.

Charlotte tried to speak to her sister Amanda as the summer settled and the bustle of fall set upon the Mailliard household, but each time she would begin to talk, the younger girl would turn her face and walk away, or merely speak to someone else. Even as they prepared to sleep and share the same bed at night, Amanda would not look at Charlotte's face.

If other family members noticed the strange behavior, nothing was said, for all were too engaged in more important activities than sisterly spats.

But if she had lost a sister, Charlotte had gained in other ways. She and Henry were able to meet more often as their lives seemed to cross more frequently. Since Heloise and Pauline were more and more in the company of Orlando and Alexander, Charlotte was able to volunteer for helping her mother in other ways: going to the general store, walking to neighbors' homes, all opportunities to meet Henry.

When Charlotte finally did share her plan to draw his face, Henry simply nodded and smiled. "Of course, if you wish," was his only response. He had no way of knowing what boundaries, both talent-wise and traditional, the girl was scaling in making this decision.

As he sat for her day after day, but in small snatches of time, she became more and more frustrated by her lack of ability. It had been so simple to replicate the beautiful flowers and trees that graced her drawings. She had thoroughly underestimated the challenge she undertook. As she had drawn her flowers with a general shape first, she attempted to capture the oval of his face when he would draw back the dark, wavy hair that would tumble into his eyes. She then noticed, for the first time, the two-inch scar that was just below his hairline on the right side of his forehead.

"How did you get that scar?" she questioned.

"Oh, it's nothing. I think I must have fallen, or something," Henry replied. He would not tell her the truth—that an older boy in his mother's tribe had sliced at his face when he was only five. Henry had beaten the boy in a contest of strength, and the boy had retaliated with the swipe at his eye. How could he tell this young woman, someone who had been born in the palaces of kings (he had heard the stories), someone who had been born in an exotic place called Florence, Italy, that half of his identity was something this town considered savage?

When Charlotte was satisfied with the empty shape she had drawn with her graphite, she then attempted the eyes. How insurmountable a task this was. She had never before noticed that a person's eyes are not exactly the same, nor that one side of a face mirrored the other. Day after day as she tried to refine her work, she was discouraged and near the point of abandoning her project. Yet as each new day would come, she resolved to redo her drawing.

A new appreciation awakened within her, as she studied the Raphael that now hung within the Mailliard home. How expressive and exquisite the eyes, what stories they told with their poignancy. If only she could begin to capture that same depth, truly the focal point of any drawing, she would achieve success.

Though the eyes were the focal point of her drawing, the other features were no less important: Henry's sharp, angular nose, his wide mouth, the high cheekbones that were unlike any facial structure she had seen before.

As the summer days shortened and the cool of fall mornings became ever more pervasive, the relationship between the two young people had turned to true friendship, not just one inspired by looks. Though Charlotte could not help but be stirred each time she saw his face, she had begun to share the stories of her past, telling Henry of the journey that had occurred just last year, but now seemed eons ago. She described to him the elegant homes she had lived in, the royalty she had seen, Pointe Breeze with cousin Antoine and Uncle Louis, the trip down the Ohio River, the stories connected to the places along the journey. She told him of the young woman in Boston, the horror of the slave market in Louisville.

To Henry, it was as if a new world was being revealed. With every story she told and the emotion that she conveyed, he wanted to sweep her into his arms and protect her from all the evils and dangers of the world.

"Henry, there is one thing I have never told you. I was in your home, the one the Coopers live in now. Mama and I helped Missus Cooper give birth to her child. I, I saw the place where your mother is buried. I wondered who that grave belonged to. And then I learned it was your mother. How sad for you! And then, your father . . ." Charlotte's voice trailed off, and she wondered if she had said too much.

"The truth is," Henry's voice faltered, "I cannot remember the details of their faces. So many times I close my eyes and try to force myself to see them, but all I can think of is how tall they were, some of the words they would say to me. I can recall my father's voice sometimes, but I cannot hear the voice of my mother."

"I needed to have your talent to draw, Charlotte," he continued quietly.

"But, you see, I don't have the talent! I try so hard and it looks nothing like you. You see," Charlotte almost shouted, shoving her rough drawing into his hand.

He held the drawing and smoothed the edge of one corner that she had inadvertently creased. He looked at the sketch with a sense of wonder. He had seen his face in the crude mirrors whose surfaces waved, creating distorted images, and recognized in this representation that it was his face.

"I cannot draw your eyes, Henry. I must keep working . . . but then maybe I will never be able to capture the beauty and story that I see in your face," Charlotte confessed.

The look in her eyes was so intent and distraught that Henry could not resist the need to pull her into his body. Holding the sketch with his left hand, he pressed it towards his body and drew her to him. The top of her head touched the bottom of his chin, and he gently and slowly touched his lips to her hair. She raised her face to him and he kissed her forehead, the ridge of her nose, and then very lightly her lips.

Charlotte felt his strength and the most disturbing, yet wonderful tingling in the very pit of her stomach.

Henry stepped away quickly. "I am so sorry, Charlotte. Please forgive me. I did not intend to do that." What if someone had seen them? How foolish and silly to jeopardize their friendship.

"Henry, please, there is nothing to forgive. I didn't really seem to be running away, did I? But I think I should return now though. I'm sure Mama will have some chore for me to do," said Charlotte.

"Yes, and I must get back to the store. We will both be missed."

He returned the drawing to her, and she carefully gathered the materials that she had brought. As they walked away from the creek, their hands touched, and they returned each other's smiles.

The Avenging Winter

One dreary morning early in November, as Charlotte awoke to face the chores of the day, she noted the large snowflakes that were staring to fall.

She called to her sister Amanda to come and see the beautiful snow beginning to lace the ground with its pristine whiteness. The younger girl had somewhat warmed towards Charlotte in the last few weeks, but there was an apparent listlessness about her. She seemed to have lost the spontaneity and fight in her demeanor that had been so characteristic. Charlotte was truly sorry to cause her this sadness, for she felt that she, Charlotte, was to blame. Nonetheless, she was not sorry in the least for her encounter with Henry, for even now, as she closed her eyes and recollected his kiss on her lips, that peculiar feeling in her stomach would begin. Her joy mixed with guilt, she vowed to be especially kind to Amanda and help in any way with the younger sister's assigned duties. She would even do her younger sister's mending, without Mama's knowledge of course.

"Come, Amanda, let's join Amedee outside before breakfast and see if we can make some snowballs," said Charlotte, feigning an enthusiasm she certainly didn't feel.

"No," replied a sullen Amanda automatically, burying her face in the covers of their bed.

"Please, Amanda, don't be angry. Besides, I know you can throw just as hard and fast as Amedee," cajoled Charlotte.

Her head popping up a bit, Amanda responded, "Do you really think so?" She did so want to like this sister who treated her with much more concern than Heloise and Pauline. But she had seen how Charlotte and Henry had looked at each other, and he was *her* friend first.

"Yes, yes, of course. Amedee always thinks he does everything better just because he is a boy. You don't want him to really believe that, do you?"

"Well, I guess not. Okay, then. But I just might want to throw a few snowballs at you too," challenged a revived Amanda.

"We'll see," promised Charlotte.

In the early morning air, the two sisters, now accompanied by their brothers, shouted and laughed in the fun that only a first snowfall can bring. Amedee, assisted by a very willing Leon, who idolized his big brother, ran and rolled in the soft white blanket that was already covering the bare earth.

Roused by the noise from outside, Heloise and Pauline came down from the attic to investigate. At first, the two thought they were much too sophisticated to join in the childish activities, but they abandoned that thinking as Heloise opened the door and was smacked in the face by a ball thrown by Amedee, who laughed heartily at his good fortune.

The war ensued, with sides often changing in the course of attacks. Leon laughed and ran and rolled down the hill towards the creek until a screaming Pauline noticed the three-year-old about to fall into the cold water. At the last minute, Amedee grabbed the soft hand of his brother and suddenly the reality of what had almost occurred surrounded the brother and his sisters. Abruptly, Amedee carried Leon, now screaming because he didn't want to go inside, and the subdued sisters followed. With a sudden realization, they sensed how quickly their fun could have turned into tragedy.

As if taking the cue from the Mailliard siblings, winter's innocent arrival with the first snowfall assumed an ominous tone, as the snow, which had been laced with water and perfect for packing became light and airy, belying the seriousness of its extended grip on Woodsville and, indeed, this entire area of Illinois.

The snow continued for days, with drifts nearly door-high as the strong Northern winds created artistic patterns of whiteness. As the winds and cold settled in on the plain, winter's grip tightened its hold on the lives of the settlers. Throughout November and December, residents told stories of the small community of people who had dared to ride out in the sudden onslaught and had been found frozen in the blizzard. Horses and riders had become quickly covered with ice if they tried to cross creeks. Needing to be warmed quickly by changing blankets, both would come to their stables looking as if they were strange pieces of art in some grotesque museum.

Charlotte's 15th birthday and Christmas passed still in winter's grip. The monotony of dark days was relieved only briefly as the Gallet and Mailliard families joined on Sundays and Christmas. Fortunately, the dried fruits and meats were still plentiful and the few animals were safe in the stable, but the cold was relentless, and few ventured out their own doors. Charlotte had not seen Henry for several weeks, yet, when she could escape the rest of the family, she reached under her bed for her bag and was comforted somewhat by the crude drawing of his face. She drew another sketch of his profile from memory, always listening carefully for one of her sisters, who might start climbing the ladder to their attic.

On the first day of the new year, 1843, a week of mild weather commenced, and the settlement came alive. Neighbors who had sequestered themselves in the deep cold gathered at the general store, and supplies were purchased. Charlotte saw Henry briefly as he helped Mrs. Tripp, her mouth pursed in decided unpleasantness because she had been helped by the "half-breed." Henry did not notice the woman's reaction nor that of her disagreeable son Carl, but only sought to quickly finish their transaction and assist Charlotte with her purchases.

When their eyes met across the store, both Charlotte and Henry smiled knowingly as if recalling their encounter of last fall. Anyone surely would have seen the obvious attraction, but the store was busy and each person was intent on his or her own special needs.

"Henry, would you please help Mrs. Tripp load these wares into her wagon? We have many customers to help today?" Mary Willis said kindly, nodding in Henry's direction as she spoke.

"Yes, ma'am," he replied with a smile.

What a wonderful young man he has become, thought Mary. So helpful and honest, so willing to please. And yes, he is truly handsome. How I wish he would just once call me 'ma,' but that bridge would never be crossed, she reckoned.

As he helped Mrs. Tripp and Carl with their heavy bundles, Henry could not help but hear the constant badgering tone with which the mother addressed her son. Henry reasoned that he was truly lucky to have such people as the Willises to live with. With no more thought to their conversation, he opened the door to reenter the store just as the Mailliard women were exiting.

"Oh, Henry, how good to see you today. Have you been surviving this cruel winter?" inquired a very solicitous Heloise.

"Why, yes, Miss Heloise. I hope you and Miss Pauline and, and Miss Charlotte have also been well," responded a slightly unnerved Henry.

Carl Tripp watched the encounter between Henry and the girls and could not help but notice the smiles that were turned in Henry's direction, smiles that he had never been able to elicit from any of the Mailliard girls, not even the clumsy, young one, Amanda.

When he climbed into the driver's seat and was ready to spur the horses forward, his mother lumbered up beside her son.

As if reading his mind, Mavis Tripp said, "Yes, those Mailliard girls. All too uppity for the likes of us, but it's obvious that they are not too good to speak to a half-breed. Come on, let's get a goin' here. We've wasted enough time."

Arriving home with their fresh supplies, Amanda and the girls were thoroughly revived by the respite from winter. They had purchased fresh ribbons to adorn their petticoats and new magazines for Eloi and John (yes, Charlotte could read them also).

"Charlotte, I do believe our little trip to the store has brought some color into your face," commented a knowing Heloise.

"Yes, it is wonderful to be able to see everyone again," replied Charlotte in as even a tone as she could muster. Was Heloise aware of the looks that had passed between Henry and herself? And if she was, what of it? Sooner or later, she wanted to let the entire world know how she felt about Henry. She vowed to sneak up to the attic before daylight escaped to continue her drawings, for this time she had paid meticulous attention to Henry's handsome profile.

Eloi burst through the door of the busy home and proudly displayed four quail that he and John had been able to flush out on a walk through the warmed fields. They would enjoy a feast tonight with John and *Grandmere* and *Grandpere*.

What a few degrees of warmth, sun and melting snow can do to change one's spirits. Surely the worst of winter was behind them.

Nature had other plans, however, for the week's mild temperatures had lulled the settlers into a false sense of safety as the cold enveloped the region more cruelly and tightly than it had in the early part of the winter.

Days turned to weeks, weeks turned to the month of March, and the frigid weather remained king. Windows on the tiny house were completely covered in ice as moisture from the cabin heat froze upon contact. As the strong winds assaulted the settlers, a perceptible cold breeze could be felt in the home and items hung on walls moved visibly. The four girls had been forced to abandon the freezing attic to sleep closer to the fireplace at night. The well had frozen also, forcing the family to bring large buckets of snow inside to melt for water.

The wolves and coyotes had become increasingly brazen in their hunt for food, and chickens were attacked during the day. One settler reported that he heard scratching at the door, surely a wolf. When one man left his cabin to bring in more firewood, another would carry a rifle, ready to shoot anything that might come near.

Amedee had learned to shoot the rifle and now, nearly fifteen, he proudly displayed his prowess in assisting Papa, a Papa he had passed in height two months ago.

Though he did not share his worry with others, Eloi was greatly concerned about the ever-diminishing store of wood, for, when it was gone, they surely would freeze.

Trips to the outhouse were unheard of, so Eloi set up a small screened-in area in his and Amanda's room, where a privy pot was placed. In the morning the refuse was thrown out of the cabin, away from the well side and the area where they gathered snow for drinking purposes.

It was incredible how truly cold one could feel despite wearing all available coats and blankets. One day Charlotte could not keep her teeth from chattering despite the fact that she had been sitting close to the fire. She thought of Henry and longed to know if he was well. She had heard Papa whispering to Mama about children dying and their bodies being wrapped in blankets with snow packed around them and then left inside the houses because they could not be buried.

Perhaps no one was suffering more, however, than Mama, who Charlotte noticed was unable to eat and was visibly becoming more wan and thin with each day.

"Mama, please, you must keep your strength up," said a concerned Heloise. "Pauline and Charlotte and I will try and fix you a special broth. We can cook some of the meat and flavor it with the salt."

"No, no, I could not bear to even look at or smell it. I will eat a bit of the dried fruit. That is all I can bear right now," said Mama.

Even as she finished her words, she ran towards the privy area and the girls heard her vomiting the little food from stomach. Moreover, she often would burst into tears and cuddle and rock, much to his dismay, a wiggling Leon, who desperately tried to be released from her grip.

Charlotte conferred with Heloise. "What do you think is wrong with her? Did she get some strange disease?"

"We'll just have to wait and see. I can't imagine what we would do without Mama." It was a look of deep concern that passed between the sisters.

As the month of March progressed, winter still did not release its hold, and ice and cold sustained their grasp on the region.

After returning from a hurried trip to the general store for additional quinine for Amanda, Eloi shared with John the story of one rider who had crossed the Mississippi on horseback on the frozen river. "It was as solid as the prairie itself, the man said," he reported.

Spring at Last

Though the change was much too gradual for the settlers, signs of spring finally began to show at the start of April. People opened their doors and began reusing the outhouses, water was drawn from the wells, and the community met at the general store to exchange winter horror stories.

Eloi, the girls, and Amedee with Leon were part of the crowd that gathered at the settlers' meeting place, the general store. Owen Willis told the assembly that Woodsville had been rejected by the government as the name of the community's new post office.

"We need to recognize Ira and Asa Woods, our founders, nonetheless, for our name. Do you think Woodstock would do?" asked John Gallet.

"Woodstock," repeated Eloi. "Yes. What do you say, Ira?"

"Well, that's mighty kind of you folks. I think that will work," replied Ira for both brothers.

"So be it, and the store here will serve as our post office," added Owen.

As Charlotte roamed the aisles and corners of the store, she kept watching for Henry to appear. When he finally did come into the main part of the store, their eyes met, and they both smiled. Charlotte restrained her first impulse to run towards Henry. Perhaps his feelings had changed. She didn't want to assume anything without his reassurance. Had she just imagined the romantic scene that had occurred so many months ago? Then she heard his voice nearby, speaking to Amedee and Leon, and she cautiously moved in their direction.

"Miss Charlotte, I hope you have been well this winter. Your brother was just telling me about your mother's illness, however. I hope it is not serious," said Henry.

He spoke each word with emphasis, for he did not want to deviate from the few words he had rehearsed in his mind so many times. He kept to his script for fear of shouting to the world that he wanted to take this young woman in his arms again and kiss her and hold her forever.

"Thank you for your concern, Henry. She does not have a fever, so we hope the malady will pass," replied Charlotte. She read his face, that face she knew so well, and moved as close as she could without actually touching him. She watched him smile and speak with Amedee and pat Leon on his small blonde head. In that moment she felt as if life were absolutely perfect.

An agitated voice raised to near-shouting attracted the attention not only of Charlotte and Henry, but all gathered within the store.

"No, you're wrong, John. We've got to take care of these beasts now. It's the best time, before they get more of our chickens, our cattle, our sheep, our horses. They're wakin' up with that hunger in their bellies. Who knows when they'll take one of our kids? They already got one man." It was the voice of Emil Horton, that now commanded the audience.

"They got one man? Who was it?" asked Asa.

"It was some poor soul from Wilmington. He probably froze to death first, if that is any comfort. But the varmints took down his horse a few miles later."

"But, Emil, Wilmington's a piece away from here, north and east," said John.

"Sure, but haven't you heard them out there close to your home? Do we want to wait before it's too late? All the settlements around here are thinking about organizing one good hunt and getting rid of them once and for all," continued Emil.

The men nodded and agreed that the howling, the kind of howling that chilled a man's soul, occurred every day.

Eloi nodded, too, as his daughters watched. Charlotte knew how loathe her father was to harm anyone or anything, yet he seemed to be drawn into other men's thinking.

John finally spoke for his brother-in-law and himself. "Eloi and I agree. We should act now then. Asa, Ira, can you gather your clan? Owen, you and Henry will hunt too, won't you?"

Charlotte watched the men's faces of the men as they changed from jovial camaraderie to sternness and determination.

No one knows why the wolf stayed after its main source of food, the bison, left the Illinois prairie. Perhaps it was because they could not resist the temptation of a quick meal, or maybe stubborn pack leaders had wanted to retain their established territory. Whatever the reason, when man entered the schematic of the new frontier, the sequence of the pyramid of life was forever changed, and war ensued between the settlers and the hated predator.

As the men of Woodstock organized their part of the hunt, John Gallet and Ira Woods became accepted leaders of the pack. Thirty men, the youngest Henry Moreau, who accompanied Owen Willis, would proceed from a circle about five miles north of Woodstock towards a designated area about ten miles mostly south and slightly west, where a wolf pole had been raised. Men from other areas would also move in an established pattern from other directions toward the rallying site. They would begin in the third week of March, before the wolves' appetites had been sated, forcing the species to leave their lairs, and, more importantly, before the newborn pups would have a chance to exist outside the dens.

The men displayed an interesting array of temperaments, from the reluctant hunters such as Eloi Mailliard, to an aggressive and menacing duo of Carl Tripp and his son, young Carl. For Henry Moreau, a fine shot groomed by his father both while in the native tribe and then later in the settler home, hunting was an experience filled with conflicting emotions. Though he enjoyed the hunt, he had been taught while with his mother's tribe that each animal contained a soul and must be respected and killed cleanly. If not, then it became the hunter's responsibility to follow the wounded animal and finish the kill. He remembered how he and his father had pursued a wounded deer from dawn until nearly nightfall to make sure it would not suffer and starve to death. He also had taught the boy to respect from afar the ferocity of a wounded animal, even a deer, which, when wounded, would kill as quickly as the wolf.

It was a chance pairing that brought the Tripps and Owen and Henry together to cover their assigned territory. Carl and his son were affronted by the fact that they were teamed with the "filthy Injun," as they muttered just loud enough to be heard by the few who stood close to them. Most men just shook their heads, for, while they were not overtly friendly to Henry, they realized that the Tripps were a sorry lot. Old Carl was a drunk. Even now as they gathered early in the day, the smell of whiskey was already strong on his breath. And the whiskey did not improve his mean disposition. There was a strong rumor that he beat his son and daughter when drunk. There were often bruise marks and black eyes on the teenagers, but most folks felt you shouldn't interfere in something that wasn't your business. Besides, who wouldn't need to drink or take out frustration if you lived with the likes of Mavis, a complaining, nagging woman who never had a good word to say about anyone?

Last year, the daughter had left the town and gone east, it was said. Young Carl stayed with his parents and openly expressed his dislike for everything, eventually taking his frustration out on animals. He started by pulling legs from birds and frogs, then catching and starving feral cats, and some even said stomping the back leg of his own dog until it was no longer of use. Carl truly hated everything: the animals, the mother who constantly belittled him, the father who beat him (even though young Carl could have defended himself against the old man) and the sister who seemed to have escaped their family. But mostly, the teenager hated himself. He looked forward to killing many wolves, and hopefully making them suffer. Now, as he was forced to hunt with Willis and the Injun, he felt even more insecure. A man lacking confidence is indeed a dangerous one.

The men hunted for several hours in groups of four, searching every possible hiding place for the beasts. Occasionally, a shot could be heard in the distance as any movement in the grass gave rise to an excuse for an itchy finger. There were no reports of actual wolf sightings until early afternoon when Jacob Hartney swore that he had seen one of the beasts loping away from the Cummings' barn. Word spread quickly through the groups as messengers rode on horseback, keeping the walkers informed of happenings.

Old Carl had become completely disinterested in the proceedings and decided to, as he said, "take a breather." Fortunately, he had packed a bottle for just such a time. He sat up against a tree and graciously offered to share his liquor with Owen.

"Well, I'll tell you, Owen. I've just about had it with this here situation. A man needs to revive himself, if you know what I mean."

"I just might pass on that for now, Carl." Owen reasoned that with Carl in his group, it was best to keep your senses very keen.

It was an odd pairing, now, as the two teenagers, Henry and Carl, scouted a rocky area where settlers had moved boulders into a slight rise on a hill. Henry had seen immediately the site for what it was, a perfect setting for a wolf den. He moved cautiously a few feet behind Carl and resisted the temptation to suggest that Carl make his movements more furtive, for he realized that Carl was a person who would not be persuaded by his "half-breed" suggestions.

Now, as Carl fell over some sticks, Henry heard him swear loudly and curse his rifle, which was jammed from the impact of the fall.

As Henry moved closer to Carl, a stealthy movement off to the left arrested Henry's eye. The wolf had emerged slowly, taking its position on a precipice about ten feet above and twenty feet forward from the area where Carl and Henry were positioned. It moved with assurance and grace, and its protective instincts were keen. Henry could now see the small faces of cubs, perhaps two or three, behind their parent.

The beast looked intently at Henry, its yellow eyes with coal black centers assessing the enemy. The end of its snout and the small area under its eyes were marked by white, but the fur was a mixture of grey and tan and black, nature's perfect survival mechanism.

Henry slowly raised his rifle, waiting for a reaction from both the wolf and Carl. He did not want to kill this beautiful beast, but, if he must, he would kill as cleanly as he could. Carl swore again and violently pounded the rifle's butt against a rock, setting off a shot wildly into the air. Instantly, the wolf barred its teeth and lunged toward the duo. Henry aimed for the area in the middle of its head above the yellow eyes. The shot echoed through the cold air as the body fell with a distinct thud.

"I had it clean in my sights," yelled Carl, "but you had to take the glory, didn't you, you thievin' Injun?"

The two shots brought Owen and the now half-drunk Carl running.

"Well, lookee here," said Tripp. "We got ourselves a big one. I'll just take those ears for my own and my son's prize."

Henry said nothing as the father and son congratulated each other on the kill. Owen was silent as the Tripps cut the ears of the beast, occasionally kicking its body to show their dominance.

Young Carl stared in Henry's direction, daring the half-breed to take credit for the kill. Henry said nothing as he watched the two delight in their abuse of the dead creature. It sickened him to think that the wolf should be so defiled, even in death.

"Hey, here's a bonus. Do you see them little faces up there? Quick, Carl, get ma sack from ma horse. Let's take them pups back to the camp and have us some live-roasted wolf," said the now revived older Carl.

"Sure enough, Pa," said young Carl, running back to his father's horse.

Owen looked at Henry and shook his head, but, in that moment, Henry reached a quick decision. Three reports broke the silence as he carefully shot each of the pups at close range.

"You stupid Injun," said the father, "why did you go and spoil our fun?"

Henry remained silent but continued to stare in young Carl's direction.

A nervous laugh escaped the young Tripp as he averted his eyes from Henry. In that moment Carl vowed to somehow, someway get even with this half-breed who had saved his life, for now he hated him more than ever.

Avon

No one was quite sure how Woodsville became Avon. When the government notified the young community residents that the name Woodstock had been assigned previously to a settlement in northern Illinois, the word Avon suddenly seemed to take hold of the central Illinois town.

Perhaps it was a comfort to some of the English settlers who made their way westward from New York to have the nominal reminder of their former town. Was it the rippling of the water in Gallet Creek that reminded them of that river in their former homeland of England? Or was it the reminder of the Celtic paradise Avalon, so similar in sound and tone to Avon, which soothed the new community? Whatever the reason, the name was decided for now and for all time. And as the name became official, the town continued to prosper and grow.

The Mailliard family added its own growing factor to the town when Zenaide Mailliard was born to Eloi and Amanda in the early fall of 1843. Much to the chagrin of Heloise and Pauline, the baby was a distraction and embarrassment to the two older sisters.

"And here we were so worried about Mama, and she was just carrying the baby," complained Heloise to Pauline when the children were told that a new sibling was soon to grace their abode.

Eloi, hoping for a boy, of course, was grateful that the child seemed healthy.

Amedee and young Amanda could not be bothered with the new baby, but Charlotte, who had seen how fragile her mother's health could be, worried that her Mama's strength would be tested. The worry turned to actuality as Amanda developed the post-partum complication of a milk leg and was not able to walk or nurse the baby for several weeks. Fortunately for the Mailliard family, another new mother, Rebecca Morris, offered to become the wet nurse for the little Zenaide.

Several times during the day the child was taken to the Morris household to be nursed. Often, Charlotte was enlisted for this errand although she did not really consider the assignment a chore. She loved holding the tiny little girl close to herself, her coos and sounds so sweet and engaging. Although she was told the baby would not smile because she was too young, Charlotte swore the little one knew her voice and smiled when she carried her.

Charlotte had managed to tell Henry of her new job, and she relished the times when he could arrange to walk with her as she made her way to the Morrises. She looked at Henry's strong face and imagined a child that mixed his features—his eyes, his chiseled face—with hers, their child. Although she was not quite sixteen and still too young for marriage, how exciting would it be to have this man as her husband. The thought crept in her mind suddenly, and, although she was quite shocked, she was also pleased and incredibly happy. She wondered if this thought ever crossed Henry's mind, but would dare not ask.

"What are you thinking about, Charlotte? You seem to be smiling to yourself."

"Oh, I was just wondering if, if I will ever be a mother, although I'm still too young for all that," replied Charlotte.

"I think you would be a wonderful mother. You seem to have bonded with little Zenaide so easily," replied Henry.

"Yes, she is so precious. It is hard to believe that something this tiny will become, with God's blessing, another remarkable person who brings joy and laughter to others, hopefully, to grow into an individual to love and be loved by others," said Charlotte.

"How typical of you, Charlotte, to say something so, so thoughtful." The strong voice was silent for a few moments, and then he spoke again. "What is even more remarkable, I think, is that someone like you seems happy spending time with me. Seeing you with this baby has made me realize how much I love you. Nothing will ever change that."

They both stopped walking and looked at each other. Charlotte felt her heart had actually stopped beating for a moment, and she placed her hand over her lips to make sure she would say nothing more.

As families and the town grew, a second general store was established. The Willises welcomed the arrival of another merchandiser as their small store was literally overflowing with the swelling population. As quickly and efficiently as they filled their shelves, more products were requested, and the demand quite exhausted all three of the Willis clan. Though not quite accepted as a Willis, the town generally realized that Henry was a blessing for Mary and Owen. Yes, the boy had "that look" about him, but he was strong, a hard worker, followed the Willises' directives and seemed to be a good boy. He also was respectful and did not flaunt the fact that he read and was good with numbers. Mary Willis had made sure that he continued to read and learn all facets of their business. As she watched him in the store, he seemed to be genuinely helpful to customers, answering questions but not offering an opinion unless asked.

When the Spenser general store was opened on the west side of Main Street, Henry was sent to assist with the arrangement of goods, explaining to the new merchants, Will and Iris Spenser, how the Willises had learned to display and keep merchandise fresh and attractive. Will was a good man, had some experience with a general store in Peoria, but openly solicited the Willises' expertise.

Though some in town felt a definitely loyalty to the Willises, others lauded the spirit of American competition and were delighted that their small town now rated two general stores, a sure sign of a growing economy.

Still others, though their number was small, openly expressed a thankfulness that they no longer had to deal with the half-breed. Though the year was 1843 and the last of the Indians had been forced to leave eleven years ago, often resentments live beyond a single generation.

Clearly no one was more vocal in her relief of no longer having to go to the Willises' store than Mavis Tripp. Her sentiments concerning Henry were openly expressed to anyone within earshot. As she shared her feelings with the Spensers on her first visit to the newly opened store, Iris, struggling to retain objectivity, countered with a defense of Henry, saying how helpful he had been to her and her husband.

"Well, if I was you, I sure wouldn't leave him within earshot of your cash box. Everyone knows any Injun can't resist the temptation of takin' what isn't his," said a convinced Mavis. "Do you know he even took credit for a wolf killin' that my boy, young Carl, and his father made last spring? Yes, sir, that's my boy Carl over there right now, standin' by your pickles. He may not know how to read too well like some people, but he sure can handle a gun. We don't hold to that readin' stuff. We're just honest, plain folks."

As Mavis finished her rant, she failed to notice that a large barrel was being carried into the Spenser store. The carrier hidden behind the barrel was Henry, who had come from the Willises to give an extra barrel to the Spensers. He had heard Mavis's assault, and now, as he placed the barrel on the floor, he saw young Carl watching him closely. Neither had spoken since the incident of the wolf hunt, but Carl had not forgotten the affront, at least in his own mind, which he had suffered.

"Mrs. Spenser, is this where you wanted the barrel?" questioned Henry.

"Oh, yes, Henry, that will do fine. Your folks are so kind to loan it to us. Thank you for bringing it here," replied Iris.

"Hmph," said a disgruntled Mavis. "Carl, where are you now? I think it's time for us to be leavin'. This store has become just a little too crowded for my tastes. Carl," she yelled, "we are leavin', this minute, boy."

Young Carl skulked over to where his mother stood, and despite her public reprimand, there was a definite smirk on his face as he looked directly into Henry's eyes.

"Are you sure that you had that exact amount, Iris?" questioned Will. As soon as he had asked the question, he knew what the answer would be, for his wife took great pride in meticulously handling all the inventory records, including the money that they used to operate the store and lists of personal I.O.U.s and farmers' products that they accepted as barter. Iris even listed the names of ladies who baked pies, what kind of pies they made best and the purchasers of products. Her system, she felt, was accurate and sound business.

"Of course I know exactly what I had, $25.92, and just the denominations of bills and coins because I recount every five days just to make sure we haven't been cheated and we haven't cheated anyone else. I counted the money and wrote it on my tally sheet, dated November 15, 1843: twelve, one-dollar and two, five-dollar bank notes from the bank in Peoria, three silver dollars, eight dimes and twelve coppers. I also had a few English shillings and a couple of the Spanish coins, but I think we may be stuck with those. Folks around her seem to be leaning away from the foreign currency. So, you see, Will, I know exactly what was in the box. It looks like I only have $7, one five, no silver dollars and six dimes, so somebody just helped himself to our, let's see, $13 and twenty cents. They left the coppers alone."

"It just got so busy in the store yesterday, you know, Will, what with the customers, some buyin', some just seein', and then Henry from the Willises deliverin' the barrel." As soon as she mentioned Henry's name, Iris's face clouded in disappointment, and she shook her head.

"Now, Iris, I know what you're thinkin', and we've decided to let the past be the past. What happened a long time ago in New York does not mean anything here. He's a nice young man. He's been with the Willises for a long time. We don't want to jump to any conclusions," said Will.

"I realize that, Will, but he was right there where the cash box was sittin' and things were very busy."

Though they tried to keep their conversation muted, the few customers who were roaming through the store overheard. If there is one thing that travels more quickly than fire, it is gossip, especially gossip that fulfills the expectations of small minds.

"Well, I for one won't believe it, not for one minute. I've known Henry for so many years. He has been so helpful to us. Papa, you know what a good worker he was on our house. He never once took anything that wasn't his. I think Charlotte would definitely support the idea that he is just a perfect gentleman, wouldn't you Charlotte?" questioned a very agitated Heloise.

Charlotte sat quietly for a few moments as she tried to gather her thoughts. She didn't want to appear less than logical even though every derisive comment that she had been hearing over the last few days had shocked her deeply. She could not believe how people in town simply assumed that Henry had stolen the money from the Spensers.

"It seems to me that people are just making assumptions because they really don't want to look for other reasons. Perhaps Mrs. Spenser simply mislaid the money, or, or there is someone just playing a practical joke. What if one of us were accused of something like this? Papa, what if some day, someone would come and say, 'We don't like you French people. We saw your son Amedee take money that wasn't his.' What would you do, Papa?" questioned Charlotte.

"I would know my son," replied Eloi.

"But, Papa," said Charlotte, becoming more resolute and agitated. "You also know Henry."

"Yes, and I believe he is a fine young man. But he is not my son. And part of the problem with Henry is that he is not the Willises' son, either."

One might think, as winter settled over the small town of Avon, that the rumor swirling over the community would abate, but that was not the case. Instead, on the sparse occasions when people gathered, it seemed to be the first topic of conversation.

Did you hear how that half-breed boy stole nearly $20 from the Spensers? Did you know that the whole story about his being half-French isn't true at all? He really is one hundred percent from the Kaskaskia tribe. Do you think that the Willises put him up to it, you know, with his basic nature and all, and they actually want to put the Spensers out of business?

With the coming of spring, the gossip still persisted. Henry could not walk anywhere in town without first the silence and then the inevitable whispering. He and Charlotte would be seen together talking clandestinely, and then the gossip started to follow her.

Were her parents blind? Didn't they see how that nice young girl was attracted to the Injun? What must they be thinking? Surely the Willises will come to their senses and send him packing. That's the only way our town will ever be safe again!

Mary and Owen sat in the store that had, in past Aprils, been alive with the bustle of seed buying and a revival in community spirits as the warm weather and burgeoning buds became the first signs of new life.

However, this April was dramatically different. The few customers who did frequent the store came either to sniff out more dirt for their gossip or because they could not find what they needed at the Spenser General Store. No women brought their pies to be sold. None of Mary's homemade pickles were for sale in the barrel, for they would not be purchased.

Refusing to believe the rumors, Eloi and John Gallet continued to visit the store, but they were among the very few. Amanda Mailliard would not allow her daughters to shop at either store unless it was an absolutely necessity. She wanted no part of the controversy for herself or them, yet she was not blind to the fact that all four of her older daughters defended Henry strongly. She chose to ignore the obvious blush on Charlotte's cheeks when his name was mentioned.

Henry had managed to pass notes to Charlotte through his friend, John Gallet, who had known him since he had come to the Willises store as a baby with his parents. For John, Henry was almost a surrogate son, and Gallet knew of the mutual attraction that existed between his niece, Charlotte, and the half-breed boy. He saw no reason to thwart their affection, and now, as a confederate, he was glad to act as their sometime messenger. John had come to the boy's defense more than once, and the older man's positive thinking led him to believe that soon the mischief, the rumors would subside.

Each time Henry read one of Charlotte's messages, he realized how desperately he longed to see her beautiful face, her sweet face with the deep blue eyes that seem to penetrate to his very core. But each day became more painful as he was keenly aware of the boycott of Mary and Owen's store, something he knew he was responsible for.

As April and May passed and June blossomed in central Illinois, Henry made the only decision he felt was feasible.

After a quiet supper Henry walked onto the porch of the Willis home, his mind resolute. Mary sat looking off to the west wistfully as her rocker swished back and forth in the still of the early evening.

"Ma'am, I want to tell you that tomorrow I will be leaving you and Mr. Willis," said Henry, swallowing hard, desperately trying to keep his voice even.

Mary looked up at the face that she knew so well and began shaking her head while tears welled in her eyes. "No, no, Henry, please don't say those words, please. This will all be over soon." Even as she spoke, she realized two things: she could not change his mind, nor could she change the minds of those whose prejudice had finally found an outlet.

Owen heard their voices and put down the ax he had been sharpening. He saw Mary's face and tears, the movement of her head, and knew immediately what Henry was telling her. "I know what you're thinking and that you feel leaving is your only choice, but we can move, start again someplace. You mean too much to us, son," he said.

"No," said Henry firmly. "I won't let you do that. This is my problem, my decision. You have given me nine years of your lives, taught me everything you know, treated me as your very son. I cannot allow you to give any more than that. I am a man now, nineteen. My father was much younger than that when he faced life alone. This is the right path for me now."

For a short time there was no sound except the movement of Mary's rocker. Then Owen went back into the store and returned with a small leather bag.

"Henry, with all my heart and, I know with every breath Mary will ever take, we wish you would not leave. But I can see that we are powerless to change your mind. You are a strong young man in every sense. This is something that I have kept for you since that day your father left you with us. It is $30, small bills and coins that he gave us for your food and such. It should be yours now. We never felt we had to use any of it because, well, because we thought of you as our own son, except, of course, that you're just about a head taller than I ever was, and your eyesight is a lot keener than either of ours is or was." Owen tried to smile as he put the bag in Henry's hand.

Henry's first reaction was to shake his head, but Owen persisted. "This money is yours, Henry. There are no two ways about it. Your help in the store was more than any room or food would have cost. And you will need money as you travel. Be careful, though, don't ever display the whole amount at any one time. Well, I guess you would know that." Owen turned his head, but he could not hide the tears that were gathering in his eyes.

"It seems that all I do is cause problems," whispered Henry.

Mary almost jumped out of her rocker as she said, "Now look here, young man, if you think you can start feeling sorry for yourself and make it out there in that wild world, you are badly mistaken. I just won't hear of it."

"Yes, ma'am, I expect you are right," replied Henry.

Mary put her arms around the boy she wished had been her son. She looked up to his face and gave him one last admonition. "Don't ever think you are second rate. I don't ever want to hear any nonsense like that."

"Thank you, thank you both so very much. I have one last request before I leave in the morning," said Henry softly.

"Anything, son, just let us know what we can do," prompted Owen.

"After I leave, please don't tell Charlotte Mailliard anything about me. I would like to write to you two, but I don't want her to, to still be connected to me in any way. I'm sure she will need to make her own life, without me," said Henry forcing the words from his mouth.

"Yes, I can see that," said Owen reluctantly.

"I do want to tell her I am leaving though, so I will be gone for a while now."

"Well," said Mary, "I'll set to making some dried meats and fruits for you to take on your, your trip. I just hope and pray, though, that you will come to your senses and we will see you again soon.

But, indeed, she never did see again the only child she had ever regarded as her own.

"No, no, you can't be serious," Charlotte almost screamed as Henry told her of his decision. She put her hands to her mouth to keep from breaking into sobs.

"It's the only right thing for me to do," Henry persisted. "You can't think that I want to leave you and the Willises, but there is no other choice. Their business is almost ruined, and worse, I have seen the looks that others give you when we are together. Soon this shame will come to rest not only on you but also on your entire family. I have to leave though my heart is aching even now as I think of never seeing your face every day."

"But you will come back, won't you? Surely you don't mean to be gone forever?" Charlotte pleaded. "It is dangerous to be by yourself. You will die out there! Please, please, don't say this is true. I will die if you are not here!"

Henry put his arms around the shaking Charlotte and tried to quiet her with a soothing "there, there," but her body shook with the deep gasps that she could not stop. When she raised her face to his, he kissed her long and hard on her mouth and only then did she stop shaking.

Her voice trembling, she stepped back from him and wiped her wet cheeks with the bottom of her sleeve. "Where will you go?" she questioned. She now tried to ask the pragmatic questions to soothe the overwhelming fear. "How will you live?"

He lowered his voice and tried to speak as evenly as possible. "I will head west and cross the Mississippi, going into Iowa. I have heard the Kaskaskia have set their camps there. Perhaps they will welcome me into their community. I know I certainly will look more like their people than the people here."

"But you have not lived in that world for so many years. Are you sure you can survive a home that is so temporary, not having family to rely on?"

"Charlotte, for you, family has been an integral part of your life. For me, it has been a random luxury. I have told you I cannot even remember my parents' faces, a thought which still troubles me. And, with the Willises, I had only to think of their faces to immediately realize how mine was not the same."

They sat down then, close together, she resting her head on his shoulder, and they talked of many things—the first day they saw each other, the walks where Amanda was still included, the first time he kissed her, the long winter when they could not see each other, the parts of Shakespeare's plays she had read to him as they sat beside Gallet Creek. Here, he confessed he had not listened to the words, but to the sound of her voice and the emotion with which she had read the parts. They almost laughed when they reminisced about his reading some of Mercutio's part from *Romeo and Juliet*, a task to which her brother Amedee was definitely better suited.

As the day waned, Charlotte rose from the dry summer ground and turned to look at the beginning of a spectacular summer sunset. Henry stood behind her, his arms around her small waist. He could feel the thinness of her body as he pressed close to her. She turned her face to him again, and they kissed gently.

Charlotte stepped back and touched her hand to her lips, as if to imprint in her mind forever their kiss.

"You will write me whenever you can, please, won't you?" she questioned.

Henry opened his mouth to speak, but suddenly their world was invaded by sister Amanda's shouting. "Mama and Papa are looking for you Charlotte. You must come home right now." There was a sound of triumph in her sister's voice, the kind of tone a sister uses when she knows her sibling is in trouble. And, of course, Amanda had never forgiven Charlotte for usurping her friendship with Henry.

Amanda looked straight into Henry's face with a feeling of superiority. "Hello, Henry. Mama and Papa will not be pleased with either of you, you know. They have been worried about Charlotte."

"I am sorry about that, Amanda. Will you please tell them for us how very sorry we are to have worried them?" said Henry.

"Maybe, I don't know. I suppose Charlotte could tell them that for herself," said a miffed Amanda.

"Good bye, then, Henry," said Charlotte softly.

"I mean it. You better come right now," insisted Amanda.

Amanda turned, followed by a reluctant Charlotte. She looked back in Henry's direction as he spoke softly, "I will love you always, Charlotte."

Tears once again wet her face as she stumbled on the path toward home. Only then did she realize that he had not answered when she had asked him if he would write.

Days became weeks, weeks quickly turned into months. Each day, Charlotte would visit the Willis store and ask Mary

Willis if she had heard from Henry. In the first weeks after he had left, Mary commiserated fully with Charlotte. Both would begin to feel the tears well in their eyes as they spoke his name.

When Mary received her first letter from Henry, she wanted to share its news with the distraught girl, but she remembered her promise to her "son," and she would honor it. She would not tell Charlotte that he had found a tribe with which he was living, how the Algonquin language began to become familiar again, how he had proven himself in contests of strength, but that he was derided by other braves for helping the women with some of their tasks. Mary wondered what form that derision would take. But these fears she would not share with Charlotte, despite the girl's desperate longing for news.

She had known Charlotte for three years now, and had always felt she was thoughtful and considerate to others in addition to having an obvious beauty, stately almost, highlighted by those deep, large and penetrating blue eyes. She seemed not to be aware of the response that those eyes drew from others.

But now, the girl's entire demeanor had changed. She seemed always close to tears, even when she didn't ask about Henry. There was a listlessness and complacency about her, as if she had lost her reason for living. Yes, Mary could relate to that, for her life also felt incredibly empty as each day she would turn and expect to see the boy's face or begin to ask him to help with a task.

"This moping has got to stop. Your sister will be married in a few days. You should be happy for her," suggested Mama as she watched her third daughter move as if in a daze through her supper preparations.

Zenaide, now almost one-year-old, crawled near Charlotte's feet. Amanda had noticed that the baby was the only creature that could even begin to draw a smile from this daughter who had lost her will to live since the boy had left. Well, there was that to be thankful for, anyway, especially since Amanda discovered that, in a few short months, she would bear another child. She did not want to deal with more complications from Charlotte.

"Char, Char," the little Zenaide pleaded and raised her arms to her older sister.

Without thinking, Charlotte bent down, picked the baby up and hugged her close. Again, the tears welled in her eyes. Each time she held the little one, she thought of the walks with Henry. She breathed deeply, hoping to clear her thoughts of him, at least for a little while.

"Char, Char," the baby repeated. "Side, peez," she said.

"Yes, take her outside while I finish preparing. She is so underfoot any," agreed Mama. "But don't forget her little sweater, and one for yourself. I don't know why it has suddenly become so cold. It is just September."

Indeed, the weather had turned unusually cold, for winter should still be at least two months away. It had become so chilly overnight that a small fire had felt comfortable in the fireplace, and, now, even as she enlisted her daughter Amanda in helping with the evening meal, Mama felt glad to have the fire still warming the cabin. Its flames licked at the new logs that the young daughter had placed carefully on the still glowing embers.

At first, Amanda worked side by side with her mother in silence as they husked the ears of corn that had recently been brought from their fields. She would not talk about anything, for she too was tired of seeing Charlotte moping through her days. Henry had been her friend first, before her older sister had snatched him away. As she husked the ears, thinking of Charlotte and Henry, her mood darkened. She tore at the silks as if each sound were a slap on Charlotte's face.

Suddenly, the anger burst, and she said out loud, "I hate her. She ruined everything."

"What? What is that? Who do you hate? Young ladies do not hate anyone. Who is it you are angry with?" inquired Mama.

When the daughter remained silent, Amanda again questioned, "Come, now. Let's hear what the problem is. Are you speaking of Heloise?"

"Heloise? No, of course not," replied the daughter. In her twelve-year-old mind, the sister who was about to be married barely existed at all.

"Then who are you so angry with?" insisted Mama.

Boldly, Amanda looked in her mother's face and said, "Don't you know anything? Didn't you see anything between Charlotte and Henry? At least she has his pictures to look at."

"What are you talking about? Pictures? What kind of pictures does she have?" asked the mother.

Although she had told Charlotte that she would not tell anyone about the pictures, Amanda knew she had now gone too far. In truth, she didn't even care about what she had somewhat promised to Charlotte. Now, as her mother questioned her, Amanda almost felt relieved.

"Charlotte drew three pictures of Henry. They are hidden under our bed. Every day she takes them out and touches them. She says she closes her eyes and pretends she is touching Henry's face," the younger sister admitted.

"Bring them to me," demanded the mother. It was a voice she rarely used, but the daughter recognized a determination in the tone that she had not heard in a long time.

The daughter looked at her mother's face. Both had stopped preparing the meal and now the order was repeated. "I said bring the pictures to me."

The girl climbed the ladder to her and her older sister's room. She reached under the mattress of the side where Charlotte slept and pulled out, carefully, the three pictures of the most handsome face in the whole world, the face of a friend that had been *hers* before she had come.

Amanda saw her mother sitting angrily at their table as she carefully handed her the pictures.

Mama looked at the drawings carefully. Without question, the face was Henry's. At first she was struck by the remarkable likeness. How many hours had Charlotte been with him to capture so well his profile, that wistful, deep look in his eyes, eyes that could almost make you shudder? These drawings were wrong, wrong for so many reasons. Young ladies should not be engaged in drawing faces. Young ladies were to draw pastoral scenes or flowers. Though she herself had been trained in this area, she did not have the talent to ever recreate anything faithfully. But here, this face, without doubt, was the face of one she did not hate or even dislike, but a face that could only cause trouble.

Rising from her chair as she supported her back, Amanda Mailliard then gathered the three drawings and made the only decision she felt she could make. Laboring, she walked toward the fireplace and placed the pictures carefully into the flames.

The young man's beautiful face shriveled as the heat first browned the edges of the three pieces of paper and then consumed completely the hours of work, the labor of love that her daughter had created.

"No, no!" shouted the younger daughter. "Mama, what have you done? Why have you done this? Why are you so cruel?"

It was true, also, that, while the younger sister had envied Charlotte, she also had loved looking at the face on the pages that she too admired. She looked at the fireplace and tried uselessly to retrieve the pictures, but they had been eaten before she was even aware of her mother's intention.

"What will you tell Charlotte?" demanded the younger sister.

"What will I tell my daughter?" echoed Mama. "I will tell her that I love her and will always love her, and that I made the only decision that a caring mother could make."

At Heloise and Orlando's wedding celebration, Charlotte sat resolutely in a corner of her home. She refused to speak, she refused to dance, she would not look at either of her parents. She stared at the faces of Heloise, glowing in her bridal dress, and her new brother-in-law, but saw neither of them.

Across the room her brother Amedee danced with Mary Smith while her sullen younger sister Amanda, dressed awkwardly in one of Pauline's discarded dresses, would not raise her eyes to look in her sister's direction.

Little Zenaide came to Charlotte's side and pulled at her dress, "Dance, dance, Char, Char." Her sweet little face looked up, her soft little hand tugged at Charlotte's dress, yet the baby could not move her older sister. Instead, Charlotte took the child and swept her up into her lap. The baby wiggled from her grasp, saying, "No, no, Char, dance."

Charlotte simply shook her head, no. It is difficult to dance when one's body is not alive.

In the Tripp house, a small unkempt cabin not far from the main part of town, young Carl looked dispassionately at the pool of blood that was coming from the left side of his mother's body. She had fallen backwards when he shot her in the face. He had meant to shoot her in the mouth, but forgotten to adjust his mark since he seemed to pull to the right frequently when he fired his rifle. The shot had hit her left cheek and jaw and had blown away most of the left side of her face.

Hearing the shot's report, his father had come into the house, and young Carl, waiting for him to shut the door, aimed straight for his heart, correcting his tendency and hitting his goal.

The funny thing was, as young Carl reflected, he wasn't even happy after the half-breed left town. His ma and paw still yelled at him, embarrassing him in front of others, demanding that he do the chores they were too lazy, or too drunk, to do themselves. He was a man now, twenty years old. He decided to make things right for himself.

Now, he had only one challenge left to face. He took some heavy twine and began to unravel some of the strands, just enough to make it flexible, but still strong enough to pull a trigger. He positioned the rifle on a sturdy chair and then fastened it securely so that it would not move when the trigger was pulled. He set another chair opposite the rifle, and then folded some dirty blankets from his bed and placed them on the chair, raising the level of the seat. He now looped the string around the trigger and tested the cord's strength. A shot rang out and the bullet hit the mirror across the room, shattering it into pieces that flew several feet, one large shard settling into his left arm. The blood started to trail down his arm, yet he felt no pain, nor the wetness of the liquid.

Carl laughed at the irony. He was not stupid. In fact, he looked at his invention and complimented himself aloud, "Yes sirree, Paw. You see now how smart I am."

When Carl pulled the trigger the second time, targeting his own chest, he was also successful. The force of the blow knocked his body backwards as he and the chair landed on his dead mother, whose right eye still stared blankly at the ceiling.

Reverend Thurlow Pershing took his mission of service to his congregation very seriously, even servicing those whose Christianity seemed a bit doubtful. Among his more recalcitrant flock were the three members of the Tripp family. He was never quite sure what he would find when he visited their cabin.

On this particular clear morning, he became increasingly apprehensive at the apparent lack of activity on the Tripp property. Moreover, as he neared the house, a strong stench filled the air. His first thought was that a family of raccoons had died under the cabin. As he drove his horse closer, he felt the need to take his handkerchief from his back pocket and cover his nose. His horse whinnied and snorted and had to be prodded to move forward.

Dismounting from his ride, he approached the door cautiously and knocked. When no response came, he called to the family. "Carl, Mavis, it's Thurlow Pershing. I've come to pay a visit."

Silence. Then he turned the handle of the door and tentatively pulled it towards himself. He called once more, "Carl, Mavis, it's . . . ." There was no need to call anymore, for he then saw the three bodies on the floor, covered with maggots and flies. He had seen some death before, but, even to his relatively inexperienced eye, he assessed quickly what had occurred.

When Thurlow came back into town, he found John Gallet and Ira Woods as quickly as he possibly could and told them of the ghastly scene he had come upon at the Tripp house. The three agreed that there was only one course of action to take. They would burn the household with the bodies inside and never relay the information to others of the town. News of the family tragedy would be, of course, a terrible blot on the history of their Christian community, and would only give rise to speculative rumors.

In the early morning of September 10, 1844, the clandestine trio rode quietly toward the Tripp home and poured kerosene around the perimeter of the cabin. They did not venture inside, nor try to retrieve any of the house's contents. They knew that the fire would have to be strong enough to consume not only the furniture but also the bodies that lay inside.

As they lit their fires, the blaze quickly engulfed the structure. The flames rose into the skies as the men stood in solidarity over their decision. As if by God's intervention, when the house and its contents were consumed, the skies opened and rain extinguished the flames as quickly as they had started.

Despite the heavy downpour, the trio did not move from their vantage point on a small hill away from the house. When the rain subsided, they moved back toward the area of the home and checked what was left. The only remains were some larger bones, a few springs from beds and pieces from earthenware pots.

Gone forever was the furniture that had been clumsily made by the older Tripp, the dirty clothes that hung on the back of the door, the small sacks of meal and flour that Mavis had used in her cooking, the broken mirror that had cut young Carl's arm in the final few minutes of his life. Also consumed by the flames was the $13 (he had spent the twenty cents) that young Carl had hidden under his bed. It was as if all the misery and anger and sadness that lived here was consumed and washed away.

The Avon community gathered in the small cemetery just south of town to pay its respects to the deceased family. Yes, the Tripps were difficult people, but the town would take care of its own and remember this unhappy trio with respect.

As Reverend Pershing spoke his words, he reminded others "to judge not, lest ye be judged also." His words were somber and carefully chosen. Many times, he could speak from his heart without preparation, but on this day he knew he must be careful with his remarks and not give rise to any speculation.

John Gallet and Ira Woods nodded their approval of Thurlow's words. The assembly collectively forgave the family for their foibles and prayed sincerely that God would forgive them their sins, as well as vowing to overcome their own shortcomings.

The Mailliard family stood in silence as the words were spoken, each trying to forget some difficult incident with the Tripp family, each of them thanking God for the Mailliard family that they were a part of.

Death, the great equalizer comes to all, quickly and unexpectedly to some, only after a lingering illness to others. How ironic, Eloi thought, that, in the last week, they had learned also of the death of their beloved benefactor, King Joseph, in

Genoa, Italy, as he lay comforted by his wife, Queen Julie, and Eloi's own brother, Louis Mailliard. Birth and death, Eloi reflected, come slipping into life side by side—the other royal death across the sea, the arrival of his new daughter Mary, cradled in his wife's arms, and the three tragic deaths of the Tripp family that now they commemorated.

Others of the little community, including Mary and Owen Willis, tried to forget the contention that followed the Tripps whenever their paths crossed. And now, as Mary stood in the quiet cemetery, she again felt that chill which arose from her fear for Henry. What trial would he endure today; what challenge must he be facing just to survive?

Across from the Willises, Iris and Will Spenser nodded their greetings. The two couples had come to respect their counterparts, even though Mary felt Iris had not done enough to quell the rumors surrounding Henry. Iris thought of the few times that she had seen the Tripps, a thoroughly disagreeable lot, she realized, yet there was something truly unsettling about the boy's manner. She felt a pang in her heart for the boy, however. She remembered how his mother had spoken to him so cruelly in the store the first time she had seen him, as he stood next to the pickle jar. *As he stood next to the pickle jar*, she almost said out loud. The pickle jar, where she had set down the cash box on the morning when the money had disappeared.

Iris gasped audibly and Will turned questioningly in her direction. Had she been wrong in her assumption that Henry was the culprit? In retrospect, thinking of the boy that the Willises trusted and the Tripp boy, whose life was so difficult, she wondered if young Carl had been the thief? She looked at the faces of the Willises and the young Mailliard girl, whose name had been linked to Henry. How could she possibly tell them now what she suddenly had remembered?

Iris sighed, closed her eyes and begged God that she had not been wrong. In the end, she decided she would not speak ill of the dead and defame young Carl, who could no longer defend himself.

Part 4

Newcomer

"Charlotte, you'll never guess who has come to town," said Amanda excitedly to her still sulking daughter.

Without waiting for a response, Amanda answered her own question. "It is that very nice young man who gave you that beautiful little wooden box when we parted company. Do you remember his name? It is George Simmons. He has come right here to Avon, taken residence in one of the homes on Main Street, and, I am told, he intends to set up his trade as a carpenter *and* begin to organize pupils for a school. Isn't that wonderful? Now I just wonder why he has chosen to come to Avon, do you suppose," questioned Amanda slyly as if she and Charlotte shared a little secret.

The sullen daughter continued to stare at her mother. Except for the pragmatic functioning of daily life, Charlotte truly had not spoken to Mama since her drawings of Henry had been burned. Returning from a walk with little Zenaide on that day, Charlotte had not been able since to tolerate her mother's face. While she forgave her sister Amanda for revealing the secret of the sketches, Charlotte could not bring herself to believe that her own mother had been so unthinkably cruel. Charlotte remembered how she had screamed when she saw the ashes in the fireplace, how she swore then that she would never speak to her mother again. To think she had even commiserated with her mother when the new baby Mary was born. Yes, her mother had her husband, her children, another girl, not the desired boy both her parents had wished for. Perhaps, Charlotte thought, that was God's way of punishing Mama for her cruelty.

"So, what have you to say of this news, Charlotte? Is it not just too coincidental that this young man has come here to our town?" persisted Amanda.

Charlotte continued to stare deeply into her mother's eyes. "What do I have to say? I have nothing to say to you, *Mother.*"

She emphasized the English word "mother," rather than calling her Mama as all the children did. Charlotte wanted her mother to feel the anger that she felt not only towards every member of her family, but also for everyone in this town who had driven her love away.

"You will speak to me, Charlotte," demanded Amanda. "What I did, I did out of love for you, and yes, love for our family. Think, Charlotte, what your life, and ours, would have been if you had, had become *attached* to the half-breed."

"You speak of love. How can you know of love, and now this complete emptiness, uselessness that I feel each day? I am not alive; I do not exist because I do not see Henry. And yes, you speak of his being a half-breed. Did you know him ever to be unkind or threatening or anything but helpful?" said Charlotte, her voice rising.

"I am sorry, Charlotte, but he was part savage and nothing could change that," retorted the mother.

"Savage, savage," Charlotte laughed. "What does savage mean to you mother? This town was savage in the way it treated Henry. Now I understand how correct Franklin was in his essay. Of course, reading that essay was something you could never be bothered with. I also know another savage, one Annette Savage whom I met at Point Breeze, who was the mistress of and bore a daughter for your precious King Joseph. That is a savage I knew. What of that?" questioned Charlotte with a look of satisfaction.

"King Joseph is a man. He was a man without his ill wife for many years. A man has, has needs."

"And what does a woman have, Mother? This woman," said Charlotte pounding her heart, "has nothing. I have lost the only love I will ever have."

"Think, Charlotte, of what life would be like with your precious Henry. You would be forced from one town to the next. Suspicion would always be at your door. And your children and your family would be part of that suspicion. Can you picture yourself living in some dirty home on a dusty prairie forced to move with your *tribe*, forced from your own family? Is that a life you would want?" continued Amanda.

"Why, then, is life different for a man?" questioned the daughter. "What is life for a woman?"

"It is our lot, Charlotte, to be dependent on men. As daughters, we obey our fathers. As wives, we look to our husbands for survival. I have been exceedingly lucky to marry a man who I love, and a man approved by my family, one of my own kind," emphasized Amanda.

"I will never love anyone else," replied a defiant Charlotte.

"You are still young, seventeen. Your heart will heal. And even if it doesn't heal completely, don't be foolish enough to spend your life alone and never even try to love someone else. Do you understand what I am saying? A woman alone is a woman who is pitied and must look to her married sisters for generosity."

Charlotte continued to stare blankly at her mother, but in a way she knew what Mama said was true. A woman could not survive by herself. The only women who could be independent were rich widows. Despite all the Bonapartes' continuing generosity, she herself would never be wealthy.

"Will you at least promise me this, Charlotte? That if the Simmons boy does come to call, you will speak to him?" begged Amanda.

Charlotte remained silent for a few seconds more, but in the end she said, "Yes, mother. I will speak to him."

In the three years since Charlotte had seen George Simmons, his appearance had changed greatly. There were more character lines etched in his face, a short beard now covered the lower portion of his face, and a full brown mustache hid any remnants of youth that managed to emerge on occasions when they had spoken before. Certainly, the three years had made the young man of twenty-one seem, if possible, more serious than before. Time and experiences have a way of doing that.

Charlotte wondered how she herself had changed in the past three years. The challenge of daily life, the caring for the two younger sisters (and Mama telling the family that she was expecting another child!), the loss of her beloved Henry—all of these surely had changed her appearance.

Yet, when George called at their home in early November, 1844, he told Charlotte how happy he was to see her again, how life in Avon had agreed with her, how he had often thought of her during the past three years. On the lips of a Frenchman, the words could have revealed a budding, if not already passionate, love. But George spoke the words as only an Englishman could, with stoicism and evenness.

Despite his formality, he seemed genuinely interested in speaking again with Amedee, now sixteen, Papa's right hand man. Amedee shook George's hand vigorously, the two a study in contrasts: the young American Frenchman, easy and confident in his relationships with others; the young American Englishman, cautious and purposeful in his actions.

Yet despite his cautiousness, George seemed to be well regarded by all members of the Mailliard family. Eloi respected the young man's independence and discipline, the drive that had propelled him to not only survive but to learn a useful craft. Pauline thought of him as suitable for her sister, both of them too serious for her own tastes, however. Amanda, of course, was charming and incredibly solicitous, for she saw, without a doubt, a future son-in-law. Little Leon, now four, liked this newcomer who taught him carefully how to use a dull knife for small carvings.

Charlotte noticed how easily Zenaide took to George also. So articulate for only a year old, the little one said, "Hello, Mr. Simmons."

George smiled easily, replying, "Hello, clever one."

Sister Amanda, fourteen, assessed the face also. She would hold her final decision for a later date, but she did like his seriousness, the thoughtful and attentive way he listened to others. Though his face was not as handsome as Henry's, his reserved, cautious way reminded her of another friend who had left only a few months ago.

The young sister also realized that, though he seemed genuinely interested in everyone, the looks that he gave to Charlotte were more intense. Amanda slouched back in her chair as she reflected on herself, taller than any of her sisters, her large hands and feet certainly more suited to the tasks of men than the niceties that her mother insisted she learn. Why was it her lot in life to be placed in this woman's body and not be a boy? There were boys in town she would have liked to call her beau, yet that was not to be. Even now as she watched George's face intent on

Charlotte, she envied her sister and the easy grace that seemed so much a part of her.

"What have you been reading lately, Charlotte? I do remember the fine discussions we had when your family was traveling on the Ohio," George asked, his earnest face staring intently into hers.

"The truth is," she replied a bit abashed, "I've been so, so distracted lately that I'm afraid I neglected my reading."

Amanda, sensing that one of the younger children might interject something about Henry, quickly filled the gap in conversation. "Oh, come now, Charlotte, we all know you always have your face in some book or another. In fact, Mr. Simmons, our entire family has spent many evenings reading parts of your countryman's plays. We have had some lively readings of Shakespeare's *Romeo and Juliet.* Perhaps Amedee would grace us with Mercutio's death scene at some evening in the future."

Amedee shrugged his shoulders matter-of-factly as if to agree.

George replied, "Yes, well, I would be delighted to watch such a family event."

Shakespeare's *Romeo and Juliet*, well, yes he supposed he could sit through that, if Charlotte were part of the presentation. Shakespeare, however, was much too emotional and superficial for his tastes. He much preferred the American philosophers Emerson and Thoreau, although he also enjoyed the wit of Franklin.

Eloi listened to the conversation and studied this young man, who kept making inroads into the Mailliard family circle. He watched his face, studied the workman's hands and realized, in the small world in which they lived, he could make a good match for his dear daughter. He admired his independence, his manners, his intelligence. He wondered, however, if this young man could abide the Mailliard family's religion, for it was quite likely that his ancestry would not be willing to accommodate Catholicism.

"Tell me, Mr. Simmons, how is it I have not heard you speak of your family? Why, I am not even sure I know where they come. Were they from England, or were they born in one of the eastern states? Were they teachers as you intend to be?" inquired Eloi.

"I have two sisters, Sarah and Mary, who still live, I believe, in Hamilton, New York. My mother died shortly after I was born. My father has also been gone for many years," replied George, his words spoken as if recited from some family tombstone, cold and unemotional.

Eloi sensed the tenseness with which the reply was made and wished he had not asked the question. "We heard that you are beginning your work as a teacher. Do you have many students?" Eloi continued trying to change the topic into something the young man could address more amenably.

"I currently have seven students who will begin lessons with me in the early spring. I also hope to continue to hone my craft as a carpenter. I have a special project in mind to begin for myself along with simple requests from many kind people of the Avon community," replied George.

"How productive you are, Mr. Simmons," said Amanda. "What a wonderful husband you will make for some very lucky young woman, hopefully one from our own little town."

Charlotte stared in disbelief at her mother and the obvious insinuation she had made. Even George cleared his throat in embarrassment.

"Thank you very much for your kindness in letting me share this evening with you, Mr. and Mrs. Mailliard, Amedee, and all you Mailliard daughters. I don't want to impose myself on you anymore. I hope you will permit me the pleasure of seeing you very soon," said George as he moved towards the door.

"Charlotte, be sure to put some of that nice johnnycake you made this morning in Mr. Simmons saddlebag. We want him to start his day tomorrow with a good breakfast," said Amanda.

"Yes, Mama," replied a compliant Charlotte. Did her mother really think that anyone was fooled by her obvious plan to provide an opportunity for Charlotte to speak alone with George? Had he even ridden his horse this evening? He lived only a short distance away from the Mailliard home, the road where many French settlers lived and thus had taken on the name French Street.

Dutifully she wrapped the johnnycake in a clean cloth and walked outside with George. A beautiful November evening, calm and windless, had graced the town. A few frogs croaked their hoarse songs in nearby Gallet Creek, the laughter of young children could be heard in nearby homes, and the peace that only a small town knows seemed to infuse itself into the souls of its inhabitants.

For a few moments, Charlotte's heart seemed lighter than it had in months, but quickly her mind flashed to her Henry and the nagging question of his circumstances seized her. She wanted to be rid of this George Simmons and think only of her dear Henry.

She would not be rude, however, to this kind, young man. "I am very sorry, George, for my mother's obvious motive." Shoving the johnnycake into his hand she replied, "The truth is since I made the johnnycake, it isn't even good. I often seem to forget one ingredient or another. I am not a very good cook."

Graciously he replied, "Don't apologize for your mother or your cooking. *She* is simply a concerned mother. *You* don't have to be a good cook, for I know you have many other talents," he smiled cautiously, continuing to hold the hand that had given him the food.

"You will allow me to, to visit with your family again, I hope?" asked the earnest young man.

Feeling pangs of disloyalty, Charlotte replied as unemotionally as she could, "Yes, of course, Mr. Simmons. You may visit with my family whenever you wish. Good night, then."

"Good night, Miss Charlotte. Thank you for your kindness," said George tipping his hat and mounting his horse.

As he moved slowly onto the path towards Main Street, he thought of how strange Charlotte's voice had sounded as they parted. Yes, she had changed in three years. He couldn't quite tell what the change was, but he did know this: her voice, her intelligent eyes, the very way she moved her head to look towards his face, still made his heart quicken. In his own quiet way, he resolved to spend his life with this woman, despite the fact that her family was Catholic.

1847

"The Lord gave, and the Lord hath taken away." The visiting priest's voice still could be heard in Charlotte's head as she stood holding the hand of her new little sister Theresa, now almost two years old and, Charlotte thought, surely the last child her mother would have.

As the two sisters walked in the Avon cemetery and stood before the tombstone of Leon, little Napoleon, Charlotte closed her eyes and swore she could hear his sweet little laugh immediately echoing somewhere in the distance. Was the sound coming from Gallet Creek, that same stream of water that had almost taken his life when he was three, the place where he had been found, his face down, only two months ago?

How strange it was thought Charlotte. Leon had loved the creek, had spent so many days on its edge and, despite Mama's warnings, walked precariously and defiantly along the slippery rocks that formed its bank. In the spring, when the snows melted and the creek was deep, he was careful to walk close to Amedee. On the day he was found the creek's depth had lessened, yet it still was deep enough to claim a child of six, who apparently had slipped and fallen, a deep gash etched into his beautiful smooth forehead. The creek had always called to the child, Charlotte felt, and on that particular day when Amedee had preferred to walk to the general store with Mary Smith, a pouting Leon had said he would toss rocks by himself.

Had the creek known that she had been abandoned by one brother and like a jealous paramour now claimed forever the younger one? How melancholy and whimsical thought Charlotte to think such things, but the quiet of the cemetery lent itself to such speculation.

The little one tugging on the skirt of her dress brought Charlotte back to reality.

"I'm hungry, Char. Want to eat," Theresa said.

"Yes, it's time to go, I suppose," Charlotte said reluctantly.

She did not look forward to going back to the house and abandoning the peacefulness that she found here. At home, a strained silence pervaded. Papa and Amedee did not speak unless to discuss the plowing of the fields. Papa's loss of his only other son seemed to etch age lines into his face. But it was the loss of hearing Amedee's voice that was most stark. It was obvious her brother was steeped in guilt, for no smile, no quip escaped his lips. Mama, too, went about her chores in an uncommon stillness, so distraught over Leon, despite the noise of the two toddlers, Theresa and Mary, age three.

Zenaide, now four, also realized that Leon was gone, gone forever. She feared the creek where the body had been found, but her whispered, direct question to Charlotte when the family had stood in the cemetery, "Is he in the ground here now?" could not be avoided.

"Yes," replied Charlotte. "He is asleep forever. He is with Jesus, with God, up in Heaven."

"Will he fly like an angel? Will he watch over us, so we don't fall in the creek also?"

"Perhaps," replied Charlotte. "There are so many things I don't know."

Zenaide's startled little face (as if her Charlotte didn't know the answers to these questions) brought a smile to the older sister.

Older sister, yes, that is what she had become, the older sister, the older sister who wasn't married. Last month Pauline had married her longtime beau, Alexander McFarland, and now Charlotte felt she had become the surrogate mother to the three young girls. Unfortunately, her relationship with Amanda, despite the fact that she was now fifteen, had not strengthened, and though the two should have been a comfort to each other, in Charlotte's mind, Amanda choose deliberately to isolate herself from the family.

Moreover, Charlotte could not deny that she was being courted by George Simmons. Over the past three years she had heard the talk in town of how they were a perfectly matched young couple, how wonderful that she had come to her senses and forgotten the half-breed to whom she had once been attracted.

Yes, Charlotte knew the gossip. She knew what had been whispered about her, and Henry, and now George. What the town didn't know was that she still continued to ask Mary Willis every week about Henry.

The older woman would smile and make her standard response. "No word, Charlotte. I am so sorry I have nothing to tell you." Mary lied each time; she had promised her "son" and would not violate that promise. In her own heart she worried about Henry, but was somewhat reassured when she heard from him nearly once a month as he made his way ever westward.

Deep in her own reverie and carrying the two-year-old that had fallen asleep in her arms, Charlotte walked laboriously toward her home. She nearly bumped into George as he intercepted her path.

"Dear, Charlotte," he said, "please let me carry the child. She is really quite heavy for you it seems."

"Oh, George, yes, thank you so much. I didn't see you coming this way. I guess I was thinking so deeply about, about something else."

"Yes, of course, the terrible loss of your brother, such a handsome child. I too heard the words at the grave. I have expressed my regrets to your father, but it is you I am concerned about, for I know how, how sensitive you are."

Charlotte stopped walking and stared into the kindly eyes of this young man, who stood silently, holding the sleeping child effortlessly in his arms.

In that instant, perhaps George saw a look that he had never seen before, for Charlotte's face turned to him and smiled as if he were the only person on earth. He had waited so long for that look, and now it seemed to exist just for him.

"My dear, dear Charlotte, my timing must seem insensitive, but you must know that my feelings for you are very strong. With your permission, would you allow me to speak to your father on my behalf, on the possibility that you would consent to be my wife?" George's usual steady voice sounded tremulous, and the child in his arms stirred restlessly.

If Charlotte had wanted an excuse to change the subject, surely the child's movement could have provided one. Was it the way the child nestled more comfortably in his strong arms? Was it the way he looked so longingly into her eyes? But in that moment, she smiled and replied softly, "Yes, George, you may speak to my father. I think any woman would consider herself very lucky to have you as a husband."

Eloi welcomed George into the living room and sensed the formality of the young man's speech and voice and surmised the conversation that would soon ensue.

"My dear, George, I can only say how delighted I (and Mrs. Mailliard, of course) are to learn that Charlotte has given her permission for you to ask for her hand in marriage. I have known from the first day I met you that in manner and temperament you two are well-suited. There is, however, a bit more to Charlotte's legacy, a dowry, if you will," said Eloi.

"I expect no dowry, no gift, Mr. Mailliard. Your daughter as my bride would be the most precious gift I have ever received," interjected George quickly.

"Yes, well, it is as I expected you would say, but the matter is a bit more involved than that. As you know, my brother and I, and my wife Amanda and her family were personal servants to the Bonapartes. I know as one who is of English descent that this may be a bit, well, distasteful to you," said Eloi.

George raised his hand in mild protest as Eloi continued.

"It was not Napoleon Bonaparte himself, however, that we were indebted to, but rather his brother Joseph, the one we called the gentle Bonaparte."

Yes, thought George, gentle compared to what? His tyrant brother? But George remained silent.

Eloi continued, "For Amanda and me, our greatest connection was with Joseph's daughter, Charlotte, and her husband. It is for her, of course, that our Charlotte was named. They were, in fact, her godparents, a duty that they took very seriously. We traveled with them as they moved from Florence, to Mortefontaine near Paris, and also on visits to Point Breeze, King Joseph's home in New Jersey. They saw to her education from the time she was five, providing tutors they might have provided for their own children, had they been blessed with any. When Charlotte showed not only the capacity but also the intensity of learning and questioning her tutors' ideas, the

Bonapartes were most impressed by her intelligence. On our Charlotte's tenth birthday, they gave her a large opal, which would have been in itself, a most generous gift. But what our dear daughter has never known is, that at the time of her marriage, she is to receive an additional sixteen precious stones, opals and rubies, stones that I hid in her shoes on our trip to America. She did find them, but she does not know they are to be hers. And now George, they will also become yours."

George sat silently for a few moments, digesting the ramifications. He had no idea what the actual monetary value of such gems would be, but he was quite sure it was much more than he had managed to earn in his entire life. Furthermore, he wanted nothing to do with gifts from the Bonapartes. But suddenly another realization superseded that thought.

"And your other children, Mr. Mailliard, what gifts have they received?" asked George.

"Well, yes, there you have it. Although we have named our dear little Zenaide for another of Queen Julie and King Joseph's daughters, our Charlotte is the only one so favored by the royal family."

"Mr. Mailliard, for my part I hold no claim to this gift. I accept no dowry. I cannot speak for Charlotte, for these gems are hers to dispose of."

"Your answer does not surprise me, George. Please stay while I find Charlotte. I think you should be with us when I share this news," said Eloi.

"And these were the stones I carried in the heels of my shoes, Papa?" questioned Charlotte.

Eloi nodded his answer.

"But what of gifts to you and Mama and Uncle Louis and Antoine?"

"We have been well taken care of. We have used some of their generosity to purchase our land and build our home, to begin this new life in Avon. Louis and Antoine, as you know, have been given the Bonaparte house in Philadelphia. They are now helping King Joseph's grandson, Joseph Lucien Bonaparte, in the sale of Point Breeze. Yes, I know how you feel about their gifts."

"Amedee and my sisters, have they also received gifts?"

Eloi, smiling, paused and looked at his daughter. "No, Charlotte, you are the only one the Princess Charlotte truly knew, the one with whom they were most connected."

Charlotte sat quietly for a few moments and then calmly replied, "Papa, you now have eight children and sixteen stones. Why God has taken your other two sons, I will never understand, but at this point it seems quite clear. Each of your living children should receive equal portions of the gifts. For my part, I can only hope that someday these gifts will be used for good, not for ornaments of those who already have great riches. "

Breaking the seriousness of her words, however, she smiled. "Even though I was the courier, I will not take any special commission."

Marriage

Father Joseph married the young couple in the bride's home early Tuesday evening on May 18, 1847. The priest traveled from town to town, and, as Tuesday fit his schedule, the wedding was arranged soon after the engagement was announced. As was usual with most weddings in Avon, a notice was posted in the town's two general stores, and anyone who was available could come to the ceremony to offer good wishes to the new couple. The May evening was clear and pleasant, and several townspeople stood outside the home and chatted respectably while the ceremony ensued.

They approved of the match, so suited to each other in temperament and education, despite the obvious differences in their family backgrounds. The French Mailliards were a close-knit family, supportive of each other and hard-working. Young Simmons was also a hard worker, respected by all with whom he came into contact, despite the fact that he had never spoken of his family. Well, he would have quite the family now, marrying into the Mailliard clan, respected not only for themselves but also for Amanda's brother, John Gallet.

It was good also to ease the sorrow of young Leon's death with the joy of this union, the second of the Mailliard daughters to marry this spring.

However, one couple's wishes were not quite so effusively positive, for as Owen and Mary Willis looked at the newlyweds, they could not help but wonder, "What if . . . ?"

Mrs. Edith Churchill, who ran the rooming house where George Simmons had lived for the past three years, quietly arranged not to have any additional borders the evening of the

Mailliard/Simmons wedding, and to take a short trip to visit her sister in Peoria.

It was to this home that George brought his new wife. He showed her the room where he had lived for three years, small but neat.

When he opened the door to another much larger room, he said quietly, "This is the wedding gift I have been building for the last three years, Charlotte. I hoped from that first day in Avon, no, I really think that from the first day when you waved to me on the boat, that I would spend my life with you."

Charlotte was completely surprised by George's admission and could not think of any response. When she stepped into the room, however, she sighed in admiration and simply shook her head. "It is beautiful, George, truly beautiful."

The three-piece, maple bedroom suite was perhaps the loveliest and most-detailed furniture she had seen since leaving Mortefontaine. The peak of the headboard rose nearly three feet above the bed. Charlotte moved her hands lovingly over the smooth carvings that graced the intricate pattern, the maple leaves that were carved directly below the peak. Though less elaborate, the board at the foot of the bed bore the same delicate design. She moved to the three-draw dresser that continued this pattern, a perfect mix of two influences—French and prairie—throughout its appearance.

Charlotte touched the handkerchief boxes at either end of the dresser top and then so naturally opened them to see how deep they were. They could hold so many treasures.

"I will put that beautiful little box you made for me with my initials right between these two," she said smiling.

She then looked into the mirror, not quite seeing her entire face and bent her knees.

"Oh, no, you see, you just need to push the top and tip the bottom forward a bit. The mirror is hinged on this frame so that it moves easily," explained George.

Charlotte smiled at their reflections. "I think I shall have to tip it a bit more to see all of you," she said somewhat teasingly, for George was clearly taller than she.

Suddenly as she reflected on his height, her mind traveled to another time when she stood near to someone else who was quite taller than she.

George sensed her tenseness and then pointed to the third piece of the set. "This will be the place where we set our basin and ewer. Do you see the dowels that extend to hold the towels?" and he pulled out the small bars that he had so carefully fitted into the piece.

Recovering from her reverie, Charlotte looked into the face, the face of her husband. He was so pleased with his gift that her own wandering thoughts made her feel ashamed.

"I can't imagine how many hours you have spent on this project, George," she said, now sitting on the edge of the bed.

"Well, you must know that I certainly had a great deal of help, especially from Orlando. We drew and revised the design several times before we started cutting."

George sat down next to Charlotte and confessed, "I wanted everything to be perfect for you, for someone who has seen so much that is grand, almost like a princess."

"Oh, George," she replied laughing, "I have never been anything close to a princess. The Bonaparte children certainly made me aware of that."

"You will always be my princess, Charlotte Simmons," he said, drawing his new wife into his arms and kissing her tenderly on her lips.

In that moment, she prayed that she would be the best wife that she could to George.

But when she closed her eyes, it was not George's face she saw in her mind.

Bridal Tour

It was the dream Amanda had waited for so long. Now, with her three older daughters married, she could concentrate on the care of the three younger girls with daughter Amanda's help, of course. Yes, the fifteen-year-old certainly was not as suited to watching the little ones as Charlotte was, but she would learn. Amanda would see to it that her daughter stop these foolish ideas of trying to act like a boy, riding alone, trying to work next to Eloi.

For now, however, she would not let herself dwell too much on Amanda. She had envisioned a bridal tour for all of her three married daughters, but with Heloise expecting a child she and Orlando could not be expected to travel. But Amanda's mind was actively planning the trip for her two other married daughters and their new husbands, preparing their traveling clothes, making sure Eloi was writing to his brother. What wonderful companions they would be for each other, Amanda concluded.

Eloi watched from afar and smiled. His wife's busy arranging for Charlotte, Pauline and their husbands seemed to fill the void that was so keen after the death of Leon. Just mentioning his son's name caused a renewed pang of sorrow, but life was too challenging and filled to mourn too long. He must keep focused on his affairs, his crops, the farm animals that kept his large family well-fed.

He agreed (how could one not!) with his adorable wife that the couples should certainly begin their new lives with travel as he and Amanda had been so fortunate to do. It was the father's duty to provide for his daughters, and, fortunately, crops had been good this year. How odd, he reflected, that in the past six years they had stayed in this small, American town, they, who had made frequent crossings with Princess Charlotte and her husband, had not traveled at all.

Now, his children, at least Charlotte and Pauline, would benefit from their Bonaparte connection once again, not in monetary gifts, per se, but through hospitality. For Eloi's brother Louis and nephew Antoine had invited the newlyweds to come to their home in Philadelphia, and had secured a most gracious invitation from King Joseph's grandson, Joseph Lucien Bonaparte, the opportunity to visit Point Breeze. Though Joseph Lucien was actively engaged in trying to sell the property, he felt some liveliness in the estate would be most welcome. The prince (all referred to him as one although he would not have that official title until his father died) told Antoine he would look forward to seeing Charlotte Mailliard, his compatriot in classes once again.

"Really, compatriot? That was his word? I thought of him simply as the spoiled boy, who along with his younger brother, used to poke at me with the tips of their epees," commented a surprised Charlotte. "Well, he has found someone better to tease, I'm sure."

"Evidently, he must really want to atone for that teasing, for all four of you travelers have been invited to be the Prince's guests at the Astor House in New York for two weeks. I'm sure you will all find that to be quite an exciting visit," concluded Eloi.

As the small bags containing their belongings were strapped to the coach, the two couples waved their good-byes to the assembled family—Pauline bubbling and radiant with the cheerful Alexander lifting her cautiously into her seat, Charlotte smiling and tentative as she gave her precious Zenaide one last hug and then allowing George to assist her into her seat. Eloi hugged his two sons-in-law while a subdued Amedee shook the hands of his new brothers.

Could a mother want for two more handsome young couples than her own dear, dear daughters and their two well-regarded husbands? How fortunate she was, how truly blessed thought Amanda. Yes, the girls would be gone for many months, but the experiences they would have would carry them throughout their lives. She remembered her own travel during her and Eloi's early years together as they followed King Joseph's precious daughter Charlotte and her cousin and husband Napoleon Louis. That all seemed so incredibly long ago, she mused. Now, she must think of the daughters and son here in Avon and hope that they, too, would find spouses so well-suited.

Her own Charlotte, obviously, had finally resolved her silly infatuation with the half-breed, and despite the fact that she often saw Charlotte speak with Mary Willis, Amanda felt that chapter was closed forever.

They traveled to Peoria and then followed the path of the Illinois River. At LaSalle they began to see glimpses of the canal whose construction had begun in 1836 and which would eventually join the river to the Great Lakes. As they followed the path northward to Chicago, the talk among the newlyweds turned often to the work that was being done on the waterway. What a wonderful boon it would be for the farmers of communities like Avon to bring their grain more easily to the east. But they had heard also of the loss of lives, the lives of the Irish and German immigrants, whose toil would complete the ninety-six mile canal.

"It is always the loss of the least-paid who pay the highest price," said George. "I have seen that too often."

"Aye," agreed Alexander. "My father often spoke of the same sacrifices in his native land."

"Come, come, now, you two, we are having such a pleasant time. Don't you serious men spoil our fun, right Charlotte?" inserted Pauline, who was slightly miffed at the ominous tone of the conversation. She waited anxiously for her sister to affirm her objection.

"I think as we travel, we will see things that will cause us to appreciate the lives we have and wonder why we, unlike others, have been so blessed," added Charlotte after a few moments of strained silence.

George reached for Charlotte's hand and once again realized how truly fortunate he was to have met this young woman on a summer day only six years ago.

When they arrived in Chicago in early July, the heat of the thriving city, nearing 20,000 inhabitants, only mildly stilled the anticipation that all four of the young people felt. Suddenly, however, as George and Alexander moved their bags from the coach towards the entrance of the rooming house, a downpour unleashed itself on the dusty streets. Thunder and lightning filled the skies, the horses snorted their complaints and travelers moved quickly to their destinations.

For two days the couples were confined indoors due to the severity of the storm. George ventured out only to purchase a copy of the newspaper that had begun its publication just this year. In the *Tribune* he read the local news, reporting on the progress of the new canal, and then the articles that supported the abolitionist views of many.

When Chicago finally began to move again, the dusty streets were replaced with mud roads that impeded the progress of a bustling community. Mud was so deep in the roads that it gushed onto the wood walkways adjacent to buildings. As the couples moved into the town and began to visit the shops, it became very apparent that their apparel would never quite be the same, for shoes were caked with mud and Charlotte and Pauline's dresses were soaked with mire, despite the careful lifting of their skirts. Often George and Alexander carried their wives over the worst of the muck.

As they passed one store that dealt with leather goods, Pauline suggested that she and her sister buy boots for their husbands. "They are so beautiful," she said, "and we would never see anything like that in Avon or even Peoria. And besides, they would be very practical since you will be doing all this walking in mud."

"They are much too expensive. I really don't need them," said George quickly.

"But, George, you gave me such a beautiful gift. I think Pauline's suggestion is a good one. One beautiful gift surely deserves another one," said Charlotte.

"They do look quite graaand," added Alexander, stressing the word as his father used to.

In the end the young men allowed their wives to purchase the boots, but George felt uncomfortable about the buy, for it was Mailliard family money, not his own, that had been used to buy them.

On the fifth day after their arrival in Chicago, the couples set on their trip through the Great Lakes that would take them to their destination of New York. The clement weather was indeed an asset to the overall trip that would take ten days on the steamship.

Whenever they went on the vessel, appreciative eyes turned in their direction as their youth and good looks became a magnet to all onlookers. In the dining room, comments were passed on the attractiveness of the young women—obviously sisters, although while one was taller and more strikingly beautiful, the other had a more soulful appearance. The young men were also handsome, each in his way, though the fiery red hair of the one named MacFarland seemed to suit his gregarious personality, while the other one, Simmons, was assuredly more conservative.

Yet, on the evening when they sat at Captain Sumner's table, Simmons was the one who was more verbal, sharing some of the experiences he had had while a carpenter on an Ohio River steamship.

"Really, Mr. Simmons, how interesting, and now here you are as a guest on our fine line. Surely you have made your fortune in the west?" questioned the captain.

"Actually, it is the good fortune of my wife and her sister's family to have been in service to one of the, the wealthy families in Europe," replied George.

"Yes, one could say that," chimed in Alexander. "I would certainly call the Bonaparte family one of the more wealthy and, well, interesting families in Europe."

"The Bonapartes! Oh my, interesting to say the least," responded the captain. "Will your travels take you to France, then?"

"Oh, no," answered Pauline, "not so far. We are going to Bordentown, where I was born, on the grounds of Point Breeze, where my uncle worked for King Joseph. We will stay there with my uncle and our cousin and hopefully see King Joseph's grandson, Prince Joseph Lucien."

"Is that where you were also born, Mrs. Simmons?" asked the captain as he looked directly into Charlotte's eyes.

"No, Captain Sumner," responded Charlotte. "I was born in Florence, Italy."

"Well, gentlemen," replied the captain, "it appears you two have certainly married into some very interesting history, and, if you don't mind my saying, two of the most refined and lovely young ladies I have met in many a day. What a pleasure for me to have shared this meal. But now, I must end my evening and return to my duties. My very best wishes to you in your travels."

George and Alexander rose and shook hands with the captain as he left for the evening. In that moment George felt a great uneasiness as he projected, for the first time since his marriage, the uncomfortable prospect of meeting with one that was addressed as "prince," in addition to actually being related to the infamous Napoleon Bonaparte.

For two days they traveled in much less grand style on the Erie Canal the three hundred fifty miles from Buffalo to Albany. Since its completion in 1825, the canal had already been enlarged in 1832. The project, derisively called Clinton's Ditch, had been a hotly contested topic in the New York governor's race, but, with DeWitt Clinton's victory and vision, the link that had been sought to join the Atlantic Ocean to the Great Lakes finally came to fruition.

For George, the trip was not his first on the canal, for he had traveled its path earlier in his life when he left his home area of Hamilton. Sharing this information with his new family, Charlotte commented that, perhaps, he would like to return to his roots and visit his own family, but George's short, negative response was most definitive. She had learned early in their relationship that whatever had happened to George before their meeting might never be revealed.

Switching to a sailing vessel, they traveled south on the Hudson River from Albany to New York, landing at the Battery, the stopping point for many vessels including those that brought daily the influx of European immigrants. Many of the newcomers shared the same native land, Germany, as the now famous John

Jacob Astor, whose fortune had been realized from fur and investment.

It was to Astor's former home that the travelers now made their way from the Battery up Broadway to the renamed residence, the Park Hotel. From their carriage, for as far as their eyes could see, block upon block of three and four-story buildings amazed the young couples. For Alexander, whose twenty some years had been in either Indiana or Illinois, the city of New York, nearly 350,000 people, the view was truly overwhelming. For Pauline, who "oohed" and "aahed" in near cadence with the clop of the horses on the street, there was a distinct request to "never, never" return to Avon. George mentally compared this city to those he had seen in his travels on the Ohio. Yes, he admitted to himself, the vastness was quite remarkable.

Charlotte peered from the coach intently, noticing not only the tall steeple of St. Paul's, but also the walkers on the busy streets, their many different styles of dress, the variety of vehicles, from elegant carriages to simple pushcarts, the occasionally single dog scouring for scraps along the street. Her eyes, though accustomed to the scenes of many large cities, Florence and Paris included, never ceased to look beyond the structures of buildings into the faces of those who crossed her path. Two young gentlemen on horseback in top hats, white pants and long coats suddenly caught her eye and doffed their hats, smiling at the beautiful young woman.

"Come, come, Charlotte," teased Pauline, "we must no longer flirt with gentlemen, for we are old, married ladies now."

Charlotte laughed and wished in so many ways that she could find lightness in life as easily as her older sister.

When they finally arrived at the hotel, the girls and Alexander moved quickly with anticipation towards the prospect of a pleasurable experience. George hung back with definite reticence, his discomfort at entering a place that was obviously for the affluent becoming more intense. He walked behind the threesome, the nervousness of his situation easily seen in the tightness of his jaw, had any of his fellow travelers stopped to notice.

He gazed upward at the building's six stories, the entrance guarded by Doric columns. Is it truly possible that this structure had once been the residence of one man? The disparity between those who have and those who have not was truly amazing and disturbing.

Approaching the desk of the hotel, Alexander spoke first. "Good afternoon, sir. I am Alexander McFarland, this is my brother-in-law, George Simmons, and, with pleasure, may I present our lovely wives, Pauline and Charlotte Mailliard. I believe we will be staying in this beautiful residence as guests of Prince Joseph Lucien Bonaparte.

Frederick Hague lifted his eyes from his register and astutely began to assess the appearance of the quartet. Yes, yes, he had been told in advance to expect the guests. He certainly had met and respected Louis Mailliard for his relationship with and service to the Bonaparte family. He had heard the young prince speak highly of the risk Mailliard had taken in transporting many of the royal family's treasures. Now, as he began to appraise these visitors, as he did all visitors who had come to this hotel for the last eleven years, he wondered just what challenges he and his staff would face.

He looked directly into the green eyes of the young McFarland and said evenly, "Yes, Mr. McFarland, we have been informed that you will be here as guests of the prince. My staff and I are here to serve you, of course." It was his stock response, but he could not help but feel a bit wary of these possible country ruffians and their wives, despite the Bonaparte connection, who might not respect this most esteemed establishment.

Realizing he must also make his introduction, George stepped forward. "Good afternoon, sir. I am George Simmons. My wife is Charlotte Mailliard Simmons." He struggled to maintain an even voice, despite feeling overwhelmed by the opulence of the surroundings.

Charlotte and Pauline remained a respectful distance from the desk while their husbands handled the arrangements for their rooms. Pauline's eyes surveyed the surroundings with obvious admiration while Charlotte tried to be as inconspicuous as possible. She realized that with each foray the four made on this adventure, George's tenseness seemed to increase.

As the young men signed the register, Hague now looked to the two young women who stood close to their husbands. Yes, quite attractive, their clothes were certainly not of the highest quality, though carefully made. Their bonnets shaded their faces, but not enough to prevent him from discerning that there was a definite liveliness to one, while the other seemed more reserved. However, when that one looked directly into his own eyes, he felt she had the power to probe his very thoughts.

She moved towards the desk and spoke softly, "Thank you, sir, for being so kind to us. We feel incredibly fortunate to be able to stay in your hotel," said Charlotte.

"My dear young lady, though I have worked for the Astor family for many years, I must say it is not my hotel. But while you are here, we hope we can make your stay very enjoyable," replied Hague. Ah, he thought, though some have the money to buy respect, there are others who simply evoke that response from others. This young woman certainly was one of those.

Realizing that the good fortune of this experience might never occur again, the quartet embarked on absorbing and seeing as much of New York as their energies could sustain. They visited the city's Gallery of the Fine Arts, founded only three years earlier. They toured the Custom House on Wall Street, where 3000 vessels yearly brought over $20,000,000 in duty into the coffers of the U.S. Treasury.

As they walked the streets, they shopped at cigar stores and clothing stores, at Genin, the Hatter. "Young gentlemen must really have a top hat," advised their new friend, Frederick Hague.

They purchased foods at the open markets, and George and Alexander sampled oysters from stands along the streets while Charlotte and Pauline emphatically shook their heads "no" at the epicurean delicacy.

At the Minerva Room on Broadway, they were amazed by the scale model of New York that accurately captured the thousands of metropolis's structures. The completed miniature, twenty by twenty-four feet, crowned with a Gothic canopy of fifteen feet, was one of the city's main attractions. William Cullen Bryant of the *Post* assured editors in other cities "that it was indeed an accurate representation." The model encompassed all structures below Thirty-Second Street and part of Brooklyn and Governor's Island.

There was, however, the one exhibit that the four travelers as many, many other visitors to the vast city could not avoid. That, of course, was none other than P. T. Barnum's American Museum, at the corner of Broadway and Ann streets. For a mere twenty-five cents, one could find information, entertainment, fantasy and even the grotesque. The five-story structure held exhibits for every taste, including menageries, aquaria, and taxidermy exhibits. In the Lecture Room, one could enjoy a Shakespearean play, or, in another area, view the photos of previous Barnum exhibits—Tom Thumb, known as the General, who was only two feet tall; the bearded lady; and Chang and Eng, the Siamese twins. All classes of humanity, from immigrants to tourists, middle-class and working class, gathered to be amazed, awed or repulsed by the experience. To accommodate all, the museum opened its doors for fifteen hours, six days a week.

On Sunday, Charlotte and Pauline, escorted by Alexander and George, of course, attended Mass on Barclay Street at St. Peter's Church, which had been built over a four year period, from 1836 to 1840. Although he was not Catholic, Alexander graciously agreed to accompany the women into the church, though he also confessed to a bit of curiosity about the Catholic service.

George would not enter the church, however. He had stated clearly to Charlotte that he would not interfere with her religion, but also that he would not participate in any way, the one exception, of course, their marriage when a priest had officiated.

Charlotte noted again the firmness in George's anti-Catholic stance. Yes, it was America, a commingling of ancestries and religions, yet she knew first-hand how prejudice reared its ugly head. Her mind thought of Henry once again, and the "what if" weighed in on her mind

No, no, she thought. I must not go there. It is disloyal to George.

Once the service was ended and the trio alighted from the church, Pauline, grabbing her husband's arm and smiling, questioned him about the experience. "So, my dear, have you survived this religious adventure?"

"Well, there certainly is a lot of getting up and down, I must say. But the message is basically the same—do good works, love your neighbor," he mused.

George, rejoining the group from his stroll, was silent.

Charlotte took his arm and smiled. "I hope we have not kept you waiting too long," she added.

"No, of course not. I have enjoyed touring this area, looking and studying the faces and hearing the accents. It has been most interesting," said George.

He did not inquire about the service and the topic of religion was ended, at least for now.

In the last days of their stay, the four ventured farther into New York's history, as they saw the Deaf and Dumb Asylum and the boarding house known as the Sailor's Home. Each of these charitable institutions was something of which the city was proud. Yet the visitors were also warned to be wary of the district known as Five Points, slums that had spread past Grand Street and were now creeping towards Tompkins Square.

George commented on the disparity of wealth and the misery of those that do not share in that promise of optimism. Charlotte agreed, saying that in every city she had ever seen, poverty was as much a staple as a vendor on a street corner.

"Yes," agreed George, "and that underbelly of the world feeds the discontent of any country."

"Oh, you two, come, let's be thankful for all we have, but not let seriousness spoil the last day. We need to be grateful, yes, but we can't do anything to change the world. We have one last thing to do before we leave. Remember, you promised, gentlemen, we would have our images captured by that nice Mr. Brady that lives in the Astor. You do remember his name, the artist that Mr. Hague told us about?" said Pauline.

Promises remembered, the two couples visited the studio of Mathew B. Brady, a skilled artist in the technical medium called daguerreotype. Here, portraitures of the famous and not so famous were captured on a camera obscura and then developed in mercury vapors. Although many were working in this new medium, Brady's studio, which opened in 1844, had achieved notoriety not only because he had captured the faces of the famous—presidents, business leaders, stars of the stage, writers and artists—but also because he replicated the common man and woman—seamstresses, carpenters, in fact anyone who wished to see his or her image reproduced.

As they walked into the building, the four were amazed at the plush surroundings, with velvet tapestry hangings, chandeliers and the faces of kings, queens and the commoners gracing the walls. They walked throughout the facility, looking at the variety of serious and stark faces that stared back at them.

Charlotte stopped at the visage of one Indian chief and could not help but think again of her first love. To her, the seemingly wild countenance of the figure was an alarming reminder of the life that Henry must now be enduring. Suddenly, her forgotten disgust for her parents, the town, anyone who had contributed to his leaving swelled within. She closed her eyes and forced herself to remember every detail of his face, and then she felt a keen loss of the pictures she had sketched, the loss her mother was responsible for.

As if reading her thoughts, Pauline touched her elbow and said, “It is over, Charlotte. George is a good man, despite his occasional reticence to show his emotions.”

Charlotte jumped at her sister’s touch and said quickly, “Some things are never over.”

“Don’t be a silly girl now, sister. It is your turn to have your and George’s portrait sitting. Be good.”

Charlotte retorted, “Aren’t I always?”

Pauline said nothing but led her sister away from the face of the Indian and towards her husband.

Mr. Brady often had to remind his subjects of the seriousness of life and for them to strike an appropriate pose (yes, those McFarlands had presented a bit of a challenge), but this second couple did not have to be reminded of the product he wished to effect. The young man, Simmons, a typical reserved Englishman, sat tall and unbent on the chair, with the young woman standing behind. Looking at the variety of his subjects, he had seen beauty and confidence, often pride and arrogance, and, occasionally, what seemed to him malevolence and despair. But here before him, though obviously young and wholesome, this twosome seemed to be, though not stern, weighted by a burden that rested in their eyes—yes indeed, the right visages for his work.

Alexander whistled as the open carriage traveling on the narrow road reached the place in the well-worn path where the buildings of Point Breeze became visible.

"And this is the place where your uncle was the caretaker?" he asked.

Pauline quickly replied, "Not the caretaker, really, but more of a steward overseeing the property. He often traveled with the king, or count, as he was called here in America. This is where I was born and where our parents lived for a time. I haven't been here for nine years. Somehow, it seemed much larger when I was a child."

George was silent but thought, larger? How could one person own, control, have so much? His right hand clasped more tightly on the side of the carriage.

"Our uncle is not here now, but has gone to Florence to help settle affairs there. But our cousin is here helping the prince to sell the estate. We will stay with him in the steward's residence. You can see it now, barely, the much smaller building to the side of the estate itself," added Charlotte, sensing the tenseness in George's demeanor.

As the horses' hooves became silent on the brick drive, and a young person of much their own age emerged from the building, both Pauline and Charlotte gathered their skirts and anxiously waited to be helped down.

"Dear cousins, how good to see you," shouted an excited Antoine as he ran to the carriage. "Come, come, it has been so many years, my laughing Pauline and my much serious Charlotte," he said as he hugged them tightly and kissed their cheeks.

"And the husbands, of course. Please, forgive me, Antoine Mailliard, the older cousin as you can see," he laughed and shook the hands of Alexander and George. "Mr. McFarland and Mr. Simmons, how wonderful to meet you, how lucky you are to marry such beautiful ladies, of course, my dear cousins. As you can see, they have all the beauty in the family."

"It is our pleasure to meet you, sir, and please call me Alexander. The generosity of your family and the Bonapartes has been quite remarkable, I must say."

"Yes, also, let me echo my brother-in-law's 'thank you,'" added George. "I can only say that I have been most overwhelmed by all our, our adventures. And please, do call me George. May I also address you as Antoine?"

"Oh, yes, by all means. The formalities are behind us, as we are simply family. We want you to be most comfortable and make this your home, but I have heard of the professions that you both are engaged in, gentlemen, and with your permission, I would like to use your skills on the estate. There is so much that has been neglected in the last few years due to our travel to Europe. Now, we would like to restore things to their original beauty, if possible, since the property will be sold. George, I have heard that you are quite the carpenter, and Alexander, quite the wagon maker. Both areas are in need of much attention. Perhaps you will oversee the work, and, by the time the prince arrives in two weeks, the estate will be closer to what it once was," said Antoine.

In the end, however, George and Alexander did not simply, oversee the work, but performed most of the necessary changes themselves. George saw to the repairing of the interior wood—floors and doors that had been damaged by misuse, drawers that had warped from their original shapes and needed to be sanded or modified. Alexander, not only repaired the estate's vehicles, four carriages and farm wagons, but repaired the barn where they were stored. After weeks of indulgence, both young men seemed revitalized by their physical labor and accomplishments.

The days passed with manual work done by all four, the men at their specialties, the women assisting in the repair of draperies and coverlets on the beds. In the evening, however, they were free to peruse the Count's extensive library. Charlotte and Pauline, of course, had seen its contents, but George and Alexander were awed by not only the number but the variety of authors that were collected. Yes, the Europeans were there, especially the French, but also found were contributions from the Russians, the novelist Nikolai Gogol and the poet Alexander Pushkin. Since neither of the young men had been exposed to foreign languages, they could only read the translations. Nonetheless, the variety of selections was astounding.

George could not overcome the thought, however, that all this had been gotten on the backs of others. Still, while he was at this place, he vowed to read what he could. And, the section of American writers was, indeed, no less lacking, than any other. For here were not only his favorites—Franklin, Emerson and his younger disciple Thoreau—but also the new novel by Cooper, *The Deerslayer*.

One early evening, George resolved to seclude himself in this wonderful library and become part of the world of Natty Bumpo and Chingachgook. So deeply was he engrossed in his reading that he did not hear the sound of the library door open. Suddenly, he jumped up, for standing before him was a young man of much his own age. George's book slipped to the floor.

"Oh, dear, I did not mean to startle you. I am most pleased to see you are enjoying some of my grandfather's selections. I assume you are one of the Mailliard girls' husbands. Let's see," said the stranger, grabbing his chin with his left hand and assessing George, "I would say, from your serious look, you would be the choice of the studious Charlotte. Permit me to introduce myself. I am Joseph Lucien Bonaparte."

George, moving forward, shook the extended hand of the young man. He had never before met anyone whom he should address as "prince."

"Yes, George Simmons, sir, er, prince, I should say," said George nervously as he nodded. Yes, definitely a Bonaparte in stature, not very tall, with dark curly locks falling nearly to his shoulders, and an assured air of confidence that comes from being raised with wealth.

"I hear you have been setting to rights much of my grandfather's home in need of repair, for which I am most grateful," said Joseph Lucien.

"It is such a small way to repay all your kindnesses, Prince, the experience of New York, the privilege to avail ourselves of this library," said George. He would be polite despite his personal feelings.

"The irony is, there is really no way, you see, for us to repay the service that the Mailliards gave to my family. There were, of course, the perilous journeys that Louis made, but did you know that he was also with my grandfather when he died in Florence three years ago? So, yes, there is really no way to repay him."

"So, please, while you here, enjoy this library. I assume you are a reader, as was, is, Charlotte. What was it that had your attention so intensely?" asked Joseph Lucien.

"Oh, my, yes," said George reaching down and retrieving the book. "It was Cooper's *The Deerslayer.* It seems to purvey that which is, well, American, I suppose. "

"True, true, but, George, I hope I may address you as such, have you read the French authors, philosophers, Diderot and Voltaire?" asked Joseph Lucien.

"No, you see, my French is nonexistent," admitted George. Perhaps it was the first time in his life that George realized a gap in his self-education.

"That will be no problem, of course, for I believe we have translations in German and English, at least of Voltaire's *Candide.* I am sorry to say I do not read the German. I'm not sure if there is an Italian version. That might be a bit much for Rome, for the Pope to abide, don't you think, George?" asked Joseph Lucien light-heartedly.

"But, are you not Catholic also?" asked George.

"Well, of course, in fact my younger brother is so interested in things of the church he is thinking of becoming a priest. But, we are French Catholics, you see. You do recall my dear uncle, shall we say, upstaging Pope Pius VII, by crowning himself the emperor? Did he really grab the crown from the pontiff's hands, or had they agreed on the procedure beforehand? Either way, it is a good story, and it shows that, yes, we are Catholic, but we are French first. Is it not the same for you, or your family, George? Are you not English before you are Anglican, possibly?" asked Joseph Lucien.

George restrained his emotions, but simply said, "I am English only in my ancestry, definitely not Anglican, Prince. I attest to no formal religion."

"Excellent then, you will truly enjoy *Candide,*" said Joseph Lucien lightly, not realizing how his comments had stung the religious nerve of one George Simmons.

"That is precisely my point with organized religion, if you all forgive my saying so. It is the hypocrisy of preaching the word of

Jesus Christ and then lusting for control, power or personal gain."

George paced nervously as he spoke more adamantly than Charlotte, who was sitting tensely in one of the library settees, had ever heard him speak before. Alexander studied George's face but said nothing while Pauline sighed almost loudly enough for everyone in the large room to hear. Antoine seemed to nod a slight affirmation.

The only one to speak was Joseph Lucien. "So, then, I assume, George, that you believe all who attend church are hypocritical?" He knew he was baiting George, but Joseph Lucien was not one to avoid a good argument.

"Of course not. I just believe that those who attend a church and accept unconditionally the teachings of that faith and its ministers are, well, simplistic. Surely you must agree that Rome is often interested in control and power, aligning itself with the strong, acting to preserve its survival," defended George.

"Yes, there is that. But there is also, I believe, a goodness in the teachings of Jesus Christ, and those teachings have been spread and nourished by the Catholic Church," continued Joseph Lucien.

"Oh, yes, and then there was also the 'goodness' of the Spanish Inquisition," laughed Antoine, hoping to lighten the rising tension in the discussion.

"Gone, all gone now for at least three hundred years, and besides that was the avidity of those Spaniards gone amok," said Joseph Lucien.

"Yes, and many so-called 'holy wars.' I have seen also how some have professed to believe in Jesus Christ, who read the Bible, who force others to do the same, and then mistreat those they supposedly love." George's voice grew more intense.

Then regaining his composure, he continued, "Surely, in this country, we have the prime example of this, in this continued practice of slavery, which is defended by those who claim to be staunch Christians."

George, looking in his wife's direction, saw her face suddenly effect a very melancholy look, and he nodded to her. "Charlotte and I have seen the awful spectacle of the selling of slaves in Louisville, while we were traveling on the Ohio."

Pauline, suddenly alert, stared at her sister. "Oh, Charlotte, how horrible. We have only heard the stories. How in the world did Papa allow you to be exposed to such cruelty?" she questioned.

"Don't blame, Papa. We had stopped at an open market in the evening, and I foolishly wandered away and got pushed along in the crowd. I will never forget the faces of those being sold, especially the woman who was just my age, whose young child clung to her. And then the look, the arrogance of the man who bought her."

Charlotte looked directly in her husband's eyes, nodding her head "no," hoping he would say no more. She did not want to share the ridiculousness of the act when she had outbid the buyer by one dollar.

"So, Antoine, you seem to have resigned yourself to be part of the Bonaparte circle, despite that I once detected your discomfort with all of this," Charlotte waved her hand over the land as she and her cousin sat on the estate's lawn."

"Well, I see you did not forget my, what shall we say, tenseness when I described many of the furnishings in the Count's home. Yes, I suppose I have become more tolerant in my outlook. Life is complicated, is it not? I am well aware of Napoleon's treachery and his thirst for power. But his brother was, at least in my estimation, a different man. Even on this estate, he shared the lands with his neighbors. And yes, he was very generous to my father and me. I stay here also because of my father. He needs me. I hope a day will come when I can give or help others the way I have been helped."

"Well, of course, our gentle Joseph did have that little liaison with Annette Savage," added Antoine smiling, "but then his wife simply refused to be with him. I know that is not an excuse for disloyalty, but one's heart can certainly become lonely. Speaking of not being alone, I am very happy for you and your sister. Your George is a good man, Charlotte, as is Alexander. You have both chosen well. Sometimes, as we know, the heart does not always choose wisely, but this is not so with my two cousins," said Antoine, removing his hat and wiping the sweat from his brow.

She said nothing, but methodically smoothed her sketch of the water lilies that had become curled at the edges, the humidity from the warm day distorting the delicate paper.

"Oh, dear," continued Antoine, "have I treaded on dangerous ground? Your silence is not a good sign."

"He is an honorable man, a man any woman would be proud to have as a husband," answered Charlotte, responding as if she were reciting a line she had rehearsed many times.

"But your heart is somewhere else," added Antoine, taking Charlotte's small right hand in his and bringing it tenderly to his lips.

"How is it, Antoine, that I can speak to you so easily, without fear of what you think of me? Yes, I loved another, and still feel his presence strongly. He was, is, half-French, half-Indian. Ironic, don't you think after our discussion about 'savages' the last time we came to Point Breeze?"

"And when you looked at his face, your breath stopped and you could not believe that this same person could love you?"

"Yes," replied Charlotte softly, "and you speak as if you know exactly that feeling."

"I did once, her name was Louisa, and our parents could not have been happier. But she died last year, unable to survive diphtheria."

"I am so sorry," said Charlotte. "I had no idea."

"Yes, it is very difficult, but perhaps that is why the project with the estate has been good for me. It occupies so much of my time. But for you, with your love, I can only imagine how your parents did not approve, of course."

"Yes, there was that, although Papa never said anything. But more than that, the town drove him away. He was accused of stealing some money, and he was an easy target for the fear and hate that many feel against the Indians. I know he never could have taken the money, for he was most honest and kind and truly a friend, not only to me, but to all of us. But he did look more Indian than French. Perhaps if he had not had that certain look. Well, it is too late now. He has gone forever," concluded Charlotte.

From across the small pond where George was fishing contently, he waved to his wife and her cousin and wondered what topic seemed to be so engrossing. He noticed Antoine kissing his wife's hand solicitously, and suddenly George felt a most uncommon stab of jealously. No, he would not think in that direction. He should realize, at this point, that these French were certainly demonstrative in their actions and speech. He contented himself with the idea that their discussion was just some family matter.

Their formal goodbyes expressed to Joseph Lucien and hugs and handshakes given to cousin Antoine, the travelers drove quietly away from Point Breeze, each deep in the reverie of capturing, in their minds, the experience of Point Breeze.

Pauline wiped the tears from her eyes and vowed she would always remember this place, for she knew she would never encounter such grandeur again.

Alexander studied the white chateau, vowing to remember the astonishing structure with its spacious rooms and incredible contents, a place where he had been treated as if he were a guest.

George's eyes surveyed the entire scene with its grounds and buildings, and recalled appreciatively the library and the reading of books that he could only have imagined in his wildest dreams. His guilt of enjoying the Bonapartes' largesse was offset by what seemed to be the cordiality of Prince Lucien.

Charlotte's eyes were captured by the rising sun as it rose higher on the back side of the estate, and she thought how wonderful it was that Joseph Lucien had become such a gracious host and gentlemen. With a wistful look on her face, she knew she would truly miss her cousin and the possibility that she would never speak to him again. But then, smiling, she reached for her husband's hand.

Part 5

Family

Though they spoke in whispers, Charlotte could hear the conversation clearly as the doctor told George that the infant's lungs were not fully developed.

"She has just been born too soon. I'm not sure how long she will be able to live. I'm sorry. There's really nothing I can do."

Charlotte continued to pretend she was asleep. The birth had not been difficult, perhaps only two or three difficult pains before she told her mother the baby was coming. The water had broken and then the pains came quickly. She wondered if something might be wrong. By her calculation, it was only her eighth month.

She remembered that day, a year after they'd returned from the bridal tour, when she had missed bleeding for the first time in seven years. Suddenly ordinary sights became abhorrent. She recalled gagging as she plucked the feathers from the chicken and began to gut the bird. She had done the chore so many times before without a second thought, but then, as if overnight, she could not bear to look at the carcass.

Then the smells became unbearable—the pen for the animals was especially intolerable. She also would hold a handkerchief close to her nose as she walked to the outhouse. The outhouse itself, never a pleasant encounter of course, was now a chore beyond belief.

But as the pregnancy progressed and she and George and then the entire family knew of the expected child, the nausea subsided. The realization that she would join her older sisters as they too had become mothers brought a satisfaction that she had not experienced before.

Now, Charlotte tried to rouse herself from her extreme exhaustion. She called George softly to the bed.

"Oh, my dear, Charlotte, are you in a great deal of pain? The child, a girl, you heard, I believe, is, is very small."

She nodded and tried to speak. "She must have a name, now, before, before, something happens," said Charlotte, trying to sound stronger than she actually felt.

"Yes, yes, of course, you are right. We will call her Charlotte," he said trying to smile, "because she is as beautiful and delicate as her mother."

She shook her head. "No, she must be her own," was all she could think to say.

"Then what of your second name, Louise? Will that be alright?"

"Yes," she whispered, reaching for George's hand. "George, the baby, would you allow her to be baptized?"

George said nothing at first. He had dreaded this moment, but as he looked at his wife, so fragile, so small in the bed, he could not refuse. "Yes, of course," he replied.

"It must be done, now, before, before she cannot breathe."

He laid the infant next to his wife, left his house and went to find her relatives.

A short time later as the group stood at the foot of the bed, Eloi, pouring a small amount of water over the child's head, with Amanda and Amedee standing close by, pronounced the words over his new granddaughter, "I baptize you in the name of the Father and of the Son and of the Holy Ghost."

"Louise, you must be careful now, no running," said Charlotte softly.

The child, who had just turned one-year-old, was really not capable of running fully, yet each time she seemed close to a more rapid pace, Charlotte quickly tried to hold her back. Indeed any undue exercise seemed to bring about spells where little Louise could not get her breath easily. Once when she laughed heartily at a silly face that seven-year-old Zenaide had made at her, the little one gasped loudly and started to turn blue. As she fell forward before Zenaide could catch her, she was able to catch her breath just in time to start crying loudly.

"Oh, no, no, no," said Zenaide almost shouting, "I didn't want anything to happen to you. I'm so sorry, Charlotte. Please forgive me, little Louise," Zeniade continued as she tried to comfort the baby with gentle rocking.

"Zenaide, it's alright. Don't worry. It seems to happen very frequently," said Charlotte.

And indeed the incidents did increase, as Charlotte reflected. Now the baby needed to be watched almost constantly to avoid any challenge to the undeveloped lungs. Mama had suggested that Amanda would be helpful in assisting Charlotte with the baby. Secretly Mama hoped that Amanda, now eighteen, might soften her coarse ways around a new baby. The younger sisters, Mary and Theresa, six and five respectively, seemed quite able to fend for themselves with Zenaide's supervision. Therefore, it was decided by Mama that Amanda should assist Charlotte with the new child.

It was a role Amanda did not relish. While she did not dislike the baby, she certainly would have enjoyed other chores more—gardening, harvesting grapes, strawberries, cherries—chores that were more physical and outdoors, but this was not to be. Each day as she spent time with her older sister's new child, she felt a resentment growing more strongly as she realized the lifestyle of her married sisters would never be hers.

"Thank you, Amanda. It is so very kind of you to give your time to me each afternoon," said Charlotte. "Perhaps today you could simply sit outside with Louise while I try to do some preserving of the fruits for the food cellar. Louise does have a way of getting into everything and being underfoot."

"Yes, I suppose," replied Amanda in a very non-committal tone. She could watch the child and run after her if need be. As little as Louise was that should not be too much of a challenge.

Amanda carried the small child outside and sat on the cleared area in front of her sister's home. She thought wistfully of Henry, who had been gone now for five years. If only Charlotte had not spoiled that friendship, perhaps he could have been her own beau. In her reverie she closed her eyes and tried to recall the details of his face. She smiled to herself as she recalled the little conspiracies and secrets that she had shared with him, all before Charlotte had come of course.

She remembered the day that Mama had burned Charlotte's drawings. The funny thing was that Charlotte was not as mad at her as she had been at Mama. Well, why should she be mad? After all, Charlotte had found someone new and completely forgotten about Henry.

Amanda opened her eyes and sighed heavily, thinking of many things, but certainly not little Louise. She looked around and called for the child. "Louise, Louise, where are you? Don't be hiding now."

She stood up and looked around, becoming more concerned. Where had the little one gone?

Suddenly Charlotte came out of the house and called to Amanda. "Everything alright out there, Amanda? You two are certainly being quiet."

"Yes, yes, we're fine," replied Amanda. Where had that child gone?

Panicked, Amanda peered around the cabin and started to run to the back of the home. "Louise, Louise, come now. Aunt Amanda is looking for you." Why had she been so careless? Could she not do anything right?

She ran towards the creek, Gallet Creek, the one where little Leon had drowned only a few years earlier. "Dear God, please, please help me find her," she whispered.

Amanda saw the color of her pale yellow dress first, and then the child herself, who sat precariously close to the side of the creek. Swiftly, Amanda grabbed Louise and scooped her up running back to the house.

Charlotte, close behind, had watched the scene play as her panic increased. She could not help the outburst before it escaped from her lips. "What were you thinking, Amanda? You know how fragile Louise is. What would I have done if something had happened to her?"

Amanda, upset with herself for her own laxity and scared as she had never been scared before, shouted back in frustration, "You, you, it's always about you! You and Heloise and Pauline or Zenaide and Mary or Theresa. It's never about what I want!" She pushed the child into her sister's arms and stomped away from the house.

Untying the team from the post, she climbed swiftly onto the bench of the wagon and drove the horses north, away from town.

Charlotte ran for a few steps after her sister, but was unable to pursue very far. "Amanda, please come back. It's not your fault. I know how quickly she can move when she wants to. Please."

The words were not heard, however. Charlotte only saw the trail of dust that followed the wagon.

It was a path she had taken many times before even when Mama had told her time and time again that ladies did not drive wagons. Now, she drove the team recklessly, and her anger and resentment were a fuel that the animals responded to as she urged them even faster. As the tears rushed down her cheeks, her vision was clouded, and Amanda released her right hand from the reins to wipe her eyes just as the wagon's back right wheel struck a rock.

The team continued to race down the path, but Amanda was jolted from her seat and her body flew in the air as if it she were doing a huge somersault. She was not afraid in the few moments she was suspended. She only felt relief, as if a terrible weight had been forever lifted from her soul.

But, as her body fell to the earth, her head took the impact first and in that moment her neck snapped.

It was Uncle John Gallet who came upon the team first, and then his niece, the niece that he wished had been his own child, the one whom he had taught to ride and harvest and do all the "boy things" she seemed to like so well.

He closed the eyes, the hazel-colored eyes that, in death, stared at the cloudless blue sky, and then he cradled the head and shoulders in his own arms, sobbing as he had never cried before.

George held Charlotte's hand as the group stood around the small mound that covered Louise's body, the body that after two years just seemed to exhaust itself from the challenge of breathing. Despite the peaceful manner of her death and the inevitability of her short life, the stabbing ache that each of her parents felt was not eased.

Amanda and Eloi along with Pauline and Alexander and Heloise and Orlando stood close to the newly-bereaved parents and tried to soothe them with caressing touches to Charlotte—a kiss on her cheek, a tight hug—and pats on George's shoulders.

Zenaide had been holding the hands of her two little sisters, but now she rushed to Charlotte, grasping her around the waist. "She was so sweet, Charlotte. I loved her so much. We all did. She was like a miniature you."

Papa spoke directly to his weeping daughter. "There is no way to ever heal your heart completely, but time lessens the ache and the demands of life force us to go on."

Charlotte and George both nodded their assents.

Mama, whose life had now been impacted by the death of three of her children, thought how each death had affected her differently. Jules, in France, had been ill for at least two weeks before he finally succumbed to the fever. She then remembered the ache, the shock of her adorable Leon, little Napoleon, which had evaporated her very strength for such a time that she was truly unable to care for the little girls. And then, just a few months ago, the sudden death of her Amanda, the child she always had felt a stranger to, the daughter she could not understand. Despite being her namesake, that daughter's death had touched Amanda the least. The lack of feeling brought the guilt once again, but she did not dwell on that thought for long. So many deaths, including recently, her own parents, seemed to numb the senses.

A respectful distance away, the townspeople had also come to share their thoughts with George and Charlotte. Among those present, Mary and Owen Willis offered their sympathies to the parents of little Louise.

As they walked away, Mary spoke quietly to her husband. "Odd, don't you feel, Owen, that some just seem destined to bear more sorrow than others. Perhaps we were simply saved much sorrow by not having our own children. And then, of course, we have Henry," she said smiling.

Owen nodded his agreement.

Yes, they had their Henry, their loyal "adopted" son, who never failed to write to them and now seemed to be sharing, on a regular basis, the good fortune, the gold strike that he and other partners had found in California. California, it seemed, was more forgiving to a person of Henry's ancestry, and his hard work had resulted in considerable profits, which Henry did not squander as so many others did. Rather, he kept a small amount of money for himself and then sent the rest to Avon.

In return, he asked only to hear the news of the town. The Willises knew exactly what he wished to know. They included all the town news, but always concluded with specific news about Charlotte, trying to be as gentle as possible in the relaying of that information.

They both hoped that somewhere in that far place called California, Henry would find someone to love and replace Charlotte, but as of yet that had not occurred.

"Charlotte, you must read this new book that cousin Antoine has sent to us. It absolutely will make you want to tell Papa to take out his gun and shoot those horrible, horrible slave owners and overseers. I cannot understand how *anyone* can possibly defend this horrible practice!" said a most enraged Zenaide.

Charlotte rose slowly from the rocker, a wide smile on her face as she greeted her impassioned sister. She couldn't have been so stirred by anything when she was ten, could she? That seemed like such a long time ago. Lately, all she had thought about was the child growing inside her, a busy little child, indeed, whose feet she sometimes felt kicking her ribs as it reached the days when it would be born, soon after the new year.

"So tell me about this book. Are you the first one to read it?" inquired Charlotte.

"Yes, I grabbed it away from Papa when it slid from his lap one evening as he was reading, and then I told him I wasn't giving it back until I finished it. That was only two days ago. I just couldn't stop reading. Even when Mama reminded me to do my chores, I hid from her so she wouldn't see me reading. You know how Mama always has something for you to do," confided Zenaide.

"Yes, of course," replied Charlotte smiling. That is what mothers seem to do. But tell me, what is this momentous novel about?" inquired Charlotte.

"Well, it is all about how the families of negroes are sold, just like any other thing you might buy at the store. And the families are split apart, and people are beaten, and they try to escape, but then they are captured and the worst thing is then they are 'sold down the river.' That means the Mississippi, of course, and the farther south you go, the meaner the slave owners are. It's all so horrible. I will be an abolitionist when I grow up," said Zenaide, without appearing to pause for a breath.

Perhaps Charlotte would have smiled at the passion of one so young had she herself not been privy to the actual horror of a slave market only a few years before.

"Yes, it is a terrible practice. So, you must tell me, Zenaide, what is the name of this remarkable book?"

"It is called *Uncle Tom's Cabin.* You wait and see, Charlotte. Everyone will read it and things will have to change. They just will!" Zenaide said adamantly.

Sometimes the words of even the very young can be prophetic, for in a few short years a very tall president was reported to have said to one Harriet Beecher Stowe, "So, you're the little girl who started this big war?"

Changing Times

The railroad planners came first to the growing community of Avon in 1853. They talked with the town's leading men—the Woods brothers, John Gallet and the town's newly elected justice of the peace, George Simmons. Avon would be one stop on the new railroad that would travel from Quincy to Galesburg, a distance of 99.91 miles.

From Quincy through Macomb and Avon and north to Galesburg and all the flat, vast prairies in between, the men toiled laying the tracks and building the Iron Horse, which would forever change the face of the nation.

Working for the Northern Cross branch of the railroad headed by Nehemiah Bushnell, former military man William Sidell was the lead engineer for the project, assisted by recent Irish immigrant, William Fennessy. Men from Avon worked on the construction alongside those who were strangers to town. Those from other communities soon took up their residences with local families, including John Gallet, who housed three of the workers including Fennessy.

During the three years of the construction, Union Township, which included Avon, increased in population over fifty percent from nine hundred to fifteen hundred.

The Simmons family, however, experienced the death of their second daughter, little Carlotine, who died at exactly the same age as her earlier sibling. Once again, George had agreed to the name and baptism of this child. When her passing occurred, during the diphtheria outbreak in the winter of 1856, his silent resentment grew as a wedge between him and his wife.

George said nothing of the death to Charlotte or her family, but retreated into himself. His bitterness sought an outlet, and, briefly, he thought of becoming a member of Illinois's growing Know-Nothing Party. When he was summarily rejected entry, because his wife was Catholic, he shook his head at his own ill judgment in even considering the membership.

Springfield resident, Abraham Lincoln, encapsulated George's thoughts as the lawyer told the newspapers, "When the Know-Nothings get control, it will read 'all men are created equal, except negroes, and foreigners, and Catholics'."

George knew his anti-Catholic feelings were complicated by the hypocritical religion that had played in his early life, yet he could not combat the gnawing as his wife's religion ate constantly at his thoughts.

Also, it seemed to him that their Catholicism was being strengthened as the French families of Avon, the Hectornes and the Poisets, had been reinforced by the likes of two French émigrés, Joe Tudor and Leopold Stocker. These two gentlemen had come to America later in life as the Bonaparte influence waned in Europe. Like Louis Mailliard, Leopold Stocker had served King Joseph closely, as his personal valet-de-chambre. Leopold invested his money in a furniture store, but his energetic and lively personality added significantly to the French of Avon as he promoted Sunday evening songfests and get-togethers.

Indeed, Sunday became a day of family gatherings as the community would picnic close to the new tracks and inspect the progress of the railroad that had been accomplished during the week. The home gatherings would then commence, but George would not participate in what he called frivolity. Though Charlotte initially tried to cajole him into joining, she abandoned her efforts when she realized they were fruitless.

"I do not mind if you go, however," he said trying to smile.

Charlotte thanked him for allowing her these Sunday evenings, yet she resented his moroseness. Had she also not lost a second daughter? Furthermore, on second thought, she even resented the very idea that she should need to be allowed to go. She loved the dancing and singing. When she was with her family, the weight of her losses was diminished. Was she not free to make her own decisions?

Yet, despite the congeniality and lightheartedness of the Sunday gatherings, the topic of others' freedom invariably invaded the conversation.

"Do you know that I have heard some of our very neighbors, those particularly who have migrated from the South, defend the practice of slavery even to this day?" commented Uncle John. "They claim that the matter of the 'peculiar institution,' in other words slavery, is a clear question of states' rights."

Eloi nodded while Alexander and Orlando shook their heads in disgust.

Thirteen-year-old Zenaide, standing close to the men's corner, looked them clearly in the eyes and questioned her male family members. "So, what do you gentlemen intend to do about it?"

"Yes, what shall we do about it? That is the terrible question. We have sidestepped the issue for so many years, but surely it is now coming to a head," continued John.

Joe Tudor, whose English was extremely limited, removed his pipe for a few moments and said only with his thick accent, "A war with one's own, *non, non.*"

Amedee chimed in quickly, "Well, yes, I guess there was that bloody thing called the French Revolution. But lucky for us, there was also Napoleon, right Papa."

Usually quiet in these conversations, Eloi now spoke softly. "Yes, there is that, Amedee. But my dear Zenaide, I do remember another child of my mine who, when she was just your age, tried to act very openly against this horrible thing called slavery."

Then, quietly, in halting speech, Eloi recounted Charlotte's action at the slave market in Louisville, concluding his story by saying that he had never been so proud and scared in his entire life.

"My sister Charlotte did that?" Zenaide questioned.

Somehow, the older sister whom she loved dearly but who seemed often so passionless was certainly not capable of such action. A new sense of admiration welled in Zenaide, and she was sure that another woman in her family would take up the cause against slavery.

She called to her sister and motioned her to come to her side. "Charlotte, Papa has told us the story of what you tried to do at the slave auction in Louisville. Why have you never told me of this?" asked Zenaide somewhat indignantly, for she had always considered this older sister, despite their age difference, to be her confidante, her ally in thought.

"Why have I not told you? Well, because now as I look back, it was so futile, so incredibly useless. This young woman, with her child at her side, was just my age, Zenaide, just my age, and she had obviously been, been used by a white man. The lightness of her child's skin clearly attested to that ignominy. And then the wounds. I can picture them so plainly—as if someone had taken very sharp nails and run them down her face. They were so deep. Three lines, they looked like lightning streaks, down her right cheek."

Charlotte shuddered unconsciously as if she were witnessing the horror anew.

"Oh, Charlotte, how horrible!" said Zenaide. "It is just like *Uncle Tom's Cabin*, and it is taking place every day, still. And we do nothing!"

The dancing and music had suddenly stopped while Zenaide's voice rang throughout the small room.

Amanda was very embarrassed by her daughter's outburst and sighed heavily, shaking her head. What was she to do with these daughters who persisted in acting so unladylike?

As Charlotte began to walk the short distance from her parents' home to her own, Amedee called to her. "Charlotte, wait for us. We'll walk you home."

Amedee was still courting Mary Smith, as he had been for many years. Many in the town, including Mary's parents, wondered why they had not married.

"Good evening, Mary," said Charlotte. "I haven't seen you for a while. Have you been well?"

"Oh, yes, thank you," said Mary. "I've just been doing some traveling with my parents. Amedee told me about the abolition talk that your family was engaged in. I must say it was all the talk in Chicago and Philadelphia, too. I just hope there isn't any war. War always results in death, the death of all our young, strong men," she said, looking longingly at Amedee.

Charlotte thought, yes, that was true. How old was her brother now? Well, just a year younger than she, of course, twenty-eight. If she remembered correctly, Mary was perhaps three or four years younger, really time for both of them to be married. Oh, my, was she really becoming her Mama?

Amedee took Mary's small, delicate hand in his, but turned his question towards his sister. "So, you really bid on a slave, did you?"

"Yes. I know it was a foolish thing to do, but at thirteen, fourteen, perhaps we have the courage to do things we would think twice about as we get older."

"Yes, isn't that true. However, I'm sure if I had seen the incident, I would not have had the same reaction. But if I had known what you had done, I would have teased you unmercifully at the time and only been interested in having my own fun at your expense," he admitted with a sigh.

"You would have reacted in a way to make me realize my stupidity, for isn't that a younger brother's role?" replied Charlotte. But, as soon as she said it, she regretted the words, for Amedee's temperament had been visibly changed by the death of their younger brother.

"I'm sorry, Amedee. I should have not made the reference to younger brothers," said Charlotte.

"Yes, I know, Charlotte. You are much too kind a heart for that. Besides, I relive that day with every waking moment without prompting from someone else," said Amedee.

"Well, we are here now," he said. "Please tell George we missed him this evening and that perhaps he will think of joining us another Sunday."

"Yes, I will, and forgive yourself. It is time. I long for that boy named Amedee, who made my life miserable when I was younger," said Charlotte. "Good night, Mary."

Except for the lone candle that lit the area where George sat, the room was nearly dark on this Sunday evening. George was so absorbed in his reading that he had not even noticed Charlotte come into the room.

"What is it that you are so engaged in, George?" his wife questioned.

"Oh my, yes, I am so glad you are here. I have been reading the writings of Frederick Douglass from the *North Star*. What a drive this man has had to become so educated and to inform the world of the need for the end to slavery," said George with a very impassioned voice. "But, forgive me. I don't want to spoil the merriment of your evening."

"But you see George, merriment as you call it, is not the only function of the evening. In fact, slavery and abolition and the possibility of war were all discussed. Papa even told the story of the Louisville slave market. Zenaide, dear Zenaide and her passion, was quite shocked that her much older sister had dared to be so bold."

George pushed his reading aside and slowly stood to face his wife. "I think, in that moment, Charlotte, in Louisville, I realized how deeply that I loved you." He pushed back a dark wisp of hair that had fallen across her face when she removed her bonnet. "And . . . there is no question in my heart that I will always love you."

Smiling, Charlotte moved slowly towards her husband and rested her head on his chest. She said nothing.

He lifted her face and kissed her tenderly.

With pride, George looked at the two-story structure that he had helped to build, a place where he was a teacher. It consisted of four rooms, three rooms on the first floor for the lower grades and a room on the upper floor for a high school, certainly a progressive accomplishment for any town in the year 1857. It was a school where his niece, Addie McFarland, would attend and where he hoped that someday his new daughter Hortensia would be a student.

Though the turmoil of the question of slavery plagued the nation and still controlled the talk of any town gathering, for George and Charlotte the year had been kind—good crops, a healthy daughter and the promise of another child in the spring.

Yes, he had conceded to another Catholic baptism. Life must have its trade-offs. For himself, he would never be a religious man. But his wife seemed to find an incomprehensible joy in the rites of her church. For now, he would swallow his pride and thank *someone* for his blessings.

All of Avon had indeed prospered despite the specter that loomed nationwide, for the railroad had been the key that provided easy access for farm products and cattle to be transported to the north, to the growing market of Chicago. The railroad had brought new towns into existence where prairies once reigned: Bushnell, named for the president of the railroad and Bardolph, both south of Avon, arose from the fields.

The Fifth Debate

The two senatorial candidates could not have been more different if they had arisen from different species. The one, fiery, small in stature, sophisticated, well-connected, successful at several levels of government, and called, not unkindly, the "Little Giant." The strong voice of Democrat Stephen A. Douglas penetrated in several circles of the state government, and now he looked forward to continuing his term in the United States Senate. His expansionist policy supported a growing, thriving nation—and if slavery were the price, so be it.

The other, physically a giant, came from storybook humble beginnings, if indeed such lack of creature comforts could be called storybook. A short term in the U.S. Congress had been rather lackluster, and then a law practice in Springfield had been barely enough to pay his debts.

But, suddenly, he had risen to prominence as his client list grew in number and importance and his homey, yet cogent, manner of speaking and presenting an argument had gained him statewide recognition. His crowning achievement came on June 16 of this year, 1858, as he criticized the U.S. Supreme Court decision in the Dred Scott case as an excuse to legalize slavery in every state. Dred Scott, now living in a free state had appealed for his freedom, but the nation's chief judicial body ruled that though he lived in a free state, he would remain a slave.

Abraham Lincoln's words "A house divided against itself cannot stand. . . . I believe this government cannot endure, permanently, half slave and half free," resonated with the newly formed Republican Party, and he became their nominee to challenge Douglas, who confidently expected to be elected to his third term. Capitalizing on his opponent's confidence, Lincoln challenged Douglas to a series of debates to be held in each of the state's seven districts.

A bit less than thirty miles from the town of Avon, Knox College in Galesburg, chosen as the site for the fifth debate, was a setting that definitely favored Lincoln's anti-slavery stand. The college had been founded in 1837 by reformers who deeply opposed slavery and promoted the potential of all, including women and people of color. Knox College was also known as a "freedom station" in the system of the Underground Railroad, assisting negroes in escaping north to Canada to avoid the Fugitive Slave Law of 1850, which required northerners to return runaway slaves to their masters. The old First Church in Galesburg also provided hiding places for the slaves as did many prairie homes that stood ready to receive fugitives at any time of day or night.

October in Illinois can often display the warm temperament of the passing of summer with bright blue, welcoming skies, pushing the promise of a challenging upcoming winter from the corners of apprehensive minds. Sometimes, however, the weather can portend the specter of what is to come, the cold rain turning to sleet then to the snow that reigns for endless months.

Thursday, October 7, served as an ominous precursor of winter. Rain had drenched the dirt roads the day before, and now a cold, raw wind ravaged the central plain, daring to assault any intrepid traveler that might venture out.

The elements had not deterred, however, several residents of Avon, who, like inhabitants from many other communities, felt the need to hear these two men who might actually settle this slavery question forever. Many folks from Avon had decided to take the train that would travel from their town to Galesburg. Then, however, there would be a fair walk to Knox College itself.

Therefore, Charlotte, George, and, of course, Zenaide chose to ride their wagon to the debate. Although the weather deterred many, they would not be stopped by the elements. Charlotte, despite the birth of Emile just a few short months ago, insisted that she be part of the venture. She felt, like many others, that to miss this event was tantamount to missing, well, Napoleon himself, had that opportunity ever presented itself.

How strange, she thought, that once upon a time, she had resented the fact that she had to leave Europe. Now, however, as she grew older and thought of her two young children, how proud she felt to be in this country, where decisions were made, for better or worse, not by a single man, or even a select chosen few, but by men of all classes.

Well, there was *that*, of course, as Zenaide never failed to remind those who would listen: the fact that women were not allowed to vote. How ridiculous that, in this country, all adults, regardless of race or gender, were not given suffrage. Though she was only fifteen, she vowed that "sometime in my lifetime, I too will have the privilege to vote."

"One argument at a time, Zenaide. But I'm sure that will come before too long," comforted Charlotte.

Hortensia and Emile would be left with Pauline, whose older children would help with their tending. God bless, Pauline, thought Charlotte. Though her older sister did not seem interested in the politics of the time, she was always ready to watch the children. She easily adapted to an additional two or three without complaining of little ones being underfoot.

They had prepared food for the journey to Galesburg, of course. No one knew how long the debate would take, at least three to four hours, and travel each way could take two to three hours depending on luck, so food would be a necessity. Charlotte placed the food carefully in a basket—dried meats and fruits, johnnycake—and George made sure that two large jugs of water and a tin cup were also packed in the floor of the wagon.

Many wagons set out from Avon on that day, a fortunate circumstance for Charlotte, George and Zenaide, for when they were two miles north of town, the front right wheel of their vehicle became lodged in a deep rut of mud. As George urged the horses to pull the vehicle forward, he heard the crack of the wheel, and suddenly all three passengers were tipping to the right and then falling in the mud as all contents were sent sprawling to the ground. George quickly caught his wife, but the food basket flew several feet from the path and then bounced quickly down to a small stream, its contents lost in the weeds and muck.

"Are you alright?" George said solicitously.

"I, I think so," replied Charlotte, beginning to wipe the wet mud from her face with the handkerchief she always carried in her pocket. "Zenaide, where . . . oh, no," continued Charlotte.

For there sat Zenaide, quite unhurt, except for her pride, smack in the middle of one very large mud puddle, her once white gloves now supporting her body.

"How will we ever get to the debate now?" she bemoaned.

In spite of the seriousness of what had just happened, Charlotte could not help a small laugh. Perhaps it was the relief that no one was hurt or the extremely dramatic look on her sister's face, but somehow, Charlotte's snicker just could not be stifled.

Zenaide was shocked by her sister's reaction, but, as she tried to get up, she slipped once again, and suddenly both sisters were laughing.

George shook his head. Sometimes when these two were together there was no telling what they would do, but now he truly appreciated their light-hearted acceptance of the misfortune that had occurred.

"Well, my laughing ladies, I assume that since neither of you are hurt, you will have the strength to walk home. I expect we are only one or two miles from town," said George, a smile on his face. "I have found the jugs of water, but our food is all gone."

Zenaide, very serious now, cried out, "No, no, we can't turn back. Surely someone will have room in their wagon to take us with them."

No sooner had those words been said then another wagon came upon them.

To Charlotte, Zenaide whispered, "Oh, no, it's the Babbitts with that pesty son of theirs, Harry."

"Howdy there, George, it seems you've had a bit of trouble," said the affable Jonathan Babbitt as he brought his wagon next to the Simmons.

"Yes, I told my wife and her sister that we can walk easily back to town, but they insist on going on to Galesburg for the debate, regardless of our somewhat muddy appearance," replied George.

"Well, you are certainly welcome to join up with us, right Ann? It seems there are quite a few of us on the road, but I'm just glad we caught up with you first since we do have the room in our wagon," continued Jonathan.

Zenaide gave her sister a look that conveyed both disgust and panic, a look that implored, "Can't we wait for someone else?"

But before she registered a vocal rejection, her brother-in-law said, "Well, that is mighty kind of you and Ann, Jonathan. I'm sure my women would be very grateful."

Charlotte sensed the immediate tension within Zenaide and inwardly smiled, thinking how grateful she was to not be fifteen.

And then, just as she thought of herself at fifteen, there it was again—the image of Henry's face, the sound of his voice, the touch of her finger down the line of his nose—always followed by a great sense of emptiness.

She looked at the group around her and suddenly had the overwhelming sensation that this world was not real, that she would wake up from a dream. This was not where she should be. *He* should be getting back into the wagon with her, not all the strangers around her, beside her.

"Charlotte, Charlotte, are you alright?" said Ann. "Maybe you were more shaken up than you thought. You have such a strange look on your face."

Focusing on the present, Charlotte regained her composure. "Of course, yes, I'm sorry. I was just thinking how, how fortunate it was that the children were not with us."

George acknowledged his gratefulness to Jonathan. "How lucky we were to have you folks come along just when you did. I suppose that wagon of mine will still be sitting here tomorrow. I think I should be able to hitch my team up with yours. I hope the four boys can get along."

Young Harry assisted the men, but Charlotte noticed that he was more interested in looking at her younger sister.

"It's good to see you, Nin," said Harry. "I'm so glad you weren't hurt when your wagon tipped. You seemed to have gotten a might dirty though."

"Well, yes, but then I don't suppose Mr. Lincoln will mind as long as we cheer loudly enough for him," replied Zenaide with just enough emphasis on the "Mr. Lincoln" to let everyone know where she stood.

"So, it's Lincoln you're for, George? Hmm, the man is a trouble maker in my book," chimed in Jonathan, now beginning to take his seat on the front bench and grabbing the reins of the horses from George and his son.

"Yes, I do believe in Lincoln's ideas, Jonathan. And, Harry, what was that name I heard you call my wife's sister?" George asked directly to the young Babbitt.

"Oh, yes, Mr. Simmons. We don't mean any disrespect. It's just Zenaide" (he deliberately said the name slowly, almost turning it into three syllables) "jes seems so, well, not American. So the kids at school have begun to call her Nin."

"I see," said George. "And how do you feel about that, Miss Nin?" said George teasingly.

"I suppose I really don't care what my name is as long as people know how I feel about things."

"And that, my dear sister," chimed in Charlotte, "is something I'm sure they will always know."

As the six travelers renewed their journey to Galesburg, the gentlemen in front, the ladies in the back, the conversation was confined to the respective genders. The gentlemen, George and Jonathan, continued their talk of politics while a somewhat disinterested Harry frequently stole glances to the young lady who now was riding in his wagon.

On the rear bench Charlotte and Ann commiserated about the inclement weather while a gracious Ann offered to share the food that she had brought for her family.

"That is such a kind offer, Ann. I'm afraid our food was lost when the wagon tipped. Well, now some of our little, wild creatures will have a nice feast courtesy of the Simmons. I do hope they appreciate the cloth napkin I provided," quipped Charlotte, who sat between her sister and Ann. She hoped her light-hearted comment would hide the dark feelings that had surfaced earlier.

Zenaide, her arms folded, refused to take part in the women's conversation, and only occasionally allowed herself to look forward and stare at the back of the head of one Harry Babbitt, whose attractive brown waves were hidden, only slightly, under his cap.

"I did hear that your brother Amedee and Mary Smith were married a few weeks ago. And it's about time I might add. And that nice Will Fennessy, the engineer from the railroad, has married Jonas Woods's daughter Cornelia and bought a farm right outside of town. Isn't it wonderful hearing about our young people marrying?" questioned Ann amiably.

"Well, marriage might be alright for some, but it certainly isn't in my plans. There are just too many important things to do," answered Zenaide, her blues eyes blazing and speaking loudly enough to ensure that the occupants of the front bench would hear.

As the wagons and train reached their destination, the south front of the main building of Knox College, the size of the crowd seemed unaffected by the stiff winds that continued to blow. The decision was made to move to the east side of the building to shield the speakers from the force of the gale, so the temporary platform on the south side was disassembled and then moved. Accordingly, the crowd, now pushing 10,000, shifted collectively to its left.

The density of the crowd was quite overwhelming as people pushed their vehicles and bodies into position for the main show. Students housed in the East Bricks dormitory hung out their windows, while other spectators positioned themselves on the roof. Banners, many of which had been destroyed by the wind, flew throughout the crowd, while a prominent one, KNOX COLLEGE FOR LINCOLN, hanging over the erected platform, continued to blow vigorously. The whipping of the fabric of the huge U.S. flag on the stage punctuated the noise of the crowd, which rose with every passing minute.

Parking their wagon to the right of the stage, Jonathan and George hitched the horses as securely as possible to one of several posts that had been provided for the day. As the women alighted from the vehicle with Harry's help, he quickly asked Zenaide if he could accompany her as she walked through the crowd.

"It could be a mite dangerous out there, Nin. I wouldn't want you to get crushed or anything," he said.

"Well, I suppose, if you want. But the real debate won't start for a while, so I thought I would just walk around. Perhaps I will go to this college someday. You're welcome to come. It is a free country, after all. Well, that is if your skin is white and you are a male," Zenaide added quickly.

"You do seem to get yourself riled up over so many things," said Harry.

"Well, yes, and why not? Do you agree with slavery? Can you imagine what it would be like to have a child of your own ripped from your arms and *sold* to someone? Yes, I think everyone should get upset about that. Have you ever even seen a negro? They are people, you know. In fact, there are some here today. They are sitting over there on the south side. I dare you to go over and talk to them, Harry Babbitt, for that's just what I intend to do," said a defiant Zenaide, walking quickly, but secretly hoping that Harry would follow, for she wasn't quite sure how to engage a negro in conversation.

Of the nearly 5,000 people of Galesburg, only a very small percentage was negro, most of whom had come with the advent of the train. Now, the small group, bent on hearing Mr. Lincoln speak, gathered in their own little corner on the south side of the building. Several, out of force of habit, carried papers proving they were free. Though their inroads in the Galesburg community and Knox College had been generally positive—two of their own, Hiram Revels and Barnabas Root, had even been students at the college—one could never be too careful.

As Zenaide approached the cluster of dark-skinned people, her footsteps became increasingly slower, Harry now only a few paces behind her.

With a deep breath and renewed determination, also not wanting to show her fear to Harry, she decided to greet the group as she would any other strangers.

"Good afternoon, sirs and ladies. I'm so glad you decided to come to hear the speech from our Mr. Lincoln. My friend Harry and I are really looking forward to this afternoon, especially if that wind dies down a bit," she said, smiling, opening her wide eyes and quite startling the group. "My name is Zenaide, Zenaide Mailliard, but Harry calls me Nin."

Harry nodded his affirmation, but was too tongue-tied to speak.

Finally, a tall, slightly bent man turned to look directly at Zenaide and spoke as if he had been designated by the entire group to speak. "Well, now isn't that very nice of you to offer us a good day, Miss Zenaide. My name is Jonas," his deep resonate voice replied. "We, too, are looking forward to the debate."

Slowly the entire group of negroes turned toward the two white children and smiled, nodding in their direction. Zenaide smiled back with as much assurance as she could muster, glad that she now felt Harry's strong hand in hers.

"Good afternoon, folks," said Harry haltingly. "I do hope we aren't disturbing you."

Thank you, thank you, Harry, for now she was utterly without a follow-up to her opening comment—at least for a few seconds.

"Harry has come with his parents, Jonathan and Ann Babbitt, and I have come with my sister and brother-in-law, Charlotte and George Simmons."

"Simmons?" questioned Jonas.

Suddenly, a tall woman who had been tending to some smaller children in the back and to the left of the gathering started walking towards Jonas. She had heard the conversation ensue and was curious to see the two friendly, if unlikely, visitors. As she approached Zenaide and Harry, she clasped her hand to her mouth to keep from crying out, but the words escaped her lips, "No, no, it cannot be. It is too long ago. Your face, it is the same face," said the woman.

She now turned towards Zenaide and Henry and as she stood looking directly at them, only a short distance between them, Zenaide almost screamed, for she saw three old scars, like lightening streaks, running down the woman's right cheek. "It's you, the girl, woman from Louisville."

Taking the startled woman's hands in hers, Zenaide said, "Please, stay right here. Please don't move. I must bring my sister."

Zenaide, with a confused Harry beside her, made her way as best as she could through the crowd that seemed even denser than before. She ran through small clusters of people, people still picnicking, people engaged in heated political discussions.

Finally, she saw them and began yelling, "Charlotte, Charlotte, come quickly. I have found her," said Zenaide, now nearly out of breath.

Charlotte and Ann had finished gathering the leftovers from the food and were speaking quietly when Charlotte heard her sister and saw the startled look on her face. She grabbed her sister's hand, "My goodness, Zenaide, what is it? Who have you found?" she questioned.

Zenaide held her chest, trying to find enough air to speak. "Of course, I cannot be sure, but I just saw a negro woman with those scars on her right cheek, and when she saw me, she must have thought it was you because she said, 'It is the same face'."

Two pieces of dried meat that Charlotte had begun to rewrap in cloth fell from her hands. "Take me to her," she said.

When the two women, one with white skin, the other with skin of a darker hue, saw each other, the tears began. "Savannah, Savannah, it is you. You are safe, and free."

"Yes, it is me. For so many years I have thought of your face, your kind face with those eyes that reflected my own sorrow. I have wanted to say 'thank you' for so long, and now, here, the Lord has granted me that wish. I don't even know your name," said Savannah.

"It is Charlotte, Charlotte Simmons. But, I must hear your story. And, of course, this is my sister, much younger sister, Zenaide. To see you again, to know you, you have survived. That is truly a blessing."

The three women sat down then together and though the cold wind continued to blow, it was unheard and unfelt as Savannah's story unfolded. She had been taken from Louisville to a farm near Richmond, owned by the Parker family. Clayton, the man that Charlotte had seen so long ago, was not as unkind as he could have been, but she was his for many, many years. His was a privileged life, given to much drinking and gambling with an occasional duel to relieve his boredom, he said. She hated the thought of the duels, for she never knew what would happen to her and her sons if Clayton were killed. In 1854, however, he was killed in just such a duel, but the terms of his will provided for her freedom, hers and their son.

"How did you come to Galesburg?" asked Charlotte.

"Despite our freedom, the dangers in the South from those who would take us back into slavery are, to this day, very real, but I was fortunate in finding a free man who protected me. He spent many years looking for his wife and daughter, who had been kidnapped years ago. His daughter would have been twenty-five this year. He never found them, but he did help my son and me. With the help of the Underground Railroad, we came to this town," said Savannah smiling. "Here in Galesburg is where my life began."

Cautiously, softly, Charlotte asked, "Forgive me, but I must ask about your son, the one that, that was with you that day in Louisville."

"Yes, my little Elias. We were lucky in that we were not separated for many years, but his impatience could not abide his life anymore and he tried to escape. I was told he died trying to swim the Ohio. He was thirteen when he left," said Savannah.

Zenaide, who had been sitting strangely silent, allowed the unwiped tears to roll down her cheeks.

"I know what it is like to grieve for children, for I have lost two young daughters. But to be lost in that way, to have lived as you have lived, I can only say that I am profoundly sorry," said Charlotte.

"I do have my other son, however, and my husband, Jonas. Josiah, come here, please. There is someone I want you to meet," said Savannah.

As a tall, young man came towards Charlotte, it was with great restraint that she kept from gasping. Zenaide's eyes also grew large indeed, for she had seen many things today, but certainly nothing as remarkable as the boy named Josiah.

"How do you do, ma'am, miss? Is there something I can do for you?" Though his voice had the same intonation as his mother's and his lips were larger than a white man's, the wavy, light brown hair and stark blue eyes belonged clearly to the man who had fathered him.

Charlotte had seen those eyes and all their lust and cruelty once in Louisville, but here they conveyed a most different story.

"Josiah, I do love that name. I do remember it, I believe, from the Declaration of Independence," said Charlotte.

"Yes, ma'am, Josiah Bartlett from New Hampshire, one of the signers of that great document," said the young man.

"My Josiah is quite the reader, I must say, an advantage of being the master's son," said Savannah. "We hope he will soon be a student at Knox College."

Zenaide was clearly quite impressed. How was it that she had not bothered to recognize the signers of that document?

"Charlotte, Zenaide, oh, there you two are. It is almost time for the debaters to arrive. I have been searching for you. Harry finally led me here," said George, but as he spoke, he, too, recognized the woman from long ago.

"Savannah, this is my husband, George Simmons. He was also there that night in Louisville," said Charlotte.

"Yes, how nice to meet you here. We were all so, so young back then," said George.

"I would like you, to meet my husband, Jonas, Jonas Williams.

"I knew a Jonas Williams, once. He worked with me on the steamship *Prairie.* Surely it cannot be the same man?" asked George.

When Jonas was called over, the two men simply shook their heads in amazement. But as they drew near enough to shake hands, they both stopped. Perhaps in another time, another place, these two men of similar intellect and common experience could have shared their pasts. They could have spoken of the captain, the snags they had avoided, the splendor of the Ohio—but now, here, in this setting, their respective skin colors made them dance an expected step.

Jonas would not speak until spoken to.

George broke the silence. "It seems, Jonas, we are here for the same reason."

"Yes, sir, Mr. Simmons."

The women stared in disbelief at the men's reaction to each other. Is it the fear of friendship, intimacy or the loss of face that causes some to close doors that others can open so easily?

"We must be going now, ladies," said George somewhat nervously. "It is almost time for the main speakers to arrive."

Zenaide said nothing, but again grasped Savannah's hands as if to apologize for all her suffering.

"You must promise to write to me, Savannah Williams, and I to you," said Charlotte. "Have I told you I live in Avon? I will pray for you. Please do the same for me."

And then the two women, united by one small, brave act of kindness, hugged each other.

As two o'clock, the appointed hour of debate neared, Editor Reed of Alexis, a small town just north of Galesburg, completed his welcome speech to the assembly. Then the band played and the glee club sang, and when they finished and the two, four-horse carriages brought Stephen Douglas and Abraham Lincoln to the stage, a large cheer like the sound of thunder arose from the throng. Three companies of militia, which had escorted the orators, took their place in the crowd as people tightened their ranks and allowed for the official procession to make its way to the front door of Old Main.

As Douglas and Lincoln stepped through an open window and onto the platform, the tall lawyer remarked that he had now gone through Knox College. The crowd nudged each other in good humor and laughter, and then held a collective breath waiting for the debaters' words to penetrate the air. The speeches would be recorded in shorthand and then reported to newspapers throughout the country.

As agreed beforehand, Douglas would speak first, which he did for one hour, in his powerful stentorian voice. Addressing the crowd as "Ladies and Gentlemen," he reviewed the provisions of the 1850 Compromise, the Kansas and Nebraska bill of 1854 and avowed popular sovereignty and supported all states as equals, old and new, free and slave. He derided the Republican Party for its sectionalism filled with "Northern passion, Northern pride, Northern ambition, and Northern prejudices against Southern People, the Southern states, and Southern institutions."[6]

Douglas then turned his attack directly to Lincoln himself accusing his opponent of duplicity by saying that, if Lincoln included all negroes as equal men as stated in the Declaration of Independence, then why had he called them the inferior race in his speech in Charleston? Douglas said his opponent had one speech for southern Illinois and its counties and another for the northern part and its counties. He stated "this Government was made by our fathers on the white basis. . . . Humanity requires and Christianity commands, that you shall extend to every inferior being, and every dependent being, all the privileges, immunities, and advantages which can be granted to them, consistent with the safety of society, [but] . . . [e]ach State must do as it pleases."[7]

George and Charlotte stared at each other and nodded as Douglas spoke. The theme of his anti-abolitionist speech was not unexpected.

As if reading her husband's thoughts, Charlotte said quietly, "I wonder if Mr. Douglas would speak of rape and abuse as consistent with Christianity?"

When Abraham Lincoln arose to speak, the anticipation of the crowd had been thoroughly whetted. However, even some of the Springfield man's strong supporters were very apprehensive, for though they may have hated the substance of Douglas's speech, there was no question that the incumbent was a remarkable and durable speaker.

If he had been intimidated by the ardor of (as he was called familiarly) the "little giant's" speech, Lincoln gave no sign, for he casually slipped off his cloak and handed it to a man behind him. Later when the crowd dispersed, many reported that they had heard him say, "Hold this while I stone Stephen," while others swore that he had said, "The days and the years of the wicked are short."[8]

Stretched to his full height, his arms seem to dangle awkwardly, and at first he paced back and forth as if unprepared to address his opponent. When he did begin to speak, even his voice seemed thin and ineffectual when compared to the splendor of his much shorter opponent. But within a few minutes, he achieved his stride, his arguments and humor emanating from within his soul, and he held the standing crowd rapt for the next hour and a half.

"My Fellow-citizens," he began . . . Lincoln admitted that the great writer of the Declaration of Independence was indeed an owner of slaves, but also added that the founding father "trembled for his country when he remembered that God was just."[9]

He rebutted Douglas's accusation that he gave different speeches to various parts of the state, saying that all of his and his opponent's speeches were printed in both the north and the south. Frequently referring to Douglas as the judge, Lincoln refuted his label of the Republican Party as a sectional party, saying there was nothing in the platform of the party that Douglas, nor those from the South, had attacked.

"I see the day rapidly approaching when this pill of sectionalism, which he has been thrusting down the throats of Republicans for years past, will be crowded down his own throat.[10]. . . . [T]he Judge is not in favor of making any difference between slavery and liberty" and that he doesn't "care whether slavery is voted up or down."[11]

The crowd continued its cheering and applauding with each point, but when Lincoln included his story of the drowned fisherman, whose body was filled with eels, and the fisherman's wife in reference to a suspected collusion between Douglas and two of his friends, they yelled their enthusiasm.

Lincoln's voiced echoed the wife's callous response as she replied to the question of the body: "Well, take the eels out of the pockets and set [him] again."[12]

This was the Lincoln the crowd expected and loved, and his performance did not disappoint. He then defended his position on the Dred Scott decision, something for which Douglas had berated him since Lincoln had openly criticized Chief Justice Roger Taney. Lincoln criticized Douglas's expansionism without regard to the subsequent spread of slavery, reminding the crowd that Douglas had once said that he didn't care whether slavery be "voted up or down."[13]

If that were the case, Lincoln suggested that the United States would then make slaves of all the non-whites of Mexico and South America, wherever expansion would take place. For an hour and a half, Lincoln refuted every argument that Douglas had made.

Perhaps it was the cold of the day that now penetrated the core of every man, woman and child who had stood for nearly three hours, or perhaps their expectations had been fulfilled by what they heard, but when Douglas stood to rebut his opponent, for nearly a half hour, he wisely requested there be no applause to stop his speech. He vigorously, however, refuted Lincoln's charges of impropriety, walking over to his opponent and shaking his fist four times in Lincoln's face. Douglas accused all who opposed the law and particularly the highest law of the land as those who would "raise . . .mobs"[14] to overthrow that law. He concluded by prophesying that without law, "violence [will] overturn the government of laws."[15]

It was over, and as the men in the crowd prepared their horses and wagons to leave and the women collected their baskets and children, for many the day still presented the challenges of returning to their homes. Though a few would remain with relatives and friends in Galesburg, the majority of the huge assembly must wend its way home over many miles of rutted and rain-soaked roads, home to the jobs they had set aside for one day, home to the lives that challenged their survival each day.

The Babbitt and Simmons horses now seemed ready to feel their legs move again as they became one in a long line of wagons heading south from Galesburg to Avon and beyond, to Bushnell, Bardolph and Macomb. As the sun began its descent into the lower sky, wagons moved as quickly as possible to reach their destinations before nightfall.

"Well, George, that was quite the spectacle, wouldn't you say?" questioned Jonathan.

"Yes, I believe there is a definite choice to be made here," replied George, not really sure where this discussion would lead.

"I can't say that I agree with everything Abe says, but he does have a way of spinnin' a tale, doesn't he?" continued Jonathan.

"Yes, he does that," said George.

From the rear of the wagon, Ann suddenly spoke up. "Now you boys just keep in mind what you're about up there and get those horses to movin'. I'm sure we're all a bit tired, and I, for one, am very hungry."

With that Jonathan clicked his tongue, sent a loud "giddy-up" to his team of four and the wagon picked up speed. Harry, once again between the two men, turned towards Zenaide to make sure she was still seated since the rush had jerked everyone.

"Hang on there, ladies. We're going to go as fast as these old boys can safely go," said Jonathan loudly.

Though there was occasional conversation, each passenger seemed to be mulling over the day's events. As they arrived home, the Simmons expressed their sincere thanks to the good neighbors who had come to their rescue, shared their vehicle and food and allowed them to witness an event that they felt would change the destiny of their state.

Charlotte did not mention her meeting with Savannah to the Babbitts, for she was sure their son would relate that incident in great detail.

Ann Babbitt felt that Charlotte was a nice lady, but certainly given to some strange spells. But that younger sister, well, wasn't she just the most outspoken young person there ever was!

Zenaide vowed to meet every negro she could and atone for all the suffering they had experienced at the hands of their white masters.

Harry Babbitt still could not believe the uncommon stroke of good fortune that had allowed him to spend almost all of the day with Miss Nin Mailliard.

"George, I have been thinking of Douglas's accusation, and apparently it is true, that Lincoln said the negroes are an inferior race. What do you think of that statement?" questioned a concerned Charlotte.

"It's funny, Charlotte, that that is the very same idea churning over in my mind. It does amaze me how we often react so similarly," he replied.

Charlotte nodded in agreement. "I wonder if Mr. Lincoln was narrowing his battles, trying to not diminish the cruelty of slavery but to concentrate on preserving the Union, as he said. For my own part, I would say that Savannah and Jonas and her son Josiah are in no way inferior to us or anyone. Can you imagine the courage it has taken for them to merely survive?"

"Courage isn't a strong enough word," said George. "And then there is Frederick Douglass, self-taught I might add, and his brilliant mind. That certainly doesn't imply inferiority."

"But, of course, these are the only negroes we know. There is obviously an entire race. To my way of thinking, in the end each person must be judged for who they are individually, no more or less. But to keep all in slavery due to a chance of skin color, that is so very, very wrong," said Charlotte.

"Charlotte, that is the character of your mind that is so amazing. You view things so logically, you question where questions need to be asked. That is why . . . ," George paused.

"Why what, George? Why you cannot understand how I can accept my Catholicism? I admit I do question things about my faith. But to be completely honest, religion is a closed door with you, your prejudice. I have surmised that in your home, religion was forced on you without the true spirit of Jesus Christ, of love and understanding and peace. But, don't you see, though many have used religion to support their own agenda, the goodness of the tenets of Christianity cannot be denied," said Charlotte.

"Perhaps. For myself, I believe that men, people, can be either good or evil depending on their own character, without the promise of a reward or the specter of a hell hanging over their heads," replied George strongly.

"I see. Then it follows that all who do believe in an afterlife are simpletons, lacking in self-worth, but needing more guidance than is contained in their own beings. They lack spirit," said Charlotte, her voice becoming more intense with each point.

"No, I cannot ever say you lack spirit, or courage, Charlotte. In fact, what you did in Louisville took intense courage. But I also feel that when you did what you did, *you* knew it was the right thing to do, not because you were a follower of Jesus Christ," replied George gently, desperately trying to make his point. "And I lacked the courage to back you but merely searched for your father to take you away before something terrible happened to you. In fact, I often wonder if I will ever be able to match the courage that you display, your openness, your willingness to let others know by your actions what is right." George's voice was low, steeped in self-recrimination.

"Today, for example, when I saw Jonas, I . . . ."

"Yes, you thought too much. But, it is not courage that you are lacking, for without courage you would not have left your home, made your way independently in this world, working, educating yourself. That is definitely courageous. But when faced with a new situation, I believe you immediately think of the consequences. Then you proceed. While I, for better or worse, react impulsively. Perhaps that is because of where we come from, our countries of origin. Do you think the reason could be that simplistic?" asked Charlotte.

"Maybe that is so. It is very hard to change the conditions of one's birth and the environments that influence our early years. Tell me, Charlotte, though, what are your prejudices, besides, of course, all those whose ancestors come from England," queried a smiling George.

She returned George's smile.

"My prejudices, oh dear, let me see. I'm sure I have many, but after today I can only think of one: I am prejudiced against those who will not at least listen to another's point of view, who accept the views of only those who agree or support their opinions and never even bother to consider the *possibility* that they are incorrect. But I do know this: on the issue of slavery, there is only one conclusion. It is wrong, ungodly, unchristian, unholy, and anyone who believes otherwise is, well, going straight to hell," concluded Charlotte.

George smiled, shook his head, and then, putting his arms around his wife's waist, he said, "How did I ever get so lucky?"

They stood there on the porch of their home and looked to the west, where the sun had disappeared below the horizon. The day's strong wind had subsided, and the evening had warmed. Although the air was still, there was a tenseness in the tranquility that could not be denied.

A House Divided

Charlotte bent down and opened the door to the cook stove to check if the fire was warm enough for the morning meal that she had begun to prepare. Emile and Hortensia were within sight which would make things a bit easier to accomplish since she wouldn't have to chase after them. She did feel, however, that her little Emile trailed almost too close to her sometimes despite the fact that he was four.

Hortensia, though only a year older, was so much more independent. Charlotte smiled at the girl sitting in the corner, creating conversations now, as she often did, between her two little dolls. Charlotte thought, laughing to herself, was it always a curse of these Mailliard, well, now, Mailliard/Simmons women to be imbued with this sense of self-reliance?

Unconsciously, she began singing a line from a French song, "*Partant pour la Syrie le jeune et beau Du Mois.*"

Hortensia looked up from her dolls. "What are you singing, Mama? Are those the French words you say sometimes?" Her beautiful, little face was so intense as if worried that something had happened to her Mama to speak so strangely.

"Yes, it is a French song I use to sing long ago," replied Charlotte.

"It seems so sad. What does it mean, Mama?" said the little voice, her head tipped slightly, her blue eyes large and concerned.

"It is about a young soldier who longs to be home," Charlotte said.

"Do our soldiers want to be home?" asked Hortensia.

Even a five-year-old can sense the weightiness of conversation, the talk of war and death and illness, and, yes, wanting to be home since the war had gripped the nation for over a year.

From her own childhood, Charlotte remembered when Princess Charlotte had been crying about someone's death.

To comfort her namesake, she had replied, "Please don't cry. Death means nothing."

How silly she thought, for now she felt death was everything and everywhere, a permanent separation, a loss beyond words, a sudden, cruel twist of indiscriminate fate that struck some, spared others. She and George had lost their two girls, and now this terrible war had already subjected many young lives to death's clutches.

Events had occurred so quickly, it seemed, but wasn't that always the way as one aged? Was it just four years ago? She thought of the debate they had attended, Lincoln's surprising loss in the senatorial race (even though he had won the popular vote), then his more surprising presidential nomination and election against his former "Little Giant" opponent.

But even before Lincoln made his inaugural speech in March of the previous year, South Carolina, a state whose population was sixty percent slaves, had already seceded from the Union. Jefferson Davis had preceded Lincoln's inauguration with his own, in February, as president of the Confederate States of America, which not only included South Carolina but also Mississippi, Florida, Alabama, Georgia, Louisiana and Texas.

Despite assuring the South that he had no intention of abolishing slavery in states where it existed, and thus hoping that calm would reign throughout the nation, Lincoln also warned that an individual state could not make the decision to separate itself from the Union. He would protect the Union from those who would try to seize its property. In a few short weeks following that speech, he sent orders to the military that Fort Sumter in South Carolina, and Fort Pickens, Florida, were to be reinforced.

When Jefferson Davis's Confederate army fired upon Fort Sumter in Charleston, South Carolina, on April 12, it signaled the start of open conflict and a quick victory for the newly formed secessionist states. Then Virginia, Arkansas, Tennessee and North Carolina quickly followed suit and joined the Confederacy

Illinois responded with a patriotic rush of 10,000 volunteers within days of war's start. Gatherings were organized by people in many of the towns to raise money for the cause. Entertainment was provided, some ladies played their pianos and sang, others brought food to sell, hand-made items were donated and then sold. In all the state raised a surprising $1,000,000.

Since they were limiting the merchandise in their own store due to their age, Mary and Owen Willis hosted one such gathering in Avon. Charlotte, who struggled to finish some lace she had been tatting, donated not only that cap, but, as many women in her family and town, knitted woolen socks for the army. Others donated dishes of food and desserts to be auctioned off.

Since their connection three years ago in Galesburg, Charlotte had been writing to Savannah Williams, not only exchanging news but also recipes. For her donation at one of Avon's fundraisers, Charlotte decided to use Savannah's beaten biscuits recipe. Charlotte had noticed that lately, however, there was a definite worried tone to Savannah's letters, relating that although Josiah continued attending Knox College, the negro community as a whole had closed its ranks due to Northern accusations that they had caused the war.

The war, which the North had thought would be short, stretched into the end of its first year. As the townspeople waited for news via the telegraph in the general store or the newspapers that would arrive from Peoria and Springfield, the shock of the Union's army utter defeat at a place in Virginia called Bull Run surprised the people of Avon and all of Illinois. The North's larger population and advanced industrial capabilities had been seen as definite advantages. However, what the North had not factored was the resolve of the South against the threat to its very way of life.

In Avon, the town read about the personal tragedy of the Lincolns when the death of their son Willie occurred in February. That news was followed by the Confederate army forcing the Union army to retreat across the Potomac in March, and the battle of Shiloh, where nearly 2000 Union soldiers were lost, another 8,000 wounded and nearly 3000 were missing. Though the Union army under General Ulysses Grant regained control of the area, his army was so depleted he could not pursue the rebels.

Charlotte looked at the numbers of the dead and wounded and could not help but fear George's decision concerning the war. Despite Charlotte's gentle reminder of his age, thirty-nine, he was determined that, once the fall harvest was completed, he, along with several others from Avon, would join the cause.

The fervor for the war had not diminished within the town, for that spirit was kept alive at the Willis general store, which now served as an unofficial gathering center for army supplies and food for the families of the Union volunteers. Despite Mary's rheumatism that severely stifled her activity and Owen's decline in health, the two kept managing the army supplies with a staff of volunteers, including members of the Mailliard families. The town's animosity towards the Willises due to Henry all but disappeared over the many years.

On several days of the week, Charlotte and Zenaide would come to the store to organize the many donations that the town continued to amass. Each time Mary saw the two sisters, who were quite far apart in age, but so similar in appearance and temperament, she could not help but feel an overwhelming sense of melancholy. The younger one may have a bit more fire, she surmised. Or was it just that Charlotte had suffered the loss of two children, and now was a mother to the two youngsters who often trailed her?

Each time she entered the Willis store, Charlotte could not quell the feeling that Henry would come around a stack of groceries or supplies and suddenly be there in front of her as he had the first day she had seen his face. His face, if he were even still alive, what would that face look like now?

For her part Mary Willis could not feel that, but for one cruel act of fate, she would have been linked to these sisters and the entire Mailliard family. The children with Charlotte could have been her grandchildren, but the connection was not to be. Henry, her dear Henry, now gone so many years, never failed to write to them, but now, with each passing day of the war, Mary and Owen both realized that indeed his life was increasingly threatened. He continued to send the money that he was now earning as part of the California Union army. The Willises dutifully kept all of Henry's funds in a separate box, hopeful that, someday it would be opened upon his return. However, when the families of war widows, those whose husbands had gone to war, were in need, they supplemented food donations with cash from Henry's box, as they called it. How fitting, thought Mary, that her "son," an orphan as they both had been, was now able to help others in their time of need.

"Emile, Hortensia, come children. It is time for us to go home. Say your good-byes to Mr. and Mrs. Willis, now," said Charlotte smiling.

"How you are growing! Each time I see you, you are getting closer to being as tall as I am. Please, come give me a hug before you leave," said Mary.

As Hortensia smiled and moved quickly to give the older woman, like another *grandmere* she thought, a hug, and Emile trailed more cautiously behind, the door of the store was suddenly thrown open.

"Charlotte, Zenaide, are you here?" shouted Amedee.

"Yes, we're here, Amedee. What is it?" asked Charlotte, although the look on her brother's face told her immediately that it was something serious. Her first thought was for her parents, for they both seemed to be failing with each passing day.

Grabbing her hands in his, Amedee said, "It's George, Charlotte. He was thrown from his horse and his back is hurt, badly."

Charlotte ran out the door with Zenaide trailing behind, holding Hortensia and Emile by their hands.

Mary sat down in her chair by the counter of the store and said out loud, "Dear God, don't let anyone else be lost to that dear girl."

"We'd like you to be part of the group of ladies to help with, well, their personal things in the store. Do you think you could do that, Charlotte, you and Zenaide? Would it be possible for you to find someone to stay with George and the children?" asked a concerned Stephen Tompkins.

A longtime resident of Avon, Tompkins seemed the one to turn to when official business needed to be done, if George was not available.

"You were friends I know, and there was a connection at one time, I heard."

A connection, is that what they call it now? thought Charlotte. "Yes, I think I can ask either of my other sisters at home to come and be with the children. George will most likely rest this afternoon. It seems to help with the pain a bit," she replied.

Yes, the pain. It had been six weeks since the accident. At first, George lay deathly pale in the bed unable to move, barely speaking, barely eating. The pain had been so intense he often groaned despite his resolve not to do so. She would notice him biting his lip to keep from making noises, and then sweat would bead on his face and run down the sides of his face. The doctor offered to give George some laudanum to help ease the pain, but both George and Charlotte had heard of the addictive qualities of the drug. Yes, although they kept it in their home, George had severely limited his intake to only one dose every four or five days. On those days he was able to get the rest his body so desperately needed to recover.

The doctor had also told them that George might never be able to walk again. A back injury could not be treated in any way that he knew. Only time would tell.

Apparently, six weeks was not time enough, for George's recovery had not progressed. Each morning he would begin anew with the hope that today would be a better day, but within a half hour of pretending that there had not been an injury, the pain once again became intense. He insisted on walking to the outhouse instead of using the chamber pot and seeing his wife deal with his waste, yet each trip was agony.

Six weeks had also passed in the war, during which time newspapers had reported on the Seven Days' Battles. Then, one day when the driver who brought the papers opened the door to the Willis store, he found them both dead. Mary lay in her bed with a startled expression on her face, and Owen was found a few steps away on the floor face down as if he had been rushing to her side.

Death, thought Charlotte, death everywhere. Today she, Zenaide and some other ladies would now go through the private rooms of Mary and Owen, like uncomfortable thieves prying into the suddenly opened windows of their lives.

"George," she whispered, "I will be going to the Willises to help organize and dispose of their belongings. I've brought you some fresh water in the pitcher, and Mary and Theresa are here to watch the children. I'm hoping that reading will put them to sleep for a while. The day has turned into quite a warm one. I hope you are comfortable."

"Please, don't worry. There is nothing you can do for me. I hope I can rest," he said, trying to manage a smile. "Go along now."

Charlotte grabbed her bonnet from the back of the door and gave her children a kiss on their cheeks.

"You must promise to be good for Aunt Mary and Aunt Theresa. Mama is going to the store."

"Mama, will Papa ever be able to walk again?" asked a very pensive Hortensia.

"Mama, how did Papa fall off his horse?" asked Emile his brow wrinkling in a way that made Charlotte want to hug him fiercely and wipe away the obvious worry in his voice. Even her younger child had sensed that Papa was more than "just sick."

"Well, Emile, sometimes accidents just happen. Papa is a very strong rider on his horse, but something frightened the horse that day, and when it reared up, Papa fell off and hit his back on the ground and the rocks were very hard. But you must not worry, he will get better. We must be patient. Do you know what that means, Emile, to be patient?" asked Charlotte.

"Does it mean that I shouldn't ask questions, Mama?" replied the little voice.

"No, my dear, you may always ask questions, if you speak politely and respectfully and wait your turn. You must also remember to say 'thank you' and 'please' when you want to know something," said Charlotte.

"Thank you, Mama," said the little boy cheerfully. Mama always seemed to have the best smiles.

"Be good, now. I must catch up to Aunt Zenaide."

It felt so strange to be in the very rooms where Mary and Owen Willis had spent their private lives. The front of the building was their store, open to everyone, but here, in these back two rooms, were their papers and letters, their clothes in one medium-sized dresser, the assortment of treatments for various ills—quinine, bitters, tincture of aconite for Mary's joints—on the top of that dresser. Charlotte began packing the clothes into a box. Later, she would air them on her line at home and then distribute them where they would be most beneficial. Socks would be sent to the army along with Owen's serviceable clothes.

She found their wedding certificate and could not help but notice that they had married the same year as her parents, 1823. Her parents had been so blessed with ten children, seven still living, but the Willises had not been so fortunate. Except, of course, for Henry.

As Charlotte and Zenaide entered the second room in the back of the building, it was clear that, at one time, there was another resident here. The small bed was still covered with a quilt, but now it contained tiers of boxes used for storing army supplies. A dresser, smaller than theirs, must have once contained *his* clothes.

Charlotte stood in front of the dresser, loath to open the three narrow drawers. If she were to see any of Henry's clothes, well, she wasn't sure how she would react. Of course, she knew how she would act, she reminded herself, as if nothing were amiss. Even with Zenaide there were things that could not be shared.

"This just doesn't feel right, does it Charlotte?" said Zenaide, a sadness in her voice as she too entered the second room. "I know someone needs to do this job, but I still feel so strange about being in their private rooms. It is so sad that they never had any children of their own, isn't it?"

"Yes, it is, although there was a young man that lived with them for eight years. His name was Henry Moreau," said Charlotte, trying to keep her voice as even as possible.

"I do remember hearing that name a few times, I think, but then I think Mama would say something like, 'no more, I will hear no more.' I don't know something like that. It seems like a good French name, though. Was he French also?" questioned the sister.

"Only half, his mother was an Indian."

"Really? Do you know I have never even seen an Indian? Sometimes I really feel as if I know absolutely nothing. Charlotte, what's wrong? Are you getting worried about leaving George alone?" said an alarmed Zenaide, noticing the strange expression on her sister's face. "Here, let me finish that."

Zenaide moved towards the dresser that Charlotte had stood in front of for what seemed like several minutes and began to empty the drawers.

"Well, it just seems as if Mary stored some ribbons in here to keep them clean, I suppose. Oh, there's also this metal box with a letter tied to it. 'In case of our deaths, please give to our friend Stephen Tompkins'. This is just like a mystery. Wouldn't you love to see what's in here?" continued Zenaide. "But we can't, of course."

Charlotte said nothing, allowing herself time to recover while her sister continued to work.

"Mr. Tompkins, it seems we found something that you're going to be in charge of," called Zenaide in a strong voice as she started walking to the front of the building.

Charlotte steadied herself on the edge of the dresser, put the last of the ribbons in a box, and then left the room.

Dear Stephen,

If you are reading this letter, it probably means that Mary and I have left this Earth and gone, hopefully, to our eternal reward. We put you in charge of disposing of our goods as you see fit, but with a preference to give anything you feel is serviceable to our Union army.

The money in this box we have saved from the amount sent to us by our dear "son," Henry Moreau. He was our pride and joy for the eight years he lived with us, and there is not a day that passes when we know that he was so wrongly accused of taking money from the Spensers. That is history, however, and though Henry may never return to this town because of it, Mary and I hold no ill will against anyone. I guess it was just a time when some people were distrusted. We would like the money to be used for families of soldiers and other families as you see fit. We do love our town of Avon and always felt that our community should take care of its own.

We also ask that you never tell anyone that Henry is still alive, nor allow anyone to contact him. That was Henry's wish. But we do ask that you tell him that we have gone, so his letters to us will stop. In the last few years, he has been part of the army in California. Any letters we received from him we felt we had to burn.

Thank you.

Owen Willis *May 6, 1861*

Stephen read the letter several times before he could wholly digest its contents and the responsibility that had been thrust upon him. He was astounded when he counted the money and found the incredible sum of nearly $3000 packed tightly in the tin box.

The heat of summer had not dimmed the avidity of the Confederate forces, and in early September the newspapers carried the story of the second battle of Bull Run, another horribly bloody battle in which 25,000 plus soldiers from both sides became casualties: 3200 dead, 16,000 wounded and nearly 6000 Union soldiers missing. President Lincoln replaced General John Pope with General George McClellan following the horrible Union defeat.

As Charlotte read the newspaper to her husband, she commented, "It is a good given name, don't you think? He should do well." She tried to lighten the seriousness of the mood despite the tragic news in a desperate attempt to ease George's pain.

George smiled and leaned forward from his rocker, reaching for her hand. But, as he did so, he could not hide the wince of pain that registered on his face.

"It all happened so fast, Charlotte. And now everything is changed. I wake each day and hope things will be different, but they are not. I feel I must investigate any possibility of getting better, and I have been in contact with a doctor in Quincy, Samuel Carter, who has been helping war veterans with their injuries. He has agreed to examine me and see if his treatment can be of help. I am not sure what that treatment would be, but I think I, we, need to try something."

"Your family, your wonderful family, has been so kind during this injury, helping with our crops, bringing water into our home, watching the children so you can help me. I know that without them, we would be quite lost. I never realized what a system of support they are. It is good to have a large family. God willing, we may have another healthy child. Is it January that you think the child will come?" asked George.

"Yes," said Charlotte smiling. I feel it will be a strong one, for its kicking is just as strong as Emile's was, even at this stage

"Would you feel well enough to travel with me, Charlotte? You don't feel it would be a risk, do you?"

"I think it would be very easy for me to convince Mary and Theresa to come here and stay in our home for a short time," said Charlotte smiling. If there was any hope on earth for George to recover, she would gladly risk a small trip to Quincy.

When they left a few short days later, the summer heat had reached its peak. With Amedee and Alexander's help, George sat in the wagon that would take the Simmonses to the train.

Sweat rolling down his face, Amedee said, "I can't remember such a spell of weather. The fields are so dry the dust just seems to rise up like a cloud with the slightest breeze. I hope the wheat isn't burned before we harvest it."

"Amedee and Alexander, thank you again," said George. "I'm not sure what we would do without your help."

"It's nothing that you wouldn't have done for us," said Alexander smiling. "Perhaps by the time you return, the heat will break. We will be back to pick you up in ten days. That will be enough time, don't you think?"

"If I am not better by the end of that time, I'm afraid I never will be," said George.

"The good news, Mr. Simmons, is that you have been able to even walk a few steps. The back is composed of many bones, as you know, but the other significant component of its makeup, we believe, is that it holds the many nerves that control the arms and legs. You are one of the lucky ones since you not only have feeling in but also the ability to use those limbs. It is a strange thing about these nerves. I have prescribed laudanum for many of the amputees who claim to have significant pain—in a leg that no longer exists. But that, of course, is not your case," said Dr. Carter.

Did George detect an insinuation that his injury was not as noble as one received in the war? No, that was ridiculous. He was being too sensitive, feeling guilty because he had not enlisted. This hospital, as many others, was overwhelmed with those being treated for war injuries. Ironically, those who had had their limbs amputated in the battlefield were more likely to survive since the rate of infection was much less before transport. Often, such field amputations were done a mere fifteen or twenty minutes after the injury had been inflicted. If the soldier survived, he could then be transported to a nearby hospital, were one available.

Life was so incredible unpredictable, George reflected. He had been spared the war, spared by the chance occurrence of his horse being spooked by an uncommon rattler that had strayed from its home.

"Is there any treatment you can suggest?" George asked.

"Based on the bruising, which you say was extensive and now seems to have faded, and the fact that you could make this trip, I believe you may continue to improve. Perhaps you could try to ease your pain with warm treatments, for, even if you heal now, you will surely be pained by rheumatism as you age. Of course, the pain can always be eased with the laudanum, but you know that I advise caution with its use. The fortunate thing is that you have a wife who has traveled with you, and from our conversation her family seems to have helped you with your crops. Do what you feel you can. Broken bones need time to heal, and the nerves in those bones, well, who knows? But I do know for sure that healing cannot be rushed, and when, and if, they do heal, they need time to regain their strength. That is all I can tell you. How old are you now, Mr. Simmons?" asked Dr. Carter.

"Thirty-nine," replied George.

"Well, you generally seem to be in good health, but of course you are no longer young. Did I see that your wife was expecting a child?" continued the doctor.

"Yes, it will be our fifth, although we lost two girls when they were each two years old," said George.

"Pray for a son, Mr. Simmons. He will be needed," concluded the doctor.

"Yes, well, my wife does the praying in our family," replied George.

The trip back to Avon was not that difficult for George, for Charlotte easily arranged the wagon, the fare, the help needed to assist George to the train. The journey was not too long, only four hours, but the continued unusual weather proved to be the greatest challenge. As the engine labored along the tracks, the heat from the steam spread throughout the train cars, increasing every passenger's discomfort.

George moved almost constantly in his seat, trying to find a position that would bring him some comfort. If he settled in one position, within a few seconds the pain would strengthen once again. He tried to read the *Quincy Herald* newspaper that Charlotte had purchased at the station, but his mind was too distracted by his discomfort to allow for concentration.

Charlotte's voice, which relayed the stories of General McClellan's victories at South Mountain and Crampton's Cap, was lost in the noise of the engine, and the wind and the dryness of the air accentuated George's increasing pain. Though he appreciated the speed of the train, all he could think of was getting to his home and lying on his bed, and taking a dose of laudanum.

"George, are you alright? We've passed Bushnell. We'll be home soon. I can't wait until we see the children," said Charlotte lightly. She had tried so hard to distract him from the pain she knew he must be experiencing. Not too much longer, she thought.

"I can see Amedee now, George," said Charlotte. "I'm so glad he is here to help us. Oh, I see Papa, too. My, that is unusual. I'm surprised he has come in this heat."

Amedee took the bag from Charlotte and helped George move down the steps of the train. Her brother's face was set and he said nothing.

"Papa, it is so good to be home. But why are you here? I'm so surprised to see you out in the afternoon," said Charlotte. "I hope the children are napping."

"Yes, dear. Did your trip go well? Was the doctor able to help George?" asked Eloi.

George said, "The doctor told me I was one of the lucky ones and may continue to improve, but I have to be patient."

Amedee drove the wagon east toward their road, the one townspeople still quaintly called French street. The afternoon was still, and as Charlotte looked off to the end of town towards the south, the air seemed to wave in wafts of heat. She unbuttoned the two top buttons of her dress and could feel the perspiration running down her back and between her breasts.

"Amedee, my, you are a quiet one this afternoon. Has the weather gotten to you also?" asked Charlotte.

"Yes, the fields have been dry, the ground very hard," he said mechanically.

"I was hoping the children would be awake when we got home. I cannot wait to see them," she said.

"Come, Charlotte, George, we want you to, to have a cold glass of water with us before we take you home," said Eloi.

"Oh, Papa, that is very considerate, but we just want to go home now. It has been a tiring experience for us both," said Charlotte.

George nodded slightly, grateful that his wife had expressed his thoughts for him.

"Please, Charlotte, George, you must come with us now," replied a somber Eloi.

The wagon stopped in front of Eloi and Amanda's home, and the door opened slowly. Zenaide, holding Emile's hand stepped onto the porch. She said nothing but Charlotte noticed her sister's free hand as it opened and closed in a fist.

Charlotte nearly shouted her question. "Where is Mama?"

Mama now labored to the door and answered softly, "I am here, Charlotte."

Then Charlotte knew. As if someone had slapped her face, she brought her hand to her mouth and moaned, "No, no, please tell me my Hortensia is sleeping." But even as she asked, she knew the answer. She let her body slump down on the porch step while Eloi sat down beside her.

George, despite Amedee's help, had nearly fallen in his path as he tried to climb the two steps onto the porch.

"Lean on me, George. We are going inside," said Amedee.

They were all there, waiting, as if the weight of their news could be diffused by sheer number. Uncle John sat at the table. Mary and Theresa, their faces weighted with anxiety, held pitchers of water, and then, as if by cue, began to pour mechanically into the glasses arranged on the table. Heloise and Orlando with Pauline and Alexander stood motionless near the fireplace.

"Sit down, Charlotte and George, please," said Eloi softly.

Amanda moved to the table, sat beside Charlotte and held her daughter's hands.

John now spoke, his voice strange, as if his words had been rehearsed. "We sat together at this table the very evening you left. We had tried to lighten the situation for Hortensia and Emile's concern, for they, especially Hortensia, were so concerned about your train ride and what would happen with their Papa. We were singing songs, silly songs and then all laughing, when Hortensia gasped and could not breathe. We assumed she had some food caught in her throat and it would not get out. It simply would not get out," he repeated, his voice rising in intensity and volume. "We are so sorry, so very, very sorry."

The room was silent. Charlotte shook her head. George, seated in the rocker close to the door, stared at nothing. Zenaide held Emile in her arms, and even the child seemed to hold his breath, waiting, as they all were, silently, waiting for a clap of thunder or a strong gust of wind to break the ear-splitting sound of nothing.

Amedee then stepped towards his sister and brother-in-law and said, "We had no choice. We had to bury her. Even in the root cellar, the heat . . ." He stopped. "She is next to her sisters, Charlotte. I am so sorry."

"Please, help me, us, go to her grave now," said George almost inaudibly.

"Yes, please," said Charlotte.

It was a somber procession that walked to the cemetery at the south edge of town. George leaned on his brothers-in-law; Charlotte walked slowly with her parents, who insisted on being part of the solemn group. Then the other family members followed: John with his cane, Zeniade with Emile and all the sisters, their husbands and children. And, as they walked, their ranks grew with the neighbors from French street, then the Babbits and the Woods and the other townspeople came, hoping that they could diminish the grief that had once again affected their own, Charlotte and George.

They reached the cemetery that was home to the three graves of the Simmons children. The older two markers of the first two daughters had faded somewhat, but they still told their story alongside their sister, newly laid to rest:

Louisa Marina Simmons 1849-1851
Carlotine Simmons 1854-1856
Hortensia Maria Simmons 1857-1862

It was the strong voice of Alexander that broke the silence as he began the song that had come to embody the sorrow of the Civil War and all death. The gusting, dry wind could not drown the strength of the words, "Amazing Grace, how sweet the sound, that saved a wretch like me . . . ."

As Charlotte read to George the news of the battle of Antietam Creek in Maryland, where over 23,300 had been lost in one day, she could not help but empathize with those left behind by the losses, as she and George now struggled to cope with their loss. Charlotte busied herself with the chores of each day filling each minute with work, work that would exhaust her so that she could sleep at night.

George had not spoken Hortensia's name since their return from Quincy. Charlotte knew he was not sleeping at night, for despite her weariness, his slightest movement seemed to wake her, and then the stab of their loss would assault her once again, and she would lie awake for hours.

During the day she would not let Emile from her sight, yet George seemed to not notice him at all.

One late afternoon she told George she was leaving to visit Pauline for a while and was taking Emile with her.

He replied with one word, "Yes," and continued to sit immobile in the rocker, where he spent much of his day.

She could feel the frustration growing within him, the frustration of not being able to do the work that should be done now, the subsequent dependency upon others that hurt his pride, the inexplicable, sudden loss of their beautiful daughter.

As she walked out the door, she took a few steps towards her sister's home, but then changed direction and walked south to the cemetery. Each time she thought of Hortensia's death, her grief became more acute. She had not been able to hold her precious child one last time, to say good-bye with a kiss or a touch.

When they reached the cemetery, Charlotte's pace became more determined. Emile's little legs tried very hard to keep up with his Mama.

"This isn't the way to Aunt Pauline's house," said Emile.

"I know it isn't, dear. I thought we might want to visit with Hortensia."

"But she isn't in that place where we were the other day. I haven't seen her in a while. I miss her, Mama. Did she go to visit someone?"

"Yes, she is staying with God now, in Heaven. Heaven is a wonderful place."

"I should want to go to Heaven too," said Emile.

"No, no, not yet. You must not say that, Emile," shouted Charlotte, slumping to the ground and grabbing her son in her arms, holding him so tightly he could barely breathe.

The child did not squirm as he might have done any other time. He merely said, "Alright, Mama, I'm here now. I won't go visit anyone else."

"Yes, you are here, little man, aren't you?" said Charlotte as she released the little boy and held him at arm's length. Please, God, she thought, let me be grateful for each day that I have the gift of this child.

"Come, Emile, and kneel down beside me now. We will say a prayer for Hortensia and the other little sisters you didn't know."

She knelt in front of the three graves, the one still heaving with its cover of new earth, the others flat and leveled by time. She prayed that Hortensia would feel the power of a mother's love and that they both could be at peace.

"Mama and I have been praying for my sisters," announced Emile, very proud to share his news.

George turned his head toward his son and asked stonily, "And what did you pray?"

The little boy looked quizzically at his father. "Well, we just knelt down on the ground. It was very hard and it hurt my knees. But I was, was patient," said Emile proudly.

"So you forced the child to kneel with you, Charlotte?" George's voice sounded very strange.

Charlotte turned her head quickly towards her husband and answered. "I suppose so. It is a comfort to pray, George."

"Comfort?" He questioned. "And tell me what comfort does your praying bring you, Charlotte? What comfort does your God, your Catholic religion give you? When I think of you down on your knees, going to church, gyrating with the rest of your Papists, it makes me ill. Does it heal your heart, your pain? Tell me, does it?"

It was as if all the frustration of his life, of his coping with the injury over the last four months, of the loss and grieving for his daughters had suddenly erupted in this one moment.

Charlotte had never heard him speak so strongly, had never heard him utter an unkind word to anyone. She stared at this face she had known for so long, and it was the face of someone she had never seen before.

"Well, I am waiting. Tell me, what comfort does your popery provide?"

Charlotte wanted to yell back in anger, to remind him that *she* was the one who had borne these daughters, the one who had nursed them, who had fed them, who had rocked them when they were ill. She breathed deeply, however, and staring directly into his eyes, she forced her voice to be steady, steady and logical.

"It gives me comfort, George, to know that I am not alone, that I can share my grief with God. It gives me comfort as I hope it comforts all who have suffered the loss of someone dear, to share my grief with family, yes, if you wish, my Catholic family. I am sorry, George, that apparently you have never been close enough to anyone to feel you can share your sorrow. It is a choice you have made, George, a choice to be alone. For that, you are to be pitied, not for the other misfortunes that you have experienced."

Emile looked at the faces of his parents, and the sound of their voices made him shiver. He wanted to go sit by his sister and have her say, "It's alright, Emile. I'm here." But his sister wasn't here. When was she going to come home from this place called heaven?

Charlotte did not know the field in which she was standing. She peered into the distance and could not recognize any of the homes. Was this west of the train tracks? But when she turned around there wasn't any track. She continued to walk and passed a stream, but it wasn't Gallet Creek. Was it possible that there were so many parts of Avon that she had never seen?

And then she heard the sound of a young voice, the laughter of a child, the sweetest sound in the world. She kept moving toward the sound, and just when it seemed as if she were getting close, it moved away.

"Hello," she called. "Don't run away, please. Are you lost?"

The laughter seemed to be getting closer again, and then there was a shed. As Charlotte turned the corner around the shed, she saw the child ahead of her, skipping and running, and she saw the yellow sash of the child's dress trailing behind, so close it was almost within reach.

"Please, wait," Charlotte called.

She could hear the child breathing now, and when she reached the walnut tree, the child sat on the other side of its large trunk.

The laughter was more sporadic now, and Charlotte knew who the child was.

She reached around the tree and grasped the child's hand and felt the tenderness of the skin she knew so well.

The child peered around the trunk and looked into her eyes and smiled.

Charlotte opened her arms to the child, who allowed her mother to enfold her.

Charlotte smelled the sweet scent of the child's perspiration on the top of her head. She felt the smooth skin of the child's forearm and traced her fingers to the palm of the child's hand, bringing that hand to her mouth and kissing each of its fingers.

Charlotte asked, "Why did you have to go away?"

The child did not answer, but continued to smile.

"Have you come to say good-bye?" Charlotte asked.

Charlotte felt the child slipping away, and then she was sitting in the rocker and the doll, Hortensia's doll, which she had been holding, fell from her lap.

Her first thought was to share the dream with George, but then she remembered the words that they had spoken—his words, her words, her very cruel words. She went into the children's room and placed the doll back on her daughter's empty bed. Across the room Emile was sleeping soundly. She touched his brow and, despite the warmth of the day, drew the covers more closely around his shoulders.

Then she went into their room. George seemed to be asleep, but she could not be sure, for his face was turned to the wall. Quietly, she removed the shawl from her shoulders and slipped under the covers. She hoped the movement would not disturb him.

Charlotte's birthday, her thirty-fifth, passed without celebration and was followed two weeks later by Christmas. The three Simmons ate their Christmas dinner with the rest of the family at Eloi and Amanda's home. The Mailliard grandchildren, eight of them now, seemed so pleased with the homemade treats and toys that they received. Normally, George would have carved the children some soldiers for the boys or dolls for the girls, and then Charlotte would have clothed them with costumes, but not this year.

For George did no carving. He sat apart from the group, apart from conversation and the laughter that, despite their loss and the continuing war, seemed to quiet for a while the sorrow outside the Mailliard door. Charlotte, now nearing her fifth child's delivery time, always felt her spirits lifted when she was with her siblings, Uncle John, and, of course, Mama and Papa.

As they walked the short distance back to their own home, Charlotte dreaded the return to the silence that reigned there. Though they had spoken to each other since the outburst, their conversation was cursory, stemmed from necessity and pertained only to the running of the house and care for Emile.

Now, as Charlotte held Emile's mittened hand in hers and walked slowly to keep from striding ahead of her husband, the crunch of the snow was a welcome sound on the crisp December evening.

"Charlotte, do you realize how truly lucky you are to have the family that you have? And I, I am lucky to have you as my connection to that family," said George deliberately. "Life can change so quickly. We shouldn't waste any time with regrets."

Charlotte stopped suddenly. George's words did not include "I'm sorry," but they were a leap towards a return to the easy conversation that had always been a part of their lives.

"I have known how important family is for a long time, George. Our own little family too, though my heart still feels a stab of pain whenever I think of our girls. But, to know we have others to share our burdens with, that is a blessing," said Charlotte.

She wanted to add, I have missed you, George. You have shut everyone out of your life, but she felt she must tread cautiously.

"Yes, I am part of that burden," he said slowly.

"Only when you think you are," she replied quickly.

They had stopped, and suddenly Emile wiggled free from Charlotte's hand and ran ahead, throwing handfuls of the light snow up in the air.

"My words were hateful, Charlotte."

"And mine equally so," she replied.

When they returned to their home and Emile was sleeping in his bed, Charlotte began the task that she performed almost every evening since their return from Quincy. She stoked the fire, boiled the water with the rags, reached into the pot with her wooden spoon, and then wrung as much of the water as she could quickly into a pail, trying not to waste any drops. Then she moved to their bed and placed the warm rags on George's back. After they cooled a few minutes later, she would then massage, as strongly as she possibly could, the area from which the pain still emanated. Tonight she did not mind the pain of her own sore and chafed hands, and the task seemed easier than usual.

Zenaide brought the news as quickly as she could to Charlotte and George, news that President Lincoln had issued a document called the Emancipation Proclamation, which declared that all slaves were free. Several measures had already been enacted to end slavery, but this solidified the abolitionist fervor that gripped the Northern Republicans.

Charlotte tried to greet Zenaide with the same enthusiasm, but her mind was elsewhere. Since early this morning, she had been queasy, and for the last several hours the pain in her back had become quite intense. It was strange how each birth carried its own signature. After five, one would think there would be a pattern, but just as each child had its own personality, each birth followed its own path. One thing she resolved, however, one way or another, this would be her last pregnancy.

"Zenaide, please run and get Pauline and Heloise. I think the baby is about to be born. And take Emile with you please," said Charlotte, trying to keep her voice as calm as possible.

"Good-bye, Emile. You're going to spend the day with Aunt Zenaide and your cousins. Try to stay warm in *grandmere's* house, now," said Charlotte.

"Is Papa staying here?" asked Emile.

"Yes, he is going to be helping Aunt Pauline and Aunt Heloise," said Charlotte. "Run along now."

There was no time to waste.

"George, come quickly. I need you. Now."

George had helped, somewhat, in the birth of Emile, but he wasn't sure if he could manage alone. He helped Charlotte move to their bedroom, and then removed first her petticoat and the linen, that had already become moistened with the water from the birth canal. He threw a sheet over her legs for modesty's sake, and then bravely said, "I'm sure your sisters will be here soon."

"It doesn't matter, George. There is no time. I can feel the baby coming now. Make sure your hands are clean and get the fresh blanket that I have been keeping on the dresser. Oh, Lord, it's very close now. This baby is not waiting," said Charlotte through her pain.

George steadied himself at the end of the bed, and with one more push from Charlotte, the baby slipped onto the blanket, the cord trailing behind. "It's a boy," he said happily. Deciding to wait for one of his sisters-in-law to cut the cord, he put the newborn at the end of the bed.

Charlotte strained to see the child, but her wet head collapsed onto the pillow. She smiled at the father, who now held his new son. "My two Georges," she said, for she had decided on the name two weeks ago. She also had made up her mind that she would not insist that this child be baptized into the Catholic faith, at least for now. Life does come with compromises.

"I'll need a name in this blank, soldier," said Corporal Westin as he reviewed the papers of one of the new arrivals to Camp Meigs.

Since their arrival in Readville, Massachusetts, a few days ago, this soldier and his fellow enlistees from California had made quite an impression on the army. Their path from the west had taken a most adventurous route to become part of what would be called Company A of the 2nd Massachusetts Cavalry, known as the California Hundred.

Although they had been part of the federal army in California, as the war lingered, this unit wanted to do more than stave off the remaining natives or guard wagon trains. Using their own money, the experienced group of fighters—sharp shooters, skilled riders—left San Francisco on December 11th, 1862. They traveled through the Isthmus of Panama and up the eastern seaboard to New York and then on to Boston. There would be further preparation in basic training, and then they would travel to Fort Monroe, Virginia, and be placed on active duty.

The corporal looked up from the paper that this enlistee had signed, attesting to his horsemanship and good health. Yes, he certainly seemed fit, though he might be a bit older than most soldiers he had seen. He was taller than most, too, and despite the beard and moustache that most of the unit had, there was something just a bit different about him. Name, too, he had never seen a name like that before.

"You really need to have someone to notify, you know. It's always a good thing. Are your parents gone?" questioned the corporal.

The tall man started to say something, but then just said, "Yes, they're dead."

"Well, sorry to hear. How about an aunt, or a sister maybe?"

The soldier thought a few seconds more, and then he said, "Yes, my sister," and he filled in the line on the form.

"I tell you, George, I don't like it. I don't like it, not one bit." It was the voice of Jonathan Babbit that echoed through the building that was once the Willis general store. His comment expressed loudly what many men, and the women at home, had spoken of with friends or spouses.

Now the assembled men nodded their heads and mumbled their disapproval.

George tried to keep the conversation logical. "It's true, gentlemen. The draft will be unpopular, and for me personally, I will be the one enforcing it. But what is the President to do? Shall we let the South have its way, making those who have lost their lives already be lost for nothing?"

"I've sent one son to this bloody war. I don't want to lose another one, one way or another," said Otis Taylor.

"Yes, and twenty to forty-five. Forty-five? Why a man is lucky if he can still survive a winter or has two good legs left to walk on. Sorry, George, I meant no reference to you," continued Jonathan.

"And what about our crops?" continued Otis.

Orlando and Alexander stood in the back of the room, waiting for the opportunity to support their brother-in-law. It was Alexander who spoke. "We can accept the law begrudgingly, or we can react like men. I, for one, don't want to have some Johnny Reb in my backyard tellin' my children they have to start whistlin' Dixie."

Orlando then added, "And as far as crops go, you know we help each other make do. That's what we've always done in this town, support each other. Steve Tompkins has distributed the

Willises money to help those families whose men are off to war. God bless Mary and Owen for thinking of others so kindly."

"There is the exemption, of course," continued George.

"Well, that is even more of an insult. Which of us has $300 to give to the government, so we don't have to go to war? Isn't a poor man's blood just as valuable as a rich man's?" added a disgruntled Otis. "It seems as if 'Czar Abraham' has done it again."

Otis loved to quote from the *Illinois Register*, the Springfield newspaper which had opposed Lincoln since his election and throughout the war.

"I thought someone might have some ammunition ready from that source," said George, "so in fairness, may I counteract that slur with an editorial from the *Journal*, our other Springfield newspaper?"

Without waiting for a response, George picked up the paper and began, "Statements of the *Register* are coolly coquetting with treason and with fiendish and infernal malignity endeavoring to paralyze the arm of the Government upon the maintenance of which depends the preservation of our liberties."

Putting the paper down and looking into the eyes of the assembled men, George continued. "Look, the army needs money as much as it needs men. I'm sorry this doesn't seem equitable to you, Otis. No one ever said life is fair, nor any law perfectly suited to every man, but I do believe our President is trying to do his best. He does not make decisions without consulting his entire cabinet, a very diverse cabinet I might add composed of men with good minds. For myself, I will do my best to set my affairs in order, and then enlist."

"But, George," said Alexander, "you still can't ride a horse. I know you have gotten better, or at least you seem to be in less pain, but can you see yourself marching through swamps? Have you even walked a mile since your accident?"

Otis somewhat relented. "George, when push comes to shove, we know what the right thing to do is. Plain and simple, you have said your piece. We know our Northern cause is the right one. It's just that every one of us knows someone who has been lost. And now the thought of more of our boys going, well, it hurts, especially in cases where a family has sent one boy already or where the father has left children under the care of the oldest son, who now would have to be conscripted."

"I realize that, Otis. But here's a thought I would like to put forth. Steve, are the funds from the Willises still plentiful enough to give money to save boys from the draft who are needed by their families?"

"Well, I think we could pay for two, or maybe three. I'm sure Mary and Owen would have agreed to that," replied Steve.

"Otis, Jonathan, Steve, would you be willing to work with me to decide which boys to save from this draft? I wouldn't want to be the sole decider in these matters, but, in my role as justice of the peace, I feel I could be the organizer," said George.

Orlando and Alexander nodded their approval.

Otis said, "I think it's a good idea, George. A few heads together are always better than one."

"Charlotte, I know you disapprove of my going into the war, but you have to lead by example. I cannot expect others to go when I am not going myself," said George. "Others have young children and crops to tend too."

"Of course they do, George. But I know this also: they do not have a constant pain in their right leg, a pain that will become worse with lack of care. We have read of the conditions in the army. There is not enough food or adequate clothing on either side. More than that, George, would you really be the type of soldier on whom others could depend? I'm sorry, that is the truth. I don't want to hurt your pride, but the accident has changed your strength," she answered.

George looked at his wife. He knew that she was right. He raised his cane and brought it down hard.

"A man's pride is a fragile thing, and I know very keenly that your pride has been wounded by your dependency on others, but this decision would be completely foolhardy. But there is something . . . ," said Charlotte.

He watched his wife go into their bedroom, and as she walked away, he hung his head.

From the top of her dresser, Charlotte lifted the small wooden box, George's gift to her, the box, on which he had engraved her initials. She picked it up carefully and removed the top. Inside, lying snugly in the comfort of the red velvet lining, were the two rubies, her gift from the Bonaparte family, from Napoleon's niece.

"If you are suggesting what I think you are suggesting, I won't have it," said George as she returned to their kitchen.

"Why not?" said Charlotte smiling. "Don't you see the wonderful irony in this whole episode? Riches, however obtained, used for what? To adorn dresses, the necks or fingers of the privileged, now used to help free the most underprivileged, to save the ideas of the finest government that man has ever designed."

"But it is your legacy."

"That is exactly right. It is my legacy to do as I see fit. I don't see much use for the stones in their present form. I think we both know that money and riches are not the sources of our happiness. They are lying in their beds in the next room, or they live down the street, or on the next street," said Charlotte.

"But my leading by example," continued George.

"And you have done that very well throughout your life. Well, most of that life, I think," she said, smiling to ease the tenseness.

"Charlotte, I don't know what to say."

"Say nothing. I will speak to Steve Tompkins in the morning, and I know he will assist me in selling the gems. We may get less or more than $300 for the stones. If it is not enough, somehow we will find the extra money. If it is more, than we will help out some other family. That will ease your conscience, I hope. But most of all, let us pray that this nightmare of war will end soon."

A total of fifty-five Illinois men paid the $300 to avoid conscription. Amedee was one of these after his mother tearfully implored him, pleading that she would not lose her only remaining son. Eloi echoed her request, and Amedee sold his legacy to avoid the draft.

The grumbling against the law persisted throughout the state and among some residents of many towns, such as Avon.

However, despite the unpopularity of the law, the state's population, which was one-thirteenth of the North's, gave one-tenth of the soldiers to the Union cause. They fought first in Tennessee, and then in July went to Mississippi and fought with other troops alongside Ulysses S. Grant for six weeks at the battle of Vicksburg. That battle gave the North control of the Mississippi, and an earlier one in July at a place called Gettysburg in Pennsylvania, not far from Philadelphia, prevented Lee's forces from crossing the Potomac, arresting his threat to Washington. For the first time, the North had taken the offense in the conflict.

Philadelphia, yes thought Charlotte, and the mail so sparse she worried about the effects of the war on her uncle and cousin. How long ago that visit now seemed! Her cousin's last letter had come nearly four months ago, and in it Antoine had written about how he was working at the Satterlee Hospital, where he assisted in the library and tended to the barbering of wounded soldiers. The institution was not far from their home because he needed to be with his father each day. How like Antoine to make himself useful, but still be watchful and devoted to Uncle Louis.

Charlotte had seen enough of the wounded during her short visit to Quincy to know that each day must be a challenge.

It was Antoine's very letter, however, that sparked another response from Zenaide.

"I am going to work in the hospital in Cairo, Charlotte. I know Mama and Papa do not approve, but I am twenty now, and they still have Mary and Theresa to help them," said Zenaide. "I have been idle too long and this is a way that I can actually do something. I have heard of a woman from Galesburg, a Mary Ann Bickerdyke, who has given her life to helping the wounded soldiers. I hope she might accept me as a volunteer."

"Cairo? Oh, Zenaide, it is so far. I will be so worried for you," replied Charlotte. "Mama and Papa will be lost without you, and, and so will I. And what about your, your friends?"

"I know what you are implying, dear sister. But you see, Charlotte, sometimes normal life must be put on hold. And if fate had made me a male, I would be going to the war right now. How can we ever obtain the right to vote if we are not ready to do what we can?" said Zenaide adamantly.

"But nursing, what do you know of nursing?"

"There are many ways to help besides administering to physical wounds. Do you know that this Mrs. Bickerdyke was sent by the people of Galesburg just to make sure that their soldiers had the supplies they needed? In fact, that will be my introduction to her. I will prepare boxes of clothes and medicine to take with me. I also could help write letters for soldiers. I will do anything I can. And I will go with others. I won't be alone," she said smiling, trying to reassure her sister.

"Where will you stay?"

"There are boarding houses for women, and there is an order of nuns who have also been working at the hospital."

"I am proud of you, my dear Zenaide. But not a day will go by that I won't pray to God to keep you safe," said Charlotte.

"And I for you, and all those whose lives have been so horribly affected by this war."

Contention over the war did not cease. While newspapers in Springfield and Chicago openly supported or ridiculed the President's actions, and while frequently demonstrations following those publications could be volatile, the draft riots in New York were openly bloody. In New York, the state's disenfranchised Democrat Party forecasted the specter of emancipated slaves traveling north and usurping the jobs of Irish and German workers. With the Emancipation Proclamation, tempers grew, and as the summer heat sizzled, July grew ugly.

Two days following the enactment of a conscription law, five days of rioting, beginning on Monday, July 13, 1863, scarred the city of New York. At first only military and government buildings were targets, but as the fervor and discontent grew, negroes were attacked and beaten. The orphanage for negro children, located at Fifth Avenue between Forty-Third and Forty-Fourth Streets and housing over two hundred children, was burned to the ground. The rioters took anything useful and then moved quickly to set the institution aflame. The chief engineer of the fire department tried to save the building, but the fire was too intense. When one Irish man berated the mob for its actions, he was beaten.

Then the mob moved to the docks, where it attacked the negroes working on the vessels. There on the waterfront they hanged William Jones and burned his body. The lynchings totaled eleven in all. Bodies were mutilated and sometimes thrown into the river.

In some cases however, humanity prevailed. In one such instance, Irish neighbors protected a black drugstore owner from the mob.

Charlotte and George read with sorrow the report of the July tragedy.

"We've been to this city. We have seen the orphanage and some of the places that they speak of," said Charlotte. "How can people be so evil? These are people that could be our neighbors."

"Is there ever an explanation for evil? Remember our discussion, Charlotte, of why people do what they do? When I read of these happenings, however, I must believe that the very devil himself is to blame," said George.

It was to be the day of national Thanksgiving as decreed by President Lincoln, Thursday, November 26, 1863. The President designated the Thanksgiving Day for a year of plentiful crops and a hope that the war would soon come to an end.

As the Mailliards, their married children and spouses, Mary and Theresa, and Uncle John gathered in the home, it was a day filled with not only thanksgiving but sorrow for the scourge that still plagued the land. Eloi, Amanda and John sat at the table with their children; younger children sat in the laps of their parents. George, the youngest grandchild, squirmed as his mother held him closely, but then he, too, was quieted when the group held hands and prayed.

Eloi began the prayer. "Dear Lord, we are grateful for the bounty of your gifts, for this family, for this food. Please keep us safe and watch over our dear daughter Zenaide, who is in your care." He nodded to his brother-in-law.

John added, "Dear Lord, we pray that our land will be freed from this war and somehow repair itself after this suffering. We pray for our President, and we pray for all soldiers who cannot share in this day, who have endured suffering beyond the scope of our own experience. Amen."

It had been decided that, except for the blessing, the talk at the table would not be of the war, but the topic was so intense that often a remark would slip, and then an awkward silence would follow. The silence was often filled by comments on the wonderful food: the quail, the wild turkey, the bread dressing, the pies, the ever-present johnnycake.

When the meal was finished, Mary and Theresa, with their sisters and sister-in-law, began the cleanup as the men moved outside to the porch. Lighting their pipes, the men now burst forth with a steady stream of talk about the war, talk that had been stifled during dinner.

"Did you see the text of the President's speech at Gettysburg?" began George.

"Yes," said Alexander, "a speech of short length, less than two minutes they say, yet quite remarkable in its content."

"And followed by a speech that was over two hours," added Amedee. "Can you imagine that, and in November to boot?"

"Yes, and though that speech was recorded in the paper, it is Lincoln's that is causing the most stir. I can almost hear him saying those words," said George, "that rather unremarkable voice that seems to touch at the very souls of those to whom he speaks: 'The world will little note, nor long remember,' " quoted George. "Somehow I don't feel that is going to be the case," he added.

The War Will Be Over By Christmas

It was the horribly ironic aphorism that had been widely accepted in April, 1861, at the onset of the war. The Union was so confident that the saying, "The war will be over by Christmas," was repeated throughout newspapers, town meetings, with neighbors and at the supper tables of farmers, store keepers, laborers of any sort.

But as the war stretched through its third Christmas, the retort morphed to, "And Christmas of what year?"

Shortly before this Christmas, Charlotte received a letter from Savannah saying that Josiah had joined the first Illinois negro division of the Union army, the 29th US Colored Infantry. They were scheduled to leave Quincy after training in April. Josiah had looked forward to this for so long, "the chance to serve our President," as Savannah said, had finally come. "He has left Knox College, but with God's blessing, he will return soon."

Despite the ongoing strife and unpopular calls for additional troops, in June, President Lincoln was soundly nominated for a second term and the Republican Party was renamed to the Union Party. The President then named General Grant Commander of the Union armies, and the fight now seemed to focus on General Lee's forces in Virginia with battles at Spotsylvania, Cold Harbor and Petersburg in Tennessee.

In July, a short letter from Zenaide told the Mailliards that she had been accepted as a nurse at the hospital in Cairo and that her physical health was "not impacted by contagion." But at the end of her note, she admitted that she would never be able to forget the suffering she had seen. "It is impossible to imagine how the human body can be so ravaged by a single shot, and then the inevitable infection occurs. And now the heat and humidity of this summer will surely bring its own challenges."

Yes, thought Charlotte, we know the July heat and humidity here, but in southern Illinois, Cairo, on the Mississippi, it had no rival. She wiped the perspiration that was rolling freely down her face as she lifted water to the stove and considered boiling some of the summer fruit, turning them into spreads.

Behind the house she could hear the voices of Emile and his two little friends, Ira and Aaron, playing loudly in the yard. How different was the play of these children compared to her little nieces and her little Hortensia, who clung to their dolls and mocked the duties of their mother—cooking, washing clothes, sewing, mending, always the mending.

Little George was somewhere underfoot nearby. He was so quick now that it was quite a challenge to keep a constant eye on him, but then she heard his cry and saw the open front door (the door she had opened due to the heat), and she dropped the pitcher of water, spilling it all over the wood plank floor.

Dear God, she thought, please no, no. Keep him safe.

"George, George, where are you?" she yelled, her voice filled with alarm.

"He's jes with us, Maw."

Some time in the near future she would speak to Emile about calling her "maw." She wanted him to call her Mama as she still called her mother, but not today, not in front of his little friends.

When she came to the back of the house, she was taken by complete surprise. The three boys had piled small logs in a square, or as near to it as they could manage, around little George, who sat very pleased in the center, happy to have such attention from the bigger boys. They carried sticks like rifles over their shoulders and marched around the logs.

"Look here, Maw. We have caught ourselves Johnny Reb, sneakin' into our yard, so we put him in a stockade, and if he tries to escape we intend to shoot him down," said Emile proudly. He raised his stick, pointed at his brother and said, "Bang, bang, I gotcha' you Reb. You're dead, for sure."

Charlotte's face expressed all the feeling of anger and sorrow that one could imagine, strong enough for even a six-year-old to perceive. She raised her hand to her mouth and shook her head "no."

Emile was now very worried. "Maw, we didn't mean anything by it. We were jes pretendin' to be soldiers. We didn't hurt George, really."

Seeing his mother racing towards him, and now tired of the game, little George raised his arms, puckered his bottom lip and began to cry.

"I'm sorry, little Georgie. We'll let you go," said an apologetic Emile.

"Miz Simmons, I swear we did not even poke him with our sticks," said Ira, a thought that had indeed crossed his six-year-old mind.

Charlotte knew she had to tread carefully, for Emile was usually very reserved and cautious in his actions. She didn't want to discourage his imagination.

She held her youngest child and began rocking him. "I know, boys. It's just so sad, so sad that you have to play at war," said Charlotte, shaking her head and walking back to her door.

"Yer maw is a nice lady, Emile, but I still want to be a soldier when I grow up and kill me all the Rebs I can," said Ira.

"Me too," echoed the little friends.

"I do appreciate this, Charlotte. I knew I could count on you to deliver the food and money. The doctor says I should stay off this twisted knee for a bit longer. I would have asked Zenaide for her help, but of course she is in Cairo. How is she, by the way?" asked Steve Tompkins.

"Her letters are very sad, but everything is so sad, isn't it?" replied Charlotte. "Yes, and here another of our war widows needs our help. I hope we can make it through to help as many as possible."

"Well, I do have $20 for Mary Brewster," said Steve, "and that should help quite a bit."

"Yes, and I have the food—some of the preserves, the eggs and milk my sisters gathered," said Charlotte. "I hope it will be enough. The money from the Willises will run out soon, I would think. The store hadn't been that profitable for a long time."

"Well, no, but there is the money from . . . ," and then Steve stopped mid-sentence, a strange look on his face.

"The money from where, Steve? Have others been donating their gems to the war cause?" she asked with a wry smile on her face.

"No, I'm not the source. I've already said more than I should have," replied Steve.

It was one of those moments in life when you feel as if a whip has suddenly hit your cheek, or you have opened a door and been blinded by the angle of the sun striking your eyes. Charlotte suddenly knew the source of the money.

"You must tell me, Steve, please. The money has come from Henry Moreau, hasn't it?" she demanded. Her voice was strong and unrelenting, and she stared squarely into Steve's face.

"Charlotte, please, don't, don't stir up any problems," he pleaded.

"Problems for whom, Steve?"

"I'm just honoring Mary and Owen's request. Don't ask more."

Charlotte sighed heavily. "Your silence has given me my answer. You probably have surmised that my 'connection' with Henry Moreau was an inconvenience for this entire town, my own family included."

She picked up the food basket and the small money sack and left the store. The door slammed as Steve hung his head.

Henry was alive! He had been in contact with the Willises all these years. Why had Mary lied to her? Why had she never told the truth?

Charlotte's mind raced as she walked towards the Brewster home, not thinking of anything but that face that had been so loved, the lips that had touched hers, the kiss that had sent her stomach into a delicious turmoil. All these years, sending money from what—jobs?—so that the Willises ended with more than they could ever spend. Yes, the irony, sending money to the town that had never shown him much love.

Would she ever see him again? Where was he? But then, suddenly, she slowed her pace. And if he came to Avon today, then what? She unconsciously smoothed her hair, tidying it the best she could under her bonnet, the hair with the ever-increasing gray strands that crept into her hairline. She looked at her hands, chapped by the years of work in the garden, the cooking, the sewing, the mending, the massaging of George's back.

And what of George? What of the children she had borne? You cannot go back, you made a decision, a commitment, and she did love George, unquestionably loved her children, but . . . There are many kinds of love. There is the love that is a duty and the one that comes from an admiration of character, love that grows and nourishes over time. But there is nothing that can replace the love that grabs one's heart so violently that it takes your breath away. How arrogant, though, she thought. Surely, Henry would have found someone else to love, someone as she had. But yet, even after all these years, the connection, yes, connection, could not be forgotten, could not be severed.

Unknowingly, she had passed the Brewster house, and now, as she realized her mistake, she retraced her steps. There sat the two children on their porch, Emmy and Helen, their dark hair and eyes smiling appreciatively at the lady who their Mama said was bringing them food and, perhaps, some little treats.

"Hiya', Miz Simmons, we've been waitin' for you," said Emmy. "I think I saw you go right by our place when I was hopin' that your basket was for us."

"Yes, wasn't that silly of me," said Charlotte. "I guess I just wasn't thinking right. I do that sometimes."

She smiled at the little girls (those sweet little girls) and gave them each a big hug.

She could not escape, however, the thought that, somewhere, Henry was alive.

As the summer heat piqued in July and August, the Union campaigns led by two generals, Philip Sheridan and William T. Sherman, became ever more pivotal in achieving the North's victory. Though land supply lines were seriously threatened and harbors inaccessible since most of 1862, the Confederate army did not lack the courage to push north and, at times, come within sight of Washington. Led by General Jubal Early, 15,000 rebel forces advanced to the Potomac but were repelled by Sheridan's forces, including the 2nd Massachusetts Cavalry, who were using the new Spencer repeating carbine, which allowed an able marksman to fire seven shots without reloading. The following month, Sheridan moved his forces into the Shenandoah Valley, a strategic area that supplied the South with meat and grain.

Meanwhile, General Sherman marched his troops from Tennessee to Georgia, encountering Confederate General Joseph Johnston, who contained the Union army, which was twice the size of the Southern army. Curiously, Jefferson Davis then replaced Johnston with General John Bell Hood. The decision was a disastrous one, and Sherman drove Hood to the edge of Atlanta.

President Lincoln's reelection campaign wavered as the Democratic candidate and former Union general, George McClellan, was touted as the peace candidate. The North wanted an end to the war, but was it worth the price of splitting the country?

"Hard war" became the thrust of the two Union generals as Sheridan and Sherman not only occupied, but destroyed anything of value to the Southern troops. Sheridan ordered the burning of crops in the rich Shenandoah Valley. Sherman occupied Atlanta on September 1.

Prior to the November election, the Springfield *Register* continued its diatribe against the incumbent president.

As Charlotte stood at the fire feeding it logs to begin heating water, George read from the Democratic paper. "Listen to this, Charlotte, they say President Lincoln is guilty of crimes and high taxes. I guess they won't be happy until he is gone."

"Do you think these victories in Atlanta and the Shenandoah will help his chances at re-election? It would be so incredibly foolish to change courses now. Everything the North has gained would be lost," replied Charlotte.

"Of course, that would be the logical conclusion, but we know that emotions often rule before logic," he said smiling. "Even in this town, we still have Lincoln detractors. Those who migrated here from the South are steeped in the very culture they abandoned. But, we'll know soon the outcome of the election."

On November 8, every able-bodied man in Avon cast his vote at the town hall, where George served as the justice of the peace. Despite the grumblings against "Honest Abe," all sixteen of Illinois's electoral votes went to the President, who won by over 400,000 popular votes. The recent battle victories had apparently put the incumbent into the win column.

Sherman's hard war policy continued as he ordered the civilians of Atlanta to leave and then burned the city. He then began the march to the sea, cutting a swath sixty miles wide and three hundred miles long, destroying everything of military value in its wake: bridges, factories, railroads with Sherman's signature neckties (bent rails around trees). Though looting was not part of the order, once a destructive mood infused itself into an army, who could say how men would respond? And destruction was the course it took.

As the news was reported back to the North, the people were divided once again. "It's war, what do you expect?" many said. Others proffered, "But how will we restore ourselves to one nation?"

At Christmas, Charlotte and George walked the short distance to the gathering at her parents' home. They brought their small gifts, the soldiers and stick dolls that George had carved for their nephews and nieces. Reluctantly Charlotte had labored over the little blue uniforms for the soldiers. There was no use fighting the fact that the war had insinuated its way into all minds, even the very young. In addition to his first words of "Mama" and "Papa," little George also knew, "webel."

Prior to Christmas day, the Mailliard family had packed boxes with non-perishable food and clothing to be sent to the troops. Gathering for the Christmas meal, the entire family joined to thank God for their blessings, to pray for the end to the war, and to pray for the continued health of Zenaide, still at the hospital in Cairo.

Alexander added his own thanks. "I just want to thank General Sherman for his own special present for President Lincoln, Savannah, Georgia."

"Here, here," chimed in Amedee.

Charlotte's said nothing, but wondered how different life would be if one of the Southern generals had reported back to Jefferson Davis that he had taken Chicago or Springfield or Peoria. What if Jubal Early had reached Washington and burned it to the ground? She remained quiet, but felt that, somehow, despite being victorious, the North would pay dearly.

Her thoughts were interrupted as her father stood slowly. "I do have a joyous announcement to make. I'm sure everyone knows Albert, Mary's friend, shall we say. He has spoken with me and in the very early spring, our dear Mary will become Mrs. Albert Churchill.

Mama wept, of course, and Charlotte patted her hand, but although she outwardly showed affection to her mother, whenever beaus were mentioned, she could not forget her first love and what her Mama had done. Charlotte still could not accept that the burning of Henry's sketches was anything less than cruel.

Looking at the warmth of her family table, her nieces and nephews, her two little boys, she could not help but wonder if there would be a Christmas gathering somewhere for Henry.

The winter days brought their usual challenges. If the snows were too foreboding, Emile would not trudge to the school where his father had once been a teacher. However, lessons occurred nonetheless, with both Charlotte and George participating in the youngster's reading and ciphering, one of the advantages (or in Emile's mind, one of the disadvantages) of having parents who insisted on education. Yet, even with a focus away from the war issues, the youngster's mind was arrested by the pictures of the soldiers in *Harper's Weekly*, and he asked his father to read him about the Feds and Johnny Reb.

Charlotte wondered how her little girls might have reacted to the war atmosphere. She tried not to be wistful, yet they would have been ten, eight and six now, and learning their mother's skills. Perhaps she would have already schooled Carlotine in the sketching of leaves and flowers. And yet it was not to be. She must thank God each day that she had two boys, and her husband seemed to be growing stronger each month. He vowed that, with the spring, he would be ready to lead his own team of oxen.

Winter brought increasing hardship for the armies as supplies and food dwindled. Sheridan's troops spent the cold months on patrol duty. Then, in February, they burned Loudoun County in Virginia, an area that had aided Colonel John Mosby's raiders. They slugged through three hundred miles of rain and mud, fighting and destroying what stood in their paths as they marched eastward to join the Army of the Potomac against Lee's forces. On March 31st, they were at the battle of Dinwiddlie Court House, and then at the battle of Five Forks on April 1st. Sheridan's forces captured Lee's supply train at Appomattox Station. Rumors passed through the armies that Lee had abandoned the Confederate capitol of Richmond.

Meanwhile, Sherman focused his surge in the Carolinas. In February, Colombia, South Carolina, was ravaged by fire. Moving into North Carolina, Sherman had retreated somewhat from his hard war policy and did not inflict the devastation that followed his forces when they had moved through Georgia and South Carolina.

It was the *Springfield Journal* that proudly carried the news that the first flag raised over Richmond was from Illinois and that President Lincoln, with his son Tad, travelled down the canal on April 4th with a bare modicum of twelve sailors as guards in the still smoldering city.

Charlotte, however, did not learn of the swift-moving events of early April. As she stood looking at the soot-stained window of her kitchen on the first days of the fourth month, she considered cleaning the panes that had only recently shed their ice lines after having dripped through most of the winter.

"Mama, would you come and check my sums on my arithmetic board?" said a plaintive Emile. He had learned that this was the correct way to address his mother, especially when he needed her help.

Charlotte turned to look at her son and then, as if a sword had pierced her left side, she cried out in pain and fell to the floor, hitting the back of her head sharply on the edge of the table.

"Mama, mama, what's wrong?" shouted Emile.

His mother made no response, and instinctively he sensed something terrible had happened.

"Georgie, Georgie, come over here," he ordered his little brother.

Little George looked up curiously at his brother, picked up his two little soldier dolls and walked towards his brother.

"Georgie, you stay here right next to Mama. Do you hear? You have to stay right here," ordered Emile. "I'm going to get someone to help, Mama."

"Me too," said the little blonde boy decidedly.

"No, you must stay here. Mama needs you to be with her. You must promise to stay with her. Okay?"

"Okay," said the toddler as he sat down next to his mother.

Emile ran to the door, and making sure that it closed tightly behind him, raced to Aunt Pauline's house.

Georgie tugged on his mother's sleeve. "Get up, Mama. Get up," he repeated.

But Charlotte did not move.

For four days Charlotte lay on her bed without moving, neither opening her eyes nor moaning as if in pain. The doctor could not determine why she was unconscious. Her breathing grew more shallow with each passing day.

"Well, yes, she does have quite a knot on the back of her head, but I've seen many blows to the head that are worse, and the person is still conscious. I just don't understand the length of time she has been out. Have you tried just yelling her name?"

"Yes, yes, several times—when I first came in the house, when I carried her to the bed, when I tried to shake her hands, her body. She just seems to not be here," said George.

"I know you have had your own pain, George, but do you think you could manage to carry on as normally as possible with the children? Keep your conversations with the boys constant, as if nothing is awry. I'll come back to check on her, but, you see, there is nothing I can do."

She heard the voices first and then wondered if she were simply dreaming. Or was she dead? She didn't know what awaited one on the other side, but perhaps that was what had happened. When she opened her eyes, her vision was fuzzy. She tried moving her head, but the pain made her wince. The images became sharper, though, and the trappings of the room were surely her own.

She tried calling her husband's name, but the sound was raspy, her throat incredibly dry.

"Charlotte, dear God, Charlotte, are you awake?"

Charlotte knew the voice, but surely she was being tricked. And yet, the face slowly coming into focus could not be denied.

Zenaide, grinning widely, sat down gently on the side of her sister's bed.

"Is it really you, Zenaide? Or have I gone to Heaven?" asked Charlotte softly.

"I am here, Charlotte. I came home," replied Zenaide. "You must drink some water now. Your body has been through, well, no one is sure what. But you have quite a lump on the back of your head."

Unconsciously, Charlotte's hand went to the very spot where a large knot protruded from her skull. "Ooh, that must be why my head feels the way it does. Where are the boys and George?"

"Don't worry. He has taken the boys out for a short walk. George seems to be much better than when I saw him the last time," said Zenaide.

"Are you home to stay?" asked Charlotte.

"Yes, I believe so. What do you remember, Charlotte, before you fell?"

"I was standing in front of the window yesterday, and then Emile asked me to help him with something. I remember a pain, yes, a pain in my side, and . . . that's all."

"Well, let's see if we can get some more of that water down, before anything else. Then we'll try some small bits of food," said Zenaide.

"And look at you, the nurse. I am so proud," said Charlotte smiling. She tried to raise herself with her arms and they shook from the weight. "Why am I so weak?" she questioned.

"You haven't drunk nor eaten anything for, a while. Don't worry, you'll feel better in a bit," said Zenaide.

"What day of the week is it?" asked Charlotte.

"Let's see if you can dangle those legs over the side of the bed without feeling dizzy," said Zenaide.

"Zenaide, please tell me, what day is this?" said Charlotte looking desperately into her sister's eyes and trying to use her big sister voice.

Zenaide hugged her sister with her left arm. "It is Wednesday, Charlotte. The bump on your head caused you to sleep for a few days."

"Four days?" questioned Charlotte. She touched the side where she had felt the pain, gently at first, then with more force. That pain was gone.

"I want you to sit here, now, and I will bring you some soup. We're going to ease you back into life, and then I'll get you caught up on everything that has happened," said Zenaide.

It was an incredible picture that graced the pages of *Harper's Weekly* on Palm Sunday, April 9: on the left, Jesus, the symbol of peace, riding into Jerusalem; on the right, Lee's surrender to Grant, and the hope that peace would once again come to the nation.

When the townspeople of Avon heard the news, some of them wept, others drove their wagons, waving proudly the American flag and letting out war hoops as they raced through the town. Many more dropped to their knees in thanksgiving that this terrible chapter of American history was finally coming to a close. Boys still played at capturing the rebels.

Charlotte sat on the porch of her home, still weakened by the malady that no one could explain. The bump was becoming less prominent, and, with it, the head pain. She watched her little boys and thanked God that they were too young to have been involved in the terrible war. She and George laughed as little Georgie tried to emulate his big brother in yells and shouts.

"I cannot believe it is finally over," said George. "It seems to have been going on for so much of our lives."

Zenaide joined their celebration. "It will truly be an Easter Sunday that we shall never forget."

Legacy

In some churches the Easter lilies that had already been placed on the altars were painted black to signify the shock and mourning that gripped the nation. The small Catholic gathering in Avon did not have the lilies but many blooming prairie flowers were gathered to adorn the makeshift altar in the Mailliard home. Perhaps there would be a Catholic church someday, but on this Easter Sunday it was not to be.

The visiting priest had revised his prepared sermon, and now likened the dead President to Jesus, a martyr sacrificed for his people, one who had saved his nation and then was brutally taken away. "But like Jesus Christ himself, let us believe that his message of peace and forgiveness will continue though he may be gone."

When the Mass concluded, the assembled group shared the blessed food and then the conjectures of "how," "why," and "what now" stirred the thoughts of many.

"There is no one who can take this man's place, I fear," proffered John.

"I know nothing of this man named Johnson, sorry to say," added George, who joined his wife's family after the religious service. "Only time will tell how he leads us in this task of healing our country, but how could anyone replace Lincoln?"

Charlotte and George did not make the journey to Springfield to see the body of the fallen leader. Charlotte was still a bit weak, and both she and George felt the trip, which required nearly a week's travel, would be quite taxing on her health. They also determined that the care of ever-busy little George was quite an imposition to be thrust on anyone else. George also was adamant about preparing his own acres this year. He would not rely upon others to do his work, and this was a critical time for seeding.

Yes, all these ideas were true and spoken, but the unspoken reality was that they feared leaving their two sons. It was difficult to forgo the thoughts of their last ominous trip to Quincy and the stark news that had awaited them upon return. No, they would not leave their children.

Many in Avon, however, did make the journey to Springfield. A caravan of wagons began the trek in the last week of April, traveling the nearly ninety miles that would take them to the state's capitol. Among those making the journey were the Babbitts, whose older son John had been lost during the war. Jonathan and Ann felt that seeing the dead President might bring closure to their loss. The family of Samuel Taylor, who also was killed in the conflict, was among their fellow travelers. The Mailliards did not make the journey. However, when Harry Babbitt invited Zenaide to join his family, she gratefully accepted. The train with the President's body was scheduled to arrive in Springfield on Wednesday, May 3.

As both Springfield newspapers reported the timeline for the burial rites and filled their pages with copious stories surrounding the death, they also both lauded the deeds of the fallen leader. Ironically, the *Register*, which had berated every decision Lincoln had made, now referred to the man as "kindly" and "beloved of his neighbors." The *Journal* said it had lost a friend. "Here his virtues were appreciated and the struggles by which he so worthily arose to such distinction, as well as the difficulties with which he has to contend with through four years of the most stupendous war, were fully understood."

After lying in state in the nation's capital, the body was transferred to a nine-car train that left Washington on April 21, 1865. It traced a route through many of the land's major cities, traveling nearly 1,700 miles. The train would stop, and the body would be displayed. Some claimed that it was viewed by nearly 1.3 million people. However, even more remarkable was the estimate that twelve million stood at attention, sometimes in the wee hours of the morning, beside the tracks, often with black arches draped across them, as the cortege moved with the right of way, winding its way to the adopted home of the man called Honest Abe. Three hundred passengers rode with the remains not only of Lincoln but the coffin of his son Willie, who had been disinterred in Washington and would now be reburied with his father.

At Chicago on May 1st, the procession went down Michigan Avenue, then Lake and Clark Streets to Court House Square. Here the coffin was open for public viewing and by Tuesday morning the discoloration in the body was becoming distressful. At eight p.m., the hearse brought the body back to the depot of the St. Louis and Alton Railroad, and then the last leg of the journey was begun. Traveling south and west, it passed through several small towns including Joliet, where 12,000 mourners gathered at midnight.

The Avon contingent had reached its destination with time to spare to view the President, in the State House's Hall of Representatives, the same room where Lincoln had made his "House Divided" speech. The body had been restored by a local undertaker using chalk and amber, and then shortly after 10 a.m., the mourners began to pass solemnly.

Zenaide and Harry silently looked at their fallen leader, the man they had seen just a few years before, the man who had been vital and eloquent and joking, in that debate at Galesburg. Zenaide instinctively made the sign of the cross over herself and bowed her head, unable to fight back the tears that flowed copiously. She would not give herself the luxury of open sobs, but many others could not restrain themselves, and that sound and the shuffle of feet and the rustle of skirts were the only breaks in the silence.

On the morning of May 4th, more mourners stood in line, and then the State House closed, and the President began his final, small journey. The coffin, loaned to Springfield by the city of St. Louis, was moved to a hearse finished in gold, silver and crystal. At 11:30, the procession, led by Major-General Joseph Hooker, commenced from the State House, past Lincoln's home, past the Governor's Mansion and then onto the road to the cemetery.

As the parade came to the area where Zenaide and Harry stood, she was struck by the ornateness of the hearse's design, which was, to her mind, incongruous to the simplicity of Lincoln himself. It was draped with velvet trappings, and the eight dark plumes that rose from its top seemed to remind her of a calliope she had once seen.

Following the hearse, the President's horse, Old Bob, now symbolically riderless with empty boots turned inward, was draped in a black blanket. Bands played solemn songs sporadically, but the constant sound was the unbroken, mournful roll of drums.

The silent crowd grew as the procession moved on the designated serpentine path toward the cemetery. Some, however, could journey no farther, for the day had dawned unusually hot and humid for so early in May.

The older Babbitts remained in the center of Springfield. But Zenaide and Harry moved on together. She could feel the weight of her heavy black dress, bonnet and gloves (she had needed to borrow from her sisters to have the appropriate attire), but that weight was nothing compared to the heaviness in her heart. At times the dryness in her mouth seemed overwhelming, and she leaned unconsciously on Harry for support, but they were determined to be a part of the final ceremony.

Having completed the additional two miles to the site, the two coffins, one grand, the other poignantly small, were laid upon the marble slab inside the tomb. Somewhere in the crowd, Zenaide heard that Lincoln's son Robert and his cousin, John Hanks, were in attendance, but her slight body could not see above the ever-increasing throng, which now moved towards the final altar. Many mourners who had preceded the cortege had already positioned themselves above the tomb to view the ceremony more easily.

Methodist minister Bishop Matthew Simpson, a strong supporter of the former President, addressed the crowd, and though his voice was rasping, Zenaide would forever remember his closing words: "He made all men feel a sense of himself—a recognition of individuality. . . . They saw in him a man who they believed would do what is right, regardless of all consequences."[16]

Yes, thought Zenaide, and now our President has paid with the greatest consequence of all.

Dr. Phineas Densmore, who had preached the funeral sermon at the White House four days after Lincoln's death, read the benediction.

As iron gates and the heavy wooden doors of the tomb closed, Zenaide felt that a chapter of her life was closed, and she wondered if she could ever feel life again. For so long she had needed to quiet so many emotions in order to survive. Now, at twenty-two, she was not sure if she would truly live again.

Zenaide and Charlotte spent many days together when the immediacy of their lives did not demand the care of others. Zenaide exchanged one nursing responsibility for another as Eloi and Amanda moved more slowly with each day, and the challenges of having given birth to ten children had seriously compromised Amanda's strength. More and more Zenaide became the child on whom they relied.

Charlotte grew stronger with each day and tried to assume the routine that had been her life before her illness—caring for the boys, seeding and then caring for the garden which was their primary source of food. Emile prided himself on his ability to take direction, and even good-naturedly tried to show little George what were weeds and what were plants, though all growing things were still quite indiscernible to the toddler.

"What a joy he is becoming," Charlotte said to George of their older son one afternoon in early June. "He is thoughtful, caring, aware of others, probably much as you were when you were his age."

"That is so very long ago, and I have tried so hard all my life not to remember those times. But if I had been a considerate child, then I am sure it was due to my mother," said George.

Perhaps in time, Charlotte thought, she would be able to break through the wall that still seemed to surround George, but for now she felt a first step had been taken with this small revelation.

Lost in their own reflections, both were startled by the sudden knock on the door.

George rose to answer, and then, with a pleasant smile, welcomed his sister-in-law. "Ah, yes, would that be Miss Nin Mailliard?"

"Yes, it is," replied Zenaide. "That name seems to have been forgotten, for a while, at least. I hope I am not disturbing anything. I just wanted to share a gift with you that I have received from cousin Antoine. I'm sure you will both enjoy it. It's a book called *Drum Taps* by Walt Whitman. Antoine felt it would be particularly interesting to me since the poet also worked as a nurse during the war."

"I do believe we have heard that," replied George. "But I think it would be good for you and Charlotte to visit for a while. I have promised to take the boys for a walk to check on the crops."

After George had left with the boys, Zenaide put her bag on the table and sat down quietly.

Charlotte continued her cleaning of the strawberries that she had collected in the morning. They might have been a bit unripe, but she and the boys couldn't wait to taste the sweet juiciness after a long winter of dried fruits.

As she turned to face Zenaide, she was shocked by the look on the younger woman's face. "What's wrong? Are Mama and Papa that ill?" questioned Charlotte.

"No, today is no worse than any other day for them. You know, the difficulty in moving, Mama's labored breathing at times, but . . ." Zenaide's voice trailed off.

"But what? Tell me, please. What can I do to help? With all of us sisters, we surely can relieve the burden of our parents that seems to have fallen on you. It is only right that we all take turns. I will talk to them, and we will decide on a schedule," said Charlotte decidedly.

"Oh, Charlotte, how so like you, to try and correct what you see is wrong. That is not why I came." Trying to smile, she continued, her voice now very low. "Do you have a remedy for someone who feels dead inside?" She walked to the front of the home and stared out the window.

"You feel dead inside? Dead because of what you saw at the hospital?" asked Charlotte.

Since Zenaide's return from Cairo, whenever anyone would ask her about her experiences, she would simply speak in generalities, talking of the bravery of the soldiers, the care of the nurses and doctors, and always minimizing any of her own contributions. Perhaps now, Charlotte thought, she might be ready to speak a bit more and unburden the weight of what she must be carrying inside.

"The hospital, yes, and then today the *Journal* reported on what the number of casulties might be, dead not only from battle, but from the disease and the starvation that went on in the prison camps. Did you know that nearly 30,000 soldiers from Illinois were lost? The nation, both North and South, may have lost over 600,000? Think of the populations of entire cities being gone—because of the pursuit of a system that was so incredibly, morally wrong. The murder of President Lincoln was only one more mortal sin in a world given to evil." The younger sister sat down at the table and hung her head.

"Zenaide, I know it is all terrible, too terrible to think about, but I do have something good to share with you. Do you remember Savannah's son, Josiah? I received a letter from her a few days ago and learned that he has come home from the war. He is well and will go back to Knox College."

The older sister would not, however, add that Savannah had also told of the many ways in which her son had been reminded that he had been a slave and therefore inferior from the white officers who refused to lead the negro regiments, to the Southern soldiers who refused to engage them in battle, to the lower pay that he received.

"Savannah is overjoyed that he has come home and can begin his life anew," continued Charlotte.

"Charlotte, I can read your face only too well. I know the inequities that the negro troops suffered. It was just this month, June, yes, nearly two months after Lee's surrender, that Congress declared that pay and medical services for negro troops should be equal to whites."

"What medical services will they receive?" continued Zenaide. "How do you repair a man who holds his own intestines in his hand? Or another who slips on the floor because it is pooled with blood? Or another whose jaw has disappeared from his face? Or that you cannot stand to see one more black leg or foot or arm thrown on a pile of discarded limbs? I'm sorry, Charlotte. I shouldn't burden you with these things. It is just that, when I lie down at night, these are the things I see," said Zenaide.

"You are not burdening me. I am your sister," said Charlotte, gently taking her sister's hands in hers. "You are the brave one, Zenaide, to offer to help."

"Oh, no, how very wrong you are. I was never brave. Do you know that I learned to breathe through my mouth to try and combat the smell of dead flesh, the smell that hung in every corner of the hospital? I tried to turn my face to my sleeve, to smell the stink of my own sweat to avoid the smell of death. They would try to dictate their letters to me even though many were unable to speak. And when I tried to sleep at night, and I could hear the crying and the moaning, I prayed for their deaths, Charlotte. I prayed for their deaths."

Charlotte rose from her chair and now knelt in front of her sister. "I am so sorry. You have suffered so much."

"I am no different from anyone else."

"And you have brought me poems about war? Perhaps we will save those for another day," said Charlotte.

"No, no, that's the strange thing. When I read from this book, I feel a kind of peace. I have marked one page in particular. Will you read it, Charlotte, please?" said Zenaide, wiping her face and handing the opened book to her sister.

Charlotte read through the poem once silently, and then, steadying her voice, she read:

A sight in camp in the daybreak gray and dim,
As from my tent I emerge so early sleepless,
As slow I walk in the cool fresh air the path near by the hospital tent
Three forms I see on stretchers lying, brought out there untended lying
Over each the blanket spread, ample brownish woolen blanket, Gray and heavy blanket, folding, covering all.
Curious I halt and silent stand,
Then with light fingers I from the face of the nearest the first just lift the blanket;
Who are you elderly man so gaunt and grim, with well-gray'd hair, and flesh all sunken about the eyes?
Who are you my dear comrade?
Then to the second I step-and who are you my child and darling?
Who are you sweet boy with cheeks yet blooming?
Then to the third-a face nor child nor old, very calm, as of
beautiful yellow-white ivory;
Young man I think I know you-I think this face is the face of the
Christ himself,
Dead and divine and brother of all, and here again he lies.[17]

Both sisters sat silently for a while, holding hands.

Charlotte spoke first. "I do not know how you will feel alive again, but I do know, that somehow, we go on. We are very lucky. We have family who love us, who want to share our grief, who know the depth of our sorrow. You, we, are not alone."

"And you have lost three daughters. I know you have grieved," said Zenaide.

"I will grieve every day of my life, but I also rejoice in knowing what joy they brought me while they were here. I swore I would try very hard to appreciate every day that I have with my two little boys and husband and all of you."

Zenaide, nodding in agreement, rose as did Charlotte. No more words were necessary.

Charlotte returned to the chore of cleaning the berries and sprinkled them lightly with sugar, just enough to bring the juice out.

"Miz Simmons, it's me, Sam Douglas. Ya got yerself a very special letter," called a voice from Charlotte's porch.

She answered the door quickly, her apron still on.

"Yes, ma'am, good afternoon to ya," said Sam taking off his hat. "I ran all the way over here from the post office 'cuz the letter comes from the United States Government, the Department of War," he said proudly, shoving the envelope into her hand.

Charlotte looked at the envelope, the return address, her name, Mrs. Charlotte Simmons, Avon, Illinois, and when she felt it press against her hand, it was as if her flesh were on fire.

Sam stood in her kitchen, a look of expectancy and confidence on his face. Any other time he had delivered a letter such as this, the person had opened it immediately. It always made him feel very special to share in the news. But Miz Simmons just stood there with a strange look on her face.

Charlotte turned her back to Sam and slipped the envelope into her apron's pocket.

"Well, you are just the luckiest person, Mr. Sam Douglas, because I have this minute cleaned and sugared some fresh strawberries, and I bet they would be very tasty over some biscuits with fresh milk. Would you like some?" she said cheerfully.

"I don't mind if I do," said Sam, removing his hat and making himself comfortable at the kitchen table.

Charlotte asked him about his family, his mother and father, his two older brothers who had stayed home from the war to help their paw, as Sam called him. He told her of his two younger sisters, who were bright girls, "They already know how to read," he said proudly. "You know, Miz Simmons, readin' never's been too easy for me," he admitted.

"That's okay. Everybody has their own talents." She had heard that Sam was not exactly a quick learner. He continued to sit at the table and relish every bite, some milk occasionally dripping down his chin—all the while the letter burning in her pocket.

"Would you like a second helping?" *Please say no.*

"Well, are you sure there's enough? They sure are good," said an appreciative Sam.

"I wouldn't have offered them if I didn't have enough," she said politely.

Sam ate most of the strawberries, and after the second helping, he patted his stomach contentedly and said, "You do grow the best strawberries, Miz Simmons."

"Thank you, Sam. I just hope you weren't needed for anything else at the post office," said Charlotte. She could almost feel the heat from her pocket penetrating her thigh.

"Oh, my, yes. I've had such a nice time visitin' with you. I guess I got a little side-tracked."

Sam shuffled his feet a bit and then rose from his chair, backing out the door. "Good-bye, then, Miz Simmons. I hope to see you again, and thank you for those wonderful strawberries."

He was very proud of himself for remembering to say "thank you." Miz Simmons was certainly a fine lady, yes sir, a fine lady.

Putting his hat back on, he started walking quickly back to town. "By golly," he said out loud to no one, "She never did open that letter."

My Dearest Charlotte,

You must be wondering why, after so many years, I have asked my thoughts be conveyed to you, and yet I must be honest and say that hardly a day has gone by that your face has not been in my mind. I cannot enter a new place or town without unconsciously searching through a crowd to see your eyes, your smile and that look of concern that would cause my heart to ache.

I also must confess that I have learned of the events in your life through the letters from Mary and Owen, but I insisted that they never relate the happenings of my life because it was so uncertain. More importantly, though, I feared that, if you knew I was well, you might still have felt a bond with me, a bond that we both knew was not wise. Please forgive my presumption in assuming that your feeling for me was as strong as mine for you, and yet I cannot help but think that it was.

When we were young, the love and concern that you gave to me opened a door that was closed when my parents left my life. Though the kindness of Mary and Owen was so generous, it was through you, Charlotte, that I saw that love was possible. However, even if the innuendo against me had not been made, I am afraid that a true union between us would not have been tolerated. It was a different time, and I could never have done anything to hurt you.

Through the letters from the Willises, I have learned of your marriage to a man who is kind and well-regarded by the community, the tragedy of the loss of your daughters, but the joy of the birth of your son. Your happiness brings a peace to my life.

I traveled for many years and lived in California. I came to realize that people can be strong or weak, good or bad in every setting and community. I joined the army, where my skills were valued. The war has been a terrible scar on this nation, but I feel that, somehow, the decency of this country will survive this test.

My hope is that love and respect, which I knew because of you, and the kindness that surrounded me as I lived with Mary and Owen, will win over suspicion and fear and greed that eat at the core of any society, whether a small town or a nation.

I thank an angel named Rachel who has written my words for me.

May God bless you and reward your goodness.

Henry

The words of Lieutenant Henry Moreau told to Rachel Carson,
May 15, 1865

The letter was folded inside the formal announcement.

To the sister of Lieutenant Henry Moreau

We regret to inform you that Lieutenant Henry Moreau of the Massachusetts 2nd Regiment Cavalry, died on May 16, 1865, of wounds received during the battle of Five Forks in Virginia, during the first days of April.

He served with bravery and honor.

Edwin M. Stanton, Secretary of War

The words were beginning to smear as Charlotte realized that the water from her tears was fading the print. She grabbed for a clean dry rag that was lying on the table and tried to blot those tears, but her hands shook so violently that she could not control them. She reread each piece several times, the letter first, trying to hear his voice, easily remembering his face. How like Henry to try to protect her, to thank her for her "love and respect," to see goodness despite the unkindness that he had encountered, to say her "happiness brought peace" to his life. He had not even known of the birth of little George.

The formal words of the official letter were so cold in contrast. Did Mr. Stanton truly "regret"? Was every soldier's family told their loved one served with "bravery and honor"?

What more could be said? That he had suffered for a month and a half before his death? That he didn't moan very much at night and was appreciated as a patient? That his life meant something?

Charlotte took the letter with Mr. Stanton's name and began tearing it into very small pieces. She walked to the fireplace and carefully placed each scrap onto the logs where they fell innocently and would soon be consumed by the fire that she would start.

She wiped her hands on her apron and then smoothed Henry's letter gently and began folding it as she walked to her bedroom. She reached for the wood box, the one with her initials, the one she had received from George, and then delicately and securely placed the letter inside on the red velvet lining. She made sure the lid closed tightly, and then, opening the second drawer of the dresser, the drawer that always stuck a bit, she put the box in the back left corner.

As she walked out onto her porch, she grabbed the doorway and steadied herself, feeling as if she had lived an entire lifetime in one afternoon.

She sat down in her rocker and breathed deeply, her body still shaking sporadically. She looked at the tall pink daisies that had begun to bloom last week. She had warned the boys to stay away because the bees enjoyed sucking the nectar, and their stings would definitely hurt.

But this afternoon there were no bees. Instead, Charlotte noticed the beautiful, large butterflies, the Monarch butterflies, that had come in their small flock to glean their nourishment from their sister flowers. The beautiful orange and yellow tones of their wings accented with stripes of black, created a pattern of delicate elegance. Their antennae moved cautiously, sensing their surroundings, and their legs moved through the brown seeds at the center of each daisy. Did their legs tickle those centers? They moved from daisy to daisy. Some flew to a new flowerbed, and only a few were left on Charlotte's daisies.

Don't leave just yet. She remembered, then, when she had been a little girl in France, perhaps five or six, and she had wanted to keep a small yellow butterfly that had landed on one of the roses in the garden. She grasped its soft wings between her thumb and index finger and, holding it up to her face, she saw how its legs grappled helplessly to escape. She put the butterfly under a jar that she had found in the kitchen, determined to keep the butterfly for herself. But in the morning, when she quickly ran outside to see the beautiful little creature, it was dead. She tried to blow gently on it, to move some petals of the rose towards its legs, but it would not breathe, and instead lay unmoving. She then took the poor creature, placed it on the ground, covered it lightly with dirt, and said the "Our Father."

Today, she would not attempt to capture any of the butterflies, though she could almost feel the soft velvet of their delicate wings. She looked at them closely and tried to etch the picture of their delicate bodies in her mind. She thanked God for the pleasure of sharing these creatures, if only for a short time. And then the butterflies moved away, fading from her view as they flew towards the sun.

Her eye was caught by the sight of a man with one small boy on his shoulders, and an older child, leading his father and brother, carrying a long stick.

The man waved, and then the older boy followed his example. Charlotte returned the wave as George had on that boat many years ago. She smiled and decided she would splash some water on her face before she resumed her chores. Her men were coming home for the noon meal.

Epilogue

In a letter to her sixteen-year-old granddaughter and namesake, Charlotte Simmons, then eighty-three, recalls the experiences of her early life in Europe and tells of her family's background and their connection to the Bonapartes.

While living in Florence, Italy, she remembers the ermine cloak of Queen Hortense more than the woman's face. She tells of seeing many of the members of the royal family including the Princess for whom she was named. They were pleased with her Italian "childish talk" and rewarded her with candy and cake and fruit.

When the Princess's husband died and the young Charlotte saw her crying, she cried with her. When they asked the child if she understood what death meant, she replied that "death meant nothing."

Charlotte remembers sitting on the lap of Louis Napoleon, afterward Napoleon III, who played with Charlotte, as he loved children.

Charlotte tells her granddaughter of how she had been passing in the hall of the palace when the two young princes, who were fencing, ran after her, scaring her quite badly, for which their mother severely scolded them.

She recalls one visit to Paris to the mansion of Madame Clary, daughter of Madame de Villineuve, at the Swedish mansion in Paris, and, while in Paris, how her father Eloi often rode with the two princes as an escort.

Charlotte's grandmother, Therese Gallet, had been chaperone to Joseph Bonaparte's two daughters, Zenaide and Charlotte. Amanda Gallet, daughter of Therese Gallet, at the age of seventeen accompanied her mother, who attended Princess Charlotte, in a visit to Point Breeze, Bordentown, New Jersey. There Amanda met her future husband, Eloi Mailliard, the younger of two Mailliard brothers employed by Joseph

Bonaparte. The older Mailliard brother, Louis, was the executor for the will of King Joseph, or as he was called in America, the Comte de Survilliers. The wife of Joseph Bonaparte, Queen Julie, did not live in America due to her delicate health, instead residing in Florence for twenty years as an invalid.

Charlotte also recalls the castle at Survillier, where she lived for six years, before coming to America. She says it was "the best time of my youth" in that large mansion, which had been built by the Moors and contained many fine gardens.

She does not address what happened to the painting "Ecce Homo," although many asked her of its whereabouts. To this day, it has not been found.

In this poignant letter to her granddaughter, later to be the grandmother of my own husband, she does not log any memories of her husband, who had died in 1892.

Charlotte Louise Josephine Mailliard Simmons died in Avon in 1921, at the age of ninety-three and six months.

Zenaide Mailliard married James Harrison Babbitt, son of Jonathan Babbitt, in 1887, at the age of forty-four. She did not have any children but became known to her community as "Aunt Nin."

In 1937, after being recognized as Avon's oldest resident, she died at the age of ninety-four. Among those who attended her funeral was Mrs. Richard Kirtley of Bushnell, Ilinois, my future mother-in-law.

Charlotte L. J. Simmons
1900

Acknowledgements

This project could not have been started without the generous help of Margaret Hickerson of Avon, Illinois, who opened the Avon Library one summer morning in 2005, so I could begin my research. She directed me to *The Founding of Avon*, the 1937 publication that contained many invaluable recollections of the town's first settlers and their immediate descendants. She also located obituaries of Charlotte Mailliard Simmons, George Simmons and Zenaide Mailliard Babbitt, which gave in-depth profiles of these three individuals at the focus of the story. In addition, Mrs. Hickerson suggested additional book resources that provided details of 19th century Illinois prairie life.

The more I immersed myself in this project, the more my husband Rich was there to not only provide verbal encouragement but also to retrace together some of the very ground on which this story unfolded. We stepped out together on the east side of Old Main at Knox College in Galesburg, Illinois, where the famous fifth debate took place between Abraham Lincoln and Stephen Douglas. To place our steps on the very site where that great leader stood was indeed one of the most awe-inspiring aspects of this research.

Rich and I also paused at the site of the Ohio River at Louisville and were overwhelmed by the expanse of that river and the incredible courage that some of the "forced immigrants" to this nation choose to attempt to cross to achieve that one goal which humankind has always aspired to, the freedom to make one's own choices.

In the last part of research, Rich and I walked the ground of the Avon Cemetery, where several years before we had stood as his maternal grandparents were laid to rest. On this last visit, however, we were absorbed by the markers of his early ancestors, the Mailliards and the Simmons, whose stories now absorbed my life. We noted with poignancy how they had buried not only their parents but often their children.

Rich has been and always will be my "BFF."

The further I moved in this story, my children; Craig, Colleen and Carolyn, were there to offer their encouragement and their constructive critiquing. My grandchildren also offered their support, and one granddaughter calling from her college campus in Springfield, Illinois, provided impetus for another source, Eliza Farnham's *Life in Prairie Land.*

Dr. Kit O'Toole persuaded me to have confidence in this project and guided me through publishing decisions.

To my fellow teachers, Peg Cain and Patty Filomeno, thank you also for your guidance and encouragement in bringing this work to fruition.

A very special thanks goes to Erik Igoe, of the University of Illinois, Springfield, whose journeyman's editing of this project was invaluable.

Gene and Gail Laulunen, owners of Midwest Outdoors Publishing, Burr Ridge, Illinois, graciously offered their facilities as their graphic artist, Jesse Saenz, assisted by Dina Gervasi, designed the cover.

My friends, with whom I have shared this idea, were there to urge me to finish the project, encouraging me by expressing their desire to read the final work. To them, I also am most grateful.

As with all historical fiction, I have taken the liberty of defining the characters of this story with, what I feel, is a plausible course of action. Where the cause of deaths was not recorded, I created dramatic occurrences to reinforce ideas already inherent in the story. Obviously, I also created fictional characters to move the dynamics of the plot.

During my research, I did not learn of any slave markets in Louisville. Kentucky slave markets were located in the Bluegrass area of that state near Lexington. However, for purposes of the story, I needed to portray that scene as the Mailliard family traveled on the Ohio. My apologies are extended to Louisville for that skewing of history.

Jacob Abbott's book, *Maria Antoinette*, was not written until 1849, and therefore could not have been read by Charlotte in 1841. However, Charlotte's margin notes, written sometime later in life, still give credence to the poignant feeling of solitude that seemed to be keen during some point in her life.

There were also two conflicting records of the exact year when Charlotte came to America, one saying 1838, the other 1841. I choose the later date, the summer before her fouteenth birthday, for I felt it was a more critical time in a young woman's life, a young woman who had been raised in a privileged world and then suddenly transported to the western frontier of this young nation.

Any resemblance between the fictional characters of this novel and actual people and events is purely coincidental.

Lastly, as I explored the life of these settlers and the times in which they lived, I felt that each of them had a compelling story to tell. This tale has been but one.

October 30, 2012

Character List

Historical

Eloi and Amanda Gallet Mailliard

Their children:

Heloise, b. 1824, m. Orlando Woods

Pauline, b. 1825, m. Alexander McFarland

Charlotte, b. 1827, m. George Simmons

Children: Louise Maria, b 1849

Carlotine, b. 1854

Hortensia Maria, b. 1857

Emile, b. 1858

George, b. 1863

Amedee, b. 1829, m. Mary E. Smith

Jules, b. 1830

Amanda, b. 1832

Napoleon, b. 1840

Zenaide, b. 1843, m. James Harrison Babbitt

Mary, b. 1844, m. Albert J. Churchill

Theresa, b. 1845, m. Charles Stevens

Gabriel and Therese Gallet, parents of Amanda Gallet Mailliard

John Gallet, son of Gabriel and Therese Gallet

Louis Mailliard, older brother of Eloi Mailliard

Antoine Mailliard, son of Louis

The Bonaparte Family

Joseph Bonaparte, brother of Napoleon Bonaparte, known as King of Spain and Naples, then as Count Survillier at Point Breeze, New Jersey

His wife Queen Julie

Their daughters, Zenaide and Charlotte

Joseph Lucien Charles Napoleon Bonaparte, eldest child of Zenaide and Charles Lucien Bonaparte, and Grandson of Joseph Bonaparte

Annette Savage, mistress of Joseph Bonaparte

In Woodsville/Avon

The Woods brothers, first settlers
Jonathan and (Ann?) Babbitt, parents of James Harrison Babbitt
Stephen Tompkins
Leopold Stocker, friend to the Mailliards, and former valet-de-chamber to Joseph Bonaparte
The Hectornes and Poisets, French immigrants
W. T. R. Fennessy, civil engineer

Fictional

Savannah
Clayton Parker

Henri Moreau
Fair Moon, wife of Henri
Henry Moreau, son of Henri & Fair Moon, also known as Swift Eagle

Owen and Mary Willis
Carl and Mavis Tripp and their son, young Carl
Will and Iris Spenser
Thurlow Pershing

Jonas Williams
Josiah Parker

Sam Douglas

Notes

1. Connelly, The Gentle Bonaparte, book title.

2. I will try to do my best. (online translation)

3. Connelly, The Gentle Bonaparte, p. 292.

4. Pearce and Nugent, The Ohio River, cover jacket.

5. Bricker, "From Palace to Log Cabin," n.p.

6. "Fifth Joint Debate at Galesburg. Mr. Douglas's Speech," p. 4.

7. "Fifth Joint Debate at Galesburg. Mr. Douglas's Speech," p. 6.

8. Calkins, They Broke the Prairie, p. 291.

9. "Fifth Joint Debate at Galesburg. Mr. Lincoln's Reply," p. 1.

10. "Fifth Joint Debate at Galesburg. Mr. Lincoln's Reply," p. 3.

11. "Fifth Joint Debate at Galesburg. Mr. Lincoln's Reply," p. 4.

12. Calkins, They Broke the Prairie, p. 292.

13. "Fifth Joint Debate at Galesburg. Mr. Lincoln's Reply," p. 8.

14. "Fifth Joint Debate at Galesburg. Mr. Douglas's Reply," p. 4.

15. "Fifth Joint Debate at Galesburg. Mr. Douglas's Reply, p. 5.

16. Kunhardt and Kunhardt, Twenty Days, p. 301.

17. Whitman, "A Sight in Camp," from Leaves of Grass/Drum Taps.

Works Consulted

Abbott, Jacob. Maria Antoinette. New York: Harper, 1901. (Originally published in 1849)

"Abraham Lincoln Library of Congress 2011 Calendar."

"Abraham Lincoln's Funeral Train." <http://home.att.net/~rjnorton/Lincoln51.html > 19 Feb 2009.

"Africans in America/Part 4/Lincoln's 'House Divided' Speech." <http://www.pbs.org/wgbh/aia/part4/4h2934t.html> 12 Jan 2011.

"Alton, Illinois – Civil War Era – Confederate Prison: Alton in the Civil War." <http://www.altonweb.com/history/civilwar/confed/index.html> 26 Feb 2009.

" 'Aunt Nin' Babbitt, Avon's Oldest Resident, Dies at Age of Ninety-Four." (Obituary) n.d., n.p., n.p.

"Battle of Dinwiddie Court House >> History Net." 29 Aug 2006. <http://www.historynet.com/battle-of-dinwiddie-court-house.htm> 11Feb 2011.

"Blessings in Disguise." Harper's Weekly. 4 Feb 1865. <http://www.sonofthesouth.net/leefoundation/the-civil-war.htm> 14 Mar 2009.

Bluemer, R. G. Here Comes the Boats! A History of Canal Boats and Steamboats in the Illinois Valley.
Grand Village P: Granville, Ill., 2005.

"Boats: Westward Expansion." <http://www.promtega.org/csu/30026/boats.htm> 14 Feb 2006.

Bogce, Allan G. From Prairie to Corn Belt. Ames, Iowa: Iowa State University P, 1994.

"Bonaparte House." <http://www.ushistory.org/districts/washingtonsquare/bonap.ht m> 16 Apr 2008.

"Bonaparte Mementos Treasured by Families in Area." The Daily Register-Mail, Galesburg, Ill. 26 Jan 1955. 8.

"Bonapartes, The, Olga's Gallery." <http://www.abcgallery.com/bio/bonaparte.html> 15 May 2005.

Bricker, Harriet. "From Palace to Log Cabin." n.d., n.p., n.p.

"Building on Our Progress: City of Perth Amboy, New Jersey." 25 May 2007. <http://www.ci.perthamboy.nj.us/html/city_history.html> 30 May 2007.

"California and the Civil War: 2nd Regiment of Cavalry, Massachussetts Volunteers, The." <http://www.militarymuseum.org/2ndMassCav.html> 2 Feb 2011.

Calkins, Earnest Elmo. They Broke the Prairie. Westport, Conn: Greenwood P, 1937.

"Cave-In-Rock State Park." Department of Natural Resources 2008. <http: //dnr.state.il.us/lands/Landmgt/PARKS/R5/CAVEROCK.HTM> 16 Feb 2008.

"Celebrating a Proud History." <http://www.knox.edu/x6285.xml> 15 May 2005.

"Coming of the Railroad, The: The First in Fulton County." The Centennial History of Avon. 1937. n.d., .n.p., n.p.

Chapman, Charles. History of Fulton County, Illinois. Peoria: Chapman, 2010.

Chrastina, Paul. "No Plan to Free Slaves, Lincoln Assures Crowd." Old News. June-July 2010. 1-2.

"Communication During the Civil War." <http://googleads.g.doubleclick.net/pagead/ads?client=ca-pub-687184075270882&dt=123 87184075270882&dt=123> 14 Mar 2009.

Connelly, Owen. The Gentle Bonaparte. New York, Macmillan, 1968.

Couri, Dr. Peter J., Jr. "Peoria: The First European Settlement in Illinois." Peoria Area Tricentennial Celebration, September 1991-September 1992. Peoria, Illinois: Peoria Historical Society. <http://www.peoriahistoricalsociety.org/peohistoryfr.html> 9 Feb 2009.

Crawford, Mark. "Battle of Dinwiddie Court House." America's Civil War. Mar 1999. <http://www.historynet.com/battle-of-dinwiddie-court-house.htm> 12 Feb 2011.

Cronin, William. Nature's Metropolis Chicago and the Great West. New York: Norton, 1991.

"Daguerreotype." <http://www.metmuseum.org/toah/hd/adag/hd_adag.htm> 01 Nov 2010.

Dayton, Fred Irving. Steamboat Days. New York: Tudor, 1939.

"Declaration of Independence, The." <http://www.ushistory.org/declaration/document/index.htm> 10 Feb 2007.

DeMay, Nora. Email Communication on French Translation. Nazareth Academy Language Dept. LaGrange Park, Illinois. 27 Jan 2011.

Demorest, Rose. Pittsburgh A Bicentennial Tribute 1758-1958. Carnegie Library of Pittsburgh. <http://www.clpgh.org/research/pittsburgh/history/demorest.ht ml> 12 Nov 2008.

Donahue, James. "Early Atlantic Liner." <http://perdurabo10.tripod.com/id969.html> 9 Mar 2006.

"Early Industrialization." <http://www.ohiohistorycentral.org/entry.php?rec=1562> 14 Feb 2006.

"Eloi D. Mailliard." Biographical Sketch, n.d., n.p., n.d.

Farnham, Eliza W. Life in Prairie Land. Chicago: U of Illinois Press, 1988.

"Fifth Joint Debate at Galesburg: Mr. Douglas's Reply." 7 Oct 1858. <http://www.bartleby.com/251/53.html> 28 Jan 2011.

"Fifth Joint Debate at Galesburg: Mr. Lincoln's Reply." 7 Oct 1858. <http://www.bartleby.com/251/52.html> 28 Jan 2011.

"Fifth Lincoln-Douglas Debate, The." <http://catalog.knox.edu/archives/local_hist/ld_debate.htm> 15 May 2005.

"First Brick School Building, The." The Centennial History of Avon. 1937. n.d., n.p., n.p.

"Francois-Pascal-Simon Gerard: Marie-Julie Bonaparte, Queen of Spain, with Her Two Daughters." <http://www.abcgallery.com/D/david/gerard14.htmL> 24 Feb 2008.

Franklin, Benjamin. Poor Richard's Almanack. Mount Vernon, Peter Pauper P, n.d.

_____. "Remarks Concerning the Savages of North America." The Norton Anthology of American Literature. Nina Baym, ed. New York: Norton, 1999.

Freeman, Elise, Wynell Burroughs Schamel, and Jean West. "The Fight for Equal Rights: A Recruiting Poster for Black Soldiers in the Civil War." Social Education 56, 2 (February 1992): 118-120. Revised and updated in 1999 by Budge Weidman) <http://www.archives.gov/education/lessons/blacks-civil-war/> 21 Jan 2011.

Garside, Nan. Personal Interview on Art During 19th Century. Nazareth Academy Art Dept. LaGrange Park, Illinois.21 Feb 08.

"George Simmons." (Obituary) n.d., n.p., n.p.

Goodwin, Doris Kearns. Team of Rivals: The Political Genius of Abraham Lincoln. New York: Simon & Schuster, 2005.

Gray, Christopher. "Where Lincoln Tossed and Turned." 24 Sep 2009. <http://www.nytimes.com/2009/09/27/realestate/27/scapesready.html> 19 Apr 2011.

Handlin, Oscar. Boston's Immigrants, 1790-1880. Cambridge, MA, Belknap Press of Harvard UP, 1991.

Hansen, Liane. "'Amazing Grace': A New Book Traces the History of a Beloved Hymn." <http://www.npr.org/templates/story/story.php?storyId=89406 0> 16 Feb 2011.

Harris, Leslie M. "The New York City Draft Riots of 1863," from In the Shadow of Slavery: African Americans in New York City, 1626-1863. 2003. <http://www.press.uchicago.edu/Misc/Chicago/317749.html> 18 Feb 2011.

"Harvesting the River: History: Settlement: Meredosia, Illinois – Illinois StateMuseum." <http://www.museum.state.il.us/RiverWeb/harvesting/history/settlement/ Meredosia.html> 11 Feb 2009.

"Hearse Used for the Springfield Procession." (Picture) <http://rogerjnorton.com/Lincoln51.html> 7 Mar 2011.

"History of St. Charles, Native American History." <http://www.st-charles.il.us/native.htm> 19 Feb 2009.

"History of the City of Beardstown." <http://www.beardstown.lib.il.us/community/history.html> 11 Feb 2009.

Holmberg, Tom. "Point Breeze: Joseph Bonaparte's Home in America." <http://www.napoleonseries.org/articles/biographies/joseph.cfm> 3 May 2005.

Holzer, Harold, ed. Lincoln As I Knew Him. Chapel Hill: Algonquin Books, 2009.

Hughes, Kristine. Everyday Life in Regency and Victorian England From 1811-1901. Cincinnati: Writer's Digest Books, 1998.

"Illinois Historical Digitization Projects: Search Results." <http://Lincoln.lib.niu.edu/cgi-bin/search2t?word=crowd&CONJUNCT=6&DISTANCE =&PR. . .> 15 May 2005.

"Irish Famine of 1840 Liverpool Flooded With Immigrants." <http://www.answers.com/topic/history-of-birmingham> 28 Feb 2007.

"Irish in America, The: 1840s-1930s." <http://xroads.virginia.edu/~ug03/omara-alwala/IrishKennedys.html> 12 Feb 2008.

Jensen, Richard. J. Illinois A History. New York: Norton, 1978.

"Joseph Bonaparte at Point Breeze." <http://flatrock.org.nz/topics/new jersey/new_ jerseys_ ex_king.htm.> 27 Feb 2007.

"Joseph Bonaparte at Point Breeze-Suite 101.com Images." <http://www.suite101.com/view_image.cfm/2083780> 22 Dec 2010.

"KET's Underground Railroad: Kentucky and the Question of Slavery." <http://www.ket.org/underground/history/questionof.htm> 15 May 2005.

Kouwenhoven, John A. The Columbia Historical Portrait of New York. Garden City, N.J.: Doubleday, 1953.

Kreider, Dr. H. W. "Pioneer Days in Union Township with Troy as Commercial Center." The Centennial History of Avon. 1937. n.d., n.p., n.p.

Kunhardt, Dorothy and Philip B. Kunhardt, Jr. Twenty Days. New York: Harper and Row, 1965.

Lapansky-Werner, Emma J. "Teamed Up with the PAS: Images of Black Philadelphia." <http://www.hsp.org/default.aspx?id=816> 16 Apr 2008.

"Lived to a Ripe Old Age: Peaceful Demise of Mrs. Charlotte Simmons Closes a Long and Well-Spent Life." (Obituary), n.d., n.p., n. p.

Lincoln, Abraham. Writings of Abraham Lincoln Vol. IV. Arthur Brooks Lapsley, ed. New York: P. F. Collier, 1905.

Loewen, James W. "The First to Secede." American Heritage. Winter 2011. 13-16.

McCutcheon, Marc. Everyday Life in the 1800s: CA Guide for Writers, Students, & Historians. Cincinnati: Writer's Digest Books, 1993.

Meserve, Dorothy Kunhardt and Philip B. Kunhardt, Jr. Twenty Days. New York: Harper and Row, 1965.

Miller, Edward A., Jr. The Black Civil War Soldiers of Illinois. Colombia, SC: U of South Carolina P, 1998.

"Mr. Lincoln's White House/Rev. Phineas D. Gurley (1816-1868)." <http://www.mrlincolnswhitehouse.org/content_inside.asp?ID=49&subjectID=2> 11 Mar 2011.

Musgrave, Jon. "Black Kidnappings in Southeastern Illinois." <http://www.illinoishistory.com/ugrr.html> 13 Nov 2008.

"Named for Princess: Mrs. Charlotte Simmons." Copies of Clippings from Edith Gallet Simmons Barthel of St. Louis, Mo., to Mrs. Charlotte Simmons Olson Riggins of Avon, Ill. n.d., n.p., n.p.

"Native Americans." <http://www.museum.state.il.us/muslink/nat_amer/post/htmls/soc_family.html> 19 Feb 2009.

Neece, Eugenie C. "From Palace in France to Log Cabin in Illinois: The Story of the Early French Families in Avon." The Centennial History of Avon. 1937. n.d., n.p., n.p.

"New Jersey's Ex-King and the Crown Jewels." Aug 1987. <http://flatrock.org.nz/topics/new_jersey/new_jerseys_ex_king. htm > 22 Feb 2006.

Newman, Richard S. "The Pennsylvania Abolition Society: Restoring a Group to Glory." <http://www.hsp.org/default.aspx?id=815> 16 Apr 2008.

"Ohio's Underground Railroad to Freedom." <http://www.dnr.state.oh.us/parks/explore/magazine/sprsum96UNDERGRR.htm> 22 Feb 2006.

"Old Main, Galesburg, IL. USA." <http:www.outfitters.com/Illinois/knox/old-main.html> 15 May 2005.

"Our History." <http://www.knox.edu/x720.xml> 11 Jun 2005.

Owens, Patricia Ann. "Lincoln and the Springfield Newspapers During the Civil War." <http://www.lib.niu.edu/1997/iht429729.html> 21 Jan 2011.

Owens, Peter. "St. Lawrence River History." <http://www.vsr.cape.com/~powens/riverhistory.htm> 20 Jul 2009.

Paine, Thomas. Collected Writings. New York: Penguin Putnam, 1955.

"Palm Sunday Editorial Cartoon." <http://cartoons.osu.edu/nast/images/Palm_Sunday_50.jpg> 5 Mar 2011.

Pearce, John Ed and Richard Nugent. The Ohio River. Lexington, Ky.: U Press of Kentucky, 1989.

Peattie, Donald Culross. A Prairie Grove. New York: Simon & Schuster, 1938.

"Peoria History – The French." <http://www.peoriahistoricalsociety.org/peohistoryfr.html> 9 Feb 2009.

"Philadelphia in the Civil War." <http://files.usgwarchives.net/pa/philadelphia/military/pcw0002.txt> 2 Feb 2011.

Pierson, George Wilson. Tocqueville in America. Baltimore: Johns Hopkins UP, 1938.

"Point Breeze: Joseph Bonaparte's American." <http://www.encyclopedia.com/doc/1G1-92545137.html> 18 Feb 2008.

Pool, Daniel. What Jane Austen Ate and Charles Dickens Knew. New York: Simon & Schuster, 1993.

"Ralph Waldo Emerson – Texts: Self-Reliance." <http://www.emersoncentral.com/selfreliance.htm> 18 Nov 2008.

Reardon, Patrick T. "Lincoln's Last Trip." The Chicago Tribune. 6 Dec 2009. 5:1.

Rew, Kay Jenkins. "Foot Passengers & Livestock Welcomed on 19th Century Turnpikes." <http://www.paturnpike.com/newsletters/summer98/page-8.htm> 13 Apr 2008.

Ross, Harvey Lee. <u>The Early Pioneers and Pioneer Events of the State of Illinois</u>. Astoria, Illinois: Stevens Publishing C, 1970.

Sandburg, Carl. <u>Abraham Lincoln The Prairie Years, Volume Two</u>. New York: Harcourt, Brace, 1926.

Schwartz, Stephan A. "Dr. Franklin's Plan." <http://www.america.gov/st/pubs-english/2005/June20050606135614Pssnikwad0.888515> 19 Nov 2008.

"Ships of the World: An Historical Encyclopedia - - Britannia." <http://college.hmco.com/history/readerscomp/ships/html/sh_014600_britannia. htm> 9 Mar 2006.

Snapp, William L. <u>Early Days in Greenbush: With Biographical Sketches of the Old Settlers</u>. Springfield, Ill.: Rokker, 1905.

"St. Lawrence Seaway." <http://www.u-s-history.com/pages/h1788.html> 20 Jul 2009.

Stowe, Harriet Beecher. <u>Uncle Tom's Cabin</u>. New York: Knopf, 1994.

Stroud, Patricia Tyson. "Point Breeze: Joseph Bonaparte's American – Estate of Former King in New Jersey; Art, Furniture Collections." <http://www.findarticles.com/p/articles/mi_m1026/is_4_162/ai_92545137/print> 15 May 2005.

"Taming the Wilderness: Rivers." <http://www.connerprairie.org.historyonline/tamriver.html> 14 Feb 2006.

Tompkins, Julia P. "The Founding of Avon." <u>The Centennial History of Avon</u>. 1937. n.d., n.p., n.p.

Townsend, William H. <u>Lincoln and the Bluegrass: Slavery and Civil War in Kentucky</u>. Lexington, Ky: University P of Kentucky, 1955.

Twain, Mark. <u>Life on the Mississippi</u>. Mineola, NY: Dover, 2000.

"Units from Illinois During the Civil War."
< http://www.illinoiscivilwar.org/units_num.html> 14 Feb 2011.

"Urban Woes."
<http://legacy.www.nypl.org/research/chss/spe/art/print/exhibits/movingup/label vi.htm> 01 Nov 2010.

VandeCreek, Drew E., Ph.D. "Native American Relations."
<http://lincoln.lib.niu.edu/nativeamericanpr.html> 9 Feb 2009.

Varhola, Michael J. Everyday Life During the Civil War. Cincinnati, Writer's Digest, 1999.

Voltaire. Candide. New York: Halcyon, 1936.

Whitman, Walt. "A Sight in Camp" from Leaves of Grass/Drum Taps.
<http://www.americanpoems.com/poets/waltwhitman/13261>
11 Mar 2011.

Wieland, Sarah. "Mother Bickerdyke: Heroine of the Civil War." From Arthur Charles Cole, The Era of the Civil War, 1848-1870; Victor Hicken, Illinois in the Civil War; Robert P. Howard, Illinois: A History of the Prairie State. <http://www.lib.niu.edu/1994/ihy940239.html>
25 Feb 2011.

"William T. Sherman – Strategies – CivilWarWiki."
<http://civilwarwiki.net/wiki/William -T.Sherman-Strategies>
1 Mar 2011.

Young, David. "The Illinois and Michigan Canal Link Great Lakes, Mississippi River." <http.www.chicagotribune.com/news/politics/chi-chicagodays-canal-story,0,5540099,pri…> 16 Oct 2010.

Young, David. M. The Iron Horse and the Windy City: How Railroads Shaped Chicago. DeKalb, Illinois: Northern Illinois UP, 2005.